AURYA'S VOW

The song was joyful in content; it was a song of home and children and life in a place of peace. But the sorceress Aurya did not want to listen to it. She bit her lip to keep from shouting, as she thought:

"I swear by the great Morrigan, Goddess-Mother, Keeper of Life and Bringer of Death, I swear by all the black power of the nether-realms, that I shall get free. I will pull this Realm down, stone by stone, until nothing remains. Until no one dares oppose me again. I shall unleash a fury such as this kingdom has never known.

"All this I swear by every breath I take. Nothing will stop me, not even death . . ."

PRAISE FOR REBECCA NEASON'S
THE THIRTEENTH SCROLL

"A satisfying story that provokes readers to examine the meaning of truth in their own hearts."   —*Booklist*

"The kingdom of Aghamore is territory worth exploring at length . . . with fascinating creatures and terrains. . . . This is a narrative that deserves to be played out in full."
—*SF Site*

"Refreshing . . . There are a few surprises built into the plot."
—*Science Fiction Chronicle*

"The action is well paced . . . intriguing . . . recommended."
—*Voya*

Also by Rebecca Neason

The Thirteenth Scroll

Available from Warner Aspect

THE
TRUEST
POWER

REBECCA NEASON

WARNER BOOKS

An AOL Time Warner Company

WARNER BOOKS EDITION

Cover design by Don Puckey
Cover illustration by Daniel Craig
Hand lettering by Carol Russo Design

Aspect® name and logo are registered trademarks of Warner Books, Inc.

Warner Books, Inc.
1271 Avenue of the Americas
New York, NY 10020

Visit our Web site at
www.twbookmark.com.

 An AOL Time Warner Company

Printed in the United States of America

First Printing: December 2002

10 9 8 7 6 5 4 3 2 1

To Betsy Mitchell, editor and friend.

I will miss you.

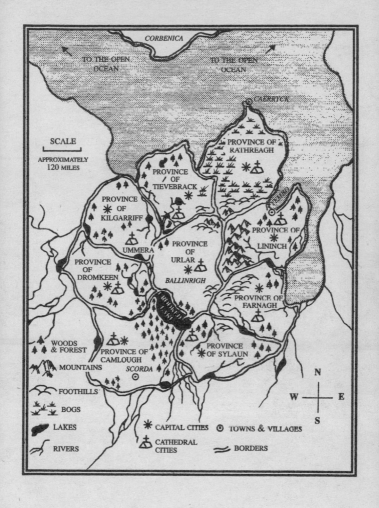

THE
TRUEST
POWER

Chapter One

L ysandra sat on the stone bench at the center of her garden, enjoying a moment of stillness. This was one of those rare spaces in activity where it felt as if the whole world was holding its breath. No bee buzzed or bird chirped; no creature, human or animal, moved; no tree rustled in the afternoon breeze. There was nothing but warmth and silence and peace. These moments never lasted more than a few heartbeats. Soon, the waiting world would exhale, and the activity of *life* would begin again. But for this brief instant, Lysandra's spirit basked in the preternatural silence and was refreshed.

There, a bird made the first call . . . a bee flew to the next flower . . . the moment was gone in a soft but unmistakable passing. Lysandra, too, exhaled. From within her cottage, she heard the sound of voices —first Selia's, then Renan's response. Soon, footsteps entered the growing richness of being, ones Lysandra recognized as much with her heart as with her ears.

She moved slightly to one side, making room for Renan to join her on the bench. She did not bother to call upon her *Sight;* although once it was a spurious gift that came and went by a pattern she could neither name nor control, now she had but to need it, and it was there. But she did not need it for Renan. His footsteps, like his presence, were now almost as well-known to her as her own.

When they had met, his thoughts and emotions had been completely shielded from her. It had been a unique relief to Lysandra. For the last ten years, the nearness of other humans had been a painful experience in which her mind was bombarded by all the thoughts, all the needs and hopes, fears and sorrows humans unwittingly projected. Most human minds were like a sieve through which all these, and more, ran in a constant, unstoppable flow—and she caught them all. It was a large part of why she chose and protected her solitude.

But now, like her *Sight,* this had changed. Now she could control the thoughts she let touch her—and with that control, she no longer had to fear the presence of people in her life. It was a gift that promised her a freedom she thought she had lost ten years ago, when she lost all the other pieces of the life she had always known.

Just as her mind was shielded from unwelcome contact, Renan's was open to her. His thoughts and feelings ran along the current of their deep and mutual feelings for each other, so that Lysandra could feel the inner essence of the man sitting by her side.

At the moment he was confused—and a little discouraged. As he sat there quietly in the sunlight, neither of them said a word for a long moment. Then, finally, she felt him beginning to relax.

Lysandra turned toward him. "Selia?" she said, asking a number of questions with that single word.

"Selia," Renan replied, answering them all.

During the last three weeks, as they rested from their long journey past and for the task ahead, Selia had withdrawn more and more into herself. Lysandra, knowing the shock of losing the life one thought to have, had at first given the younger woman supportive silence in which to make her adjustments of mind and heart. But that luxury was past. June was now upon them, and the summer months of dry weather meant the Barons would be on the move.

It was time they were moving as well—back to Ballinrigh. Both she and Renan felt a deep certainty that whatever was next on Selia's path to the throne could only be accomplished in the kingdom's capital city.

At least this time we know where we're going, Lysandra thought as she stood. Someone needed to point that out—again—to Selia . . . and Lysandra knew that this time it had to be her.

Renan, kind and solicitous, was a great one to offer comfort. With him, Lysandra did not hesitate to share her worries and fears. But comfort was no longer what Selia needed. She needed to put aside both sentiment and personal choices, and look ahead with a clear, determined eye. There was too much at stake for any of them to let personal preferences interfere with what had to be done. Selia had shown her strength in the Realm of the Cryf, when dealing with Aurya and Giraldus—it was time she did so again. Lysandra only hoped she could emulate the gentle firmness her own mother had so often used with her.

The memory of her mother came easily now. The long years in which her heart was dead and cold, buried beneath the crushing weight of her sorrow, were over. Grief was healed, as was the guilt that she had unwittingly carried for so long—guilt that she should still live while those she had loved died trying to save her.

The healing had come from many places, had worn many faces—three of whom were with her now. There was Cloud-Dancer, first and always. From the day he had come into her life, an abandoned six-week-old wolf pup with a broken leg, his joyous devotion and loyalty had begun to chip away the hard shell in which she had encased her inner self. Guard, companion, friend—he had been the first and only being she loved in a long, long time.

Then Renan came into her life—or she into his. Although, at first, she had hated the compulsion that drove her to leave this cottage, that led her first to Ballinrigh and then to Rathreagh to find Selia, she knew now it had been a gift from the Divine Hand. In Ballinrigh she had met Renan— *Father* Renan, priest of the little parish in which she had sought refuge only minutes after entering the city.

Viewed in hindsight, the events of that long trek to the kingdom's great capital, and of the even longer one that followed, were nothing short of miraculous. True, she had her *Sight* to guide her and Cloud-Dancer's presence to keep her safe. But she was still a blind woman walking alone, save for the wolf's company. There could have been danger behind every tree or around any bend in the road.

Instead, she had encountered only honesty and beauty as she traveled. When she did reach Ballinrigh and faced the one truly dangerous moment of her journey, the place of sanctuary at hand contained the one person she needed to find. If those two men had not tried to attack and rob her— gaining only the protective fury of a wolf for their troubles— she might have wandered the streets of Ballinrigh until, money gone, she was forced to abandon her search without ever finding Renan or discovering why she was there.

But she had found Renan. He alone, of all the city's inhabitants, had known what she did not—who she was and the purpose behind her presence there. He revealed to Lysandra the Thirteenth Scroll· of Tambryn and explained to her what it meant. But that was not the greatest gift he had brought to her life. Although it seemed so at the time, Lysandra now knew that what Renan had truly given her was love.

Somewhere, some*when,* along their difficult journey, helpful stranger had turned to friend—and friendship had blossomed into that rarest flower of true and everlasting love. The dark wall behind which she had hidden the deepest part of herself, where she had once believed it would and must always remain, had crumbled bit by bit.

But the pieces, so long in place, had not come easily

down. It was not until she had to battle her way back from the depths of dark magic cast by their enemy, back into the light of life again, that she had finally let the wall around her heart tumble. Within the Light that had become her chosen reality, no Darkness—of magic or of self—could survive.

But Renan was still a priest; the love Lysandra felt for and from him would remain unspoken. Lysandra told herself that did not matter. Love existed—and the friendship, which they could share, was all the deeper for it.

There were other places and people through whom her healing had come. There was Eiddig, the aged Guide and leader of the Cryf, the forgotten beings who lived in their wondrous Realm beneath Aghamore's mountains and whose souls were as beautiful as their appearance was strange. Their name meant the Strong, and that is what they were— possessed of amazing strength in their compact, hair-covered bodies and, above all, strong in their belief of the One whom they called simply the Divine.

No one had demonstrated this strength more surely than Talog, the young Cryf Guide-in-Training who had left the underground Realm to travel with Lysandra and Renan as they searched for Selia. While all of the Cryf had impressed Lysandra with the faith and the compassion that created their amazing, harmonious society, none had done more than Talog. Terrified to travel Up-world, as the Cryf called the surface land of Aghamore, and in physical pain from the brightness of the sun he had never before seen, Talog had proved himself invaluable time and again. Lysandra knew they would never have succeeded in finding or getting Selia to safety without him.

And there was Selia herself. She, too, had helped heal Lysandra in ways the older woman was still discovering. Both the Thirteenth Scroll of Tambryn and the Holy Words of the Cryf named Selia the *Font of Wisdom*. When their minds had touched that first time, Selia's own gifts—

unrecognized and unwanted by the girl—had served as a catalyst to unlock Lysandra's undiscovered potential. Together, they had been able to banish the Darkness that had so nearly destroyed Lysandra and bring her back into life again.

It was then that Lysandra's *Sight,* that wondrous inner vision that had allowed her to live and function as a healer through all the long years of solitude, had blossomed. But for nearly ten years, her *Sight* had come and gone of its own accord, and though she had learned to use it, she could find no way to control it.

Nor was what the *Sight* revealed the same as physical vision. There were moments when it would erupt into colors and images, showing her all that her eyes had learned to do without—but most of the time her *Sight* came in patterns of light and shadow that dwelt within the heart of living auras. It had taken her a long time to perfect her understanding and use.

Now, however, her *Sight* was under her control, coming or going at her summoning. It also came with color now, and gave her true images whenever she needed, images she combined with the auras for even greater healing skills.

Along with her *Sight,* Lysandra now possessed the gift of Far-Seeing, where her inner vision revealed things at a distance. And, as the Scroll of Tambryn had named her, she was also Prophecy's Hand; her *Sight* now looked into the future as well as the present.

Amazing as all this was to her, there was one gift so awe-inspiring that Lysandra hardly dared think on it. Each time she did, she was still stunned that she should have been its instrument. Manifest through both her *Sight* and touch, it was the gift of true healing, and it had come only once—to heal Eiddig from the wound of Aurya's dagger.

Had this been a gift from the great Divine on whom the Cryf called with such unbending faith, a one-time miracle given for the sake of a beloved servant? Or, Lysandra scarcely dared to believe, was this given to *her,* a supernatural fulfillment of who and what she was meant to be?

This question, like so many others, had whirled through her thoughts throughout the three weeks since they had returned to her cottage. As yet, she had no answer, and she was certain there would be none while they remained here. It had been important to stop and rest and to regain their strength, as important as it had once been to leave. But now the time to leave had come again. Lysandra knew it; Renan knew it— it was only Selia who would not accept it.

Cloud-Dancer brushed against Lysandra's thigh as she put her hand to the door latch. As always, his presence made her smile, and she automatically reached down, running her fingers into the thick, soft silver-and-white fur that covered his head and neck. Together, they entered the cottage, leaving Renan alone in the sun-washed garden.

Lysandra heard the younger woman in the kitchen. This had become a favorite place of Selia's, the kitchen and the medicine pantry beyond where Lysandra set the herbs to dry and stored the prepared unguents and syrups, salves and simples for use. Their production seemed to fascinate Selia. Although Lysandra was grateful for the help and glad to teach both Selia and Renan what she knew, it was not Selia's destiny to spend her coming years as a healer's apprentice.

While Cloud-Dancer went to curl up in his favorite spot by the fireplace, Lysandra headed for the kitchen. She summoned up her *Sight* so that she could watch Selia as they spoke. It was not that she thought the younger woman would try to deceive her—but she might try to deceive herself, and Lysandra needed to be aware and help her accept the truth.

It would not be easy. Unlike most humans, Selia possessed the ability to keep her inner self carefully hidden away, even from Lysandra. How much of this was innate and how much had been learned through her pain-filled childhood, Lysandra did not know. But what her empathy might miss, her *Sight* would not, and Lysandra intended to make full use of it now. Honed through a decade of practice, Lysandra would be able to read Selia's true emotions on her face, and in the changes to the aura that surrounded her.

When she entered the kitchen, and Selia turned to greet her, her aura was clear, bright as sunlight reflecting on a mountain lake. But Lysandra knew it would not last, and she was sorry for that, sorry that she must be the one to destroy Selia's happy, contented humor.

"The marigold salve is almost finished," she told Lysandra proudly. "I'll be sealing the pots soon, if you want to look at it first."

"No," Lysandra replied, heading for the cupboard where she kept her dishes stored. "I'm sure you've done it right. You've learned a great deal in the short time you've been here. But come, let's have some tea. There are things we must say."

Cups now in hand, she turned and *saw* that Selia's aura had already begun to darken, as if a bank of clouds was moving to block her inner sun. *She knows what is coming,* Lysandra thought. *Of course she does . . . her own heart is telling her, just as ours are telling Renan and me. How can I get her to listen to what she knows but does not want to hear?*

Lysandra put the mugs down and opened the cupboard where she kept the herbs she used for tea. She chose her favorite, a blend of wood betony and chamomile she kept already mixed. Betony strengthened both the body and mind, and chamomile relaxed while promoting clear thoughts and insight.

A kettle of hot water was always on the back of the stove, ready for use. Lysandra bent her attention to the necessities of the tea, studiously ignoring the continued darkening of Selia's humor. Finally, steaming mugs in hand, she went to the table and sat, willing her own calm to reach out and at least touch, if not envelop, her companion.

"Bring the honey with you," she said in an even voice

that, though soft, was a tone that left no room for argument. *My mother's voice,* Lysandra thought with a small and wistful smile, grateful that she could think of her family again. That, too, was part of her healing.

Selia brought the honey as asked, her footsteps speaking her reluctance as clearly as any word. For a few minutes more, the silence continued as each woman fixed her tea the way she liked it. Then, finally, Selia drew a deep breath.

"I know what you're going to say," she began. "Father Renan has already said it. 'It's time to go, to leave here and continue with the task ahead.' But I don't want to go—and I don't want to finish anything that will make me be Queen."

Lysandra said nothing. She sipped her tea and waited, letting Selia say everything, logical or otherwise, that was boiling around inside her.

"You live a good life," Selia continued when Lysandra did not speak. "You help others here—people, animals, anyone who comes to you. The good you accomplish is *tangible.* That's something I want—not some abstract 'good of the kingdom.' I want to stay here, to learn what you do and help you do it. I've thought all about it, and I don't see any reason . . . eventually you'll need someone here. I mean, you're not old or anything—yet—but what if you were injured or sick? You need to have someone here, instead of living all alone . . ."

Her voice trailed off into the silence of both women unconvinced. Again, Lysandra waited passively, giving Selia a chance to continue if she wanted. But now the younger woman said nothing.

"Yes," Lysandra affirmed softly. "I do live a good life here. Peaceful, meaningful . . . but it is *my* life, Selia, and you cannot live it. Your own life awaits."

Selia pushed her chair back abruptly and began to pace. "I don't *want* that life," she said as she walked. "I don't care about prophecies and Holy Words—or about what my being Queen *might* mean. I don't know how to be a Queen."

"And that is one of the greatest gifts you'll bring to the people," Lysandra answered. "This kingdom has had too many rulers who thought they knew what being a sovereign meant—and to them it meant only power and profit. They ruled with greed instead of wisdom, and for their own pleasure instead of the people's good.

"But if it is too 'abstract' for you," Lysandra quoted Selia's word back to her, "to think of the mothers who have put their children to bed hungry because the tax collectors have taken every penny they needed to buy food, or what it will mean to this kingdom to suffer a civil war until one Baron vanquishes the others and claims the crown—then think of Eiddig, Talog, and the others. They put their lives in jeopardy for your safety. Will you tell them by your actions that all their efforts, all the sacrifices of those who died in the battle with Aurya's and Giraldus's soldiers—defending *you*—was for nothing? Surely you're not that much of a coward."

"I *am* a coward," Selia said sharply. "I'm afraid to leave here, to go to Ballinrigh, to see all those people who might be suffering just as you said. And I'm *afraid* to be Queen. What if I'm no good at it, and the people suffer more because of me?"

There, Lysandra thought as she watched the cloud of self-deception lift from Selia's aura. *Now the real reason is out, and we can deal with it.*

"Selia," she said aloud, "sit down and listen to me."

Reluctantly, the younger woman again came to the table. Once she was seated, Lysandra took her hands, again remembering how often her mother had sat in such a way with her. The circle now completed as she gave the comfort she had once received.

"Fear of the unknown does not make you a coward—unless you let it keep you from moving forward. And fear of failure can be what spurs us to our greatest efforts. But both are a choice, made every day. You're not a child to think life is all one way, always only good or bad. Every day and many times within each day, we are faced with the choice to go one way or the other, to add success to success or failure to failure—or to turn our failure into success."

"But—" Selia began.

Lysandra shook her head to stop her from continuing. "You have a great gift within you," she said, "a Divinely ordered gift. You *are* the Font of Wisdom. You know it, as do I, Renan, the Cryf—even Aurya and Giraldus. To leave that gift languishing here in obscurity would be more than a shame . . . and that, too, you know. It would be living a lie, and that is the ultimate failure."

Slowly, through the link of their touch, Lysandra now reached her mind for Selia's. Their minds united, as they had before, as they ever would. Truth met Wisdom in that place beyond words. Despite what Selia had said earlier, she was not a coward—nor could she turn away from prophecy delivered on the wings of Truth.

Lysandra's *Sight* suddenly gazed into the future that might yet be, and at the fork in the road upon which their destination relied. Through that gaze of prophetic *Sight,* Lysandra showed it all to Selia: if they stayed here, as she said she wanted, death awaited. Not for them—not yet—but for countless others. Soldiers dying in battle; families torn apart by war; children trampled beneath heedless, galloping hooves; mothers and sisters raped, fathers killed; all of Aghamore's Provinces turned into one, blood-soaked killing field . . .

This was civil war. But its aftermath was no less terrible. It mattered not who won the war; even with Giraldus and Aurya gone, this kingdom would become a place of Darkness. The scars upon the landscape would be as nothing compared to the wounds on the hearts and lives of the people—and they would not heal for many generations.

And there was the other road, the one that led them now to Ballinrigh. It, too, was filled with danger—to them and to this kingdom—but the distant end was far different. Lysandra could not *see* its end clearly; the road twisted and turned, branched and rejoined the main path again with the many choices that might still be made along the way.

But by the single act of acceptance—of herself, her fate and purpose—by acting in faith and going to Ballinrigh now, the Darkness that could destroy the kingdom would be averted and Truth would have the chance to take its rightful place.

It was Selia who broke the contact with Lysandra's mind. She withdrew her hands from Lysandra's grasp and stood, going over to the nearby window that looked out on the garden and the forest beyond. Lysandra waited. All barriers between them were now down, and she could feel the girl's silent quandary even as she watched it pulsate through the aura surrounding Selia's body.

The younger woman still did not want to go, but neither was she heartless. Slowly, the turmoil ceased; her own inner civil war of duty versus desire ended in unconditional surrender.

"How soon must we leave?" she asked.

"Tomorrow, the next day at the latest," Lysandra answered. "The longer we wait, the closer the Darkness draws."

"I'll be ready in the morning," Selia replied, still not turning from the window.

Lysandra could feel the young woman's deep attraction to the peace that view accorded—and she shared the feeling. She did not envy Selia's destiny; neither power nor riches held the slightest appeal to Lysandra. Nor did they to Selia, who had thought to live a quiet life of prayer amid the holy Sisters of St. Gabriel in the little convent outside the fishing village of Caerryck on the northern tip of Rathreagh.

There will be compensations for that lost life, Lysandra thought, but did not say. She knew Selia was not yet ready to hear it. In time, Selia would rediscover joy—even amid the duties of a Queen. As the life she was meant to live, in time it would become as fulfilling and as meaningful to her as Lysandra's had become over the years.

That much Lysandra could *see*—but such assurances would be meaningless to Selia right now. There was only one thing that mattered to her today, and that was finding the strength to endure her present task.

Lysandra finished her tea and stood. She would go back outside to Renan and leave Selia to make her peace with the life to which she had just committed.

Chapter Two

Elon Gallivin, Bishop-ordinary of the Province of Kilgarriff, was worried; he still had heard nothing from Giraldus and Aurya. Their scroll-guided journey to find the child whom Tambryn's writings had named the Font of Wisdom should have taken no more than two or three weeks. They had left before the end of April, and it was now June, yet they had neither returned nor sent him any message to explain their delay.

Elon had sent his spies on errands through the northern part of the kingdom. They had brought back news of places Giraldus and Aurya had stopped, places like Yembo in Lininch and Fintra in Rathreagh—but those sightings had been weeks old. It was as if Giraldus and Aurya had simply disappeared.

If they did not return soon, all the hard work Elon had

done to ensure Giraldus had the Church's support to make him the next High King would go for naught. Already, he feared, the backing of the other bishops, including the Archbishop, was beginning to waver.

Elon got up from behind his desk and began to pace the room. This study at his Residence in Ummera was large enough for him to take several unimpeded steps, despite the ornate furnishings and bookshelves. He walked from the fireplace on one wall to the bay window that filled the wall directly opposite, and back again. The pacing helped him think—and not about the many papers piled on his desk.

He knew he had a decision to make, and it was not one that came easily, for it ran contrary to the plan that had been almost three decades in fomenting. Yet, if Giraldus and Aurya did not return within the next few days, he must find the way to disassociate himself from them and salvage as much of his reputation—and his plan—as possible.

Twenty-eight years ago, he had seduced Aurya's mother in accordance with a carefully researched and followed ritual of power, in service to the dark god Leshtau, who had been worshiped centuries ago in a land half the world away. But time and distance meant nothing to the forces he was summoning in the act—as Aurya herself proved.

Nine months later, she had been born. Of her mother, Elon gave not another thought; he cared only for the child, a creature of magic destined to wield such power as Elon could only dream. Elon's own power was in his voice, and he had used it to ensure that Aurya's mother would never betray him. He implanted an order of silence deep within her mind, and it had held throughout the remainder of her life. Not even Aurya knew that he was her father.

But he knew, and through his spies he had kept watch over her progress. He knew about the early and growing rift between mother and daughter that had caused Aurya to leave home by the age of twelve. At that young age, she had turned her back on the woman toward whom she felt only apathy at best, disgust at worst, who was too consumed by her own guilt to give her ill-conceived child any glimmer of maternal care or affection.

Elon knew, too, about the "witch of the hills," old Kizzie, who had become Aurya's teacher in the ways of magic. From a distance, he had kept watch on how Aurya progressed in her studies. He knew when Kizzie died. He had been there personally, hidden in a thick clump of tree-shaded underbrush, distant enough to be safe from the wild powers she was unleashing, to watch Aurya as she summoned the fire that consumed her teacher's body and sent her spirit free into the universe.

It had been a turning point in Aurya's life, for with that conjuring of power all the forces by which she was conceived were awakened. On that day, the magic that was her destiny fully claimed her as its own.

Aurya had been seventeen. For the next year she had lived by her wits, and Elon had neither interfered nor stepped forward to help her. Eventually, she began to travel with a gypsy band as a fortune-teller. It kept her fed and sheltered, finally bringing her to the Summer Faire at Adaraith, the capital city of Kilgarriff.

Elon had been there, too, dressed in humble clothes he had borrowed from his manservant, Thomas. Walking unrecognized among the people, he saw the exceptional beauty Aurya had become, with her long, raven-dark hair, sapphire eyes, and skin of rose and cream so translucent that it looked lit from within. Nor was he the only one who saw it. Everywhere Aurya went, people—men—stopped to stare at her.

The Baron of Kilgarriff, attending the Faire to open the festivities, was no exception. From the first moment Giraldus saw her, standing and watching him, then disappearing into the crowd, he could not take his eyes from her. That Aurya had brains as well as beauty showed in the way she played the lusty young Baron. She made him think he was the hunter when, in fact, he was the prey. Nor did she make the mistake too often made by young women of giving away the prize too early. Before Aurya had "allowed herself" to be coaxed into the Baron's bed, she had made certain he was completely besotted, hers in both body and soul.

Elon had applauded the play as he continued to watch from a distance, using spies of his own within the Baron's household. All the while, he was waiting for the right time and the right way for contact between them to be initiated—and the plan begun all those years ago to be brought to fruition.

It had come at last with the death of King Anri this last September. Anri, like his uncle King Osaze, who ruled before him, had left no bodily issue to inherit the crown. Now, by the law of Aghamore, any one of the Barons, as Heads of the Ruling Houses that were of direct descent from the first King's nine sons, was equal in the Line of Succession.

But none of them had the advantages of Baron Giraldus of Kilgarriff. He was a soldier, tried and true, possessed of a strong arm and a stronger army . . . and he would bring that strength to the throne. But Giraldus was not the only one who could make such claims. Among the Barons of the Eight Outer Provinces, one or two were better suited to handling books than leading men; hesitant, perhaps even squeamish, at the thought of fighting. But most had been as well trained in the arts of war and leadership as had Giraldus.

Yet none other had a sorceress as a consort. Aurya's powers were known—and feared—throughout the kingdom and beyond. With Giraldus on the throne and Aurya by his side, no enemy of Aghamore would dare think of invasion. Considering the weakened state in which Osaze and Anri had left the kingdom, it was an important assurance to make.

Yet while Aurya's magic added to Giraldus's strength, there were those within Aghamore who looked upon it, and his unsanctified union with her, as the greatest impediment to his ascension to the throne. Aurya's enmity to the Church was as well-known as her powers. Elon was aware that his peers within the College of Bishops, including the Archbishop himself, who, without a King to govern, was currently the highest authority in the land, viewed Aurya—and through her, Giraldus—as completely unsuitable to wear the crown or sit upon the throne of Aghamore.

It was this knowledge that brought the next part of Elon's long-fomented plan into play.

It was he who had brought the Thirteenth Scroll of Tambryn to the Baron and his lady, and set them on their quest to find the child it called the Font of Wisdom—the one true threat to their rise to power. As far as Elon knew, he was the only one in the kingdom to possess a full set of Tambryn's writings. A onetime monk, a mystic and Seer, Tambryn's prophetic visions had at first delighted, then bitterly offended both the secular and sacred authorities. In the end, the Church had declared him, and his writings, heretical. While he escaped their punishment, all the copies of his scrolls were collected and burned.

Elon had found and purchased the scrolls in his possession thirty years ago, from a merchant far away from Aghamore. Recognizing the power in their accuracy, he had started on the road that led to his present alliance with Giraldus and Aurya. He had brought the scroll to Aurya, knowing that she, too, would see and understand its worth; it was for this purpose she had been conceived.

Their quest to find and destroy the Font of Wisdom was not for Giraldus's sake alone. Elon was not that altruistic. He did not care about the good of the kingdom—and his interest, his *plan,* for Giraldus and Aurya's future was only because it was the best way to get what *he* wanted.

When Giraldus's House ascended, Elon would, too; he would gain the triple-crowned mitre of the Archbishop. This, alone, was the cause for which he worked so diligently . . . and not for faith, or for the call to service—but for recognition, for wealth, and for the power that were his rightful due.

While he awaited the triumphant return of Giraldus and Aurya, he secured the Church's support for the Baron of Kilgarriff to become the next High King of Aghamore. It had been no easy task to convince six of the nine bishops, including the Archbishop, the Primus of the Church in Aghamore, that Aurya had renounced her magic and turned with full contrition to seek both absolution and admittance into the body of the Church. Giraldus, he told them, had done the same.

The lies had come easily to him, for he knew what the other bishops wanted to hear. He had finally convinced them that Aurya and Giraldus were on a secret pilgrimage of reparation and upon returning would seek both baptism and the formalizing of their relationship under the Sacrament of Holy Matrimony.

Now, however, he was in danger of losing everything, and Elon was not going to let that happen. He strode over to the bellpull that hung by the fireplace and yanked it twice. Within minutes, Johann, his officious and slightly irritating majordomo, knocked once on his door and entered.

Pompous though he might be, he was also extremely efficient, which was why Elon retained his services. But aside from giving the man orders and knowing they would be quickly carried out, Elon dealt with Johann as little as possible.

"Yes, Your Grace," Johann said, giving Elon a slight bow.

"I'm looking for Thomas," Elon said. "Do you know where he is?"

"Thomas has gone into the town," Johann replied with a sniff that expressed exactly what he thought of Thomas and of the man's close association with the bishop. "He *claimed* it was on an errand for Your Grace. If that is not true—"

"Yes, that's right," Elon cut him off. "We arranged it last

night . . . I had forgotten. Very well, when he returns please send him to me."

"Yes, Your Grace. Was there anything else?"

"No . . . yes, what time is luncheon?"

"Twelve-thirty, Your Grace, same as every day."

Elon glanced at the pendulum clock on the far wall. It was eleven o'clock now. "Thank you, Johann. That will be all."

"Very well, Your Grace," the servant said, giving Elon another small, formal bow.

Elon always found something about the way Johann gave such bows, like his constant addressing Elon as "Your Grace" in nearly every sentence, to be annoying. Both were correct, and from no one else did Elon object to them. But, although the tone of both act and voice seemed correct, from Johann they came across with disdain, even a slight sarcasm—as if under this guise of respect, he was actually proclaiming his innate superiority to everyone . . . including Elon.

Elon watched him leave, glad when the door shut behind him. The bishop then went back to his desk and pulled another bell cord, this one summoning his secretary. A moment later, another soft knock sounded, and a young deacon entered.

Elon was seated now and looking busy, with papers in hand and others spread out before him. "Yes, Lymin," he said, "I wish to be undisturbed for the next hour. *No one* is to enter or even knock until time for the midday Office, when the staff assembles in the chapel. Until then, you're to see I am left strictly alone. Do you understand—*strictly alone*."

"Yes, Your Grace," Lymin answered earnestly. "Strictly alone. Anything else?"

"No, that's all—but I make it your personal responsibility to see this is carried out as I wish."

"Yes, Your Grace," the young deacon answered, backing out of the room.

Once the door had closed again, Elon stood and sprang quickly into action. He had only an hour for what he wanted to do. Thomas, he knew, was not in Ummera on an errand of either his own or Elon's. But those words, which Johann had repeated with such contempt, had told the bishop exactly where his manservant was and what he was doing.

Elon stepped over to the bookshelf near the fireplace, removed three books from the second shelf, and pulled the hidden lever behind them. Immediately, a latch released, and the bookshelf swung out, revealing a passageway behind. Inside were stairs that would take him to his bedroom suite and through there he would enter his other and very secret study.

Thomas, who had been with Elon for nearly a quarter of a century, was the only other person who knew of this secret room and its contents. He was also the only one, besides Elon, who had a key. The room was kept locked at all times, even when occupied, in case some other servant should accidentally chance upon the hidden door. To his knowledge, no one else had ever found it, but Elon could take no chances.

Inside this secret chamber, Elon kept the books and other articles that would have cost him everything—his wealth, his power, his status within the Church, even his life—had word of its existence leaked out. It was where Thomas would be, studying the books Elon had put out for him, doing the mental exercises as he had been instructed and honing the potential power they had both only recently realized he possessed.

Elon took the steps two at a time, quickly ascending to the door that opened into the large, walk-in wardrobe where his vestments and other clothing hung. From there, first making certain no other servant was busy cleaning his rooms, he crossed to the wall panel beside his bed, found the place within the ornate molding that was actually a keyhole in disguise, and let himself into the little room.

A small fire blazed in the brazier, and a single lamp

burned beside the chair where Thomas sat, his eyes closed in concentration. They flew open with Elon's entry.

Thomas jumped to his feet, barely catching the ancient book that had been open across his lap. "Your . . . Your Grace," he stammered nervously. "I'm just doing as you instructed. I'm—"

"Relax, Thomas," Elon said, with a wave of his hand. "I'm delighted you're here. I have something I would like us to try, something that needs your . . . talents. It will show us how far you've progressed these last few weeks."

Thomas's delight now showed on his face as clearly as his worry had a moment before. He again took his seat.

"Is this all right?" he asked Elon. "Or would you rather I sat elsewhere?"

"That will be fine, Thomas. Perfect," Elon said as he crossed the room to stand behind Thomas's chair. He then turned it slightly, so it would better face the fire.

What they were about to try, they had practiced often, using a candle as a point of focus. Elon now hoped that using the fire might reveal more, showing Thomas a bigger, more detailed picture that might answer Elon's most burning question.

"Just relax," he said as he stood behind the chair and placed his hands on Thomas's shoulders. "You know what we're doing . . . we've done it many a time before. Relax . . . breathe into it. Let your mind go silent, still. Let your breath expand to carry it outward. All you see are the flames; all you hear are my voice and the sound of your own breath. Relax, Thomas . . . relax and let yourself see what the flames reveal . . ."

Elon was keeping his voice low and steady. He could feel it working as, beneath his hands, all the tension left his servant's shoulders. Sometimes, when he and Thomas worked this way, the physical contact allowed him to share a shadowed portion of whatever vision appeared. That was Elon's hope today.

But so far, there was nothing; no parting of the flames, no sudden feeling of timelessness communicated itself through their bond—servant to master, student to teacher.

After another moment, Elon lifted his hands. Thomas gave no recognition of the change, as he kept his eyes steadily focused forward. He would, until Elon's voice released him. The bishop came around so he could watch Thomas's face, hoping that would give him at least some indication of revelation that contact had not.

Thomas's eyes were wide, unblinking—but also unfocused. Elon knew then that Thomas, too, beheld no vision in the flames. Blowing his air out sharply, Elon sat back in his chair and steepled his fingers, thinking.

Perhaps, with a flame this big, he needs more specific direction, Elon thought, hoping it was insight and not desperation that guided him.

"Remain relaxed," he now began again, his voice at its most lulling pitch, using every bit of the skill he had honed into it over the years. "See the flames. For now, they are only flames as your breath flows in and out. Let your breath be a river; it fills you and releases you. With each breath, your body becomes more anchored—and your mind becomes more free. You are free of time. You are free of distance. The river of breath carries you out, along its currents to the place you want to go. . . ."

Elon matched his words to the rhythm of Thomas's breathing, connecting the two into one powerful tool. He closely watched his servant's reaction, seeing the last traces of tension and unrealized effort leave the younger man's body. In an automatic attempt to obey Elon's commands, Thomas had been trying to force his mind along the pathway to power, rather than opening his mind and letting the vision come to him.

Conscious and subconscious now melded into unified silence. *Now,* Elon thought, *he is truly ready.*

"The flames are your window, Thomas," he directed.

"Look closely as you think of Lady Aurya. See the path she has traveled as a trail of light passing through shadow. Focus on the light and let the shadow fall away. Do you see it now, Thomas?"

Slowly, the manservant nodded. "Very good, Thomas," Elon continued. "You are doing well. Remain relaxed as your mind follows the trail. Let it take you forward. Remember, time means nothing—you are not bound by it. Distance does not exist for you. There is nothing holding you back as you follow Lady Aurya's trail. Where are you now?"

"On a river." Thomas's words held no inflection, nothing to give Elon any indication if this was Aurya's travels on the "river of breath" he had instructed Thomas to follow, or a true river of physical existence. He wished, briefly, that he had used another image; Aghamore was a kingdom of numerous rivers and waterways.

For now, he would believe the latter. "Does the river have a name, Thomas?" he asked.

"I don't know," came the reply. "It is a large river, wide. The rafts are not swift enough. Must go faster . . . they're getting away . . ."

Ah, Elon thought triumphantly, as he realized what had happened. Thomas had indeed found Aurya—and was now following the trail of her thoughts, magic touching magic.

"Keep following, Thomas," he instructed. "Stay with the rafts. Tell me what is happening."

"Hurry . . . hurry." Thomas's voice was suddenly higher, as if coming from a woman's throat. "The mountains ahead . . . yes, we'll go in there. What's that sound? Growing louder . . . what? Birds, hundreds and hundreds . . . so loud . . . *here* are the voices of Tambryn's words . . . I was wrong before—it's *here* the 'children sing.' Into the mountains . . . hurry . . . no, leave the rafts. This way . . . Hurry . . ."

Suddenly, Thomas's eyes snapped wide open, as if with

shock. Then they closed again, and his head slumped to his chest. The connection to Aurya was broken.

How? Elon wondered. *What does it mean? A wide river, the mountains—but where . . . the mountains go through three Provinces . . . and did the river flow in or out of them? Why would the mountains sever contact like that?*

Elon shook his head; there were too many questions. This exercise had gained him nothing. He still did not know where Aurya and Giraldus were or if they had found—found and *destroyed*—the child, or if they were on their way home. They could be trapped, lost somewhere within the mountains . . . or they could be lying dead at the bottom of a ravine.

And he was out of time. The household would momentarily begin gathering in the chapel, waiting for him to lead them in the noon Office. Both he and Thomas must arrive before their absence could be noted.

"Thomas," he said quietly, "when I count to three you will awaken and remember nothing of what you have experienced until I, and I alone, tell you to remember. You will now awaken refreshed and ready to continue your duties. One . . . two . . . three."

As Elon said this last word, Thomas's head came up, and his eyes opened. He looked at Elon expectantly.

The bishop shook his head. "Later," he said. "It's nearly noon. I'll go now, back the way I came. Wait two minutes before you leave here, then go outside and come back through the servant's entrance, as if just returning from town. What was it you were to get for me?"

"I was checking on the readiness of your new red cope at Master Sallard's—which I did during my free hours yesterday. It will not be ready for three more days, at least."

Elon smiled at Thomas's foresight. *Precognition at work again?* He wondered about the talent that had made him first realize Thomas's potential.

"Very good," he said aloud. "I'll see you downstairs, then."

With that, Elon went back to the door that had become the hidden part of his bedchamber wall and retraced his path back to his downstairs study. He had barely resumed his seat at the desk when Lymin knocked on his door.

"Enter," Elon called, and again his head secretary opened the door and popped his head around.

"The household is assembling in the chapel, Your Grace."

"Yes, thank you, Lymin—I lost track of the time."

"You're welcome, Your Grace. Busy as you are, I thought you might."

Lymin's voice carried its usual cheerfulness—which sometimes grated on Elon's nerves. But it was also part of what made him such an excellent secretary, enabling him to deal well with members of the populace Elon did not wish to see. They left Lymin's cheerful presence feeling they had presented their petition to someone who cared and would see the problem dealt with in a timely manner. When Elon became Archbishop, he intended to take Lymin with him.

But when will that be? he wondered as he came around his desk to follow his secretary toward the chapel. Until he knew more about Aurya and Giraldus's whereabouts, the answer to that question remained as mysterious as Thomas's vision.

He had, however, made one decision. If he received no word from them before this week was out, he would go to Ballinrigh, to the Archbishop, and begin the process of trying to retain the old man's favor while disassociating himself from the Baron of Kilgarriff and his lady. He only hoped it could be accomplished without too much damage to his dream.

Chapter Three

All three of the humans were up with the dawn. It would take them several days to reach Ballinrigh, and it seemed appropriate to begin their journey with the start of a new day.

Cloud-Dancer still lay upon the bed, watching Lysandra with sleepy eyes that said this was not their accustomed routine. But as Renan and Selia also began to move about the cottage, and Lysandra packed a travel-bundle of her extra clothing, he jumped down and began to prance excitedly around her.

His antics made Lysandra laugh. "Yes," she told him, "we're going again."

At her voice, his prancing turned into the dance from which he had earned his name. He rose up on his hind legs, front paws alternating upward as he turned around and around. He was wont to do this often when he was a pup, especially when they were out in the garden, and Lysandra always thought he looked as if he were trying to reach the clouds.

As she watched him through her *Sight,* all the memories of those early days of his companionship flooded back. This morning, her *Sight* was full of color, granting her a gift of vision made all the fuller because of the auras her *Sight* always revealed. As she looked now at Cloud-Dancer, memories filling her mind as vividly as her Sight, she marveled at the beautiful animal he had become.

At two years old, Cloud-Dancer was just entering his prime. When she had found him, injured and abandoned, he had been a sorry sight—thin and dull-eyed from days without food, his mud-covered coat scraggly with shock and pain.

But now his coat was thick, especially around his head and neck. It shone with health, looking every bit like the silver and quartz crystal to which the Cryf had likened it. His body, though lean, was not scrawny; it was strongly muscled from the daily hunting he did for his own meat, and it radiated his vitality. His eyes shone, too—bright and clear, the same forget-me-not blue as her own.

Her bundle finished, Lysandra dropped to her knees and held out her arms. Immediately, Cloud-Dancer came to her. As she put her arms around his thick neck and hugged him, Lysandra could not help thinking that a day begun in such a wave of joy omened well for the journey—and the task—ahead.

There was a soft knock on her bedroom door. "Come," she called, and Renan entered.

"Breakfast is nearly cooked, and the water is ready for tea," he said. "What shall we have today?"

Lysandra smiled at him, still filled with the joy these moments with Cloud-Dancer had given her. "Surprise me," she told him. "Let's see how much you've learned."

Over the weeks they had known each other, Renan had been trying to learn about the herbs she used, first from the rather limited variety she had taken with her on the trip to Ballinrigh, then from the much larger supply here at the cottage. She had even promised that when they reached his parish once again and as time allowed, she would lay out an herb garden for him and provide the seed.

His knowledge was still rudimentary, and it would be interesting to see what he chose for them to begin their journey, Lysandra thought as she stood to follow him to the kitchen.

After breakfast, she would gather those seeds from her supplies and choose which herbs and medicines to take this time.

They entered the kitchen to the aroma of toasted bread, melted cheese, and sautéed wild mushrooms, whose woodsy fragrance made her mouth water. Having breakfast already cooked for her was a luxury, one she had not known since childhood—and then she did not appreciate it. But she did now, and she thought again about the omen of such a wonderful morning.

Yet not all was joyful. As she took her place at the table, Lysandra felt Selia's mood surround her like a soaked blanket thrown across a flame. It was not like the fear she felt yesterday; it was heavier, darker, like the acceptance of a prisoner facing the gallows.

Lysandra shook her head slightly. There was too much at stake to allow Selia to remain wrapped in such dismal thoughts and feelings. Lysandra knew, too well, the toll that came from mourning overlong for the passing of a once-desired life.

But unlike Lysandra after the murder of her family, Selia was not heading into the black abyss where only loneliness awaited. She was moving *toward* a life—a new life, yes, one that was different than what she expected—but it was a life of known purpose, and one she would face with counsel and companionship.

"I believe I'm becoming quite adept at preparing for a journey," Lysandra said lightly, breaking the heavy silence that surrounded Selia. "It took me only a few minutes to decide what to pack this time."

Selia remained silent, as Lysandra had thought she would, barely giving up a glance, which contained no hint of a smile. Neither Selia nor Renan had more than a few belongings. For Renan there were the clothes he wore and the ones he had once loaned to Talog. Selia had the black gown of her novice's habit, though the scapular and veil were put aside and would be returned to the convent as soon as it was possible.

To cover the gown, Lysandra had made her a long apron of a bright blue-and-white weave that a cottager had given her a year ago, after she had treated the family through a long winter's illness. There had even been enough of the material to make Selia a matching kerchief to cover her short hair. It was already beginning to lose the shorn look worn by all novices beneath their veils, and was now curling in wispy tendrils that frequently escaped the kerchief and softly encircled the young woman's face. The growing hair, like the color in the apron, lessened the severity of Selia's black gown and made her look far more her age.

Lysandra had one more dress for her, a simple shift made of a light rose-colored fabric she had also been given in payment for her care. She still had a few stitches to put to it, but she hoped to give the dress to Selia when they reached Ballinrigh. Even so, she knew these few belongings would not be enough for what was ahead.

"I still have most of the coins left from selling my mother's jewelry," Lysandra began again, this time speaking directly to Selia. "I think that when we reach the city, there will be plenty to buy what we need for some new clothes. What kind of fabric would you like?"

"You should keep your money for yourself," the girl replied, her voice apathetic.

Lysandra shook her head. "Nonsense. I've more than enough here for my needs. I've clothes to wear and cloth I've not touched yet . . . and the forest offers nothing to *buy*. But you will need new things. Think of what you'd like, and we'll look for it when we reach Ballinrigh. Or, perhaps, before. I know where there is an honest merchant," she added, thinking of the man with the booming voice but an honorable heart, who had bought her mother's jewelry, then made certain Lysandra could tell the coins apart before he paid her.

Although not all of Selia's mood changed, Lysandra felt its heaviness lift a little. The younger woman began to ponder the possibilities; as an abandoned child, raised in the convent where she had later become a novice, having new and colorful clothing made especially for her was a new experience. Even the apron she wore, with its simple blue-and-white checks, had filled her with such delight that Lysandra had started that night on the second dress, wishing she had more to offer.

Renan now brought the tea to the table. As he put the mugs down and turned back toward the stove to get the rest of their breakfast, he lightly brushed a hand across Lysandra's shoulder, silently acknowledging all she was doing—or trying to do—for Selia.

With a small smile, she picked up her mug and inhaled, trying to identify which herbs Renan had chosen. *Licorice root, that imparts strength and supports the body's reflexes,* she thought, *and there's peppermint that clears the mind so it can receive energy and insight, and . . .* she took a sip, *damiana, also for energy, but of the body not the mind.*

As Renan sat and looked at her expectantly, like a child awaiting approval, Lysandra smiled at him. Then she named the ingredients.

"Did I miss anything?" she asked.

"No, you named them all. Well?"

Lysandra nearly laughed at the eagerness in his voice. "They are wonderful choices," she told him. "I could not have done better."

She spoke no more than the truth. She might have used a slightly different combination, but Renan had chosen for the same properties as she would have done. And it was a good tasting combination—especially with a little honey added, she thought. This latter was an attribute Lysandra believed important. Even if one was taking a medicinal brew, there was no reason it could not be pleasing as well as beneficial.

Although she had no real evidence, besides her own experience, to support it, Lysandra had often thought that medicines—or teas—that were foul-tasting, lost part of their effectiveness by shocking the system.

She could feel Renan basking in her praise. Gone were the days when his feelings were hidden from her. Mutual trust and affection had opened that door partway; her newly expanded gifts had done the rest. It was good, to feel so connected to another human being, and Lysandra smiled softly as she sipped her tea, once more grateful for the good feelings of this morning. The kitchen suddenly felt filled with harmony—Renan bringing the rest of the meal to the table; Selia's mood slowly lifting. It was like a slow dawn and would take some time to crest the hilltop, but Lysandra knew that eventually it would do just that.

She thought back to herself at seventeen. That had been a terrible year, the year when her parents and Ultan, the boy she had loved and planned to marry, had been killed by the marauding gang of outlaws led by Black Bryan—and after that, her life had stopped for a long while. But even before that terrible day, life had been filled with the intensity of every emotion, the giddy highs and the heart-wrenching disappointments.

Ten years later, Lysandra could now look back and see that time for what it was. She had, in many ways, lived a charmed life, with parents who loved and provided well for her. But, at seventeen, as a girl who was neither truly child nor adult, striving to become one while still feeling the pull of the other, she had seen too little of what was around her. It was, perhaps, the most difficult of all ages, and so she was willing to give Selia the patience her own mother had so often shown her.

As they ate, Lysandra asked Renan about Ballinrigh. On her first visit there, she had seen little more than the Southgate and his church. Now, not knowing how long they would be in that city, she wanted to hear more about Aghamore's great capital.

As she hoped, Renan understood that the information was even more for Selia's benefit than for hers. He described the people and the traffic—of which, Lysandra knew, they must learn to be careful. But most of all, he spoke of the city's many attributes. He told them about Ballinrigh's shops and libraries, including one the Church kept next to the cathedral. He told them about the kingdom's greatest cathedral, about its beauty and grandeur, and about the city's other parish churches which, like his own, served the outer neighborhoods, dotting the skyline with their little cross-topped spires.

Renan also described the elegance of the Archbishop's Residence. Much of its immense size was given over to the business of the Church, serving the kingdom as a great office complex as well as the home of the Primus. Near the Residence was the great Palace of the High King. It had long ago ceased to be the fortress constructed by Liam the Builder. Though the original battlements could still be seen, like the cathedral and the Archbishop's Residence, it was a place of opulence and grandeur. The gardens of both places were open to the public, and with the coming of summer should be just entering their glory.

Lysandra found the thought of seeing these gardens enticing. But it was not her own feelings that interested her. She kept her senses alert and focused on Selia. As the moments passed, and Renan's description grew more and more enthusiastic, the girl's interest grew with them. In spite of herself, Selia's reluctance was passing as the vista of unimagined possibilities opened before her.

Finished eating, Lysandra left the table while Renan was still talking, and went into the pantry where she stored her herbs and medicines. She did not worry about Renan taking offense; they both knew Selia was his true audience. *There's so much she'll need to learn,* Lysandra thought as she ran her fingers over the neat rows of jars and bowls, and inhaled the fragrant air of drying herbs. *I can only help her so much. The rest either Renan must teach her, or she must learn for herself.*

For the first time, the true enormity of what lay ahead hit Lysandra. It made all that she had learned in this cottage, where there were no expectant and needy eyes of the kingdom to watch her, seem trivial. With her *Sight* to guide her, she had learned not only to care for herself, but to tend the garden and use its contents to heal.

But Selia had to gain the throne . . . and she had to rule the kingdom. She would need to learn its history, good and bad, about commerce, trade, and taxes, friendly neighbors, enemies, and how to deal with both, about the law of the kingdom—the letter and the spirit—and when each must be applied . . . She would also have to learn about the people surrounding her—who they were, exactly what their duties entailed, whom to trust and whom to fear . . . and, no doubt, a myriad of other particulars Lysandra could not name.

"God always fits the burden to the back," Lysandra told herself, using the axiom her mother used to quote. *Selia would not be who she is, facing what's ahead, if she did not have the gifts needed.*

It was here, she knew, she could help the younger woman. While Renan worked with Selia, teaching her about history and politics, and their many applications, Lysandra's job would be internal. Selia was the Font of Wisdom; Lysandra must help her find out just what that meant and how to call upon all the many powers within that single title.

But I'm still learning about myself, a part of her cried. With suddenly shaking fingers, she put down the jar in her hand before she could drop it. *There's still so much I don't know. How can I teach anyone else?*

Once more, she quoted her mother's words to herself. *Perhaps,* they seemed to tell her, *it is* because *you are still learning that you can teach. If it had all come easily or all at once, how could you help Selia through her struggles? You cannot give what you do not have—and that includes understanding.*

The thought brought a comfort to which Lysandra clung as she returned to the task at hand.

It was just over an hour later when Lysandra closed the door on her cottage. Renan and Selia were already waiting for her outside the garden gate. Although Lysandra did not feel the heart-wrenching sense of separation she had the last time she closed this door to walk to Ballinrigh, the finality of the sound as the door latch clicked into place sent a sudden pain through her.

Instinctively, she reached for Cloud-Dancer. As always, he was there, and the feel of his fur beneath her palm, the warmth of his solid presence beside her, eased the parting from her home. But before they stepped off the little porch, she ran her fingers more deeply into his fur. Through this strengthened physical touch, she borrowed his vision to have one last look across her garden.

She rarely used Cloud-Dancer's vision anymore since her *Sight* had expanded so dramatically. Though it now came to her each time she summoned it, most often granting a richness of color it had withheld before, it still did not replace true sight. And that was, at this moment of leave-taking, what she wanted.

Neither Renan nor Selia hurried her, as she let her shared vision glide lovingly across each stand of flowers and bed of herbs, each area where vegetable seed rested in the ground, soon to grow and provide her with food for another year. She bade them all a temporary good-bye, then lightened her touch on Cloud-Dancer, breaking the contact necessary to use his eyes. After a quick, grateful rub behind his ears, she let go, swung her walking stick purposefully forward, and stepped off the porch.

Time would not stop for her any more than it would for Selia; the future was calling to them all.

Renan held the gate open for her. "Are you all right?" he asked her softly, as she stepped through.

"Yes," she answered just as softly. "This time I know where I'm going—and I know I'll return." *And,* she added silently, *this time I'm with you.*

She heard him close and latch the gate behind her. Lysandra did not look back, would not again until the day she came joyfully back down the woodland path toward home. From this moment until then, she told herself, she would look only forward.

The forest, through which these first days of walking would be spent, was filled with the sounds of summer. Songbirds cried and answered their mates, while others, who had mated early, already had hatchlings in the nest. They hopped and twittered on branches, flew from tree to tree, singing the squawks, chirps, and trills that Lysandra automatically identified to herself.

Her companions, she doubted, heard the same as she; they were more attuned to their own passage than to the sounds of the forest. In a way, Lysandra pitied them for what they were missing, even while realizing this was the way of most sighted people. It had been her own, before her blindness had taught her about the beauty and richness that lay beyond the realm of sight.

Then her *Sight* had come, Lysandra thought, and taught her about a wholly different realm that existed somewhere between the physical and the ethereal, a new way of *seeing* that beheld truth as well as substance, intent more clearly than shape and function.

If she ever saw again with only her eyes, Lysandra feared

she would lose so much that often she no longer wished the return of "normal" vision. Where once there was grief over all she had lost, there now existed peace and gratitude for all she had been given.

This healing had come neither easily nor quickly. Through many years of her solitude, she had been afraid to heal, afraid to feel, to love, to trust any happiness that might again be destroyed—and destroy her along with it. But now she knew that joy, that *love,* was never destroyed. All that her parents had been and had been to her, all she had felt for and from them—and Ultan—was part of every beat of her heart. This knowledge brought the certainty that, just as she had healed, so would Selia.

Their stories were both different and the same, filled with loss and loneliness, with silence and sorrow. But now neither of them was alone, and now that she was here to help Selia reclaim her life, the joy, the sense of future every seventeen-year-old should have—whether Queen or commoner—was part of what fueled the new joy in Lysandra's own life.

It seemed such a long time ago now, though it had been scarcely two months, when she had sat in her cottage, sleepless with wondering why the dream was calling her to leave her solitary life and peaceful forest home. She remembered clearly thinking that, perhaps, there was but one life, one heart, she was meant to save from the suffering she had endured; that, perhaps, such a single act was enough. Perhaps it was everything.

She had not realized that, even then, the gift of prophecy within her was awakening. She *had* been called to save one life . . . but through that life, the kingdom would be saved, and through that act had come her own salvation.

Lysandra's *Sight* embraced her companions as they now walked a few steps ahead of her. It reached of its own accord, showing her their auras, which were so strong and clear, Lysandra felt them as part of herself.

Suddenly, between one step and the next, her *Sight* shifted and her newly strong prophetic power welled up inside of her. It was still so strange to her, Lysandra was unsure what to do or how to best make use of it. Nor had she a guide to teach her. She found herself wishing Eiddig were here; she had a feeling that the Cryf leader, who had spent his long and faithful life listening to the Voice of the Divine, might be able to tell her what to do.

Seconds passed. Soon, the feeling of prophecy, of future *Far-Seeing*, filled her and began to spill over. The scene before her wavered and changed. Gone were the sounds, the smells, and the beauty that her *Sight* knew as the Great Forest. Gone, too, were the auras surrounding her two companions. Instead, Lysandra felt as if she was physically transported to some other *where,* as well as some other *when.*

She *saw* Selia first, standing in the cathedral in Ballinrigh; Lysandra recognized it at once from Renan's descriptions. Though she did not *see* them, she felt the pressure of the waiting crowd, hundreds of minds all focused on Selia and what was happening to her. But then, slicing through everything else, came the sharp sense of dangers and duplicity.

Though Lysandra strained now, and tried to focus on the source of this threat, either her gift was too new for her to use it effectively, or something about the danger itself kept it from being revealed. The only thing Lysandra could *see* was Selia; the only thing she could feel from this vision was the certainty that when this moment arrived, so might Selia's death.

With a swiftness that made her dizzy, the focus of her prophecy changed from Selia to Renan. But he was changed, too; unshaven, unkempt, he knelt alone in that same cathedral, now dark and empty. Lysandra knew she was seeing the future of which he had once asked her that day in the Cryf underground, when he sat beside the Great River. On that day, his spirit had been wounded with self-accusation over the magic he had used and the part he had taken in the battle, of the men he had just wounded and killed.

She had felt his inner turmoil then, and she could feel it now, in her vision, as he prostrated himself before the altar, arms and body stretched out on the cold stone in a living shape of the cross. Although his body made no other move, although no one else appeared within this scene, Lysandra sensed that Renan, too, was in imminent danger—but his was the death of his spirit.

Why was she being shown these things? she wondered. Was she supposed to warn her companions, her friends, of what was ahead for them? Was it in her power to stop these events from happening?

Just as before, prophecy gave her no answers. Instead, her *Sight* again shifted and she *saw* only Renan and Selia walking before her through the Great Forest of Camlough. To judge by the distance now between them, several minutes must have passed. Lysandra opened her mouth to call, but before she could speak, her *Sight* grew dark. She suddenly felt as if she were floating somewhere above her body, spinning wildly.

Then, just before the spinning stopped, Lysandra heard Cloud-Dancer start his eerie, plaintive howl. It was the last thing she knew before the void closed in and her body crumpled, unconscious, to the forest floor.

Chapter Four

At that moment, Aurya was thinking of Elon just as intently as the bishop had been thinking of her. She had to think of something while her hands did the same repetitive work over and over, day after day.

This last month had been a living hell for Aurya. It was not only being stuck here, in this underground Realm beneath the northern arm of Aghamore's mountains, nor was it being a prisoner of these abominable creatures, the Cryf, and being forced into the role of a servant. Terrible as these were to Aurya, they were not what filled every moment of every day with a bleak emptiness and kept her from sleep night after night. Aurya's hell was that from the time she had entered the Realm of the Cryf, her magic had ceased to exist.

For as long as she could remember, long before she knew what it was, magic had been part of her. Its embers warmed her soul in childhood, gave its first flickering flame with puberty, grew steadily through adolescence until, as an adult, the power of magic was like a fire in her blood. Its bright blaze filled her heart and soul; strong and steady, she had only to will it forth and it was hers to command.

But now, here, there was nothing. Not even the embers of her childhood remained to warm her, and Aurya felt as if her inner soul, that secret place where identity was formed and held, had been turned into a frozen void.

There were now only two things that kept her alive and

moving through the days and nights of her captivity . . . hatred and revenge. Without them, she would have curled up on one of the nested sleeping shelves, turned her face to the wall, and waited for death to claim her. Without the searing passion of hatred, without the unyielding determination for revenge, death would have been welcomed and embraced.

Aurya spent her hours planning her revenge upon all those who put and kept her here. She worked with the same drive and intelligence she had once thrown into the study of magic. Old Kizzie, her first teacher, would have recognized the look in her eyes—though no one else, not even Giraldus, did so now.

But she rarely saw Giraldus or Maelik. The three of them were kept working in separate areas and occupations, coming together only for their early-morning and evening meals. During the day, they were taken—always under guard—to their work; at night, after supper—and still under guard— Maelik was taken to a sleeping chamber separate from the one in which she and Giraldus passed their nights.

With the guards ever present, there was little chance to talk about such private matters as escape. But Aurya knew the men desired it almost as much as she . . . *almost*. They wanted their freedom—but she wanted her magic back and *nothing* could equal that desire.

Aurya ground her teeth together as she picked up another lapful of the long plant fibers the Cryf used to make cloth. Once these fibers had been taken from inside the stem of the gorien plant, soaked in a special brine, then washed, pounded, and teased three times, they turned into a product very like wool. Then these fibers had to be carded and spun.

The first and last of the process required skills Aurya did not possess. So she sat here, hour after hour, placing wads of fibrous fluff onto the two tiny-spiked paddles in her hands, then pulling it time and again through the spikes until it changed into a material that could be spun, dyed, and woven into cloth.

It was at the uncarded stage, the stage with which Aurya worked, that the fibers were the amazingly soft material that covered their beds. The first time she had touched it Aurya had been amazed at its texture. Now, after the uncounted hours of working with the stuff, that amazement had died. She hated it as she hated everything else here.

Off in the distance, some of the Cryf females were singing in their strange tongue, sitting together in one of their work circles, each wrapped in the sarong made of gorien fibers and dyed with plant dyes, that was the female Cryf's habitual clothing. One had been offered to Aurya, but after the first day she refused to wear one.

Though most often the Cryf males wore loincloths, there were a type of loose trousers and jacket they wore in terrain where their thick hair was not enough to protect them. Sets of them were given to Maelik and Giraldus—and after the first day, Aurya insisted on them, too.

Although she gave no indication of it, Aurya was already beginning to understand much of what her captors said. Today's song, despite its minor, haunting melody, was joyful in content; it was a song of home and children and life in a place of peace—and Aurya did not want to listen to it. She bit her lower lip to keep from shouting at the Cryf females to stop. She did not want to hear their music or their tales of Cryf life any more than she wanted to eat their food, sleep on their beds, or wear their clothing.

She wanted her freedom—and her magic—back.

Don't give up on us, Elon, she thought as she put the now neatly carded fibers aside and grabbed up another lapful of fluff. *I swear by the great Morrigan, Goddess-Mother, Keeper of Life and Bringer of Death, I swear by all the black power of the nether realms, that we shall get free. Somehow. And I swear that Giraldus* will *be High King. When he is, I'll hunt down that girl who dared to condemn me to this life, and her companions, and kill them all with my own hand. Then, once I have watched their lifeblood seep away, I'll return here and pull this Realm down, stone by stone, until nothing remains of it or these . . . creatures. Then I'll turn to the rest of Aghamore. Anyone who opposes me will feel my anger, until no one dares oppose me again.*

That includes you, Elon, her thoughts continued. *Before . . . this . . . I might have compromised, I might have let you convince me to marry Giraldus for the sake of our goal. But not now. No more compromises. With anyone. Once I get my magic back, I shall unleash a fury such as this kingdom has never known. Those who wish to live will compromise with me . . . and those who don't, will receive no mercy.*

All this I swear by every breath I take. Nothing will stop me, except death . . . and possibly not even that . . . .

Giraldus, too, was thinking of escape. Like Aurya, it filled at least some portion of his thoughts every waking moment. But unlike Aurya, such thoughts had not become obsession.

As a soldier, he knew that somehow, some*when,* an opportunity would present itself. If they all continued to behave placidly, their guards would eventually relax the diligence with which they currently manned their posts, or some slip would reveal the way to the surface. If they were patient and watchful, some mistake would be made. He had only to be ready to seize the opportunity when it arose.

He was not blind to the change that had come over Aurya since entering the Realm of the Cryf. He felt the fury that raged through her and, because he loved her, he also felt the fear that her pride would have denied was there.

I'll get you out of here, Aurya, he silently promised her. It was the same promise he silently made each night as he held her, and heard the many little sounds of distress she unconsciously made in her sleep. These sounds told him what, in her pride, her words would not.

Every morning, this promise was made with his first thought; every night it was his last. Through all the hours in between, it was the thought that kept him going, kept him focused, kept him from making a rash, uncalculated dash for freedom.

He would make no move that left Aurya behind. Nor could he ask her to do something that might cost her life. He, who had been born to rule, who was the Baron of Kilgarriff, Head of the Third Ruling House of Aghamore, would rather spend his remaining years in captivity and servitude than be responsible for Aurya's death.

So he obeyed his Cryf guards and masters, doing as he was told—watching and waiting for them to make a mistake.

His work was not as mindless as Aurya's. It was dirty and smelly, hard labor that made him glad of the pools of hot mineral water in which he and all those who worked at the fishponds washed themselves each evening.

These fish were the major source of protein for the Cryf, and had he not been forced into the labor, he might well have found the arrangement fascinating. Rather than relying on the precarious occupation of fishing, where each day's catch was subject to so many changeable factors—such as season and rainfall, river conditions and the strength of this year's run—the Cryf raised the fish they would eat. It was an elaborate and obviously effective system that would have amazed Giraldus, had the circumstances under which he was viewing it been different.

His job changed according to where extra hands were needed on any particular day. Sometimes he fed the fish or cleaned out the ponds between which they were frequently moved. The ponds—there were four of them—had been hollowed out of solid rock. Whether by some watercourse that had since been diverted or by the Cryf themselves, Giraldus did not know, but they were almost twice his height and at least six times as wide.

Water filled only one pond at a time. In that one, it was kept constantly moving, simulating the motion of the river over the fish. The empty ponds were drained of water and cleaned, including all of the rocks that were strewn across the bottom of the pond in uneven layers, again imitating the riverbed. It took days for a pond to be properly cleaned, every stone removed, cleaned, and replaced. But the fish were of vital importance to the Cryf, and no chance was taken with illness or parasitic infection.

There was other work required, besides this exhausting labor. There was the harvesting of the fish. Some of the harvest was for food, which meant killing and cleaning the fish, then skinning, boning, and slicing the meat in various ways, depending on which part of the food preparation area needed it. The bones, skin, and innards were not discarded; they went into special vats to become fertilizer for the abundance of plants grown by the Cryf.

The other part of the fish harvest involved "milking" the fish—the female for her roe, the male for his semen. Some of the females' eggs were kept aside for food and pickled in special brine as a great delicacy. The rest were combined with the "milk" taken from the males, to be fertilized and hatched into the fingerlings raised in yet another series of ponds. It was an extensive and elaborate operation that Giraldus could not help but admire.

It also proved to him that their captors, despite their somewhat beastly appearance, were not animals. They were intelligent—and watchful—beings it would not be easy to fool. But that did not change his mind or lessen his determination to get Aurya free.

* * *

Like Giraldus, Sergeant Maelik was also keeping close watch for a means of escape. And like Giraldus, he had come to realize the intelligence and resourcefulness of the Cryf. Understanding one's foe was the first step to vanquishing them—so Maelik kept his ears and eyes open and his mouth closed, except to ask questions of those with whom he did his day's work.

He had become quite used to their odd manner of speech when using the "Up-worlder's tongue." He had even begun to teach some of the ones with whom he worked a more contemporary use of the language. But it was cunning and not friendship that drove him. Lulling their captors into a false sense of security could only facilitate his chance of escape.

Unlike either Aurya or Giraldus, Maelik was used to carrying out orders and to long days of hard labor. There was enough variety in what he was doing to keep him from too much boredom. There was plenty of good food to eat and a warm, dry place to sleep—which was more than he could claim with some of the jobs he had done for Giraldus. He could wait as long as it took to get free.

The Cryf society was communal, with the food production areas serving all. But there were layers within layers of work to be done. Although Maelik did not think he had seen them all, over the last weeks he had worked in many of them. He had collected the barrels of discarded fish parts, and he had cranked the large, covered vats in which that waste was turned to fertilizer. He had also collected and distributed the end product to the many brightly lit caves where the herbs and plants that filled the rest of the Cryf's needs were grown.

He had worked in those caves, too—some of which were enormous—turning the soil to mix in the fertilizer, planting seedlings, or harvesting their crop, carrying woven baskets full of vegetables, grains, herbs, tubers, or roots between caves or to the cooking area. By the end of each day, he was ready to rest.

Like Giraldus, he was glad to wash the grime from his body beneath one of the numerous small waterfalls, then soak his tired muscles in the heated pools of mineral water. Whatever was in the water somehow drained much of the soreness away and helped him sleep without the numerous aches that might have otherwise kept him awake.

All in all, if this was his prison, it was not a harsh one. Except for the guards who watched his every move, he might have occasionally forgotten he was a prisoner and enjoyed aspects of this life. The food was delicious, certainly better than any camp fare. The work, though tiring, was not unpleasant; it brought back memories of working beside his father and two older brothers on their family farm.

Thanks to that amazingly soft and fluffy material with which the Cryf covered the stone sleeping shelf at the back of the cave he now called his own, rest was easy and sleep refreshing. Maelik had often said, more in truth than in jest, that after so many years of army life, he could sleep almost anywhere. Despite its truth, it was an unnecessary talent when lying on the covered, nestlike beds of the Cryf.

The only real thing missing from this life was freedom— the feel of the sun or the breeze on his skin—and Sarai, the serving girl at his favorite pub in Adaraith, for whom he had a deep and rarely expressed fondness. He was used to being able to see her whenever he had a spare hour and could escape his duties to go into the city. Her absence was beginning to bring the depth of that fondness he felt into sharp clarity.

He had, however, lived most of his life without a woman and never truly suffered from the lack. The quick and passing lusts he felt were easily satisfied by the camp followers who were always nearby. Or so he often reminded himself; if he stayed here in the Realm of the Cryf long enough, even Sarai would no doubt fade from need and memory.

Knowing this made him wary, more of himself than of his guards. He must not let himself relax into his captivity, easy though that might be. To do so would be a betrayal of so much—not only of Sarai and the feelings for her that he sometimes admitted to himself. It would also be a betrayal of his soldier's honor . . . and *that* was something he held even more dear.

Lord Giraldus counted on him, had given him a trust that, though mostly unexpressed, was still understood between them. He counted on Maelik's ears and eyes, his experience and his wits. Maelik had never let Giraldus down, and he was not going to begin now, he thought as he hoisted yet another large basket of tubers onto his shoulders, walking with his guards along the now familiar route to the cooking area.

He smiled pleasantly, and the Cryf returned the expression as they all started down the long, stone passage. Maelik kept slightly to the fore so they could not see his how his face changed once out of their view. The smile remained in place, but his eyes narrowed as he listened to the cadence of his guards' footsteps.

The truth was, Maelik had spent more of his life in the army than out of it, and by now he could tell more about a man by his footsteps than most people could tell face-to-face. The Cryf, he had found, were no different. The way his guards walked told Maelik that they were in even more danger than he of relaxing in their task and vigilance, as did the chattering of their voices behind him.

Maelik did not have Aurya's gift for languages, but with over a month of captivity, he had begun to understand many of the Cryf words. Still smiling his cooperative façade, he concentrated on what they were saying. The words he did understand confirmed to him that he was reading the Cryf aright—if not all of them, at least the ones assigned to him. Like soldiers, like men, everywhere, they were discussing the females in their life.

Now his smile turned genuine, and not only in the recognition of that eternal male bond of woman troubles; he knew his guards would not be having such a conversation if they expected the slightest trouble from him.

Ye gabber away, me boyos, he thought, using the country speech of his youth, as he always did in his thoughts. *I'll keep a-smilin' fer ye and ye keep yer little minds a-turning on all but me. Aye — ye'll make a mistake, me boyos, and I'll be a-ready.*

Were ye ones o' mine, I'd have ye up on charges fer this lax-ness o' yer duties. But yer not o' mine, and I'll shew ye how a true soldier's mind works. Ye think I'm no trouble fer ye a-cause I smile at ye and do me work. But ye'll learn soon enough that a captive canna be a friend. When the time comes, I'll be a-teachin' ye what ye'll not soon forget — if ye live long enough. An' I'll be a-smilin' then, too, me boyos . . . .

Chapter Five

Lysandra found the trip to Ballinrigh much more enjoyable this time. The beautiful weather of June, when the air and earth were warming but still free of the burdensome heat that would come in a few more weeks, made walking a delight. And on this trip, her traveling companions were not fear and uncertainty; this time she knew where she was going and why. And if none of them yet knew exactly how they would ac-complish their goal of seeing Selia safely crowned, they at least possessed the faith that a way would be discovered.

As they approached the South-gate of Ballinrigh, Lysan-dra could not help but remember her last time here — the near tears of exhaustion and frustration, the bribe she had given the gatekeeper to allow Cloud-Dancer to enter with her. She remembered, too, the fear that had awaited her on the other side, as two men, having seen the coin she gave the gatekeeper, tried to attack and rob her.

Shocking as the attack had been, without it Lysandra doubted she would have ever found Renan. She had not entered a church in years, not since the funeral Mass for her parents; without the attack that drove her to find safety, she would never have entered one in Ballinrigh.

This time, there was no bribe demanded for her to enter. The gatekeeper knew Renan and waved them all through with a friendly greeting for the priest. It was bright daylight, too, not the closing dusk of when Lysandra had last entered.

She thought herself prepared, but as they entered the city it was as if they walked into a wall of sound and activity. She held on tightly to Cloud-Dancer's fur, partly for the reassurance it gave her—and partly to be certain he would not dash away after something that caught his attention.

I'll have to find something to use as a harness, she thought, trying not to think of what could happen to the wolf should they become separated. Pictures of disaster—of horses and carts trampling him, of city guards capturing and shooting him, of him becoming lost, confused, unable to find her or get home—pictures all born of nervousness, threatened to overwhelm her. She could hardly keep herself from running now, toward Renan's little stone church with its fenced yard and enclosed safety.

She used Cloud-Dancer's vision while they walked down the city blocks, wanting true vision to guide her. The suddenness of her own distress at first kept her from noticing her companions. When she did, she saw that while Renan was at ease with all the noise and activity, Selia was not. The fear on her face reminded Lysandra that the young woman had lived a life even more sheltered than Lysandra's own.

The little fishing village of Caerryck made Scorda, the town in which Lysandra had grown up, seem like a thriving metropolis. And for the last ten years, though she had lived a relatively isolated life in the Great Forest, Lysandra had known more outside contact through the people who came to her for healing than Selia had known in the convent where she had been raised. Overwhelmed as Lysandra felt right now, she could not imagine what a city such as this must be like for Selia.

They were almost at the church; through Cloud-Dancer's eyes, Lysandra could see its small spire poking slightly above the surrounding buildings. She reached over and put her free hand on Selia's arm to point it out to her. The girl started and trembled beneath her touch.

"Hold on just a bit longer," Lysandra said, loudly enough for Selia's ears alone. "We're almost there."

She kept her hand on Selia's arm, for the younger woman's sake quieting her own fears. Once she felt herself calm, she reached out through the mental link she and Selia always shared, especially when in physical contact, to reinforce her reassurances with her own inner sense of equanimity.

But touching Selia's mind was like jumping into a boiling cauldron. The sounds and images that surrounded them spun in a fast, distorted whirlwind that nearly swept Lysandra's own mind up into it. Although she did not let go of her grip on Cloud-Dancer's fur, she did cease the use of his vision to better concentrate her strength on calming Selia.

Lysandra took a breath. Then, as she slowly exhaled, she deepened her touch in Selia's mind, slowly letting a deep internal quiet flow from herself to the younger woman. At first, Selia's mind resisted, feeling this as yet another onslaught upon her already overtaxed senses. Then, slowly, recognition dawned, and Lysandra felt her thoughts welcomed, familiar amid all this strangeness.

Despite the conscious welcome, however, it took a few seconds for Selia's subconscious to let go and drop her barriers. But this was an act of healing, not of invasion; Lysandra was as perseveringly gentle as she would have been with any patient's need.

After a moment the barriers of fear dropped. Lysandra began to bathe Selia's mind in reassurance. She was glad that the young woman's trust in both herself and Renan provided fertile ground for the assurances she was sharing to take root and prosper.

Focusing so intently on Selia's needs, Lysandra had ceased thinking about their surroundings, about herself or what they were here to do. She was unaware that they had stopped walking until, suddenly, she heard Renan's voice.

"What's wrong?" he asked, the puzzlement in his voice more clear to Lysandra than the noise of the city around her. "Lysandra? Selia? We're almost there—why have you stopped?"

For a few more seconds, Lysandra said nothing as, mind to mind, she checked on Selia's condition. Then, healer's aspect satisfied, she withdrew both her physical and mental contact and gave Renan a little nod.

"We're fine now," she said. "I think you and I forgot how overwhelming a city can be for someone who's never seen one before . . . and Ballinrigh is a very *big* city."

"I did forget," Renan said as he stepped around Lysandra, touching her arm lightly as he passed. He went to Selia and put a fatherly arm about her shoulders.

"I'm sorry," he told her. "I should have warned you about how busy it gets here at this time of day—and I should have paid closer attention to your reaction. But we're almost to the parish, and it's much quieter there, as Lysandra can tell you. Not all the city is like here, near the gate. There are places in the heart of Ballinrigh, especially in the parks at the Palace and the Archbishop's Residence, where you hardly believe you're in a city at all."

While he talked in his gentle, reassuring—best voice, Renan had also started walking. His arm was still around Selia's shoulders, so that the young woman walked with him, moving almost without realizing it. Lysandra, still holding on to Cloud-Dancer, followed a couple of steps behind. She was listening to Renan as he pointed things out to Selia, and she was also keeping her healer's empathy extended, monitoring Selia's emotions for any sign of returning panic.

Having been calmed by Lysandra and now further soothed by Renan as they continued down the city streets, the girl was able to muster a little interest in the sights Renan was pointing out. It was a good sign and Lysandra smiled, nodding to herself. Once they finally turned the last corner and the little stone church loomed before them, an oasis of peace amid the cacophony of the city, Lysandra was certain it would take little time for Selia to fully acclimate to the setting of her new life.

Entering the Parish Church of Saint Anne was not the homecoming Renan expected. When they stepped through the front door, several things hit him at once. There were no candles burning anywhere—not before the statue of the Virgin here in the narthex, or at the statuary of the parish Patron; not even the Presence Lamp was lit beside the altar. The only light shone through the small stained-glass windows that lined the walls of the nave.

The church also smelled musty, unused, without its usual air of incense, beeswax, and wood polish. All was cold and felt abandoned—and Renan shivered with a feeling that had little to do with the temperature of the air.

I sent a letter to the office of the Archbishop, he thought as he quickly strode down the center aisle of the nave toward the sacristy to the left of the altar, to check on the sacred vessels and make certain they were safe. *Surely, the parish wasn't forgotten because of my absence. It's a small parish, true—but there are faithful souls here who need care.*

The fear that had been making his heart pound was set to rest with a quick examination of the sacristy. Chalice, paten, and extra ciborium were still in their cupboard, the vestments were all in place; not even the sacramental wine had been touched. Everything looked exactly as he had left it. Too exactly—Renan felt a growing certainty that no visiting priest had been sent to take his place.

Ilc left the sacristy and went back into the sanctuary of the altar to check within the tabernacle. Inside stood another ciborium, its bright gold shining even in the semidarkness. Taking it out and lifting its lid, he saw it still contained the extra, consecrated hosts left from the last Mass he had celebrated. Old and stale, they would need to be consumed before fresh ones could be put in their place. But that was a sacred act and would be done in the proper way and time.

For now, replacing the ciborium within the tabernacle, he closed the small, ornate door that was carved with a gilded *Agnus Dei* flanked by two seraphim. Then he lowered and lit the hanging Presence Lamp before going to rejoin the women where they waited at the back of the nave.

He walked this time down one of the side aisles, stopping to light the other lamps that stood unused in their customary niches. With each one, this little parish church where he had spent the last decade in service began to look more like itself.

"Well," he said when he reached the women, taking a deep breath to steel himself, "let's go see what shape the rectory and guesthouse are in. If they're anything like in here, they'll both need a good fire to chase away the chill, and a good cleaning, too. The church certainly does. I'd no idea this much dust could collect—or that the place would be so abandoned."

His words proved too prophetic for his own comfort as they stopped at the rectory first so Renan could stash his belongings and set a fire. Then they all headed toward the guesthouse. It, too, was in dire need of care, and Renan left the women to settle in while he went to gather some wood and kindling.

As he worked, he could barely keep his impatience in check. He wanted to be on his way back into the city; he wanted to travel around to the homes and shops of the people in the neighborhood and let them know of his return. He needed to let his people know that he had never intended for them to be left without spiritual comfort.

A few minutes later, after the fire was lit and a stack of wood laid by the hearth to keep it going, Lysandra came over to him with smile of understanding on her lips.

"Go," she said.

"What—?"

"Renan, I don't need any special gifts to tell that you're worried about your people—as you should be. You're anxious to get to your duties—even Cloud-Dancer can feel it," she added, her smile broadening.

Her words made Renan glance at the wolf. Then he nearly laughed aloud at the way Cloud-Dancer sat next to Lysandra, his head cocked slightly to one side, staring at Renan with a look of lupine puzzlement.

"Selia and I will be fine," Lysandra continued. "So go— and take as much time as you need . . . set your mind at ease."

Renan was filled with a sudden urge to pull Lysandra into his arms, to hold her and tell her how much her understanding meant to him. Instead, he shook his head.

"I should stay," he said. "This place is a mess and you shouldn't—"

Lysandra favored him with one of the truly broad and amused smiles she so rarely gave, the one that brought the little dimple to one cheek and always made his heart feel as if it jumped in his chest. She looked for all the world as if she wanted to laugh at him. But Renan did not mind. He compared this happy woman, to whom smiles came more and more easily, to the frightened, troubled, and exhausted one she had been when he first saw her sitting in the back of the church two months ago. The transformation was nothing short of miraculous, and he counted himself blessed to have had any part in it.

Finally, Lysandra did laugh. "Go," she said again. "You know you want to, you *must*—and putting this place in order will give us something to do while you're away. Go."

Renan reached out and touched her arm, the nearest thing to an embrace he would allow himself. "Thank you," was all he said before turning and hurrying out. First he must go back to the rectory and put on a clean shirt, collar, and cassock—then he would be on his way, to tell his parishioners that their wandering priest had finally returned.

But it was not only a dutiful altruism that guided his feet, as he reentered the hubbub of the city. Being out among the people who knew and trusted him was the best way to learn what was truly happening in Aghamore—not only with the Barons and bishops and the battle for the throne, but to the people of the kingdom. This evening he would celebrate a special Mass. By that time, Renan hoped to have a fair understanding of what had been going on during his absence and what the common people thought of it all.

As he walked down Ballinrigh's streets, Renan was pleased by the friendly greetings called out to him. In this part of the city, dwellings and businesses vied for space, new and old sat side by side; visitors and messengers from all parts of the kingdom were among the traffic of the Southgate. Viewing it objectively, with the eyes and ears that had become used to the quiet of Lysandra's cottage, Renan could understand why Selia had felt so overwhelmed.

Yet, despite the peace of these last weeks, he found all the noise like music he had missed, and the activity was a stylized dance performed for his enjoyment. As Lysandra had felt entering the Great Forest, Renan knew he was home.

"Hey, Father—Father Renan," a voice called.

Renan glanced around, trying to locate its source through the flow of traffic. A cart passed, and finally, across the street, he saw a young man dressed in green-and-white livery, with the patch of a winged horse on his breast, his sleeves, and on the bag he carried. His dress and bag declared him to be a Rider, a member of the messenger service with stations in every city and many towns throughout Aghamore.

Renan recognized him at once. It was Wilham Tybourne, and having caught Renan's attention, the young man was waving vigorously. He sprinted across the busy street, deftly dodging the people, animals, and carts in his way. Renan waited, smiling. He liked Wilham for his own sake, and, being a Rider, he was always full of tales from the Provinces—tales he was always happy to share—and now more than ever, Renan was eager to hear them.

Wilham was not a native of Ballinrigh, nor even of Urlar Province. He and Renan had met shortly after Wilham had first come to Ballinrigh, home of the Riders' Central Office. Out exploring the city, he had heard the bell ring for Mass and stopped at Renan's parish to attend. That had been two and a half years ago. As Wilham approached him now, Renan wondered if, nearing twenty, the young man still felt the same way about his occupation.

"It's good to see you, Wilham," Renan said, reaching out to grasp the Rider's shoulders affectionately.

Wilham returned the gesture in this male equivalent of an embrace. "Aye—and ye, Father Renan," he said, his smile matching the priest's own. "I went by yer parish a few days ago, when I arrived back 'ere, but all was dark."

Renan nodded. "I was called away—briefly. I've only just returned. And you—how long will you be in Ballinrigh this time?"

Wilham shrugged. "There ben't no way to tell," he said, still using the rural expressions with which he had grown up, despite his time away from the farm. "I may be off tomorrow or still be sittin' 'ere a week gone."

"I was just starting around to tell my parishioners I've returned and daily Mass will commence tonight. Can you walk along with me?"

"Nay," Wilham said, "but have ye eaten? There be a fair pub near, and I've both the coins and the appetite."

Renan considered. It was true that in his eagerness to be off he had neglected to eat—as, at this mention of food, his stomach was reminding him. But it was also true he had many people yet to visit. He almost declined Wilham's offer . . . yet what he might learn from an hour of Wilham's company made it too important an opportunity to miss.

So he nodded. "Thank you, Wilham," he said. "And I'll return the favor. Come to the rectory any night and join me for dinner. In fact, if you've a mind and nothing else planned, come this evening. I've two visitors staying in the guesthouse you might enjoy meeting . . . and if you come early enough, you can attend Mass first."

Wilham smiled again. "Aye," he said. "I'll do just that. But let's get us some lunch before we talk of dinner."

Selia sat in one of the front pews, staring at the altar. The cleaning rags, soap, and the beeswax and linseed oil wood polish she had found in the little closet behind the sacristy lay next to her, all but forgotten. Certain Father Renan would say Mass this evening, she had left Lysandra busy in the guesthouse and come to put the church to rights.

As of yet, however, she had done nothing more than sit here. It was not the tasks that stopped her; in fact, she welcomed them. Cleaning the church, replacing the burned-out candles, dressing the altar, even polishing the long, wooden pews, were all duties she had performed frequently at the convent that for ten years she had called home. She had also often lent a helping hand to Father Peadar as he tried to keep the ever-present layer of sand under control at the Parish of Saint Peter the Fisherman in Caerryck. These duties felt like a homecoming.

But I have no home, she thought as she continued to stare at the altar. *Again.*

She fervently wished it was a feeling with which she was unfamiliar—but it was not. Too much of her life had been spent not belonging. Even at the convent, even after so many years there, she had been something of a peculiarity.

All of the Sisters had been kind; there was no denying the sympathy they had shown her, especially when Father Peadar had first taken her there. But she had been just seven years old at the time, the youngest person there by several years, and the nuns were not certain what to do with a child in their midst. Nor were they given to displays of affection, something Selia's love-starved heart so desperately craved.

Finally, she had come to understand the strict Rule the Sisters followed. Their long silences and times of withdrawal were not aimed at her, as her mother's had been. For a long time, that memory kept her from seeing the many silent signs of welcome and approval she had received right from the start of her time in the convent. Once she did understand, she had finally discovered the sense of home and family the outside world had never offered her.

But it had been a feeling too short-lived. She was homeless again and her future just as unsettled now as in her childhood. Selia felt as if she was walking down two paths—one that belonged to her, to Selia, and one that belonged to the Font of Wisdom. The latter had a purpose and a destiny; the former knew only sorrow and disassociation. She was forced to skip back and forth between them—and she could not see far enough ahead to know if the paths ever fully merged.

Both Lysandra and Father Renan believed they did, Selia kept reminding herself. Despite their many assurances that all would eventually be well, despite the friendship that the two unstintingly gave her, this feeling of being homeless and anchorless persisted. And, if everything they believed came true, her life would change once again. Lysandra would go back to her cottage, Father Renan to his church, and she would again be left among strangers in a life she had not chosen.

Is that all I'm ever to know? she asked silently. *What must I do, what must I be, before I'm allowed a life with all the normal things, like love and family, that others take for granted? What have I done that all this is continually denied to me?*

Selia received no answer. With a sigh, she stood to begin her self-imposed tasks. Perhaps, she thought, if she took enough care of the present, the future might—for once—take care of itself.

With all the wisdom she was supposed to possess, this was the only reassurance she had to give herself . . . and from it she derived little comfort.

Chapter Six

Eiddig-Sant, Guide of the Cryf, Eldest and leader of the Council of Elders of the Fourteen Clans, sat on a large rock beside the falling water that was the birthplace of the Great River. Behind the waterfall was the entrance to the cave where the Holy Words of Dewi-Sant were kept. It was a place Eiddig had visited often in his life—to study and learn from the Holy Words, and to turn his heart inward to better hear the Voice of the Divine.

For eighty cycles of the Great River, he had been Guide for his people. He had been but twenty cycles when he began his true studies, training under the tutelage of Breda-Sant, the Guide before him. For nearly twenty more years, he had studied and trained, until Breda-Sant's cycles had ended and he had returned to the Heart of the Divine.

Now, as was the custom, Eiddig was training the one who would succeed him when his cycles had ended. His choice of student had been young Talog, son of the Fourteenth Clan, in whom the Voice of the Divine spoke with such clarity.

It was Talog who had gone with the Up-worlders as one of the Companions to find the Font of Wisdom. This was in full accord with the Holy Words of both Dewi-Sant and of the Up-world Seer, Tambryn. Yet since his return, Eiddig had sensed a change in Talog. It was this feeling that kept bringing Eiddig back here, to his favorite place, to think in solitude.

The fine mist that rose from the falling water did not penetrate the thick hair that covered most of Eiddig's body—hair that was now nearly pure white, with only hints of the rich reddish brown it had been in his youth. Nor was it nearly as thick as it had once been. But Eiddig did not care; each white hair proclaimed his age and authority as surely as the great gold-and-silver-wrapped staff he carried or the jewel-encrusted chain and badge of office he wore around his neck.

He lifted that necklace so his eyes could focus on it, hoping this talisman would bring his thoughts into focus, too. The heart of the necklace was a huge, clear diamond. Hardest of all stones, it represented the Realm of the Cryf, the strength of their union and their service to the Divine, a clear and faultless symbol of the Light of Truth, to which they were dedicated.

Around the diamond, bright-colored gemstones formed a circle. Carnelian, garnet, opal, peridot, emerald, topaz, lapis, ruby, amethyst, citrine, sapphire, tourmaline, chalcedony, and onyx—fourteen stones, each one of them different, for the fourteen clans that had been united into one people here within this great and hidden Realm.

The Ancient Wisdoms said that each of these stones held a different property, just as each of the Clans had brought a unique set of strengths and gifts into the Realm. *But which one shalt be of greatest help unto Talog?* the old Guide wondered, still wishing he could put a name to the change he sensed in the younger Cryf.

Eiddig had been hoping Talog would come to him, seek his help with whatever was troubling him. So far, it had not happened. Eiddig was beginning to feel that the younger Cryf's silence might be a declaration of its own—yet, again, he was at a loss to understand it. As he had done several times already, Eiddig tried reviewing a list of basic emotions, as if naming them might clarify the one that was Talog's great burden.

Anger . . . hatred . . . jealousy . . . envy . . . No, Eiddig was certain these were not to be found in Talog's heart. *Fear . . .* again, no . . . *remorse . . . doubt . . .* Perhaps, Eiddig conceded, knowing that doubt could be a part of faith, giving birth to the questions that could lead to true wisdom. He knew that now, looking back through the perspective that was the greatest gift of age. But did Talog? That was the question. Had his travels Up-world and the events he had both witnessed and endured, caused Talog's faith to waver?

Eiddig slowly nodded, dropping the necklace once more to his chest. He felt that he was finally on the right path. Now the greater question was the form Talog's doubts had taken and how Eiddig might help his apprentice back to the clarity of faith once more?

Again, Eiddig's thoughts touched upon the three Up-world prisoners. The same intuition that whispered to him of Talog's problem, also whispered that those three were part of it. Eiddig thought about each one separately; in the month they had been within this Realm, he had learned more about their hearts than they supposed.

He thought first about the one called Maelik, in whom the spirit of leader and follower dwelt equally. This one's heart was not as black or twisted with hate as the female's, yet neither did he possess a heart of clear purpose or a spirit of higher calling.

Mayhap, Eiddig thought, *a heart of peace mayest yet be born unto this one, if the Divine so wills. I shalt speak unto those who hath the training and the keeping of him. Mayhap they knoweth how this one's way mayest yet be turned unto the right, that his heart mayest know true joy.*

Eiddig considered Giraldus next. In this one, too, the old Guide sensed a potential goodness buried beneath layers of wrong choices and ill-focused moves.

This one walketh as a leader and yet hath been too easily led, Eiddig thought, *and not unto paths wherein the Will of the Divine mayest be found. There dwelleth in this one's heart a care unto his people, yet he hath let greed and ambition claim the greater part—and so doth a war within him rage. I shalt speak also unto those who hath the training and the keeping of him. Mayhap, by the Mercy of the Divine, a new way mayest yet be found for this one, too.*

Although Eiddig was hopeful, he was not foolish; he did not think such changes would come either quickly or easily. But She-Who-Is-Wisdom had entrusted the Cryf to guard these prisoners throughout the years remaining to them. Eiddig did not know how long Up-worlders lived, but if it was even half the number of Cryf years, then there was time for hope to have a chance of becoming reality.

But now Eiddig's thoughts turned to Aurya, and with that his hope died away. From this one he had perceived nothing but anger and hate, greed, ambition—and Darkness. His aged eyes, trained by long decades as Guide, had tried to find a glimmer of Light still residing in Aurya's spirit, even the tiniest ember that might, with care, be fanned into a flame.

But he had found nothing. He traveled often by the smaller back passages, to places where, unseen, he could watch her at her work or while interacting with either Cryf or the other Up-worlders. He saw the love in Giraldus's eyes when he looked at Aurya—and Eiddig also saw that love was not what she returned him. It was from within Aurya, Eiddig knew clearly, that the Darkness emanated . . . and it was that Darkness that had led both Giraldus and Maelik away from the heart-path they should follow.

Eiddig found himself profoundly saddened when he thought about Aurya. The darkness of her spirit was not a product of youthful mischance; it was there at her core, like a piece of fruit that appeared smooth and whole on the outside, but when sliced apart was eaten away with rot. Eiddig wondered what, in her earliest years, had caused such a terrible effect. What, or who, had killed the place in her spirit where love was born?

He had no answers—and it was the lack that drew him back to this holy place day after day, to think and pray, to try and understand how a creature such as Aurya could exist. Before now, he had always believed that every child was born in perfection and every spirit carried a spark of the Divine. He sensed it in Giraldus and Maelik—dimmed by years of neglect, but still present.

But Aurya . . . she was so completely devoid of this Divine presence that Eiddig found himself wondering if even her birth had been an unnatural, unholy event. If so, from where had she come and who would do such a thing as to curse a soul to Darkness even from the moment of its birth?

The mist from the waterfall was finally beginning to penetrate the hair that covered Eiddig's body. He stood, his knees and back stiff from the hours he had spent here, watching the water and thinking. But his mind was still too troubled to want to rejoin his people in the areas of the Realm where daily activity took place.

He decided instead to go into the cave behind the waterfall, where fissures in the rock emitted warmth into the room, rising up from the core of fire that the Holy Words said filled the earth's center. The heat would dry his hair and ease the stiffness from his ancient joints, just as the Holy Words would ease the sorrow from his heart that the thoughts of the three Up-worlders had placed there.

As he walked across the ledge of crystal that led behind the waterfall, his wide feet and long gripping toes automatically finding purchase on the water-slick rock beneath him, Eiddig consciously turned his thoughts to a more heart-pleasing subject. He thought about Renan, Cloud-Dancer, and Selia—but most of all, about Lysandra.

Art thou happy, Healer? he wondered, not for the first time since she and the others had left. *Art thou still in the home towards which thy heart didst ever look, or hast thou been called again to leave it?*

Wilt thou ever come again unto the Realm of the Cryf? he also wondered as he turned into the long, narrow passageway that led into the holiest place in all the Realm. Although he wanted to believe that he would again see the healer who, for all her blindness, saw much more clearly than any other being—Cryf or Up-worlder—he had ever encountered.

And yet, she hath her blindnesses, too, he thought, and he did not mean of her eyes. Like Talog, Eiddig found himself puzzled by the relationship between Lysandra and Renan. Their love was obvious, as was their mutual denial of the feeling. Eiddig admitted that he did not know the ways of the Up-world, but he did not believe that to deny love could be common.

At last, he stepped into the warm, well-lit interior of the cave. Here was one of the places within the Realm where the luminous stones, which were the Cryf's only light source, had been piled in tall columns, filling the corners and amplifying their radiance. Such light was necessary to read the ancient writing of the Holy Words.

At the back of the cave, ascending ledges had been carved to seat the Elders of the Clans in assembly. Toward these Eiddig walked, feeling the heat of the room already beginning its work on his body.

He stopped before the wide, deeply cut niche with the carved crystal frontpiece that held the sixteen separate volumes written in Dewi-Sant's own hand. Each volume contained the teachings, the words and wisdoms, given to the first Cryf Guide in his great visions. It was on these that Cryf life and faith were founded.

Eiddig bowed deeply, both in reverence to the Divine who had sent the visions, thereby establishing the Cryf as Its own—a holy people—and to honor Dewi-Sant, whose heart and mind were ever so fixed upon the Divine that he could receive the Holy Words to guide his people.

Reverence paid, Eiddig touched the corner of the crystal door, releasing its lock. It swung outward, revealing the ancient volumes it protected, each one of them specially bound in a manner only the Cryf could have devised or worked.

The text itself was written on paper made from the tough outer fiber of the gorien plant, the same plant whose soft inner core was turned into the nesting fabric on which they slept. This "paper" neither grew brittle nor disintegrated with the passage of the centuries. A thicker, less refined version of the same material created the front and back covers. Each of the volumes then was enclosed within a hinged box made of thin discs of stone. These were fitted together so perfectly that no air or moisture or changing temperature could reach inside. Each of these sixteen boxes was of a different color stone, and each was encrusted with the gold, silver, and gems found throughout the Realm.

But the beauty of their outer coverings was secondary in

the minds of the Cryf. The truest beauty was to be found in the words they protected. Eiddig reached in the niche and took one volume from its place. He did not look to see which one his fingers touched, but trusted the Divine to direct him to what he most needed to read. It was only after he had taken a seat on the lowest level of the ledges that he looked down at the volume in his hands.

The outer box was of deep green and red-veined bloodstone. The four corners were set with clusters of rubies. Gold scrolled-filigree sent out fingers, like rays of light through the darkness, toward the huge, square-cut garnet at the center. Each bit of stone, of precious gem or shining metal, was the most perfect example of its kind the Cryf could produce, for nothing less than perfect would befit such an exalted purpose as the protection of the Holy Words.

The bloodstone box contained the fourteenth volume. This vision, Eiddig knew, told of the future that was to be after the Font of Wisdom had been found. But it was not the future now; it was the present, the time and the dangers through which Eiddig hoped he had the wisdom to guide his people.

The old Cryf bowed his head, silently beseeching the Divine to be *his* guide as he opened the pages. He then read aloud the first passage upon which his eyes focused:

"And the path unto Wisdom be not a smooth or untroubled course, but fraught with dangers unto both body and soul. So must those who wouldst Wisdom guard be ever vigilant. The Font of Wisdom speaketh Truth unto the many, yet a single heart mayest still fall into Darkness. Therefore, must the Companions and all whom they wouldst hear, continue in watchfulness unto their own, forgetting not that deception cometh in many a fair-seeming form.

"And if thou wouldst know peace, then first seeketh thou Truth. Hide not thine eye from the inward Way. All knowing cometh of the Divine, in whom Truth and Peace ever reside.

The Divine Hand shalt open, but only unto those who hide not their inward hearts. . . ."

Eiddig stopped there. He had read, memorized, recited this passage countless times over his long life. It was a favorite of his, containing many of the dictates by which he not only tried to live, but that he tried to instill in the hearts of his people. It had never been so clear or so relevant as now.

Eiddig wished the Companions—Lysandra, Renan, and Selia—were here now, so that he could share this reading with them. It would, perhaps, warn them of a danger still to come. He knew Renan had the Scrolls of Tambryn to provide guidance—but they went only to thirteen, only to the finding of the Font of Wisdom, and not beyond. Renan had shown it to Eiddig, and he knew that of Selia's future it said only that she must gain the throne if Aghamore was to be saved from the Darkness that threatened it.

But the Thirteenth Scroll did not say how the deed was to be accomplished or give more than a general warning about the waiting dangers. As he had then, Eiddig wondered why the visions and words of the Up-world prophet stopped there. Dewi-Sant's visions went on to sixteen, not thirteen, and Tambryn's scrolls contained so much of the same truth, wisdom, and beauty as the Holy Words that the old Guide found it nearly inconceivable that the Divine would have shown so much less to the Up-world prophet.

But where wouldst such other scrolls be found? Eiddig thought, remembering what Renan had told him of Tambryn's life. *Where didst this Seer live and where die?*

Eiddig remembered that to these questions, Renan had no answers. Then, suddenly, a new thought occurred to the Guide; perhaps somewhere within Dewi-Sant's Holy Words, written of visions given centuries before Tambryn had lived, there might lie some clue to guide them to where the remaining scrolls, if they did exist, might be found. Dewi-Sant had foreseen everything else of the present situation—was there a chance he had foreseen this as well? It was certainly a chance and a solution, worth considering.

Eiddig sat back and closed his eyes. There were many passages, especially throughout these latter volumes, that had been unclear—to himself and to the other Guides who had come before. As was the nature of prophecy, many of them had only become clear at the time of their fulfillment, such as the appearance of Lysandra, Renan, and Cloud-Dancer. There were many others, intermixed within the timeless truth and wisdom of the Holy Words, still awaiting the clarification that would come only with their own fulfillment. Perhaps, he thought hopefully, the discovery of Tambryn's final scrolls—if they truly existed—was among them.

With this in mind, Eiddig opened his eyes and looked down at the volume on his lap. Then, turning to the beginning, he began to read, looking with new purpose for deeper truth within truth and meanings behind meanings.

Not all of the Companions had returned Up-world. Talog, son of the Fourteenth Clan and apprentice to Eiddig as the future Guide of the Cryf, had chosen to remain with his people after Aurya, Giraldus, and their forces had been subdued. Now, however, sitting alone on the highest shelf overlooking the Great Cavern, he wondered if he had made the right decision.

Below him, on the cavern floor, was the place where both the battle with Giraldus's soldiers and Selia's sentencing of the survivors had taken place. The bloodstains on the cavern floor, and the dais on which Selia had stood to pass her first judgment as the Font of Wisdom had all been removed—but nothing, it seemed, could remove them from Talog's mind. Waking or sleeping, he had but to close his eyes for the horror of the battle to return: the sights and sounds, the smell of fear and blood, the feel of his weapon piercing flesh, the bodies of Up-worlders and Cryf falling, dead or dying . . .

Every time he chanced a glimpse of the Up-worlders who remained as servants to the Cryf, part of him wanted to scream; he wanted to shout at them with all the fury of which he had once thought himself incapable. His whole body would then shake with rage; he hated them for their violence that had so marred his beloved Realm.

Another part of him wanted to run away, far away, leaving behind all his dark memories and imaginings. He wanted to find again the person he used to be—not the one he had become, who could not think or pray, who could find nothing in his past faith or in the Holy Words to comfort or drive away the guilt, the anger, and the terror they caused.

Talog closed his eyes. He took a deep breath, trying to ride that breath inward to a place of silence and peace, away from all the feelings and images that continued to batter his soul. But the respite he sought would not come. His life had changed into a prison in which he was every bit as much a captive as Aurya and the others. Perhaps more, for his guards were his own memories and emotions—and they were harsh, unforgiving taskmasters.

Filled again with the sudden restlessness of self-accusation, Talog stood. He needed something to do, something at which he could work until exhaustion numbed his mind and, at least for a few hours, he could sleep without dreams. *But what can I do?* he wondered. His work was usually with Eiddig—studying the Holy Words, visiting the ill, the injured, the aged, and seeing to their needs, spending time with the children to teach them the ways of the Holy Words upon which all of Cryf life was founded.

Now, however, Talog found himself shrinking away from all thoughts of such occupation that only a short time ago had filled him with purpose and delight. The Holy Words, with their teachings of the Divine's peace, of the love and reverence in with the Cryf were called to walk, were like an arrow aimed straight into Talog's heart. How could he give others comfort when his own soul was bereft?

Neither was he prepared to spend the hours beneath the scrutiny of Eiddig's too-deep-seeing eyes. To do so was only to invite questions to which the young Cryf knew he had yet no answers. How could Eiddig, who had sat so calmly, so filled with both faith and welcome in the face of approaching danger—and who had nearly lost his life at the hands of the creature of Darkness, Aurya—understand the turmoil that was tormenting Talog now?

The question brought Talog's thoughts full circle, back to the too-well-remembered battle. But now, instead of the bloodshed, he thought of Eiddig's miraculous healing at Lysandra's hands.

Mayhap, he thought, *I shouldest venture Up-world of mine own device and seek again the Healer's company. The foul humors that do now fill me hath their roots and origins within the Up-world. Mayhap, only such a return journey shalt free me from my sorrows and return unto me a measure of what hath now been taken away.*

This new thought gave Talog a sense that there might yet be a way to relieve the burden he carried. It was a welcome feeling, one to occupy his mind and take it off the memories of blood and death. But he knew he could not merely walk out of the Realm and into the Up-world without preparation. He would need clothes to cover his body, such as Renan's had during their journey, a map to guide him toward the Great Forest of which the Healer had spoken so lovingly. Then, if these could be found, he would need food and other provisions. He only hoped he could remember everything he would need for such a journey; his brief sojourn above had given him no knowledge of how such things might be obtained Up-world.

His mind churning with all the new possibilities, Talog turned toward the passage through stone that descended from the ledge's great height to the cavern floor. If not going with

Lysandra and the others when they had asked him had been a mistake, it was one he intended to rectify as quickly as possible—and, as he made the journey to rejoin his Companions, his greatest prayer would be to find *himself* again.

Chapter Seven

Colm ApBeirne, Primus of the Church in Aghamore, sat in his study at the Archbishop's Residence, staring at the letter in his hands. He had been staring at this same page for several minutes, and though his eyes had slid across it more than once, his mind had not registered a single word.

With a sigh, he put the letter aside; his eyes were not the problem. Even with the onset of these advanced years— years that stooped his back and gave his hands the slight palsied tremor of age, that caused his old bones to ache with cold so that he needed a morning fire throughout most of the year—his vision was still as clear as it had been as a boy. For that, he was more than grateful. Reading, studying, had been among his greatest joys ever since the day he had first recognized that those marks on paper *meant* something.

He had lived over eight decades now, and reading was still a wonder to him. *Here* was true magic, he often thought, that a collection of lines and squiggles, circles and dots, could be used to convey the beauty of poetry or the majesty of Divine Grace. His eyes, like his body, quickly tired, and he often fell into a doze between pages, as each evening he sat by the fire in his private study. But when he was awake and looked again at the text that had, for a few minutes, lain forgotten on his lap, for an instant he felt again like a school lad at that moment of first discovery of the beauty and mystery of the written word.

But today it seemed that reading a letter was beyond him. Unlike his eyes, his mind refused to focus. He could not clear it of the nagging whisper of doubt that had been building for the last several days. As yet, these doubts had no name. They were only an uneasiness that occasionally came upon him. But when they did, they came like a thick billow of smoke, obscuring everything else.

The Archbishop put the letter aside, sat back in his chair, closing his eyes for a moment as he heaved a great sigh. It was time to find out what his instincts—or Divine guidance—was trying to tell him. He was certainly getting nothing accomplished as things were.

With another sigh, this one prompted by the effort of movement as he pushed back his great padded chair, he stood. Then he walked over to the large window that looked out on the park that was the Residence grounds. Outside, the day was clear and bright. This part of the grounds was open to the public, and the Archbishop watched a group of children running in a game of tag; their shrill, excited laughter, blocked from his ears by distance and window, shone on their faces and rang through his mind. They seemed the quintessential symbol of a kingdom at peace.

But for how long? he wondered, and with that question all the uneasiness that had been building now sharpened into a single focus that had three names—*Elon, Giraldus,* and especially *Aurya.*

He had believed the tale Elon brought him about Aurya's conversion; even now he did not want to think one of his bishops would lie to him. But the Baron and his lady had been gone so long—too long for a simple pilgrimage. There was nowhere in this kingdom that could not be traversed and back in half the time they had been absent.

Perhaps, he thought, *if they made the pilgrimage on foot, in the sackcloth and ashes of true penitents, stopping at every church and shrine along the way* . . . But he doubted that, even in the depths of contrition, either the Baron or Lady Aurya would humble themselves to that extreme.

That meant only one of two things could be true. Either Giraldus and Aurya had chosen a destination outside Aghamore's borders—in which case they could have gone anywhere, even to the Holy Land; if so, who knew when they would return, and Aghamore could not wait forever. Or it meant that everything Elon had told him and the College of Bishops was a lie. Giraldus and Aurya could be on some errand of their own— and Elon could be working with them. If *this* was the truth, then again, who knew when they would return.

Colm ApBeirne did not want to believe this latter. Yet, for all the unworldliness he knew his brother bishops believed of him, he had been Archbishop for twenty-eight years. He had served the Church as Primus through the reign of three Kings and had served his home Province of Sylaun as Bishop-ordinary for the seventeen years before that. The Church was a spiritual body, but as much as Colm might detest the necessity, it was also a political one. In order to protect the Church and the people of the kingdom, he had been forced to play within that political arena far too long to have remained as unworldly as others believed.

Now politics had reared up again, a dragon that refused to sleep. *How long?* he asked himself again, though this time the question carried new meaning. Once the succession was settled and a new King sat upon the throne, Colm had every intention of retiring from his Office. The candle flame of his life was sputtering, and he longed to let it burn its last light within the peaceful shelter of monastic walls. He had already arranged to return to Sylaun, to the Monastery of St.

Columbkille, and end his service where he had begun it sixty-six years ago.

He had been only fifteen then, a younger son promised at birth to the Church. But for Colm ApBeirne, the choice had been the correct one; he would have eagerly entered the Church at a younger age, had his parents not needed him at home. Even when he was fifteen, his mother had been loath to let him go—but young and filled with zeal for his vocation, Colm would no longer be delayed.

Now, through the distance of age, Colm could still remember every moment of those early years. It was an idyllic time to his memory: the eight-hour monastic Office—seven times of prayer during the day and once at night, rising up in the still darkness to chant the great Canticles of Praise—the gentle silence that filled the monastery between those hours of prayer; the simple joy of gathering with his Brothers around the large stone hearth in the refectory for the daily Chapter; doing the small crafts the Community sold to bring in the little income to meet their needs for things not always donated . . . And, for Colm then as much as now, the greatest joy of all was the hours spent in the library or scriptorium, surrounded by the reading or copying of books.

Those were the actions and hours to which he longed to return. *Perhaps my longing has been too great,* he now admonished himself. *Perhaps it made me too eager to accept what I wanted to hear, but what my heart—my spirit— would have warned me was false, had I stopped to listen. Now, my eagerness may harm this kingdom I have worked so long to guide and protect.*

Yet, if not Giraldus, he also thought, *then who?* Whom would the College of Bishops support this time that they had not supported before? Elon's announcement about the conversion of the Baron and his lady had seemed God-sent at the time, unexpectedly uniting the factions into a whole.

Almost a whole, the Archbishop thought as he lowered

himself into one of the large, wing-backed chairs before the hearth, where the remnants of this morning's fire still gave the low and steady heat his body craved. *Bresal of Rathreagh and Dwyer of Camlough,* his thoughts gave name to the opposition, remembering how they had stormed from the room when the College's last vote had given the Church's support to Giraldus. *Were they right after all? Perhaps I should have heard their warnings more clearly. Perhaps I—*

Colm stopped himself. He could sit in this chair and play "if only" games all day, his thoughts running in circles of tag like the children outside . . . or he could *do* something about his doubts.

He would write to Elon and summon him again to Ballinrigh, he decided. When next they met, the Archbishop promised himself, he would be more wary. If he did not like what Elon had to say, or if Baron Giraldus and Lady Aurya did not soon return from their travels, he would again reconvene the College of Bishops. If that happened, his first letters would go to Bresal and Dwyer, and rather than the epistles of reprimand for disobedience he had been meaning to send, they would be letters of apology.

He would start with the summons of Elon. But to do so meant returning to his desk, he thought as he looked in its direction. Then his eyes were drawn back to the embers on the hearth. No, he was not yet ready to leave the circle of their immediate, radiant warmth. He would write the letter later, after the embers had died completely. They could not last too very much longer, but while they did, he intended to soak in as much of their comfort as he could.

Just over an hour later, the Archbishop awoke with a start, still sitting in his chair before the hearth. The embers had finished their slow metamorphosis and now the hearth was filled with cold, dead ash. But the lack of heat was not what had awakened him. It was a dream filled with unwelcomed images of disaster, images already fading from his waking mind.

Though the particulars of his dream were quickly paling, the wild and unsettling emotions they raised remained. He took a moment to put names to them, hoping that recognition would be enough to aid in their dismissal, like a child who upon awakening sees that its dreamed monsters did not exist in the light of day. But this exercise, one that had worked for him in the past, did not defeat the sense of dread pounding through both body and mind.

Dread, he realized, was indeed the right word. This feeling was past fear yet not as immediate as terror. There was still time, he hoped—he prayed—to circumvent the dangers threatening this kingdom.

With a little grunt, the Archbishop stood. But before he went to his desk, he walked again to his window. The children who had been playing were gone, leaving the garden-park in silence. Still caught up in the lingering traces of his dream's emotions, he did not find the silence comforting.

He continued looking out over the tranquil scene. Roses, just entering their first bloom, added long beds of color amid the greenery of flowering shrubs and trees whose springtime blossoms had come and gone. The roses were the crowning glory, the center of their beds, bordered with the brilliant white of alyssum and snow-in-summer, the soft pinks and whites of gillyflowers, and the reds, purples, and yellows of their larger cousins, carnations.

Other flower beds dotted the sweeping expanse of lawn. The brilliant jewel tones of many would not open for weeks yet. They had been chosen and timed by those who, over the years, had planted and maintained these grounds to come into their glory only after the roses were gone.

Once an avid gardener himself, Colm ApBeirne remembered his earliest years as Archbishop, when these grounds astonished him with all their hidden complexities. Companion planting had been done with a careful eye toward more than blooming times and light requirements. Colors and combinations of foliage and shape had been combined so that even in winter the gardens were possessed of a stark beauty—and when it snowed, they changed into a place of enchantment every bit as wondrous as their colorful summer beauty.

In those early years here, back before time had added such painful stiffness to his knees and back, it had been Colm's practice to end his busy, care-filled days by putting aside the robes of Archbishop. Then, donning some of the work attire of the gardeners, he would spend an hour or two with his hands in the soil. It was a meditative time that reminded him of those peace-filled years at the monastery. Within those hours of silent communion with nature, seeing and touching the wonder of Creation, he found the renewing strength to face the next day's duties.

How he wished he could do the same thing again, now. The call of it was almost more than he could ignore. But, as he shifted his weight and felt the sharp bite of arthritic knees that made even kneeling in prayer difficult, he knew again that the delights of gardening could not be his. All he could do was look from a distance and remember.

With a sigh, he turned away from the window, back toward the desk, where piles of papers awaited his attention. His life seemed made of papers—the correspondence and petitions, the copies of laws, bylaws, and canons he must continually reference in order to address the needs of those letters and petitions, the books he read for duty and the ones he read for pleasure—all these, and more, were made of paper. Paper—stuff so durable it could pass from hand to hand, place to place, or last through centuries, as some of the oldest books proved—yet paper was also fragile, easily torn, burned, destroyed by either carelessness or intent. It sometimes seemed to Colm as an excellent metaphor for life itself.

He once more sat in the grandly carved, well-padded, high-backed chair behind the equally ornate desk at which he spent the majority of his days. Perhaps, he thought with a touch of self-disdain, if he had tended himself with the same care he gave to books—or to a garden—he would not now be so physically worn and trapped inside, like an ancient manuscript stuck under protecting glass, on such a glorious day.

Or, perhaps, I would, he also thought, remembering back to his childhood when one of his grandfathers had been robust and active while the other had turned frail with age, though they both counted the same years to their lives.

It surprised him how easily thoughts of his childhood came to him now. Images of moments, of people and places he had neither seen nor thought of in well over half a century, were clearer in his mind than events of last week or last month.

The ways of the mind are strange indeed, he thought, *perhaps only truly fathomable to the One who created them. How much hidden potential is in each one of us? How many talents and abilities go unrecognized, untapped from birth to death because we do not know how—or because we fear—to discover and use them?*

It was a question he had pondered before, in both youth and age. But it was with age, with the *awareness* of how truly fleeting life was—a realization that was both the gift and burden of age—that the question took on a special poignancy.

And now another thought joined it. This thought, if said aloud, could easily be misunderstood and charged as tainted with heresy. Where it came from, he did not know—but it was here all the same, demanding attention he would never have granted in the certainty of his youth.

Perhaps, he now thought, *this is all that magic is. Perhaps magic is not evil of itself, but filled with Darkness only by the choice of its use. Could magic be no more than a talent that some individuals are either born with or have learned to use—like any talent, like a talent for music or art or mathematics?*

The Archbishop stopped himself. This was not the Church's stand upon the subject—a stand and teaching, a way of faith he was sworn to uphold. Magic was the devil's tool; this was what the Church said, and he could neither say nor teach anything else.

Not aloud, anyway.

But what did he *believe*? he wondered. He tried to chase these new thoughts away, but they refused to disappear. They went instead to that place of secret questions, of thoughts pondered in long, dark hours of sleepless nights, when dear-held values are called into question, and ponderings out of place in the brightly rational light of day become as inevitable as the next breath.

With duty now firmly replacing any more personal flights of fancy, Colm ApBeirne pulled a blank piece of stationery into place before him, took up his pen, and, after loading it in the inkwell, began to write.

> *To Elon, Bishop-ordinary, Province of Kilgarriff, our son in the Church and brother in the service of Our Lord:*
>
> *We find ourselves burdened anew by heavy concerns for the welfare of this kingdom. We therefore, of your charity and obedience, summon and ask for your immediate return to Ballinrigh, that such matters may be discussed between us.*

The Archbishop read quickly back over his words, debating whether to add more, personalizing their stark, official tone. Then he decided against it. As long as doubts remained, he preferred to tell Elon too little rather than too much. If, as he hoped, his doubts proved unfounded, then he would gladly take Elon more fully into his confidence.

And, if that happened, Colm ApBeirne would carry through on his original plan to name Elon as his successor to the role of Archbishop. Then, and only then, could he begin to ease some of the burdens of this Office from his own weary shoulders and onto those of someone with more youth and strength.

When that time came, he would welcome it, and gladly.

Chapter Eight

Though she had only been there once before, Lysandra found that the guesthouse of Renan's parish felt like an old friend. Perhaps it was because with her first arrival, it had provided a haven of safety amid the tumult that both surrounded and filled her. Or, perhaps, it was because she had heard Renan talk of this place as frequently as she no doubt had once spoken of her home. The entire place—the church, rectory, grounds, and guesthouse—was so imbued with the feel of his presence that it seemed as much her friend as he was.

Whatever the reasons, she and Cloud-Dancer both settled in with the true feeling of a second home. Not so with Selia. Through the link of minds that Lysandra was beginning to realize would always be present, Lysandra felt Selia's resistance to being comfortable, to letting herself feel at home. It was a quiet act of rebellion against the role to which destiny had called her.

Selia was once again inside the stone church, busy with

the self-imposed tasks of cleaning and polishing. Lysandra was out in the churchyard, enjoying the warmth of the sun while she walked the enclosed space, trying to decide where to put the herb garden she had told Renan she would start for him. While she walked, she pondered this strange link between her mind and Selia's. Most of the time it was like an ear or a toe, something easily forgotten or ignored. But then an emotionally charged thought or pain could make it suddenly flare, like a toe painfully stubbed.

Even with stone walls separating them, Lysandra could feel Selia's thoughts. She was aware of the sense of dislocation the girl continued to feel, and Lysandra wished she could do something to convince Selia that her future was not some punishment doled out by an unsympathetic Divine Hand. It contained the promise of all she could make it to be.

As she thought, an old axiom her mother used to quote rattled itself through Lysandra's memory. *"A man convinced against his will,"* her mother often would say when dealing with Lysandra's own kind of obstinacy, *"is of his own opinion still."* She realized this was as true of Selia. Although the young woman's *mind* wanted to accept what Lysandra and Renan told her, verified by the things she had both witnessed and done during their long journey from Caerryck, her *heart* still rebelled.

Peace will come, she had assured Selia time and again. Life, too, is a journey—and it can be a journey toward joy if you will let it. But as often as she said it, she knew they were only words to Selia, words that meant nothing to her yet.

Lysandra wished she could make the younger woman understand—but only *time* could do that. Time was both the problem facing Selia and the solution. Contrary to the sense of loneliness in her troubles that Selia felt, Lysandra did know what it felt like to lose everything and have to begin life again . . . and she knew that time does heal, does grant perspective and serenity.

But it had taken Lysandra time to learn this lesson . . . and right now, *time* was what Selia did not have. None of them did.

But you will have joy again, she thought to Selia as she walked toward the little stone mourning bench beside one of the church walls. *I have not seen* all *of your future, but that much I do know. . . .*

As Lysandra sat, with the sun still radiant before and the warmed stone behind her, she suddenly felt cocooned in comfort. She also sent what she could of this feeling back along the connection between herself and Selia, trying to be careful not to invade the younger woman's mind and yet hoping that this touch between them might soothe and encourage.

All shall be well, she thought—to herself, to Selia. The thought was more of faith and feeling than of words. It was also one she believed with all her heart.

Suddenly, a new spark entered Lysandra's mind, one that sent a burst of joy, silent and pure, through her. Renan was returning from the errands that had taken him into the city with the first light of day. Lysandra looked his way, letting her *Sight* expand until she saw him nearing the churchyard gate. His arms were filled with bundles that he shifted to free one hand and open the gate. Then he glanced around the churchyard until he saw her.

Lying contentedly by her feet, Cloud-Dancer raised his head as he heard footsteps approaching. Lysandra gently touched the top of his head, signaling that all was well. With her touch and the recognition of Renan's step, the wolf dropped his head back upon his paws and resumed his state of guarding half slumber. Lysandra then moved a little to one side, making room on the bench, and waited for Renan's arrival.

A moment later he was there. As he sat beside her, she felt his nearness as warmer even than the sun. Long seconds passed as the two of them sat, enjoying the radiant silence of their companionship. Then, at last, Renan sighed and again shifted the bundles in his arms, breaking the momentary spell.

"What is that you have?" Lysandra asked.

"Books," he replied. "I went to the cathedral's library. I thought these might help Selia. She needs to learn about the task she'll be undertaking, once all the rest of this is finished."

"What kind of books?"

"History, mostly," Renan replied. "Early history, from Liam the Builder through the reign of the House of Roetah. Then a book that gives a brief overview of all the Kings up to just before Osaze was crowned. I thought she should know which House reigned when, how they gained the throne, and what each King did during his reign. I thought that way she'd get something of the feel for what each House is now claiming—and she can, I hope, see what the best Kings did while learning to avoid the mistakes of the worst ones."

"Do you really think she's in danger of being less than a great ruler?" Lysandra said softly. "She's the Font of Wisdom. Renan, you're the one who believed in that before I did."

"And I don't doubt it now," he replied. "But I think she's young and unworldly, even with her Wisdom, and that soon she'll have many advisors all telling her different things to suit their own purposes. She'll need to have a sense of what has gone on before and what this kingdom truly needs, in order to apply her Wisdom correctly . . . and she'll need to know it for herself, not just because one advisor or another is telling her it's so."

Lysandra nodded. "That's quite a burden for shoulders so young to carry," she said.

"The welfare of an entire kingdom is a heavy burden for anyone's shoulders, regardless of age," Renan countered.

"Perhaps that's why so few do it truly well. But I believe, as I always have, that Selia will be one of those few. Remember, every life has its own share of burdens, and whether we believe it of ourselves or not, they only come when we're ready for them. In many ways, Selia is already strong enough for hers—the way she handled the sentencing of Giraldus and Aurya proved that. What she's lacking now is knowledge and experience—and the confidence that comes with them. Only time can take care of the latter, but I'm hoping these books will help with the first."

Again Lysandra nodded, acknowledging the truth in Renan's words. "What other books did you bring?" she asked.

"There's one here on the neighboring countries and our historical relationships with them, and a copy of the laws and treaties currently in place. There's also what I fear will be the most boring of the lot, a volume on statesmanship and negotiation tactics. But it was written by Oliam Grieswell, who was chief advisor to King Tynan III and is still thought by many to have been the best statesman this kingdom ever knew. Luckily, the book is fairly thin, and while rather dry and unexciting, it should be easy to read. There were many other things at the library Selia will need to complete her education, but these were the ones I thought were best to get her started. When we do discover how we're supposed to get her on the throne, I don't want anyone objecting on the basis of ignorance."

Lysandra marveled at how much Renan himself knew; she would never have been able either to choose these books or undertake Selia's education. And he was right; the girl did need to have a solid grounding in the kingdom's affairs *before* she wore the crown—not after.

"I think," Lysandra said, "this will do more for Selia than you realize. I agree she needs to learn all this and more—but I can feel how a part of her still thinks of everything that has happened as unreal, like a dream from which she soon expects to awaken. And, I think, that's because everything is either in the past or the future."

"What do you mean?" Renan asked. "We've been busy working toward the next great step all along."

"*We* have," Lysandra answered, "you and I . . . think about it, talking about it—you've studied and read Tambryn's scroll until I thought you'd wear it through. But what, truly, has Sclia had to do?"

When Renan did not answer, Lysandra continued. "When we were forced into that wild escape from Aurya and Giraldus, and later, when she had to pronounce a judgment against them, everything was immediate and she was fine. But since then, she's entered a state of emotional limbo, first at my cottage and now here. You and I, especially I, needed to rest and recover, to try and think about what came next. But Selia didn't, not really. All the doubts and fears she first felt, that seemed to disappear while we were with the Cryf and her role as the Font of Wisdom was needed, even demanded, have now returned with a renewed force. She doesn't feel any emotional connection to the future we keep telling her is coming."

"And you think these books will change that?" Renan said, not quite managing to keep the doubt from his voice.

Lysandra nodded. "I think they will give her a focus *other* than her doubts, and that they will make the idea of becoming Queen, that until now has been just a word, into something real and solid."

"I hope you're right," Renan said. "The task ahead will be difficult enough, for all of us, and especially for Selia, without having to convince her again of something I thought already settled."

Lysandra smiled softly, saying nothing more. But her thoughts were far from silent. *Is one's identity ever truly settled?* she wondered. It was not easy; it had taken her a full ten years to discover the woman she was today—a discovery not yet over, but it was possible. *If Selia will let herself,* Lysandra's thoughts continued, *she'll find she has all the strength that's needed . . . for whatever lies ahead.*

"So," she said in a lighter tone, "I think I know where your new garden should go. Come walk with me, and I'll show you."

Renan put the books aside on the bench. Then he stood and held out a hand to her.

"Lead the way," he said, as she took it, his tone matching her own. "I'm sure that if you chose it, it will be the right place indeed."

Cloud-Dancer stood with them. Then healer and priest, followed by a wolf, walked hand in hand, around the church toward the place for a garden the blind woman had chosen.

Selia received the books with less enthusiasm than Renan had hoped. When she saw the disappointment in his eyes, she tried to rally a bit more positive feeling, but knew she failed. The truth was that, while her life at the convent had educated her so that she could read and write, she knew she was no scholar. Reading and writing were chores she tried to avoid whenever possible.

But now it's not possible, she told herself as she glanced again at the titles of the books he had placed before her. Then she looked back up into his face, seeing the hopeful light that shone there as if he had just given her a present at Christmas and was eager to see if she liked it.

"But who will take care of the church while we're busy?" she asked him. "There are still things I had thought to do. The orphreys on two of your chasubles have loose stitching, and one of the fair linens is in need of repair . . . and the statuaries both need to be stripped and repolished. They both look as if it's been years, and I do know how . . ."

Her voice trailed off, silenced by the look Renan and Lysandra exchanged.

"Selia," Renan said in a gentle voice, one Selia had already learned meant what was to follow might well be unwelcome, "in the last three days you've done wonders about the church. I've never seen it looking so bright and polished. But it's time to put all that aside. There are other hands in the parish who can stitch the orphreys or clean the statuaries. None of them can be Queen. *That's* the task at which you need to work."

Selia knew he was right—knew it but did not like it. Still, she hid a sigh as she opened the first book: *The Unabridged History of the House of Roetah.*

"Why do I need to read about this House?" she asked. She might as well know the "whys," not just the "whats."

"It's the House of Liam the Builder, the first House to rule and, perhaps, the most important one in Aghamore's history," Renan answered. "It was during King Liam's time that the kingdom was divided and the Houses established. Most of our laws also come out of his time, or the reigns of the Kings directly after."

Selia nodded, ignoring the other volumes for now; this was as good a place as any to start.

Three hours later, Selia put the book aside and rubbed her tired eyes. She wished she could do the same for her tired *brain.* The book was all names and dates she doubted she would ever remember, presented in a style that made her mind want to drift—or sleep.

She had read all about the first two Kings, both named Liam, the founding of the kingdom, the division of the Provinces, how the Houses were named, about the Right of Succession, and the earliest laws of the kingdom. The book claimed that these two Kings were the greatest to have reigned throughout all of Aghamore's long history—but it gave no sense of the *men* or what made them so special. *How,* she wondered, *can I emulate what I can't understand?*

Why me? her thoughts voiced the question that had been at the heart of her unease, unrecognized until this moment, when she finally allowed herself to ask. It was a question no one had ever answered—perhaps there was no answer.

It was an exasperating feeling. Selia stood and stretched to ease the kinks from both body and brain. Then she went off in search of food and drink. *I wonder,* she thought, *if Lysandra has any special tea that will make my mind work better. She seems to have one for nearly everything else.*

Like Lysandra, Selia was aware of the subliminal link between the two of them. It was not something she needed to think of often or that flared with each passing thought. She was fairly certain that her awareness of it was far less than the healer's; such was not her gift, as it was Lysandra's.

But, if she concentrated, Selia could feel it—and through it, she knew that Lysandra was happy at whatever she was doing now. That meant, Selia thought, she was probably busy at the new garden. Almost all of the times she had felt this kind of contentment from Lysandra, it was because she was gardening.

Selia stood to go outside. Then, reluctantly, she turned back, grabbed up the book she had been reading, and took it with her out into the sunlight. The day was beautiful— something she had forgotten as she closed herself inside. The brightness of the sun, the warmth of the air, immediately made her feel less burdened.

Selia realized how much time she had spent locking herself away, always on the pretext of being busy. At the cottage, she had kept mostly in the kitchen or herbal pantry, busying herself with Lysandra's healing supplies. Here, she had found work in the cleaning of the church and its contents. In both cases, the results—and the reasons—were the same. While inside, it was easy to believe that she could hide from what lay ahead, and if she kept busy enough, everything else would go away.

Of course, it did not—it could not. And now Renan had brought her these books, and it had all come crashing in on her again. She could not run away from herself—not from the gifts and talents within her and not from the destiny that called her to make use of them.

This epiphany, this sudden acceptance, brought its own kind of relief, even amid the unanswered questions she carried.

By the time Father Peadar had found her wandering the streets of Caerryck, a lonely and abandoned child of seven, she had already learned that her "gifts" must be hidden, shunned, if she was to survive. Her own parents had cast her out because of them, saying that she must be demon-possessed to know and see and feel the things she did. Although she did not *feel* evil, Selia knew now that the child she had been, the child still within her, had believed them.

The pain of that early childhood and the emotional scars it had left had caused her to lock so much of her inner self away—the same way she was now closing herself within some building or other, hiding away in darkness. Yet knowing Renan and Lysandra—their acceptance, encouragement, and nonjudgmental friendship, their examples of bravery and the way they kept looking and working toward the greater goal—was causing her to *care* about life again.

It had been easy, in the ordered silence and discipline of the life in the convent, to pretend her gifts did not exist. Then Father Peadar had come for her; then Renan and the others were waiting, had been searching through distance and danger to find her . . .

And there was Lysandra, lying there before the altar of Father Peadar's church, desperately fighting for the life of both her body and soul. It was a battle the others in the room, save Cloud-Dancer, could neither see nor feel. But Selia could. Even when she was in the small vestry, sitting among the hanging vestments, she had felt the moment Renan entered, carrying Lysandra's inert form.

From that moment, the door to her gifts that Selia had forced shut had begun to push open again. Once their minds had touched, there was no stopping what she held inside. All that she was poured into Lysandra's mind, shifted, changed, and flowed back again into hers. Wisdom and Prophecy, each completing the other; she and Lysandra, two sides of the same gift—the Seer of Prophecy who was blind to the world and the Wielder of Wisdom who saw too much.

The door would not be shut again. Selia had been trying—but now as she walked toward where Lysandra was kneeling on the ground, trowel in hand, happily turning the dirt to make a garden, Selia knew it was impossible. She could not go back. Who she was and who she was meant to become had been chosen and set in motion by a power far greater than any mortal hand or heart could wield.

She could sometimes see the shining thread of her own life, one trailing spark amid the countless others. Even so, her heart still harbored its doubts and sent its silent "why me?" into the universe. Each time, her soul felt like it was holding its breath as it waited for the Divine answer.

But the only answer that came was a new and building sense of anticipation she did not want to acknowledge. She felt balanced on a narrow ledge, afraid to move. Behind her was who she had been; ahead was, perhaps, the solid ground of who she might become—if she could keep her footing against the buffeting winds of circumstance and change.

Selia did not know from where the image had come. The only ledges she had ever walked had been in the Realm of the Cryf, and there she had been safe. But she did not feel safe now, and the image, with its feeling of being precariously balanced amid swirling dangers, would not abate.

Lysandra raised her head and looked toward Selia, staring with her sightless, all-seeing eyes. And she smiled. Then, sitting back on her heels, she beckoned Selia closer with one dirt-smudged hand.

Clutching her book to her chest, the younger woman approached, not realizing she was holding the book like a shield until her fingers began to ache with the tightness of her grip. Lysandra kept smiling at her until, finally, some of the healer's joy traced a path along the connection between them and caused Selia to relax a little.

Just then, Renan came out of the storage room at the back of the rectory, carrying two shovels. He, too, smiled at Selia when he saw her.

How can they be so happy, she wondered, *knowing what might be ahead?*

Learn to grab the moments of happiness when they come, Selia, Lysandra's thoughts answered, letting Selia know that she had been broadcasting her feelings. *Such moments are a precious gift—and it might be a long time before the next one comes.*

But how can you just forget everything and play in the dirt, when at any moment—today, tomorrow—the Darkness could close in again?

Lysandra's soft smile broadened quickly, and just as quickly faded. *I've forgotten nothing,* her thoughts answered Selia. *But I've learned that to fill my moments with fretting over what* might *be coming doesn't prepare me for anything. It only robs me of the joy and strength I might otherwise have. Our task is not over, and danger will come. But none of us will face it alone . . . and right now, this moment, there is sunlight, and there is peace.*

Selia bowed her head against the soft admonition in Lysandra's words. She *had* been feeling alone—yet Renan and Lysandra, even Cloud-Dancer, were here with her and, she knew, would never abandon her. And there were the Cryf, Talog and Eiddig in particular. They had already done so much on her behalf, all of them—but somehow, in her thoughts about the future, Selia had let herself think only of the part that *she* must play, only of *her* future. It was not only unjust, it was self-defeating.

Whatever comes, you are not alone, Lysandra's thoughts said again, this time finding fertile soil in which to plant the seeds of this all-important truth.

Selia suddenly knew that it would be all right for her to speak aloud the question she had silently pondered throughout the day. She did not go to sit beside Lysandra, as the older woman had beckoned. Instead, Selia let her fears go as she took a seat on the little mourning bench in the sun, put her books to one side, and looked at Lysandra and Renan.

They obviously felt something from her, for they put down their gardening tools and, turning toward her, waited. Selia drew a deep breath.

"I've left Caerryck," she said, "and I've traveled from Rathreagh to Camlough, and back here to Ballinrigh, doing everything you've asked of me in between. I'm still doing what you ask—reading all these books and preparing to be Queen. So now I'm asking you something. Tell me why . . . why me? I'm no one in particular. I have no grand heritage. Why should I be chosen for this prophecy? Why should I be Queen?"

Selia waited as Renan and Lysandra exchanged looks. It felt as if time slowed, and their silent exchange lasted forever. But Selia knew it was only her eagerness for an answer, so she tried to squelch her impatience. She had waited this long to ask . . .

Finally, it was Renan who stepped toward her. "I'm not sure I can give you an answer you'll like," he said. "Prophecy often has no explanation and is not understood until long after its fulfillment. I can give you many examples where someone of humble beginnings was chosen for greatness. There was King David of the Old Testament, for example. He was a shepherd and a poet, youngest and most unimpressive of his brothers— yet he was the one chosen, and he became a great King.

"Our own King Liam," Renan continued, "about whom you've been reading . . . he began as a soldier and son of a soldier. No great family or connections, nothing to say he would found and govern a kingdom—and yet, that is exactly what he did. History is full of these stories. Do you understand what I'm trying to tell you, Selia?"

She was still wearing an unsatisfied expression, so Renan drew a breath and tried a new tack. "Selia, the truth is that all of our fates are in Divine Hands—the question only being whether or not we accept them, and whether we have the courage to *act* once Divine Will has made itself known.

"You could walk away right now, go back to Caerryck and the life you left behind. But would you be happy in that other life, now that you know where and what you are supposed to be? I doubt it. Six centuries ago, Tambryn was granted the prophecy that someone would come—and God chose that it would be you. So the only real answer I can give you is that God gives everyone gifts, and these are yours—and only the Divine Wisdom knows why."

Selia had hoped for something more exact, but as Renan spoke, she knew there was none. Why was any life what it was—hers, Lysandra's, Renan's? And how many countless others, over time, had ended up doing or being what they had never thought of for themselves? For that question, like her own, faith seemed to be the only answer.

"Thank you," she said to him.

Renan put a hand gently over the ones she had folded in her lap. "I'm sorry there isn't something more I can tell you."

"I understand," Selia said, giving him a small—a very small—smile.

Believe in yourself, Lysandra's thoughts gently touched hers, *and the reason why doesn't matter.*

Chapter Nine

Young Wilham Tybourne was the Rider who received the call to the Archbishop's Residence. The call pleased him; it exemplified everything he loved about his occupation.

He had been a Rider for three years, signing on the day after his seventeenth birthday, when he became of legal age. Never a day went by that he was not certain he had made the right choice. It was a life he loved. He could not be pressed into military service; he made a good wage—and often good tips as well—while having the freedom to ride from one end of the kingdom to the other.

He had never had to worry about food or a place to sleep, either. All but the smallest towns had at least one Rider office somewhere within their boundaries, and they always had food and a bed available—should he choose to avail himself of them. But Wilham also always had coins in his pouch to buy a meal and a bed at a local inn, where the ale was cool and the serving girls warm—a situation much to his preference.

Neither of his parents, especially his mother, had ever understood the wanderlust that filled Wilham. He had been born in the town of Traedok, twenty miles from the capital of Farnagh. As the eldest of his five siblings, his father had always expected Wilham to take over his cobbler's shop. But by the age of ten, Wilham had known such a life was not for him. He had tried to tell his father time and again, only to be disbelieved. "You'll grow out of it," his father kept insisting, "and you'll see the value of a settled life."

Wilham had wanted to please his father and had worked as his apprentice as long as he could. But by the time he was sixteen, he knew he could pretend no longer. He had turned his cobbler's tools over to Brannan, his younger brother by a year, and never picked them up again.

His father had not spoken to him for the year after that, not until the day Wilham left to join the Riders. Even now, on the few occasions Wilham had gone home, their relationship was strained—even though Brannan had proved to be every bit as skilled and content with his life as a cobbler as Wilham had not.

It had been Father Renan who had encouraged Wilham to try and mend his familial bonds. For the first two years he was a Rider, he had stayed away from Farnagh completely, letting others carry the messages to his home Province— even if the destination might prove profitable. Wilham wrote home, occasionally, to his mother or to his brothers and sisters. But he never visited.

Then he had met Father Renan and both the friendship and the counsel of the priest had begun slowly to change Wilham's attitude. Because of it, he now not only accepted any Rides into his native Province, but was also happy to carry any message sent by the Church.

He had carried letters and packages of all sizes between parishes, monasteries, and convents; he had taken good news and bad, from secular families to brothers or sisters now in the Religious Life, and answering messages back again. But he had never been summoned to the Archbishop's Residence before. Although most of the grounds were open to the public, as he walked down one of the many pathways that led past gardens and across lawns, he realized he had been missing a wonderland of beauty by never visiting there.

The heady perfume of the roses swirled all around him as he neared, making him stop and stare at them in wonder. His mother had grown roses by her kitchen door, a climbing bush that grew up the side of the house and across the eaves. Once a year, early in summer like this, the long branches became covered with a countless number of small pink blossoms, and every time the windows or doors opened, the fragrance would fill the house.

The fragrance here reminded Wilham of those days in childhood when summer seemed an enchanted time. Although these roses smelled much the same, he had never seen nor known so many types and colors existed. The marvel of the sight drove all other thoughts away until, suddenly, someone touched his arm.

Startled, Wilham swung around. He found himself facing a young monk about his own age.

"Are you the Rider we're waiting for—or are you just here on your own, to see the gardens?" the monk asked.

Wilham nodded. "I'm here for your consignment," he said. "It's just that the roses are so—"

"Amazing," the monk supplied with a smile. "Yes, they are—and especially so this year. I'm Brother Naal, one of the Archbishop's secretaries . . . one of many," he added with a slightly self-deprecating smile. "But I have young legs, so when you were noticed, I was sent to inquire. His Eminence has a letter, which he wants to give you himself. I believe he has some instructions to go with it."

"I'm sorry I've kept him waiting," Wilham said, trying to cover his surprise. He certainly never thought he would be seeing the Archbishop himself.

"I think the wait bothered Brother Mikelene much more than the Archbishop, but most things bother Brother Mikelene, so don't let that worry you."

"I never took time t' visit these gardens before," Wilham

said, as they started to walk toward the Residence. "I will now—'tis beautiful here."

"Aye," Brother Naal said, "that it is. Are you often in Ballinrigh, then?"

"As often as anywhere. I like to come back here. Although we travel all through the Nine Provinces, most Riders tend to choose a base near where they grew up. But not me. I like the noise here, the bustle. There's so many people, it's like it's changing all the time."

Brother Naal laughed. "That's exactly what many people say they don't like about it. But I agree with you. I sometimes feel like all the voices of the heavenly chorus sound in this city, filling it with a joyful noise found only here and in heaven."

Then Brother Naal laughed again, this time at his own flight of fancy. "I know," he said, "I've an odd way of thinking. Others have said so, many times, so you've no need to worry about thinking it. Odd though they are, my thoughts give me joy, and that's better than many can say."

"True enough," Wilham agreed with a little laugh of his own. He found he liked Brother Naal—and liked the "odd way of thinking" to which he so happily laid claim. Like the beauty of the roses, it was an unexpected bonus to Wilham's day.

That was another one of the many things Wilham liked about his occupation, and about the city from which he most often applied it; one never truly knew what the next encounter might bring.

Wilham had never seen the Archbishop up close or without all the glittering vestments in which he celebrated High Mass and other official functions at the great cathedral. His first thought, as he knelt to kiss the huge ring on the proffered hand, was how kind the old man looked—and how tired.

Sort of like my Granda used to, he thought as he stood, his soft brown cap in his hand, and waited to hear the particulars of his commission.

"What is your name, lad?" the Archbishop asked. It surprised Wilham; most often he was given his packet and directions, then sent on his way without the least acknowledgment of himself as a person. He represented a service and was not treated unkindly, only impersonally, as one might a ferryman or lamplighter, or anyone else who provided a service that was only missed by its absence.

"Wilham Tybourne, Your Eminence," he replied.

"Well, Wilham, have you been a Rider very long?"

"Three years last week," he replied, wondering at the question. Perhaps the Archbishop was afraid he did not know the kingdom well enough.

"I doubt there's a place in all of Aghamore I've not seen at least once," he continued, exaggerating a little and hoping to allay any concerns the old man might have. "'Tis a good life, Your Eminence."

The Archbishop smiled gently, as if he saw through Wilham's minor subterfuge and understood the reason for it. "Then you have been in Kilgarriff?" he asked.

"Aye, many times, Your Eminence."

"And to Ummera?"

"Once."

"And how quickly can you make this journey?"

Wilham thought for a moment. "Changing horses often and eating in the saddle . . . three days there and back," he said.

The Archbishop nodded, satisfied. He reached into his desk and lifted a letter, double-sealed with deep red wax.

"This letter must reach Bishop Elon with all possible speed," he said. "You are then to wait and see if there is a reply. Either way, you are to report back to me and no one else. Be certain you put this letter in the bishop's hand only, not one of his secretaries. There must be no chance of its getting delayed or misplaced before he sees it. Tell him I await his reply at once. And remember—his hand *only*."

"Yes, Your Eminence," Wilham said solemnly as he accepted the letter. Before he put it into the message pouch he carried draped across his body, he glanced at the seals. The largest one he recognized as the *Agnus Dei,* the Lamb standing upon the great Book of Seven Seals that was the emblem of the Church in Aghamore, with the keys in the upper left corner indicating the letter came from the Office of the Archbishop. The second seal was smaller and matched the ring he had kissed on the old man's hand. It was a Chi-Rho, a mark that looked like a shepherd's crook with a stylized X across it.

Although, in the last months, Wilham had carried many official-looking documents, some between the Barons of different Provinces, he had never been entrusted with anything that looked as important as this. He put it safely into his pouch, then stood a little straighter as he adjusted the strap to hold the pouch tightly to his body.

The Archbishop held out his ring, indicating the Rider's dismissal. Dropping to one knee, Wilham touched his lips to the heavy, carved garnet. Then he stood to find the Archbishop's kind gaze again upon him.

"Our Lord go with you as you travel, lad," the old man said, "and grant that your journey may be both swift and *safe*."

Wilham could feel that the Archbishop truly meant his blessing—but there was something else there, an implied warning of danger that might exist somewhere along the road. Well, there was danger nearly everywhere in Aghamore right now, he reminded himself—knowing that this, too, was part of what he loved about his chosen way of life.

Even so, the unspoken concern in the Archbishop's voice touched Wilham. His Granda had died when he was only twelve, and suddenly Wilham missed him, as he had not in several years. His Granda, his mother's father, had been the only one in the family to truly encourage Wilham to follow his own dreams.

Clearing his throat against a sudden lump of memories, Wilham thanked the Archbishop for his blessing, then hurried from the room. He had to go back to Rider Headquarters now, report his destination, then arrange for a horse and supplies. While those were being requisitioned, he thought, he would go by the Parish of St. Anne and tell Father Renan about being at the Archbishop's Residence. He did not know why exactly, but something told him Renan would want to know.

A short time later, Renan looked at the excited face of Wilham, sitting across the table from him, and tried to conceal his own sense of dread.

"The truth is, Father," Wilham was saying, "he looks so much like me old Granda that I found mesel' truly homesick. I havena' felt that way for . . . well, maybe I've never felt it. So I'm thinkin' that maybe, after this trip, I'll go see me family, like you're always sayin' I should."

Renan forced himself to smile at the young man, though he was struggling not to grab up the letter on the table between them. It was all he could do to keep from breaking open the seals Wilham had so proudly shown him, to find out why the Archbishop was writing the Bishop of Kilgarriff— Giraldus's Province.

"That's fine, Wilham," he said instead, carefully keeping his voice even. "I'm glad to hear you want to see your family again. I'm sure you'll find that all of them, even your father, will be very happy to see you, too. But," Renan hesitated just a moment, "before you do that, will you come see me again?"

"Of course. What is it, Father Renan? What's wrong?"

Renan had to decide how much to tell the young man.

Wilham was honest, he knew, and could be trusted. But much of what was currently happening — or about to happen — was difficult to explain. And, perhaps, to believe.

Renan shifted in his chair while he tried to find the right words. Across the table, Wilham's young face was lined with his concern that Father Renan, his *friend,* might be in trouble and need his help. It spoke well for the young man's heart, and Renan was truly touched.

"There could be a war coming, Wilham," Renan began.

"Aye, Father — everyone knows that. 'Twill come, I'm sure, unless the Church can think of aught to change it, like it did afore."

"I'm afraid it will take something more drastic this time." Again Renan stopped, hesitant about how to continue without giving too much away. He did not want to involve Wilham in a danger he did not have to face.

And yet — Renan was beginning to believe there was no one and nothing involved in this situation, however minor their part, without a purpose. So, breathing a little prayer for guidance, he continued.

"There are other . . . forces at work here, Wilham," he began again, "and the question has become greater than which House will next wear the crown."

"What sort o' forces? Do you mean," Wilham lowered his voice so the next word came out in a whisper, "magic? There be a rumor that Lady Aurya's gone missing — and taken Baron Giraldus with her. Some — not me, mind, but th' more superstitious like — says she's gone from this world down into the bowels o' the earth, t' enlist the aid of no less than the devil hisself, to make sure it's Giraldus what becomes King."

Now Renan found a little smile twitching at the corners of his mouth. "The bowels of the earth" might be one description for where Aurya and Giraldus were right now — though he doubted the Cryf would appreciate such a description of their wondrous Realm—but it was not the devil who was keeping the Baron and his lady there. As for the other . . .

"Yes, Wilham," Renan said honestly, "there is magic at work—and there is great *good* at work as well, though you are to mention neither to anyone. Can I trust you to do that, for our friendship's sake?"

"Aye, Father. You can trust me with anything. I'd hope you know that."

"I am trusting you, Wilham—or I'd have said nothing."

"Do you think it's about this magic," again Wilham whispered the word, "that the Archbishop's writing to the bishop in Giraldus's own Province? I mean, since the bishops all voted to support Giraldus as the next High King—"

"What?" Renan cut him off sharply. That he had *not* heard, and the words sent a chill up his spine.

"Aye," Wilham said, sounding surprised at Renan's reaction. "The proclamation was read in every parish and town hall throughout Aghamore."

"When was that?"

"A few weeks, maybe a month ago. I've heard some folk say that means there'll be no war—and others what say it'll be war for sure."

Now Renan stood. He paced the room twice and came back to stop in front of Wilham.

"Did the *entire* College vote for Giraldus?" he asked, his voice harsh and clipped with worry. "What have you heard? I need to know."

Wilham's eyes had grown wide with Renan's reaction, and the priest made himself sit again, calm down, and speak more softly.

"I was . . . gone," he told Wilham, "for several weeks. Please, this is important. What have you heard about the College of Bishops?"

As Renan watched, Wilham swallowed and blinked, trying to push past his surprise at his friend's outburst and remember what Renan had asked. Silent, Renan gave himself a mental kick. *Calm down,* he told himself. *There's nothing to be gained by being upset—or by upsetting Wilham.*

"Well," the young Rider finally began, "I wasna' there, o' course, and all I have be what rumors are whispered 'round. They say it wasna' a happy vote, not all of it anyways. They say some o' the bishops—Rathreagh, for one—stormed out, a-cursing the others for their choice. I don't know if it be true, mind, 'cause Giraldus's name was still read out in th' churches. Every Rider in th' kingdom was going to every town to deliver th' proclamation, so that much is fact. About the other, I do na' know."

Renan nodded, not replying while his mind whirled. Giraldus was the Church's choice for High King. But Giraldus was safely away. What did that mean about Elon, the Bishop of Kilgarriff? Was he in league with Giraldus and Aurya—or had he been ensorcelled? Perhaps Aurya had used a spell so he had no choice but to argue on the Baron's behalf.

And what did the Archbishop's letter contain? The answer to that question carried possibilities more frightening than Renan wanted to consider—and yet, for Aghamore's sake, he knew he must.

But not now, not here in front of Wilham. He had already said enough to the lad. Now he needed to calm Wilham before he sent him on his errand. But Renan did not regret taking the young man as much into his confidence as he had. There might well come a time when his services, his knowledge of the layout of the kingdom, and his autonomy as a Rider would prove themselves essential.

"Wilham," Renan said, "I need you to continue on your errand as if we had not spoken. Mention it to no one. Or, if they saw you enter and ask, you just tell them the truth—that I've been urging you to take time for a family visit, and you came here to tell me that you've finally decided to take that advice. Nothing more. Don't mention showing me the letter or anything I've said. Understand?"

"Yes, but—"

"This is important, Wilham. I promise that eventually I'll tell you everything. But for now, this must remain a secret between us."

"All right, Father Renan. If you say it's important, that's enough for me."

"Good lad—and thank you. One more thing . . . after you return from Kilgarriff and you've taken the Archbishop whatever reply you receive, come back here. Pay close attention to the Archbishop when you deliver the letter . . . only don't *appear* too interested. Can you do that?"

"Aye," Wilham said confidently. "It's not the first call for . . . discretion . . . I've known—though usually it's a message between lovers not bishops I'm carrying."

A little smile tweaked the corners of Renan's lips as he imagined the kind of discretion to which Wilham was referring.

"Will you be stopping at an inn or two along the way?" he asked. "To spend the night or have a meal? Anything?"

"Well, there be a pub in Ummera where the landlord makes a fine brew. I'd a thought t' wait there while the bishop readies his return letter. The Archbishop asked for m' best speed in both delivery and return—which means most of the time astride, with only a quick fire and camp each night. They be readyin' my supplies now."

"Still," Renan said, "wherever you stop, especially at the inn in Ummera, keep your ears open and your wits about you. Anything you hear, anything at all, might be important. I'll want to hear everything when you return."

Wilham nodded eagerly. "You know, Father," he said, "I can tell this is all serious-like, and I'm not treatin' it otherwise—but this be much of what I love about bein' a Rider. Each job's a different tale—not that I'll be telling this one, mind, not to anyone. It's just a-tween you and me, like you said. But it be more exciting than cobbling shoes like me Da does—where one foot's a-same as t'other."

This time Renan did let his smile show; Wilham's attitude was infectious. "Yes," he agreed, "it is more exciting than feet."

Wilham stood. He picked up the letter, put it back in his pouch, then held out his hand to Renan.

"Well, Father, I'd best be off. They'll likely have me provisions gathered and be waiting at the stables for me t' choose me mount. If old Mudlark be there, I like t' start and end m' trips w' him—he's got the smoothest gallop of any horse we own, though how a great brute like him got such a name, I'll never know."

"Probably the breeder's daughter named him when he was a new foal," Renan said, taking Wilham's proffered hand in a fond shake. "Remember to be careful, Wilham, and don't take this mission too lightly. I pray Our Lord will watch over and protect you from any dangers that might be out there."

"The Archbishop said summut like that," Wilham said a bit softly, "but I thought it was just, well, sort of a general blessing, like."

"Maybe not, Wilham—maybe not." Then Renan smiled. "And maybe so. Maybe I'm worrying over nothing. I'll see you when you get back."

"Aye," Wilham agreed, and placing his brown felt hat firmly on his head, he headed for the rectory door. "I told the Archbishop the journey would take but three days in travel, though how long it might take the Bishop of Kilgarriff t' write his reply I canna' say. But have no fear, Father Renan—I shall return as directly as I can."

With a nod, he was gone. Renan sank back into his chair, all smiles disappearing. Three days—four or five, more likely. Four or five days in which to worry and wonder and try to decide what to do next. Right now, that felt like a very long time. If Elon was in conspiracy with Aurya and Giraldus, and if the Archbishop's letter made him partner to them as well, the Darkness for Aghamore was closer than Renan thought. There was no proof that this was so, but the fear of it made Renan feel nearly ill with dread.

They needed the truth . . . now. Perhaps Lysandra would know, he thought. Perhaps something in her *Sight* or prophecy or . . . some other gift . . . could tell him what to do next. He wished something would tell them. He suddenly felt like he was stumbling around in the dark and at any moment might fall over a cliff edge into an unending chasm—taking all of Aghamore with him.

Chapter Ten

Elon Gallivin, Bishop-ordinary of Kilgarriff, stood at the window of his study. But unlike the Archbishop a few days before, Elon barely noticed the beauty of the summer day. The gardens here were also entering their summer glory. Gone were the delicate blossoms of jonquils and primroses, wood hyacinths and paper-whites, given way to the more robust jewels of lupine and tulip trees, low-growing windflowers and rhododendrons of all sizes and hues, bright carnations and sweet-scented gillyflowers that filled the air with the spicy scent of cloves.

And, of course, the roses, the precious gems of the gardens. Patterned after the gardens at the Archbishop's Residence, these roses, too, were set off in beds of white alyssum and blankets of snow-in-summer, which made them shine like finely cut rubies and amethysts, topaz, and crystals. Still dew-kissed this morning, they shimmered in the delicate balance of sunlight and soft breeze that made even the gardeners who walked among them every day stop and stare at their perfection.

But Elon saw them only in a vague and peripheral way. The only beauty he thought of was the shining gold that adorned the triple-crowned mitre of the Archbishop and how he feared it was slipping beyond his grasp. In his mind, no beauty of nature could compare with that single symbol of Office. He wanted it, and all that went with it, like his body craved the food he had rejected that morning and the sleep he had been unable to claim the past few nights.

He was about to turn away from the window, back again into the room where, he feared, he would be trapped for the rest of his sojourn of service, when he saw a Rider galloping up the garden road. The sight of a Rider was not so unusual, but the earliness of the hour and his obvious haste was enough to make Elon stop and look again.

The Rider did not slow. He galloped on past the beauty of the grounds, giving them even less attention than had the bishop, past the gardeners with barely a glance, though several of them raised a hand in greeting.

Elon watched the Rider gallop all the way to the front door. He did not have long to wait before the knock came on his study door. He quickly seated himself behind the desk before calling "Enter." Johann opened the door, his face wearing even more than its usual scorn as he announced such a common visitor, and one who dared to appear so early.

"I am sorry, Your Grace, but there is a . . . person . . . here to see you," he said, "a Rider. He *says* he comes from His Eminence, who personally instructed him to deliver the message into Your Grace's hand only. It is most unseemly that he should see Your Grace in such a . . . soiled . . . condition, but he is quite insistent."

Elon found he had little patience for his servant this morning. The Archbishop's letter could be bringing the fulfillment—or the end—of all his hopes and plans.

"Soiled or not," he said sharply, "do not keep the Archbishop's messenger waiting. Show him in at once."

Giving Elon a slight bow of obedience, Johann opened the door more widely. He gave an expressive sniff as the Rider passed him, then turned and closed the door, leaving Elon to face whatever the Archbishop had to say.

Elon's sensitive nose nearly wrinkled as much as Johann's as, coming around the desk to greet the Rider, the smell of horse sweat, road dirt, and leather hit him. But, unlike his servant, Elon hid his distaste as he held out his ring for the Rider to kiss.

After a quick genuflect, the young man stood again and reached into his deep pouch, extracting the reason for his presence.

"His Eminence, the Archbishop, said I was to put this in your hand alone," the young man said, holding the letter out so that Elon could see the double seal. "He said I was to wait for the reply, also received only from your hand."

The deep red wax on the parchment, still white with newness, looked to Elon like large clots of dried blood—blood that he feared signified the death of his dreams. He did not need to examine the imprints or the writing on the front of the letter to be certain this came from the Archbishop's own hand.

Still, he hoped he kept his face impassive as he took the letter from the Rider's hand. He could feel that his shoulders and jaw had tensed, but his fingers did not tremble and his voice, as he thanked the young man, was even and strong.

"If you'll go to the kitchens," he said, "my cooks will give you a hot meal. After such a ride so early in the day, I'm sure it will be welcome."

"Aye," Wilham agreed, "and my thanks, Your Grace."

"I'll have a reply ready as soon as possible," Elon told him, still not examining the letter in his hand. "You are welcome to remain here—my staff will see to your comfort. Or, if you leave, return midafternoon and I'll leave word that you are to be brought directly to me."

"Very well, Your Grace."

Elon did not bother to extend his ring again, but turned back toward his desk. The dismissal was obvious, and by the time Elon stepped around to take his seat again, the Rider had already left the room, closing the door with a sturdy thud behind him.

Sitting now and turning the letter over and over in his hands, Elon tried not to think of the sound as prophetic. *Damn Aurya and damn Giraldus,* he thought angrily. *Where are they? Whatever this letter says, how am I supposed to answer it when I've no idea what's going on with them? Damn . . . damn . . . damn . . .*

Elon made a decision. Although the act felt sudden, it had been the reason behind his many sleepless nights. Somehow he had to find a balance that protected him and his dreams for the future. If—*if*—Aurya and Giraldus returned soon, their mission delayed but now completed, he would carry out his part in their mutual plan. But in the meantime, he must at least *appear* to disassociate himself from them. It was the only way to keep from further imperiling his own plan.

Elon took up the sharp, sword-shaped letter opener with its ruby-encrusted hilt that lay a few inches from his fingers, slipped it beneath the hard wax, and sliced, breaking the seals. He then unfolded the letter, looked down at the thin, spidery scrawl that was the Archbishop's own handwriting, and quickly read the contents that summoned him again to Ballinrigh.

* * *

In Ballinrigh, Lysandra was once more kneeling in the dirt of what would be Renan's herb garden. Morning Prayer and Mass were over, the congregation departed, and Renan was with Selia, sitting at the table in the kitchen of the rectory discussing the books she was studying.

They had, of course, invited Lysandra to join them, but she had declined. It was Selia's task to learn the elements of history and government that would help her reign—not, thank goodness, Lysandra's.

But there was another reason Lysandra had declined their company this morning. She had felt a deep and driving need to be outdoors, away from all others. Over the last couple of days this feeling, elusive in the beginning, had been building until now it nagged at her like the throbbing of a decaying tooth. Yet, though its presence could not be denied, neither could she find the words to define it. Whatever it was made her feel unsettled, as if there was something undone, something that needed her immediate attention—something that was as much her responsibility as learning to be Queen was Selia's.

While Lysandra dug her hand trowel deep into the dirt, loosening and lifting in rhythmic motion that was both effective and meditative, Cloud-Dancer lay dozing in the sun a few feet away. She could feel his contentment; she could also feel the minds of Renan and Selia bent upon their tasks. She was vaguely aware of the myriad minds and hearts that made up the population, comfortably blocked now by the strength of her own powers.

But laid upon them, this new feeling tapped and tingled, demanding recognition, then slipping away. *What is it?* Lysandra asked herself again as she turned yet another spade of dirt. But the only answer she received was the certainty that whatever this . . . feeling . . . was trying to tell her must be discovered and dealt with as soon as possible. To ignore it could mean disaster for them all.

Shoving her trowel into the dirt, she left it there as she sat back on her heels and held out her hand for Cloud-Dancer. He hurried to her side, sliding his head beneath her fingers in a response as familiar as the gesture that summoned him. She did not want to go anywhere that needed his guidance, nor did she want to borrow his vision. She merely wanted his touch, his nearness and comfort, while she tried to fit together this new puzzle.

Cloud-Dancer was content to go no farther. He put his head on Lysandra's thigh and closed his eyes again, sending out waves of drowsy ease that made Lysandra smile. It was just what she wanted and needed. His nearness, his peaceful warmth, pushed everything else away in the same way his waking presence guarded and kept her body safe. Now she was ready.

Ready—but unsure what to do. This was all still so new to her. For a decade, over a third of her life, her *Sight* had worked one way. Although she had often wished for more perfect control over it, she had become used to its ways. Now she had that control—and more. Her *Sight* had powers within it she never imagined and she was still discovering what they were. In many ways, Lysandra felt she was back at the beginning again.

She settled herself more comfortably and waited, closing her eyes and inviting whatever might happen. It did not come all at once, but she did not expect it to. She was not, in fact, certain what she did expect, but when her *Sight* finally began to clear, it came like a reluctant dawn in which vision slowly filtered through darkness. Or, perhaps, it sailed into the light, for what Lysandra *saw* was a fleet, a vast fleet, of ships. Still in the distance, she could not count them all—but she knew there must be thousands of men crowded on their decks.

And they were coming toward Aghamore.

Eyes still closed and brow knotted with effort, she strove to expand her *Sight*. Was this a *Far-Seeing,* a vision of something happening now, or prophecy of danger to come some-time in Aghamore's unrealized future? The ships became more than shaped dots upon the open sea. They moved, rolling and pitching with wind and wave; she felt it in the pit of her stomach. They were coming to Aghamore to conquer and destroy; she felt that in the depths of her soul.

The vision was reaching full brightness now. The dawn of her *Sight* turned to daylight and, as the vision cleared, she *saw* the white sails, brilliant and shining, painted with the huge red dragon of Corbenica.

The dragon was the color of fire, the color of blood. It was the color of fear, too, a fear that took hold of Lysandra's heart. Like the light of her vision, it grew steadily, strength-ened and deepened until she could barely breathe, barely think. For one brief yet overpowering moment, fear was her entire existence as her *Sight* zoomed in, flying with the speed of an osprey's wings.

It showed her one face, hard and cold, with eyes the blue of sunlit ice, that looked greedily in Aghamore's direction. His hair, like her own, was blond—but while hers shone with the warmth of antique gold, his was the pale yellow-white of old bones. His beard, fire red, was parted in the middle in braids that reached nearly to his waist, bound on the ends with beads that were carved in runic symbols. A long scar ran from his left ear, across his cheek, disappearing beneath a red-blond mustache that fully covered his upper lip and, like his beard, was bound at the ends with carved beads.

His hands, as they gripped the rail of his ship, were gnarled with scars that ran up his bared forearms in crisscross patterns too regular to be accidental.

The rest of his body she could not see; he was draped from head to toe in the fur of a great white beast. Its forelegs were knotted across his chest, with massive paws that dan-gled, claws intact, like some ornamental celebration of con-quest and death. The beast's head formed a hood that even pushed partway back as it was, still made the man look like some fey and mythical being emerging from within the creature's body. It was a wild and terrifying sight.

Then, with a breath that forced itself as a ragged gulp into her fear-squeezed lungs, distance came again into her vision. The ships once more turned into dark specks upon the sea. Lysandra could see that there were at least twenty of them, perhaps more, all laden with men — and all heading for Aghamorc.

Something, some sense or inner voice, told her that this was no distant prophecy. This was happening *now* — and if this kingdom was to survive the invasion, it must prepare. *Now.* They no longer had time to devise, discard, revise a plan for gaining Selia's sovereignty.

Time had just become their enemy.

With a quick caress, more for her comfort than for his, Lysandra eased Cloud-Dancer's head from her thigh and stood. She had to tell Renan what she had just *seen* — and hope he would know what to do. There must be someone they could tell, someone they could convince that what she *saw* was real.

Renan will know, she told herself again as she headed for the rectory door. All of her trust, all of her hope — and all of the future for them all — was in that single thought.

Corbenica, Renan thought as he heard Lysandra's vision. He had no doubt of its accuracy — but like Lysandra, he wondered to whom they could turn.

The ancient enemy of Aghamore, it had been how long since Corbenica had last attempted an invasion — eighty years, one hundred, longer? The history book in front of Selia would say, but Renan did not take the time to look it up. What mattered was that they were coming now.

Corbenica, he thought again, as if repeating the name could somehow take away the horror and the threat of it. Tales of the Corbenicans went back centuries. Even before the Church had come to Aghamore, putting an end to blood feuds and rituals of sacrifice, the ways of the Corbenicans had been different than those of the people of Aghamore. There, Kings regularly gave their blood to feed their hungry gods, and enemies, if not tortured to death, were tossed into a pit, to be torn apart by wild beasts for the amusement of the crowd.

There were other tales too terrible for Renan to think on, let alone mention to his companions, things he had learned back in his days as a student of the arcane. Many of the books of blackest magic were of Corbenican origin.

The man whom Lysandra had seen in her vision could only be King Wirral. No one but the ruler was allowed to wear the white fur of their great northern bear, who roamed the land and ice floes, impervious to the cold. According to the Corbenican beliefs, their god had mated with the greatest of the white bears, and she gave birth to the first of the Corbenican Kings, dying to give life to the infant. When that happened, the god who was the child's father appeared and skinned the bear. He then wrapped it in the white fur, and the strength of the mother flowed into the child. Like the white fur, this strength was said to be passed down through the royal line ever since. The Kings of Corbenica claimed their sovereignty through no less than their great god, Doenaar.

Renan stood and paced the room, aware that both Selia and Lysandra were waiting for him to say something. He crossed over to the stove and poured himself a cup of the licorice and betony tea Lysandra had brewed them, glad of its strengthening properties. Perhaps, he thought, it would help him think, give him a clear head for the decisions on which they were obviously waiting.

Adding some honey to his tea and taking a large sip, more to give himself time than to quench a thirst, Renan finally turned and faced the women. He knew they had no choice but to take a chance.

"The Archbishop," he said aloud.

"What will you say to him?" Lysandra asked, as always immediately following Renan's train of thought.

"I don't know," he answered truthfully. "The truth, I suppose. What else can I tell him?"

"But the scroll—won't he—"

"Censor me?" Renan finished for her. "Refuse to listen because of it? I don't know what his reaction will be. I don't really know how much he can be trusted—I've only met him rarely, at official episcopal functions. But his reputation says he is a kind and learned man. That's the only hope I see."

As Renan came over and sat down again, he looked into the faces of his companions. They had been through so much together already, were they ready for what might come next? This was another battle, not of swords and blood as they had fought with Giraldus's soldiers, but of words and wills, of traditions and beliefs, that must be waged to clear the field for truth. This battle, he prayed, would be less horrific than the last one they faced, but it would be no less intense—or dangerous.

Would that danger be directed toward him alone, a disobedient son of the Church? Again, he hoped so; his own danger he could face. But if he could not convince the Archbishop to reexamine the scroll, if he and the others were found guilty of heresy by their possession of it, what would that mean for Selia—and Lysandra? No one had been burned as a heretic in Aghamore for 270 years; he could hardly bear the fear that the practice might begin again with the woman he loved.

Lysandra reached out and put a hand over his briefly. No word was spoken, but the gesture told him everything he needed to know. Selia, however, was another matter. Where Lysandra wordlessly understood, Selia was still unschooled.

"Why should he worry about the scroll?" she demanded. "I thought it was what guided you. If not, why am I here?"

"It is what guided us," Renan said, turning toward her,

"but it's not that simple. Nothing in this whole business, it seems, is simple."

While Renan explained Tambryn's history to Selia, his mind was busy listening to his own words and trying to judge if there were any among them he could use to the Archbishop. But, although he knew firsthand the truth of everything he was saying, he discovered no sudden, miraculous gift of oratory or persuasion within them.

When he finished Tambryn's tale, all three of them sat in silence, thinking. "He still has to know," Lysandra said finally. "He was always going to have to know. The only question was *when*—and that answer has been provided. The answer is *now*."

"Are you prepared for it?" Renan asked her. "The Archbishop will want to see and question you. It could be a long ordeal—but if he's going to believe your vision . . ."

He left the rest unsaid. Archbishop Colm ApBeirne might have a personal reputation as a kind and holy man, but they had to convince him to believe Lysandra, then to lay aside the Church's edict on the Scrolls of Tambryn and, finally, to believe in Selia and her intended role in Aghamore's future. All this might well turn a gentle interview into an inquisition.

"Selia, there's still a lot you need to learn, and we'll have to continue our lessons. Lysandra, I know how difficult it's been for you to leave your cottage again. You've both done so much already, but now it's time to step into the center ring of this kingdom's politics. Are you sure you're ready?"

"We have to be, don't we?" Selia answered. Renan was glad to hear the change that the last few days of study and focus had made in her. She was beginning to think like a Queen, putting the good of the kingdom first.

Renan waited while Lysandra remained silent. He knew that she would not speak until she had truly considered. Her words never came lightly—but when they did, they were always offered with truth at their core. Selia, who possessed all the flexibility of mind and circumstance that was the strength of youth, was the one called to earthly recognition, perhaps, even, to glory. But it was Lysandra's quiet, steady spirit on which that glory would be built.

"From those to whom much is given, much will be expected," he heard her say softly, as if only for her own ears. But it was worth repeating—for all of them.

"What was that?" he asked.

"Something my mother used to say. It means I'm ready," she said. "When will you go see the Archbishop?"

"Tomorrow morning, right after Mass. Without an appointment, I don't know how long it will take to see him—but if I get there early, perhaps he'll have a few minutes to spare me."

"Will you take the scroll with you?"

Renan shook his head. "Not yet," he said. "For now, it is your vision he needs to hear . . . and pray we can convince him to believe it."

"You will," Lysandra said, standing. "I'll let you two get back to your books. Selia needs to be as prepared as possible when she meets him."

Renan watched Lysandra hold out her hand for Cloud-Dancer and then go with him back into the sunlight. As always, he marveled at the courage she did not even know she possessed—and at the deep generosity of her heart, he thought as he remembered the wordless support of her touch upon his hand.

Then he turned back to Selia, to the books and the day's duty before him. He found Selia watching him with a concerned and thoughtful expression.

"What is it you two weren't saying?" she asked him. "What will happen when you tell the Archbishop about the scroll?"

Before he answered, Renan thought of the letter that the Archbishop had sent to the Bishop of Kilgarriff and for the hundredth time he wished he had some indication of what it might contain. He then gave Selia a wan and weary little smile.

"I wish I knew," he said. "I truly wish I knew."

Chapter Eleven

In Tigh-Lorcain, the capital city of Rathreagh, the northernmost Province of Aghamore, Baron Hueil was in the main audience chamber of his fortress awaiting the arrival of his chief military advisor. Or, that was the man's official title—head coordinator of Hueil's spies was a more accurate description of his services. And he had served his ruler well, especially over these last few months while Hueil was arranging his partnership with King Wirral of Corbenica.

The only ones in the Province who knew of this plan were Hueil himself, Jaevyn, the man for whom he was waiting, and the two operatives Jaevyn had sent to finalize the agreement between himself and King Wirral's men. Not even Hueil's daughter, Margharite, knew—though her part in what was to come was crucial.

Hueil had debated with himself for a long time before taking this final, drastic step. All through the winter, his internal battle had raged, long before he had taken Jaevyn into his confidence. Even then, with Jaevyn playing devil's advocate, it had been several weeks still before he had made his first tentative approach to King Wirral. But in all of Aghamore's long history, there had never been a King from the Ruling House of Rathreagh on the throne. Hueil was determined to change that.

Descended from Cionaod, the ninth and youngest son of King Liam the Builder, the Baron of Rathreagh governed the most land-poor Province in the kingdom. It was true that Rathreagh was the largest, but half of the land was worthless bogs or large outcroppings of stone. The usable land was limited and not overly fertile, the stones contained no remarkable gems or other minerals, the woodlands were too sparse to provide much of either timber or game. The only thing of importance for Rathreagh was fishing.

It was the one occupation at which the people of Rathreagh excelled, providing most of the fish for the kingdom, even for the King's table in Ballinrigh. The large coastline of the Province was dotted with towns and villages that lived their days to the rhythm of the sea, braving the winds and tides in small boats and fishing in much the same manner as their ancestors had done. It was an adequate living, but a dangerous and by no means a lucrative one.

Yet Hueil had found that most of the fishermen desired no other life. The call of the sea, they said, ran through their veins. Those who did not share that feeling or who hungered for wealth, glory, or merely a different emphasis of life, soon left Rathreagh to make their way in one of the other eight Provinces.

But Hueil could not leave—he was their Baron. The only way he could change his place in their kingdom was to become High King. The only way to ensure that was with the help of Aghamore's ancient enemy. And to ensure that pact did not go awry, Hueil had promised Margharite to Wirral's son, Arnallt, in marriage. Once Hueil sat upon the throne in Ballinrigh, Margharite and Arnallt would govern Rathreagh—and together they would be his heirs to the crown of the kingdom. Wirral—so Hueil hoped, prayed, and had been assured—would not destroy the kingdom his son and grandson would rule.

The Summer Solstice was fast approaching. It was Hueil's habit to hold court twice a year at different locations in the Province—at Christmas and the Summer Solstice. The people of Rathreagh then felt they had closer contact with their Baron. His presence among them assured them he knew what their lives were like and was available to hear their petitions or deal with their needs.

This year, Hueil was celebrating the Summer Solstice in the harbor city of Owenasse, one of the few larger cities in the Province—and the only one with a harbor large enough to land a fleet. It was here Wirral's army was to land on the night following the Solstice celebration. Hueil knew he would soon have to tell Margharite of his plans, but he kept putting off the inevitable, knowing she could be just as stubborn and contrary as her mother had ofttimes been.

I'll wait, he thought as he continued to pace the room, finally hearing Jaevyn's footsteps in the hallway. *I won't tell her until after Wirral has landed. Then she won't have time to upset anything. She'll have to do as she's told.*

He hoped.

But the footsteps were not Jaevyn's. Just as he thought of her fate, Margharite walked into the room—and even in the dim light, the brilliant red of her hair shone like a nimbus of fire.

Margharite's mother had also had red hair. She had been known throughout the Province for the beauty of it. Hueil had thought it the most beautiful hair he had ever seen—until Margharite was born. Beautiful as her mother was, Margharite outshone her . . . in every eye but Hueil's. To Hueil, no one could ever be more beautiful than his Caitra.

Hueil turned his thoughts quickly back to his daughter. He never let himself think of Caitra except when he was alone at night; even after all these years, her loss was too painful to do otherwise.

But the thought of his late wife would not leave him today—and he knew why. She would never have let him do what he was about to do. *If you were with me,* he thought, *everything would be different—and I have Margharite to protect. This will keep her safe, and it will give her everything.*

The assurance rang dull and flat, hollow even to himself. To chase away his doubts he thought of happier times, remembering the day his daughter was born.

Unlike most babies, she had been born with a full head of hair that only grew brighter as the years passed. Her skin was white, so softly blushed with pink, and over the years that, too, grew ever more radiant until now, as a young woman, people—in court or among the populace—could not stop themselves from turning to watch her.

The memory brought a little peace to Hueil, and the tension in his still broad shoulders relaxed a little. Hueil knew he was not the man he had been when he wooed and won the hand of his beloved Caitra. Then his hair had been bright gold, his back straight, and his broad chest had not slipped to give girth around his middle.

But now there was as much silver as gold—and he used spies and subterfuge instead of his own strength and cunning to win a battle. For a moment, one very brief moment, he felt ashamed. Then he straightened his shoulders.

I'm doing what I must to make certain I gain the throne— and to end the coming civil war quickly. That is the best thing for this Province, for this kingdom—and for Margharite.

Beside Margharite walked her almost-constant companion, Glynna. Daughter of one of Hueil's advisors, the girls had grown up together . . . and they were nearly inseparable now.

Glynna also had red hair, something not unusual for

Rathreagh. But though it was only slightly darker than Margharite's, it lacked its remarkable fire. As they approached, he saw that they wore the summer gowns he had ordered, made of mint green embroidered with white rosebuds and trimmed in eyelet lace.

The gowns differed only slightly—a square neck on Margharite's and a scoop neckline on Glynna's; Glynna's had longer sleeves and Margharite's more lace. Hanging from a hook at the waist were long ribbons, to which white lace fans were attached, so they could be easily reached, and Hueil knew that there were also matching lace parasols to protect their fair skin.

Hueil had worked very hard to keep his daughter unaware of the many burdens he carried and of how very dangerous the situation throughout Aghamore had become. He wanted her to enjoy such time of freedom as she still had. It would change soon enough. As soon as—

He gave himself a mental shake to stop this particular flow of thought. Instead, he watched the girls laughing and talking as they walked toward him. The soft green and white of the gowns, so perfect a color for the young women, made them look like sprites, full of laughter and sunshine, even in the half-lit room.

Hueil could not help but think that this was more than a trick of fabric and light; it was truest beauty, it was innocence itself, that shone . . . and he was suddenly so sorry that too soon, for Margharite at least, innocence must soon give way to duty.

As they drew nearer, Margharite suddenly ran the last few steps and threw her arms around his neck. Her embrace wiped the crumpled look of worry that had long ago become Hueil's habitual expression. For a moment, the Baron actually smiled at his daughter.

"Oh, Father," she said as she stepped back and twirled, holding out the sides of her gown. "Thank you—they're beautiful, and they're perfect for the Solstice Festival. And thank you for getting one for Glynna, too."

Hueil was pleased. "Now, would I dare get one for you and not for Glynna—your other half, I've called her often enough over the years, eh?" he teased, looking over to include the other girl.

"Aye, m'lord," Glynna said more softly than Margharite, and giving him a smile that was far more shy.

Although her father worked in close contact with Hueil, and although she and Margharite had been inseparable friends since early childhood, she still treated the Baron with an awe he could never set at ease.

"And what do you two have planned for today?" he asked.

"We're going riding," Margharite said, "after we change, of course. But we wanted to show you the gowns."

Hueil frowned. At their age, Margharite and Glynna still felt immortal, as if none of the dangers in the kingdom could ever come close or touch them. But Hueil knew better.

"Take someone with you," he told them. "Take a stable lad at least—and make sure he's armed. If you won't take a guard or two, there are several in the stables strong enough to give you some protection. But either way, you are *not* to go alone."

Hueil missed the surreptitious glance that passed between the two young women; they already knew who would go riding with them. But Margharite gave a feigned sigh, for her father's sake, as she agreed.

"And be home well before dinner," he said, as she hugged him again in farewell. Then, before she could turn away, he looked into her beautiful face and thought again how much she looked like her mother.

How would he bear it when they were both gone from him?

Once Margharite and Glynna were gone, Hueil turned again to the window and resumed waiting for Jaevyn. It took only a few more minutes until he again heard footsteps. This time, it was the sharp tap of a man's boots upon the wooden floor.

Hueil turned and saw it was indeed his approaching advisor, hurrying toward him while trying to balance long tubes in his arms. The tubes—and their contents—were the reason Hueil had called for this meeting; they contained maps of the Province of Rathreagh, of the mountains and passes, maps of the Province of Urlar, and one of the whole of Aghamore.

"You're late," Hueil said in a voice much harder than he had used just moments ago.

"I know, m'lord," Jaevyn said apologetically, "but the old map room, where two of these maps were found, is in more disarray than I imagined. I've set some of my men to cleaning and setting it to right."

"Very well," Hueil said, reaching for the maps. He hoped to find a way through the open landscape and not be limited only to the main roads; he did not wish to upset his people by having the army of Corbenica march through town after town. There would be time enough for the people to learn of the new alliance *after* Hueil sat on the throne.

Nor did he wish to give anyone the chance to ride ahead and warn the other Barons that the Corbenicans were coming. Hueil knew that surprise as well as numbers was one of his greatest weapons. Once their course was plotted, he would send riders on ahead with horses and supplies, so that the army could march with as little packing as possible and, he hoped, increase their speed still further.

"Ah, Jaevyn . . . good," he said when he opened the third tube. "I knew that complete maps of the bogs had to exist."

"Aye, m'lord," Jaevyn agreed. "But they were buried and are quite old. I'm not sure we can trust them overmuch."

"A decade or a century—how much do bogs change, really?"

"I do not know, m'lord. I just hope we do not find out that it is too much, too late."

"Oh, enough of your long looks and dire words," Hueil said with no little impatience. "This will *work,* Jaevyn. I feel it in my bones. At long last Aghamore will have a Rathreagh-born King—and the people of this Province will prosper for it. In fact, with Corbenica no longer our enemy, the whole kingdom will soon prosper. You'll see—within a year all of Aghamore will thank me for this union."

"As you say, m'lord."

Inside Hueil, a little voice was whispering in tones more dire and reluctant than Jaevyn's. But Hueil refused to listen to either of them. He was too committed to turn back, no matter what warnings his advisor—or his conscience—might utter.

He reached out and took the tubes from Jaevyn's arms, then strode toward the dais, where his throne of office stood, uncapping them as he walked. He would allow himself to think of nothing else except that very soon he would approach and claim another, much larger throne.

He would be King.

Elon was on his way to Ballinrigh. Again. He had answered the Archbishop's letter and sent the Rider on his way. But this time, Elon did not wait for his household to be gathered so he could travel in stately pomp from Ummera to the capital. He was riding on alone, in haste, and letting his household follow. He intended to be only a few hours behind the Rider and thus show the Archbishop how seriously he shared his superior's concerns.

As supercilious as Johann's hauteur made him in Elon's eyes, he could be trusted with his duties, especially with the ordering and moving of the household. He knew what and whom the bishop would need for an extended stay in Ballinrigh and, delighting in being able to strike near terror in the hearts of the junior staff, he would see that it was done with all possible haste. Elon knew he could ride out with his mind at ease—at least about that part of his life.

From Thomas, Elon had more explicit needs. Their studies and the honing of Thomas's talents were at a crucial point; it was important that certain manuals and other texts Thomas had been reading make it to Ballinrigh. Nor were Thomas's studies the only volumes Elon ordered be brought. In working to train his manservant, Elon had chanced upon a volume he had acquired many years before and, for some reason he could not remember now, had put aside and forgotten.

It came from ancient Corbenica. As he read it now, at least twenty years more experienced in such matters, he was discovering a text within a text. Perhaps, he thought, that was the reason it had been neglected; perhaps his earlier self had been unable to glean the hidden arcane knowledge it contained.

Whatever had been the reason, he was reading it now, and it was opening many new possibilities. He had always longed to taste of the power he felt within Aurya. He had always felt, too, that his voice, the one power—besides intelligence— he did possess, had to be capable of more than captivating a congregation, or persuading and seducing a woman—or even guiding a willing subject like Thomas.

The Corbenican book of the arcane hinted the promise that indeed it was. Elon might, if he was interpreting the clues correctly, possess the very ability needed to unlock and control the power of Doenaar himself.

The more Elon read, the more fascinated he became. It was not darkness the Corbenicans—and their god—saw as the place of either death or its power; it was white, the vast and unending whiteness of the frozen north, such as covered half their land and seas. Doenaar had walked this frozen death when he mated with the she-bear whose breath created it and whose coat gave it its color. After she had died giving birth to their child, Doenaar had taken her fur. By then wearing it, he had claimed and conquered the power of death and the forces of nature.

Corbenican prophecies said that the greatest servant of Doenaar would come with a voice through which the great god would once again speak to his people. This voice would compel all who heard it to listen and obey the will of Doenaar. Although others might serve the god of the frozen ways, although many others—especially the Kings of Corbenica—were required to give their blood to appease Doenaar's wrath and keep the white-death from creeping down to encompass all the land and the people, only one person each century would be born with the power to be Doenaar's voice.

Only that one, said the ancient text Elon was now reading, would be able to see and understand the hidden words it contained. And that one, Elon was beginning to believe, was himself.

What would he do with this power, if it did indeed prove to be his? Elon did not yet know. But the very possibility of it was enough to fill him with a thrill, a sense of excited anticipation such as he had never before experienced. And when he coupled that with the thought of finally attaining the goal he had held for so long, of wearing the golden, triple-crowned mitre of the Archbishop of Aghamore, there surged through him an ecstasy far sweeter than any of the earthly pleasures he was supposed to have given up for the Religious life.

It was such thoughts that made the long hours in the saddle pass quickly and gave comfort to the two nights he spent in dingy inns along the road.

Elon entered Ballinrigh by the Eastgate, midmorning on the third day since leaving his Residence in Ummera. At first, traveling neither in clerical garb nor with the retainers of his household, he was not recognized. Delayed by the gatekeeper who, in these unsettled times for the kingdom, was charged with keeping closer watch than usual, Elon paced around the small gatehouse until the servant he had sent for came and spoke for him. The gatekeeper's apology was so effusive that Elon waved a swift, halfhearted sign of blessing over the man so that he could be quickly on his way again.

The traffic in the city demanded a slower pace than Elon craved, and by the time he reached his grand House, he was grinding his teeth to keep from shouting at all of Ballinrigh's population to get out of his way. His House, too, was unprepared for the whirling energy with which he charged through its doors, calling for servants and issuing orders that came as quickly as his footsteps.

He missed Thomas's attendance and even Johann's efficiency as he waited for enough hot water to be brought to fill the bathtub in his antechamber. While he washed the sweat and grime of the road away, he ordered the best of the ceremonial cassocks he kept stored here to be brought out and aired, his boots to be cleaned, his pectoral cross of silver, garnets, and star sapphires polished. He would not go to the Archbishop looking anything other than his most competent best.

It took nearly two hours for everything to be accomplished to his satisfaction. When, at last, he stood before the polished mirror that hung on the inner door of his wardrobe, flicked away one last imagined speck of lint, and adjusted first the cross upon his chest, then the broad cincture that wrapped his slender waist, he was certain that no other prelate in the kingdom presented a more perfectly appointed presence. There was nothing unkempt or disheveled, nothing to hint at the preoccupation of a guilty conscience.

Indeed, his conscience was not guilty, for that would have meant hesitation over what he was doing. Elon felt none. He did not *care* about the dangers, not to himself or others, not of body or soul—not as long as in the end, he got what he wanted. It was this attitude that would allow him to play whatever part was necessary. He would abandon Giraldus and Aurya without so much as a backward glance, if that was what it would take to ensure he was the Archbishop's publicly named successor.

Could he do so, even knowing—as she did not—that Aurya was his daughter? Their errand was as much for his benefit, and even more at his instigation, than their own. What of that? Could he toss aside such willing tools?

And what about Thomas? his thoughts continued as he settled his biretta on top of the purple skullcap that matched his cassock and took the place of a tonsure. Would he as easily turn his back on his protégé as he was preparing to do to Aurya and Giraldus?

For Thomas, he admitted, he might—*might*—try to find an alternative. But for his association with Aurya and Giraldus, he spared not a second wavering. If denouncing them was the only way to keep the Archbishop's favor, then his decision was made and his course set.

Elon left his chamber and strode again through his large House, servants following in his wake as he issued more orders. Then, stopping only long enough at the door for one hurried servant to drape his cloak, now brushed free of any traces of road dirt, across his shoulders, Elon was out the door.

His city carriage stood waiting to receive him, its door being held by a liveried footman. The driver, too, was in place and looking his best—sitting eyes forward and at attention. Elon gave a mental nod of satisfaction. It was all part of the front he wanted to present at the Archbishop's Residence, for he knew that every nuance would be noted and reported long before he was granted audience.

Elon knew it because he would have ordered the same thing. And Colm ApBeirne, for all his scholarly mind and somewhat unworldly air, had been part of the world of politics too long not to see the opportunities that presented themselves. Elon would not make the error of underestimating his opponent. In the game he was now playing, such a mistake could be fatal.

Chapter Twelve

The Archbishop was waiting for Elon. He had, of course, already read the brief but seemingly sincere reply, hand-penned and sent back with the Rider. The words were all the right ones, and Colm ApBeirne wanted to believe well of his fellowman and fellow bishop. Yet there was something inside him, some still, small voice that continued to whisper a warning.

Reports always rolled in regarding the traffic at the Gates. Usually these reports came in general terms and went to one of his many undersecretaries as nothing more than an approximate tally of the comings and goings of the kingdom's most populous city. However, when the report of the Westgate noted the arrival of the Bishop of Kilgarriff, the news found its way to the Archbishop's ear.

He was unsure how long it would be before Elon made his appearance, and the Archbishop left orders to be alerted immediately. He was therefore ready when Elon's presence and petition for audience were announced.

But Colm ApBeirne did not admit him at once. It would do Elon no harm, he thought, to wait amid the many others of the kingdom, laity and Religious who, having no King to see them, came to the Archbishop's Residence seeking help. Perhaps, the hope whispered, an hour or two surrounded by the patience of others in need—the softly murmured prayers and words of comfort from the priests, of Brothers and Sisters who filled their time of waiting by trying to ease the burden of children who sat with their weary or aged or sometimes ailing parents, of mothers trying to control bored and sometimes hungry children, of merchants or laborers here with unsettled disputes, their pride and their hope eaten away by unfilled bellies—would remind Elon of the vows he took before God to serve all these and their countless counterparts.

A King took a similar vow at the coronation; in his long life, Colm ApBeirne had heard those words spoken three times. For two of them he had, as Archbishop and Primus of the Church in Aghamore, administered and received that vow on God's—and the people's—behalf.

Sacred though it was, that vow was less binding in heaven and on earth than those taken by clergy and Religious. A King vowed heart, mind, and body in service and protection of his people; a priest or Religious vowed their *soul* in the service of God—and no amount of wealth or power that came with Office could negate that basic truth. The wealth and power were meant to be used *for* that service, not as a personal reward either because or in place of it.

All these things went through the Archbishop's mind as he stood before the fire in his study and again reread the short letter Elon had sent in reply to his own, again trying to decide how best to deal with Kilgarriff's bishop. On his desk were some of the numerous petitions that had begun to pour in from that Province because of the extended absence of their Baron. The most common thread running through them, unstated and often hidden behind words of complaint, was *fear*. The people of Kilgarriff, bereft of their leader during this unsettled time, were afraid—for themselves, their future, for all that might happen with Giraldus gone.

Without a King, the Archbishop and the Church must find the way to lay those fears to rest.

And yet, he thought, *I've had to summon Elon here instead of being able to leave him in Kilgarriff, where the people could go to him for hope and draw comfort from his unwavering presence. Something keeps telling me not to leave him there unwatched. I want to believe in him. His words all sound so right . . .*

Perhaps they are too *right.*

Colm ApBeirne scrubbed a hand across tired eyes. It was a weariness that went far beyond his body. He had hoped and believed the future was settled when the College of Bishops dispersed. Giraldus was the Church's choice for High King, Elon was to be his own successor for Archbishop—and he could soon retire to the monastery of his youth, to spend the last portion of his earthly life in its contemplative peace. Everything within him craved that ending to his days.

Or almost everything—for he could not go there or abandon this kingdom into the hands and heart of anyone about whom he was not certain. And that meant Elon.

The Archbishop resumed his seat behind the ornate and impressive desk at which he spent so many hours. Its size did more than merely hold the huge amount of work spread out across its top. It also separated him from the petitioner on the other side. This would be no comfortable private chat before the fire. This was an official hearing by the Primus of the Church.

As ready as he could be, Colm pulled the cord that sounded a little bell at one secretary's desk. A moment later, the monk who gave service there opened the door. Their eyes met, and the Archbishop gave a little nod.

"Show him in," he said, knowing he did not need to explain whom he meant.

Another moment, then Elon entered, bringing his special energy with him. He hurried over and dropped to one knee to kiss the Archbishop's ring. Then, rising, he waited until Colm had gestured in the general direction of the chairs before taking a seat. The Archbishop noticed how differently Elon presented himself this time. He was not sitting back, confident and relaxed. Instead, Elon sat forward, as if eager for every word his superior might say.

With a flash of insight, Colm ApBeirne knew that neither meeting had shown him the real person behind the mask that the Bishop of Kilgarriff wore. Had he ever seen the *real* Elon? he wondered.

Neither man spoke immediately. Under the guise of gathering papers, Colm let Elon wait some more. He wanted Elon to feel at least some discomfort over the uncertainty of his status.

Finally ready, the old man cleared his throat. "We are most displeased, my son," he said, using the formal — and official — pronoun of his Office. "The letters and petitions from Kilgarriff pile by the hour. By the hour, this kingdom moves closer to civil war in search of a King — and Giraldus, whom you convinced this Church to support, remains absent. This state cannot continue. You said that the Baron and his lady were on pilgrimage. We have waited — the Province of Kilgarriff, even the kingdom, has waited for word of their return, contrite yet cleansed of their past sin and ready to take up the yoke of duty again, this time under obedience to God and His Church."

"Your Eminence," Elon said, spreading his hands in a gesture of helplessness, "I, too, expected the Baron's return. By now, I hoped the unrest within this kingdom would be ended under the peaceful authority of a new and duly anointed King. I know not what to tell *you*, for *I* do not know what has happened."

In these last words, the Archbishop heard the ring of truth. As for the rest of what Elon might say — on that, the Archbishop would still reserve judgment.

"If, as their spiritual director and counsel, you do not know, then I have no choice but to take action for the good of Kilgarriff and this kingdom. But before I do, I ask you plainly—is there anything more, anything at all, you can tell me about Baron Giraldus and Lady Aurya? Where did they plan to go and when to return? This is *vital*, Elon—for their sakes as well as for the people's. If they left the kingdom, many ills may have befallen them. They may be ill or captured, in need of ransom somewhere—"

"No," Elon said. "They were not leaving Aghamore. They should have returned to Kilgarriff in two, at most three weeks. I expected to hear of their return before the College was adjourned—and I have expected it every day since. As for where they were exactly or what route they took, that I do not know. There were several stops they spoke of making. But even that cannot explain their delay. Believe me, Your Eminence, I am as bewildered and upset by this as you are."

Colm heard the slight edge of desperation slip into Elon's usually cultured voice. Did he believe it? Was Elon as unsettled as he appeared—or was it a well-executed performance? And if he was truly upset, was it for the people of Kilgarriff and Aghamore he worried, as he claimed, or the threatened loss of his own elevation?

The Archbishop shook his head slightly to clear away the uncharitable thoughts that lingered. Perhaps the next few minutes would be the telling ones.

"Very well, Elon," he said. "Then I have, reluctantly, reached a decision. Until such time as circumstances change, Iain DeMarcoe, paternal cousin of Giraldus, shall govern Kilgarriff, bearing all rights and authority of Baron. I have a writ to that effect prepared, and I will personally say the words of installation, hearing his vows and duly anointing him into that Office two weeks from today at the Cathedral in Ummera. If Baron Giraldus does not return to Kilgarriff by the end of summer, or if we do not receive word of his legitimate and verifiable reason for this delay, then his authority of rights, title, lands, and state as Baron shall be forfeit, and Iain's installation shall be made permanent."

The Archbishop watched Elon very closely during this well-rehearsed speech, looking for signs within signs and expressions beneath expressions. Now he saw Elon's face change to a look of deep relief. It was all he saw — yet he still was not certain he believed it; there was still that little voice inside of him whispering a warning.

But maybe I'm wrong, his thoughts quickly countered. *Maybe I'm misjudging him with my hesitation . . .* Yet even as these thoughts circled through his brain, that still, small voice of doubt and caution issued its warning anew.

"Thank you, Your Eminence," Elon was saying, his voice now overriding Colm's internal one. "Not only for myself and the worry that I, too, have been feeling, but for all the people of Kilgarriff. Rather than send a Rider or one of your own with this news, may I be the one to deliver the writ to Lord Iain? I have not had many dealings with him in the past and do not know him well, but now Lord Iain and I must work together for the good of our Province. Let that work begin with this joyous news."

This, too, was well said. Everything from Elon was well said. But the Archbishop could think of no reason to deny a request so honorably and — it appeared — so sincerely made.

The old man nodded and picked up a large document, already folded and sealed, at his elbow. "Very well, Elon," he said. "I agree it is an auspicious note on which to begin your relationship. Let us pray it bodes well for the future."

The interview was at an end. As the Archbishop held the writ out to Elon, he rose, took it, then once more came around the desk to kiss his superior's great amethyst-and-garnet ring. Colm ApBeirne bit his tongue to keep from softening the air of dismissal, as was his usual wont. It was important that this time Elon understood the precarious place in which he stood.

The room remained silent as the Bishop of Kilgarriff rose from his knee and went to the door. Then, just as he put his hand upon the latch, the Archbishop spoke one last time.

"You will, of course, inform me immediately," he said, "should you be contacted or otherwise hear any news of Baron Giraldus that I do not."

"Of course, Your Eminence," Elon said, turning quickly back around. "Immediately."

Then, with the slightest sketch of a bow, he was gone. Once the door was firmly closed, the Archbishop let out a heavy sigh. Although he had accomplished what was needed, he felt a distinct dissatisfaction with the interview; he was no nearer truly knowing Elon's heart than he had been when the younger man entered.

How much sincerity, he asked himself, had there been in Elon's last word—and how much sarcasm? The question was not one he liked to ask, and he liked having no answer even less. Much less. But as much as he disliked having to call any of his flock, especially his bishops, into question, they were God's, the Church's—and *his* representatives. As such, they must be accountable at all times. Such lack of trustworthiness had led to problems in other times and places that were *not* going to happen in Aghamore while he wore the triple-crowned mitre.

And for how much longer must that be? he asked with yet another sigh. The little voice within him answered that it was both longer than he wanted—and as long as he must.

He pulled the cord that would again summon his secretary. The College of Bishops must now be reconvened to deal again with the question of the succession. To the common writs his secretaries would author, he would need to add personal messages to Bresal of Rathreagh and Dwyer of Camlough, the bishops who had stormed out when Giraldus was voted the Church's support. He remembered the warnings they had spoken as they left. He did not know, *exactly*, if they were right, but his internal cautions whispered that they might very well be. Unless they were all very, very careful this time, about whom they chose to support as King, the Darkness might yet close in on Aghamore.

It was at last time for their evening meal—if it was evening, Aurya thought as, under guard, she trudged back to the sleeping cave she shared each night with Giraldus. This was one of the only times a day she, Giraldus, and Maelik were allowed to be together, the only time she had *human* companionship and *human* conversation. She had not realized how much she would miss such simple things.

Yet there were things she missed even more. When Selia had passed her judgment against them, these things had been far from Aurya's mind. But now, the wind, the stars, the call of the birds, and the feel of the open were jewels more precious and coveted by her heart than all the gold or glittering stones in all the Realm of the Cryf. The sentence was for a lifetime without them—and each continued moment so bereft made Aurya vow anew to get free and take her revenge upon the one who had ordered she be kept in such a place.

It was thoughts of that revenge that kept her sane throughout the long days of the physical labor she hated, surrounded by the Cryf whom she hated even more. Her thoughts provided a voice to fill the void left by the loss of her magic, a loss that sometimes threatened to consume her with a blackness so pervasive it left room for nothing else.

She *must* get free and soon; she *must* get her magic back. She sometimes felt that if she was forced to exist much longer without it, her life would end of its own accord. Without her magic, she had neither the will nor the desire to face the long years ahead.

When she arrived at the cave, Giraldus was already there.

Maelik arrived a moment later. Both of them still had wet hair from the baths they had taken to wash away the grime of their assigned jobs. Like herself, they were wearing clothing woven of Cryf material—warm, durable, practical, and totally devoid of anything approaching style or beauty.

Their own clothing had been taken away, cleaned, and mended, then returned. But they had become symbols to Aurya, her only connection with her former life, and without her freedom and her magic, she could not bear to wear them—or think of them wearing out in this place. Once they were gone, she would be unable to replace them, and the last tenuous thread with her former life would be gone. So they sat, untouched, in one of the niches carved in the cave wall while she wore the Cryf clothing she had been given. The pullover top and trousers were usually only worn by the Cryf males, when cutting new tunnels or traveling through rough underground terrain where their own hair did not provide enough protection. When woven a particular way, known to Cryf females, the fibers of the gorien plant were nearly impossible to tear.

They fitted Aurya's height well enough, but not her girth, hanging on her so that she had to roll the sleeves and tie the waistband of the pants. For Giraldus and Maelik, it was just the opposite; they fit their girth, but barely reached past the men's knees and elbows.

They all had two sets, so that one could be worn while the other was washed. The Cryf had a passion for cleanliness that included their bodies as well as their clothes and bedding. The bathing pools were a nightly ritual, and although they smelled of minerals instead of the perfumes and oils to which Aurya was accustomed, the water was comfortably hot, and the pots of soft soap smelled pleasantly of herbs. It was the only highlight in her otherwise dreary days.

Tonight, however, something was different. As Giraldus enfolded her in the embrace with which he always welcomed their reuniting, there was a light in his eyes that told her something had happened. Otherwise, his face was unchanged, showing nothing more than his usual joy at the sight of her after their hours apart. But she knew him as their guards did not. She knew there was something more.

"What is it?" she whispered in his ear, as he hugged her tightly.

"Not yet," he whispered back. "After *they* are gone."

Gone, she knew, was a relative term. But after their food was brought and before the female Cryf arrived to escort her for her turn at the baths, the guards did withdraw a ways and leave the three humans an hour or more of relative privacy with their meal.

Aurya gave a single, tiny nod against his cheek, then disengaged herself from his arms. She went over and took her habitual place at the white stone table near the front of the cave. Maelik was already settled, and Giraldus had no sooner joined them than the food arrived. Aurya did admit that each evening, after a day of labor where food breaks were made of cold, handheld fare washed down with plain water, the evening meal of hot foods and herbal teas was very welcome—and the food, if often lacking in variety, was delicious.

Tonight, it was also spiced with anticipation, perhaps the best flavoring of all.

Her anticipation was left to rise as Giraldus calmly began passing platters around. She wanted to scream at him to get on with it, to tell her what he was hiding. As she waited, realization dawned. Giraldus was maintaining an appearance of normalcy for the sake of the guards—normal and expected, even necessary. Aurya shifted again on her seat, hardly able to bear the passing seconds. She realized that with the loss of her magic, she had also lost her control, her sense of inner silence that had given her the strength to face and master her every situation.

No, she thought, *I will not let this, too, be stripped away.* She forced herself to say nothing, to calmly break apart the round of bread upon her plate, scoop up some of the thick, spiced stew, and begin to eat. The food nearly choked her, but at least she had the appearance of being the person she had always been.

She would at least *appear* in control again.

Finally, several mouthfuls later, Giraldus spoke. His voice was low, but not a whisper; the kind of tone that went unnoticed by those not truly listening for it.

"Be careful," he began as he dipped the large spoon into the serving bowl and ladled more stew upon his platter. "Give no reaction. *None*. But I believe I've found a way out. Not today or tomorrow, but soon we will get free."

"What is it?" Maelik said in the same unremarkable tone as he put another bite into his mouth. Aurya said nothing; at the moment, the two of them were far more adept at this sort of game than she.

"I saw where they store the boats," Giraldus answered. "A glimpse only, but it's a start."

"What'll we need?" Maelik asked, taking his own second helping of stew. Aurya watched, amazed. Food had been difficult enough to swallow around the lump of anticipation while she waited for Giraldus's first announcement; now it was sticking in her throat, unable to pass beyond all her unspoken, hopeful questions.

"Food for a few days at least," Giraldus said. "Weapons—though I doubt we can get our own. Rope, if we can find any, perhaps containers for water . . . I don't know what else yet, but begin preparing any way you can."

He broke off speaking and quickly covered it with a sip of his tea as they all heard the approaching footsteps. It was the trio of females arriving to take Aurya to the bathing pools. She looked down at her plate and noticed her food was still largely untouched.

"Save me some bread and fruit for when I get back," she said loudly enough to be certain she was overheard. With the oddly styled speech they used when speaking "the Up-worlder's tongue," as they called it, she was never entirely certain just how much their guards understood. But it was a beginning to their preparations for escape. Some bread and fruit tonight, more tomorrow and perhaps some of the dried fish as well . . . then soon—*soon*—they would have enough to make their move. She did not care if the attempt brought death—that, too, was a kind of freedom.

Aurya smiled as she stood and bent to give Giraldus a kiss. "Well done," he whispered against her lips.

Briefly, for his eyes only, her smile broadened in the tiniest acknowledgment. Then she turned away and went out to meet her escort.

Chapter Thirteen

Renan had been too optimistic about seeing the Archbishop right away. He sat for three hours that first day, in the waiting area of one of the Archbishop's many secretaries, watching people come and go and listening while others talked. He slowly began to realize just how large the Archbishop's staff was and, without King or court to govern, just how busy. Most of the people who appeared each day without prior arrangements would never actually see the Archbishop. They would be directed to one staff member or other whose official function was to deal with just such a need or problem as they presented.

But Renan *had* to see the Archbishop. Finally, as the afternoon began its slow, tedious pass of more waiting, he went to inquire just how the necessary appointment could be made.

It was not easy convincing the secretary that he had a se-rious—and private—problem only the Archbishop could solve, but being a priest and from here in Ballinrigh helped.

Even so, it was nearly two more hours before Renan left the Archbishop's residence with an appointment made and confirmed for three days hence. All he had to do was wait, and use those three days to try and figure out how to con-vince the Primus of the Church of several nearly impossible things. He would be asking the Archbishop to reexamine texts that had been declared heretical, and to believe not only their content, but that Selia was the fulfillment of their prophecy and the solution to the kingdom's current danger. Then, too, there was Lysandra and the part she was predes-tined to play as Prophecy's Hand—the truth of her wondrous gift of *Sight* and her new gift of prophetic vision. Finally, Renan knew he must convince the Archbishop to take action, and to do so before either Wirral's forces could come down from the north or Aghamore could erupt in the ever-closing threat of civil war.

Also during the same three days, Renan knew he must try to find out the truth about whether the Bishop of Kilgarriff was in league with Giraldus and Aurya—something that his instinct kept whispering was likely, though he could not say why—and if the Archbishop had been somehow fooled or corrupted into siding with them. The same inner voice warn-ing him of the danger from Elon, told Renan that the Arch-bishop could be trusted. He wanted to believe it . . . but he must be sure. There was too much at risk and too little time for any mistakes.

For three days Renan had thought, prayed, read through the scroll—and talked with Lysandra. He hoped she might receive some prophetic word or vision to guide him, and he counted on her insight to help him think of something, anything, he might have missed or that might aid their cause. Finally, they decided that they must all go to the Archbishop's Residence and keep Renan's appointment together. The Archbishop needed to meet them all—and what one alone might fail to do or say, perhaps the three of them could accomplish united.

Although, as a priest of a small parish, Renan's finances were limited, he hired a small carriage to take them to the Residence. He did not want them to appear before the Archbishop tired or covered with any street dirt that might hit them on their journey. The sight of Cloud-Dancer in their midst would be startling enough without adding any additional complications.

All of them dressed in their best, which, if unfashionable by city standards, was clean—and was all they had. For Renan it did not matter; a priest's cassock and collar did not change with time or fashion. Lysandra, too, he knew, cared more about comfort, cleanliness, and utility than the dictates of others. But Selia was young, and as they stood at the door of the Residence, he could not help but wonder what she truly thought.

She was again wearing the black dress of her habit covered over with the blue-and-white apron Lysandra had given her and the matching kerchief over her still-short dark hair. The colors suited her well enough, but the clothes were simple and better suited for work around the house or in the garden than to her first presentation before the man who was, for now, the most powerful person in the kingdom.

Renan was unaware that he had been broadcasting his thoughts until Lysandra laid a hand on his arm. "No," she said softly. "It is better this way. You'll see."

Then the door opened. Renan announced his purpose and his appointment, and they were all directed inside.

The people they passed looked askance at Lysandra walking with Cloud-Dancer by her side. By the way she kept her hand on his head, Renan guessed she was using the wolf's vision to guide her. She could not miss the way people drew themselves away from the sight of her, holding their children to their sides as the three of them were directed down the various corridors to the Archbishop's office.

The outer room was large, but filled with the four desks of the Archbishop's clerics. There were no other people waiting. The women stood just inside the door as Renan went up to what looked like the main desk and again stated both his name and his appointment time.

The middle-aged monk sitting at the desk had, like so many others, been staring at Lysandra and Cloud-Dancer. Now he looked at Renan with an expression of marked disdain, his reluctance to admit them plain on his face.

"His Eminence is extremely busy," he said in the clipped tones of someone trying to hide his country origins. "You will have only a few minutes, so keep your words brief and to the point. Do you understand?"

"Of course," Renan replied.

"Is it absolutely necessary for that . . . creature . . . to accompany you?"

"It is," Lysandra said, stepping forward.

Renan, used to it now, saw the twitch of her fingers that signaled the wolf so that he walked calmly by her side and sat when she stopped. He also saw the look of both surprise, and barely concealed fear, that flashed across the secretary's face.

"Then, perhaps, you should wait for your companions out here. We cannot have the Archbishop put in danger by—"

"Nonsense," a voice from the door interrupted. They all looked, startled, seeing the Archbishop standing there. His eyes were fixed on Cloud-Dancer with a look of admiration and amazement. "Can't you see he's well trained? Use the intelligence I know you have, Geoffrey, and quit inventing problems where none exist."

The Archbishop waved Renan and the others into his office. "You'll have to forgive Geoffrey," he said as they entered. "He means well—but he's been with me for several years and sometimes he gets . . . well, overprotective. I think he's afraid that at my age, one too many shocks will send him back to the monastery."

Here, the old man gave a small smile. He made no move to go around his desk and be seated, but instead went over to stand before Lysandra, obviously fascinated by her lupine companion.

"He's a beautiful animal," the Archbishop said to her. "But he's not a dog. How did you come to have a wolf as your guide—and how did you tame him so completely?"

"I tamed him, if that's what it is, with love, Your Eminence," Lysandra said softly.

"Yes," the old man said, his voice just as soft and thoughtful, "*love* can do wonders. It's the only thing that truly can. But come, all of you, sit here by the fire with me and tell me why you're here. The reason for this appointment stated some personal problem—?"

There were two chairs before the fire, one into which the Archbishop eased himself, and there was a large settee. The two women took the couch while Renan sat in the other chair, close enough to the Archbishop to do most of the talking. The tension that had built up in the outer room was disappearing in the presence of the old man's kind and patient air.

But once they sat, Renan found that all the words he prepared and rehearsed these last three days left him. He looked into the Archbishop's waiting face and for a moment, nothing at all came to him.

"We're here," he said finally, simply, "because we don't know where else to go."

The Archbishop gave a slow nod. "Tell me, my son," he said. "Everything."

Twenty minutes later, there was a discreet knock on the door and Brother Geoffrey entered. "Your next appointment is here, Your Eminence," he announced, his glance traveling meaningfully to Renan and the others.

Before they could stand, however, the Archbishop motioned for them to stay. Then he shook his head at his secretary.

"Give everyone else new appointments," he ordered, "and clear my day. I will be busy here."

"But Your Eminence—" the secretary began. Then, at the look on the Archbishop's face, he stopped. "As you wish, Your Eminence," he finished, and backed out the door, pulling it shut with a firm and displeased sound.

The Archbishop then turned back to Renan and looked at him for a long, silent moment. So far, Renan had told him only about Lysandra's prophetic gift and the *Far-Seeing* that allowed her the vision of the Corbenican army. He could tell that the Archbishop was trying to believe him.

"Your words," the Primus said at last, "are fearful, if they are true. I am an old man and have seen too many wondrous, even miraculous things in my life to say this is impossible. But I must know more." He turned to Lysandra. "Please, daughter," he said not unkindly, "I must know all of your tale—from the beginning. Are you able to tell me?"

Renan watched the play of emotions dance swiftly across Lysandra's face. He knew that she was considering the pain that had filled her for so long, pain that was part of the memories of life and love destroyed; speaking of them, especially to a stranger, might still be difficult.

But then she nodded. "Yes, Your Eminence," she said. "We all have tales that you must hear if this kingdom is to survive."

As she said these last words, she laid an encouraging hand over the ones Selia had tightly clasped in her lap. Renan sat back and let Lysandra take over, her soft, low voice not only pleasing to the ear, but somehow lending a special air of verisimilitude to the description of her lonely life. He breathed yet another prayer of thanksgiving for her presence—both in his life and in this situation. Although it was the Font of Wisdom who would govern the future, it was Prophecy's Hand who must hold the moment if that future was ever to exist.

In the city of Vartilla, a scant fifteen miles southeast of Adaraith, Kilgarriff's capital, Elon delivered the Writ of Elevation into the hands of Lord Iain DeMarcoe. Inwardly, he had to grit his teeth to do it—but to the face of the new, and he hoped temporary, Baron he smiled and bowed and said all the appropriate words, telling Iain what a great day this was for the people of the Province.

Many, he knew, agreed with those words. Iain was a good and faithful son of the Church; his wife, family, and household were all far removed from the dark stain of magic that tainted Lady Aurya—and through her, the Baron Giraldus. This elevation, even temporarily, of Iain to the Barony would cause a great celebration.

But not for Elon. He could put on whatever face necessary, say the words required to make Iain, the Archbishop—the entire kingdom—believe it gladdened his heart even more than theirs. In truth, however, he hated it. He had always found Iain dull, colorless, overly pious, and totally lacking in anything resembling wit or fire . . . and his family, especially his "good wife," even more so.

Elon had met her six times, after the birth of each child she and Iain had so faithfully brought into the world. As soon as the required eight weeks had passed, she made what she called her "pilgrimage of thanksgiving" from Vartilla to Ummera, to be properly "churched" by the bishop in the cathedral.

The Churching of Women a few weeks after giving birth

was an old and outdated ritual, rarely practiced anymore, that had its origins in the Levitical Laws of the Old Testament. In those times, a woman was considered "unclean" until the issue of postbirthing blood had ceased. Only then, after rituals and prayers of purification, was she allowed back into society.

The Church had ceased to require this practice centuries ago, and although it was still within the Church's canons, rare was the woman who had heard of it and rarer still the one who asked for it. But Lady Drianlia appeared after each birth, dressed in somber hues, with hair properly covered as she felt befitted a matron, to have herself declared pure again by the bishop himself . . . and now, Elon saw as he stood before Lord Iain, Drianlia was pregnant again.

He suppressed a shudder as he thought of the future ahead for Kilgarriff with Iain as their Baron and Lady Drianlia as their example of wellborn and proper womanhood.

Having delivered the Archbishop's Writ and stayed an extra day to give the appearance of his blessing, Elon eagerly rode away before Iain and his household could prepare to depart. He had used the excuse of needing to begin the arrangements for Iain's installation, but the truth was he could not stand another hour in their company. One more prayer or blessing, one more joyful exclaim or congratulatory word would have stuck in his throat and choked him.

He would, as he had said, stop first in Adaraith, to officially verify and alert the household at the Baron's Fortress to Iain's change of status and imminent arrival. But it was not his intention to remain there. He would be moving indefinitely to Ballinrigh. Now that he had begun to sever his connections to Giraldus and Aurya in the Archbishop's mind, he must make himself indispensable to the Archbishop's life.

Regardless of who occupied the Baron's Fortress in Adaraith or sat on the throne in Ballinrigh, Elon was still determined that he would wear the triple-crowned mitre and that the great gold-and-silver-wrapped crozier of Archbishop, Primus, and Shepherd of the Kingdom, would be given into his hand.

Nothing has changed, he thought, more determined than ever as he rode away from Vartilla, leaving its clanging bells of celebration that sounded from every parish steeple, fading in the distance. *And no one is going to stop me. No one.*

Lord Iain, soon to be Baron—however temporarily—of Kilgarriff, also left Vartilla before his city had ended its celebration. He wished he could govern Kilgarriff from the home he already knew—but the army, the courts, and the machine of administration, were all in Adaraith. So he must be there, as well.

He knew that Drianlia would see to what must be done about the move. He could trust her in this as he did her in all things—wife and partner, confidante, and to his mind, "far above rubies." Padoric, his longtime steward, would obey Drianlia—and quietly guide her, if necessary. As for Iain, he was eager to get the wheels of *proper* government in motion. Giraldus was his cousin, direct heir and lawful Baron of Kilgarriff and as such, Iain had always obediently and outwardly supported him. To Drianlia and Padoric alone had he spoken of his doubts of Giraldus's fitness to rule.

Now, Iain thought as he rode the fifteen miles between Vartilla and Adaraith, it was *his* turn. Now the people of Kilgarriff would have a chance to see what life was like with a Baron whose highest aspirations were serving God and serving them. It was also time for the people to learn what it was like to have a *real* Baroness to lead the women and families by her example—a proper *wife* of the Baron, mother of his children, daughter of the Church, not a wild and heathen sorceress who, however beautiful, was still a practitioner of evil.

Although Iain did not wish ill to his cousin, as he neared the Baron's Fortress on the hill that was the eastern border of the city, it was for the people's sake that Iain hoped Giraldus would not return. Iain had never *sought* elevation, but now that it had come to him, he intended to put right everything that the years of Giraldus's—and Aurya's—reign had made wrong with this Province.

He was riding alone and not in state, but his face was known to many of the people, and his arrival did not go unnoticed. As he entered the city streets, people began to pour from their houses and shops, to shout both greetings and blessings as he passed. It gladdened Iain's heart to hear them and to feel their welcome. *The people, too,* he thought as he waved and smiled, *are tired of the way things have been.*

Suddenly a small girl came running out from the gathering crowd, her mother frantically scurrying after her. Iain quickly brought his horse to a halt so that the great hooves would not harm the child. Once the mother had reached her, she lifted her daughter and the girl held out a flower, a wild and slightly wilted briar-rose, to Iain. He accepted it, delighted, and gave the girl a smile as he tucked it into one buttonhole on the front of his shirt. As the father of almost seven children, such a gift from a child's hand was worth more to him than all the gold, jewels, or crowns in the kingdom.

He reached out and touched a gentle hand to the girl's cheek, his thank-you swallowed up by the approving roar of the onlookers. Then, once the mother had the child back safely out of the way, he gave another wave and continued his progress up the hill to the Fortress.

There, too, his approach had been noted. The household staff, from stableboys and sculleries to the head steward, was turned out into the large courtyard to meet him. They stood in ranks and rows, each giving a bob of a curtsy or the tug of a forelock as he rode by or glanced in their direction. Then, when Iain dismounted, a stable hand took charge of his mount while the steward stepped forward and introduced each head of staff to their new lord.

"Thank you," Iain said to the assembly, standing on the

top step of the great porch so that he could see and be seen by all. "It will take me some time to remember all your names and positions, but I will always remember my duty toward you. Whether it be God's will that I am here for a week, a year, or a lifetime, I swear that from this moment onward, the care of the people of the Province shall ever be my first and guiding thought."

"God bless Lord Iain, *new* Baron of Kilgarriff," a voice from the back shouted. It was quickly echoed by the others. After raising a hand to acknowledge it, Iain turned to go inside, motioning for the steward to walk with him.

"Tell me your name again," he said, as they walked through the great iron-hinged doors and into the huge, open foyer.

"Mathias, m'lord."

"Well, Mathias, I will rely heavily upon you, especially during these first weeks. I have a fear that there has been much neglected in this Province. I intend to set it to rights."

"I am at your service in all things, m'lord," the steward replied. "There is already a matter awaiting your attention in the Great Hall. There are several of the leading merchants from the city here, and though I tried to persuade them to give your lordship a day at least to settle in, they would not be put off. I do apologize that this has come so quickly."

"No need," Iain answered. "These men have been waiting long enough, I fear, for the proper care of their concerns. This is why God has sent me here. So let us not dawdle, Mathias. I am eager to show these men—to show all of Kilgarriff— what a good and concerned Baron can do for his people."

Iain ignored the look that flashed across Mathias's face, reminding himself that not only did the steward not know him, but it was right that the man should still be loyal to Giraldus. Nevertheless, Iain fervently believed all he had just said and was determined to prove it true.

* * *

The delegation of merchants was an angry one. They were sixteen in all, but they came bearing petitions signed by nearly every shop or innkeeper in the city. Adaraith was clearly not a happy place.

Iain listened patiently to their complaints, delivered with stammering nervousness by a few, with belligerent defiance by others. To Iain's mind, both attitudes said plainly that these men doubted their problems would find redress. They were surprised, therefore, when Iain not only promised to see to the matters immediately, but invited them along while he did so.

The army of Kilgarriff, like most armies throughout the Outer Eight Provinces, had its ranks swollen with conscripts, all waiting for the time when Giraldus would make his move to take the throne by Right of Arms. This, too, was the common state throughout the kingdom—but now with Giraldus gone, the conscripts in Kilgarriff were bored with their lack of purpose and filled with the single desire to return to the lives from which they had been forced away. They had taken to staving off their boredom, and their anger over the turn their lives had taken, by leaving the army's encampment and going into the city . . . to drink or gamble or seek whatever other entertainment might be found.

At first, the merchants and innkeepers had welcomed their additional custom. But increasingly, the revelry had turned into nightly brawls and drunkenness, and with unpaid bills for both ale and damages. The streets of Adaraith, once mostly safe under the Baron's law, were traveled cautiously after dark—and by women who valued their virtue, not at all. The merchants and innkeepers who had tried to turn the soldiers away at the door had suffered even greater damage as retribution.

Early in the delegations' speeches, Iain had sent Mathias ahead to have the troops assembled. It had taken over an hour for all the complaints to be heard, but now he led the way to the balcony that overlooked the practice yards where, he trusted, the army would be waiting.

Iain heard the merchants mumbling behind him as they walked, clearly uncertain what he would do, or if it boded well or ill that he had asked them to accompany him. Approaching the doors of the balcony, he smiled to himself. Soon the army would know, the merchants would know, and through them the city would know the difference between himself and his cousin. It was a gift, an opportunity, and one he could never have engineered so well.

When Iain stepped out onto the balcony, all noise below him ceased. He did not speak or move for a long moment, but let the men below wonder at the reason for this hasty—and complete—assembly. Finally, he stepped to the very edge of the balcony and, clasping his hands behind his back in a manner that threw out his chest and gave more mass to his otherwise unimpressive frame, he took a deep breath.

"Men of Kilgarriff," he began, sending his loudest voice to carry out over the yard. "I stand before you today by the Will of God and the lawful appointment of the Archbishop, charged to bring order and governance once more to this Province. This, by God's help, I intend to do. Kilgarriff and its welfare are my *sole* and *highest* concerns. *I* have no interest in striving for the High King's crown while the people of the Province are left without the care that is their right.

"I know that many of you are here against your wills. I, too, have a wife and family, and understand your desire to return to yours. Therefore, I promise you this—if the Baron Giraldus does not return to Kilgarriff and Adaraith by two weeks hence, those of you who were forced into the service you now hold shall be released from this duty to return freely to your former and personal lives."

At his words, a cheer erupted from below. Iain felt it as much as heard it; it was like a great wind that shook everything, even the balcony on which he stood.

He let it continue for a moment so that the men below had a chance to truly feel the joy of the announcement and all that it meant. Only then, he knew, would the rest of what he had to say have the impact he needed.

Iain now held up his hands. The men grew quiet again, eager for what else he might say.

"But," he now continued, "as this is my promise to you, so I need your promise in return. For these next two weeks, there must be no more complaints from the city. There must be no more fights or brawling; if you must drink, then it must be within reason and there must be no more *public* drunkenness; no unpaid debts, no destruction or disturbances to the peaceful commerce and lives of the people or their safety. They are the same as your mothers and daughters, your wives and children. You must treat them as you would be treated, with all the care you would give your own families.

"If you keep this pact, then in two weeks your indenture here will be ended. You will receive your pay and be free to go home. *But* . . . for every complaint I receive, a day shall be added—and for every injury suffered, a week. From this day forth, any unpaid bill will be taken from your own pay packet. Any complaint charged against one will be the responsibility of all. This is my word and promise to you, yours to me—and ours together to this city."

The cheer that went up this time began a bit more hesitantly, but within seconds it had built in strength, becoming a roar that swept up over the balcony and filled the courtyard with crashing sound. Iain turned back around and found the city delegation looked at him with surprise and wonder plain on their faces.

With a gesture, Iain summoned Mathias again to his side. "If you will present your list of bills and damages to my steward," he said, "all debts shall be paid in full from the treasury before the next two days have passed. The Archbishop sent me here to heal the wounds this Province has suffered. Whether my time here is to be temporary or permanent, I intend to spend it doing just that."

The man who had led the delegation—and been the most belligerent among the speakers—now dropped to one knee. "Forgive me, m'lord," he said, "I thought that you would be no different than your cousin. I thought all Barons were out for only their own gain."

"Get up, man," Iain told him. "Let this be a lesson learned, for all of us, of the great future the Province may know if we all work for the good of each other."

It was the delegation's turn to cheer—and Iain, who all his life had been considered second best, only the *cousin* and always thought of *after* Giraldus, gloried in it.

Chapter Fourteen

Down among the army, the air of celebration continued throughout the day. Men who had not seen their families in months, who yesterday had looked at a future in which they did not know when—or if—they would see them again, now knew they had only to wait two weeks, and they could go home. To a man, they vowed to accept Lord Iain's injunction to circumspect behavior; they would do nothing to injure their chance of timely release.

Those who were in the army voluntarily were also pleased by Lord Iain's words. They were tired of dealing with the undisciplined, the undedicated, the mass of bemoaning men who wanted to be anywhere but where they were. The career soldiers looked forward to the time when their own lives and service could return to *normal*—whatever that might be with the real Baron gone.

One person, however, was not happy—young Rhys Llewitt. He and Dafid apDoihel were the two sent back to Kilgarriff with the horses when Baron Giraldus, Lady Aurya, and the others of their company had taken to the river. Every day since then, Rhys had looked for the Baron's—and Aurya's—return. Now, with Lord Iain here, Rhys was beginning to think that day might never come.

Rhys had been ordered to absolute secrecy about the Baron's mission and whereabouts. Until now, he had obeyed that order faithfully. But he was not used to lying, and it had been difficult fending off the many questions when he returned with the Baron's horse. All he knew, he said time and again, was that he had been ordered back with the horses—and that he had no idea where Giraldus and the others had gone.

Inwardly, he kept assuring himself that what he said was true. The river could have taken them anywhere, or they could have left the river and continued in any direction on foot. But despite these many private assurances, Rhys knew his reports were half-truths at best—and he hated it.

Now, he thought, might well be the time when the rest of the truth was needed.

But he did not want to make that choice alone. While the rest of the men celebrated Lord Iain's announcement, Rhys went in search of Dafid. Having been in the army for ten years, instead of Rhys's ten months or so, the younger man hoped Dafid could tell him what to do.

He found Dafid sitting on his bunk, oil rag in hand, caring for his sword. Walking in from the excitement running through the camp, Rhys found Dafid's attitude of complacency, even boredom, surprising.

"Didn't you hear the news?" Rhys asked as he approached the older soldier.

"Aye," Dafid said simply. "It's naught to do w' me."

"But everyone will be going home soon. Lord Iain said—"

"Naught to do w' me," Dafid repeated. "I do m' duty as ordered, collect m' pay, and put most o' it aside for when m' time's up . . . and I keep m' nose out o' the rest o' it. What men come or go is naught to do w' me."

But Rhys could not settle or ignore what was going on, as Dafid obviously could. He paced a bit, back and forth before the older man, until finally Dafid put his sword aside.

"You be here for sum'ut," he said to Rhys. "You'd best out w' it a'fore you wear down the boards."

"It's about the Baron, about Giraldus and the others . . . don't you think we should go to Lord Iain and tell him what we know?"

"And just what be that, lad?"

"We know they went to Rathreagh and that they built rafts for the river—and that they were coming back here. I know we were ordered to silence, but that was before the Archbishop sent Lord Iain to take over. I'd say that makes a difference. Before Lord Iain changes everything, shouldn't he know that Baron Giraldus is coming back?"

"But they 'aven't come back, 'ave they—and who knows if they will. Not me, lad, and not you, neither. And I'll tell you the one lesson what'll get you through your years soldierin'. An order's an order. Period. We was given an order not to tell, and that's what I'll be doin'. You, too, if you've any wits to you. If they does come back, I don't plan to face 'em—especially Sergeant Maelik—havin' disobeyed. If they doesn't . . . well, then all your disobeyin' will gain you is a reputation for not bein' trustworthy. Now that's my word, lad, for good or ill."

But what about all the rest? Rhys wanted to shout. *What*

*about before the order—the magic, the ride through the night,
the child Lady Aurya said she must find? What about —?*

He could see it was no use. Dafid had made up his mind,
said his piece—and it was settled for him. Everything he had
said was right, about obeying orders and about his reputation
if he did not . . . and about facing Sergeant Maelik if—no,
when—they returned, if he had disobeyed. Rhys cringed a
little when he thought of that.

So, until he could think of something better, he accepted
Dafid's advice. For now. But if he could think of something
else to do, something that would not break his ordered silence, then with or without Dafid's help, he would act. Lady
Aurya had needed him once . . . she just might again.

Throughout most of the day, the Archbishop had remained
in his study with Renan, Lysandra, and Selia. He had all his
other duties reassigned; the Dean of the Cathedral led the
daily Offices, appointments were rescheduled or dealt with
elsewhere, food and drink were sent in so that the Archbishop could give his full attention to the tales he was hearing.

Listen he did, carefully, with the practice of his years of
hearing both the said and the messages behind the words. He
heard both the fear and the faith that had driven these three
into his presence today.

It was a strange tale, of prophecy and magic, that grew
both more wondrous and more fearsome as each told their
part. Yet Colm ApBeirne found he did not *dis*believe it.
There were things left out, he was certain; he *felt* rather than
heard the hesitation on the part of the priest—*Renan,* he reminded himself—when he reached the part about their escape upon the river. But whatever he was holding back, the
Archbishop could discern no evil within him. All that Father
Renan, all that the three of them, had done and were doing,
they firmly believed was for the good of the kingdom.

But was it truly? That was the question the Archbishop had to answer as their tales came to an end. Lysandra's blindness was obvious, and she had demonstrated her *Sight*—but what about the gift of *Far-Seeing* she claimed? Was her vision of the Corbenican invasion to be believed? And Selia— Queen of this land? She was but a slip of a girl, unworldly and untried. How could she possibly be the answer to this kingdom's woes?

As afternoon drew toward evening, he had offered the three of them rooms here at the Residence for the night while he considered the matter, but they had declined. Father Renan cited the duties at his parish, and the women preferred familiar surroundings. He had sent them home in one of his own carriages, which would also return for them at noon tomorrow.

Alone now, Colm ApBeirne, Primus of the Church in Aghamore, faced a night in which he must decide the fate and future of the kingdom. It was a heavy, wearisome burden that he felt all the way to the depths of his bones. Yet it was also one he could neither shirk nor delay. Even had he been so inclined, neither his heart nor his mind would give him rest.

The Scrolls of Tambryn—it had been many years since he had last come across any reference to those writings. He did not know quite what to make of it now. Although banned by the Church as heretical six hundred years ago, the Archbishop knew what most others, even those well placed within the hierarchy of the Church, did not. The cathedral library contained a copy of all thirteen of Tambryn's scrolls, written in the mystic's own hand.

The scrolls were locked in a special room at the back of the library where such things were hidden. The contents of that room would shock many; Tambryn was not the only person in Aghamore's history to have produced writings of which the Church did not approve. And Colm, as Archbishop, had one of the only three keys to that room.

Although Father Renan had promised to bring the Thirteenth Scroll with them when they returned, Colm knew he could not wait so long to read the prophecies for himself. By the time the three arrived at noon, he hoped to have made at least a partial decision about what they must all do.

One thing their words had made clear—Baron Giraldus and Lady Aurya were on no pilgrimage, save one of black deceit and magic. But what of Elon? the Archbishop wondered. Was he working with them, or had he been deceived by them and by his own desire to believe the best of them? That, too, was a question to which Colm knew he must soon find an answer.

He sent his servants off early, as soon as his supper had been served on a tray up in his private chambers. He wanted no disturbances, however helpfully intended, while he thought and prayed through this problem. It was like a giant kaleidoscope within his mind—all the pieces were locked together, yet constantly changing shape depending on how he looked at them.

Most of the patterns did not please him; some were far too frightening to be considered for long. There was only one that held any promise for Aghamore—and that was if Selia was exactly what she and her companions believed.

But believing something is or should be true and making it happen could be two very different things—especially with the other Barons ready to go to war, with the threat of an invasion coming from the north, and with active duplicity possibly within his own ranks.

That thought stung. It hurt him deeply until finally he knew what he must do. Donning a cloak to cover the simple cassock he habitually wore when the day's duties were done, he roused his manservant from his bed. Then, after apologizing for the late hour, he called for the smallest of his carriages to be brought around.

"Shall I come with you, Your Eminence—or, perhaps, call for some of the guards to accompany you?" Brother

Donnel asked, obviously concerned over this strange whim that had seized the Archbishop.

The old man shook his head. "No, Donnel, but thank you. You may return to your bed as soon as you've delivered my message. I'll meet the carriage myself."

Donnel turned away, and the Archbishop saw him shaking his head. "Donnel," he said as the monk, who had been with him for over five years now, put his hand to the door. "This is something I must do, and alone. But I promise you that I've not lost my wits to old age. It is important—just as it is important that you speak of it to no one."

"As you say, Your Eminence," Donnel replied without looking around.

The Archbishop knew he would be obeyed, if not quite believed. But it was better to be thought of as an old fool whose good judgment had given way to strange whims, even briefly, than not to do what his heart was saying he must.

The Residence was built on shared grounds with the cathedral, connected by covered stone walks by which the Archbishop, the members of his staff, Religious, or other visitors could travel between the two. The library was in a separate building on the other side. Perhaps, on a fine day when he could take his time, the Archbishop might have made the short journey on foot. But now, nearing midnight, both body and mind tired from his long day, he was glad of the small carriage and the driver's hand to help him in and out.

He lit only one lamp and carried that with him as he went straight to the locked room at the back. Then, withdrawing the key from one of the deep pockets in his cassock, he let himself in and began to search the shelves for the Church's copy of the Scrolls of Tambryn.

He felt strangely guided as he looked, and it took him no more than ten minutes to find them. It was the last, the thirteenth, of which Renan had spoken, but the Archbishop collected them all into one arm. Then, once more locking the door behind himself, he went as swiftly as his old muscles would take him, back to the carriage and then his home. He still had a long night ahead.

Despite his words, Donnel was waiting when the Archbishop returned. He had brought a tray with food and a pot of strong black tea to his study, built up the fire and lit an extra lamp. Although he was fairly certain that Donnel had done all this with the firm conviction that the Archbishop could not care for himself, the old man was nonetheless grateful.

But now he needed to be left alone. "Thank you, Donnel," he said as he eased himself down into his favorite chair and adjusted the cushion that supported his back. "You've done me a great kindness by all this. It's more than I will need. I have some reading I must do and now require nothing more than silence."

"But Your Eminence," Donnel said as he brought the tray within easy reach, "it is nearly one o'clock. Don't you think such studies are best saved for morning, after you've rested?"

The Archbishop shook his head. "By morning, there are things I must know, answers I must already have found."

He said this last more to himself than his servant, but Donnel understood. "I'll leave you to your urgent task then," he said, the tone of his voice once more implying that he thought the Archbishop had been suddenly overtaken by a mild dementia caused by old age.

With an affectionate little bow, he turned away—then he stopped at the door and turned back one last time. "Promise me one thing, Your Eminence," he said, both voice and face serious. "Promise that if you need anything, anything at all, you'll call me instead of doing it yourself. I'll sleep lightly this night."

"I promise, Donnel," the Archbishop assured him.

Although outwardly calm, the truth was he could hardly wait for Donnel to go and close the door behind himself. When the monk gave a slight grunt that effectively communicated his disbelief, the Archbishop did not bother to hide the amusement in his already weary smile.

The young, he thought. *He has a kind heart, but he's yet to learn that age does not have to mean dotage, and a tired body does not mean a worn-out mind. Well, I suppose I was once the same. He'll learn . . . time will teach him, as it does us all.*

Pouring himself a cup of the tea at his elbow, he unfurled the Thirteenth Scroll and began to read. Although the language was archaic, Colm ApBeirne had been a scholar long before he was a bishop, and the words translated themselves easily in his mind. Weariness of body fell away as his scholar's mind awakened to action.

I, Tambryn, monk and servant of Our Lord and His Church, write in my own hand of the thirteenth prophetic Showing vouchsafed unto me. I pray those who read these words will take heed, for dark is the prophecy they contain. But hope awaits at the end, as it ever does for all those who are guided by the Spirit and walk the Path of Truth . . . .

Brother Donnel found him the next morning, asleep in his chair, one hand still clutching the partially unrolled scroll. The Archbishop came immediately awake at the young monk's touch upon his shoulder, nor did he miss the quickly hidden look of relief his movement caused. He did not have to think hard to realize that after what Donnel considered his very strange behavior last night, he half expected to find the old man had expired during the night.

Instead, the Archbishop awoke to a sense of clearheaded purpose. There were always demands upon his time and strength, but somehow this new one invigorated rather than drained him. Despite his too-few hours of only dozing sleep, he was ready for what awaited.

"Thank you, Donnel," he said, rubbing the last vestiges of what was more a nap than a night's slumber from his eyes. "I'll take my breakfast in here—and please make the tea extra strong this morning. When you return, I'll have a list of things I need you to do. After that, I'm not to be disturbed until one half hour before noon."

With a wave of his hand, he dismissed the young man and returned to reading where sleep had stopped him. He had glanced through the other scrolls last night, and it was his second time reading the thirteenth. He could understand the fear that had caused their banishment—but with the clarity of hindsight, he also saw that what they contained had proved true.

It is time these writings get the reexamination they deserve, he thought, readjusting his seat to stretch his tired back. *Ignorance and fear might excuse their banning, but it can no longer be justified. I hope we have reached a time when fear no longer governs our every thought and action, and superstition no longer dictates faith—for that is not faith at all . . .*

Such thoughts had chased themselves through his brain all night, making him wonder what other gems of faith or knowledge might be locked away in that little room at the back of the library. About three o'clock in the morning, he had decided to appoint a council of carefully selected scholars to address the matter. His years as Archbishop might be drawing to a close—but he would not let them end in darkness after light had been revealed.

What seemed logical at three o'clock in the morning, often had its foolishness revealed with the dawn. This, however, still felt *Right*. But it did bring his thoughts back to the question of his retirement—and his successor.

Back to the question of Elon.

There were moments when the Archbishop had hoped Tambryn's prophecies would answer this question for him. But, though it was easy to identify Lysandra as Prophecy's Hand, even with the few hours he had known her, and Selia as the Font of Wisdom, the other players in this drama were named less specifically. From the long interviews yesterday and his reading last night, it was also clear that *"the dogs of Darkness that arise from the Third House, to bite at the heels of those who carry the Light within . . ."* were Giraldus and Aurya. But Elon was also of Kilgarriff; on which side was he fighting?

Until he knew, Colm ApBeirne could name no successor, either Elon or anyone else. The time until his peaceful retirement suddenly grew and extended into the indefinite. With that realization, the Archbishop's morning burst of energy waned a little, and the day felt very long indeed.

The Archbishop was not the only one for whom the night had held little rest. Elon had returned from his ride to Kilgarriff, stopped at his house here in Ballinrigh to clean the road from both his person and attire, then gone to the Residence to report of his successful meeting with Lord Iain and the presentation of the Writ of Elevation. He had gone prepared to again be humble and fair of speech, prepared to again impress the Archbishop however he must.

He had rehearsed what he would say during his hours in the saddle until, he hoped, he had perfectly planned for any question that the old man might ask. Piety, humility, surprise, distress; he had practiced these emotions and expressions, and more, until he knew himself ready, come what may.

But there had been no audience, not even briefly, not even when he explained he had just returned from an errand undertaken on the Archbishop's behalf and with his orders. No matter what Elon said, he was told only that the Archbishop was already busy and was not to be disturbed for *any* reason.

Elon had finally learned, by overhearing servants talk, that the old man was spending his day with a priest, two women—and a dog. This last struck the servants as particularly strange and was the reason behind their gossip. The words were more than strange to Elon; they filled him with a deep foreboding he could not name.

It was this sense of danger, even of possible doom, that kept him awake and pacing throughout the long night. Something, half-recognized but fully felt, kept warning him that in this company was danger to everything he wanted and dreamed of achieving.

With the dawn, Elon made a decision. Perhaps a foolish one, perhaps the only one he could make—but whatever the danger, he must know more. Somewhere within his vast and secret library must be a way of using Thomas's fledgling powers to locate Aurya and Giraldus, or to see enough of either the past or the future to discover the identities of the Archbishop's visitors and, perhaps, learn the old man's intent.

Elon was determined to find whatever trance or guidance spell necessary, and then to use it—now, today. He had to *know.*

It was the hour when the household was beginning to rouse. As usual, Thomas himself gave the first discreet knock on the bishop's door, one too soft to awake Elon if he was still sleeping.

"Come," he ordered. Thomas opened the door and stepped inside.

"Your Grace?" he said, the look on his face making it clear that he was surprised to find Elon already so active.

"I will not be coming down today, Thomas," Elon said. "Tell the others whatever you like, but keep them away. Give me a few hours, then come to the private study. I hope to have need of you by then."

"Very well, Your Grace. May I ask—"

"Not yet. Soon, I hope."

Thomas gave a slight nod and left. *And I hope that what I find will not destroy you, Thomas,* Elon thought, watching the door close. *I do not ask forgiveness from the heavens, but I ask it in advance from you—for I will pay whatever price to do what must be done, even the life of the only person I truly trust.*

Elon went to the panel beside his bed, unlocked the hidden door, and entered the secret room where arcane knowledge awaited.

Chapter Fifteen

Although Baron Hueil of Rathreagh was content to wait for the Summer Solstice before making his move, the other Barons of Aghamore were not. Throughout the long winter, the roadways of the kingdom had been kept busy by the forces of conscription gangs roaming the Provinces, searching out any able-bodied man they might have missed, and the measured tramp of drilling feet as army upon army grew and was trained. Riders, too, passed between the Provinces, carrying letters and proposals from Baron to Baron. By spring, proposals had become counterproposals, offered and answered, and one marriage contract to solidify a new partnership between Houses had been accepted, signed, and witnessed.

Now, with the Summer Solstice two days away, the Baron of Rathreagh stood alone in his treachery, as did Giraldus of Kilgarriff; the Third and Ninth Houses of Aghamore, the

Houses prophesied in Tambryn's Thirteenth Scroll, were each poised upon the precipice that might well bring disaster to either themselves or to the kingdom.

Aghamore's Second Province, Tievebrack, governed by Baron Phelan Gradaigh, House of Gathelus, found an ally in Baron Ardal Mulconry, House of Niamh, Aghamore's Sixth Province of Sylaun. They had pledged each other aid and men, that neither would be decimated in battle, and to fight the others but not one another's army. If the contest came down to the two of them, then whoever had stood strongest would have the other's pledge and sword.

The Provinces of Lininch and Farnagh, ever closely partnered by the geography of the kingdom, had formed yet another partnership. The daughter of Baron Thady Cathain, House of Ragenald, Seventh Province of Farnagh was now betrothed to the son of Baron Einar Maille, second branch of the House of Baoghil, Eighth Province of Lininch. The couple was delighted, and the fathers had vowed to do battle by each other's side—and should they win, then it would be their children and *their* heirs who would rule the kingdom.

To the south and west, in the Fourth and Fifth Provinces, the Barons had both chosen to stand alone. Dromkeen's Baron Curran OhUigio, House of Caethal and Camlough's Baron Oran Keogh, House of Nuinseann, had each refused offers of alliance, from each other or their counterparts, believing themselves prepared and strong enough to give battle on their own. Time alone would show the wisdom or folly of their decisions.

The weather now growing fine, roadways hardened in the sun, the drilling and planning of winter and spring ceased in the flurry of final preparations until, on the day before the Summer Solstice, the armies of Tievebrack and Sylaun put foot to the road to march toward Ballinrigh. Watching spies had already ridden out, carrying the word across the kingdom so that within hours of each other, the armies of every

Province, save Rathreagh and Kilgarriff, marched out as well.

The civil war in Aghamore had begun.

In Ballinrigh, the Archbishop had not yet heard of the armies marching, but he knew the day was fast approaching—too fast. He had summoned the College of Bishops to reconvene, including within the official documents to Bresal of Rathreagh and Dwyer of Camlough his personal and handwritten letters of apology, hoping to end their schism. With Giraldus no longer having the Church's support for High King, he was certain they would return, smug with triumph.

But the bishops would not reach Ballinrigh for at least a week, possibly more. By then, if everything that had come out of his meetings with Renan, Lysandra, and Selia, everything he had read for himself within the Thirteenth Scroll of Tambryn, proved true, the bishops would need only function as witnesses and celebrants of coronation.

It was, however, a rather big "if," for despite everything, as Primus of the Church, Colm ApBeirne was not certain Selia was the right person to next wear the crown of Aghamore. He was not dismissing the validity of Tambryn's prophecies; he had, in fact, come to accept their truth and their power. It was Selia herself that the Archbishop doubted. She was so young, so untried and unworldly. For all the past pain her life contained, for all the Wisdom that the scroll declared and that the Archbishop had glimpsed within her, she was still an innocent. Were her shoulders wide and strong enough to bear the mantle of sovereignty?

And she was female. That, too, presented a problem the Archbishop was uncertain how to circumvent. In all of Aghamore's long history since the time of Liam the Builder, there had been only three independent Queens. It was not against Aghamorian *law,* but it was against *custom.* Even if he and the others working on Selia's behalf could discover the way to prove her right to rule, she still must be accepted by the bishops, Barons, and the people of the kingdom.

Whatever proof was found, it had to be more than the words of an ancient text. It must be something tangible, something everyone—especially the Barons—could see and believe. Without that, Colm knew that civil war would still erupt, continue, and be the only answer to the succession. If that happened, it would not be Selia's head that finally wore the crown.

The Archbishop asked Renan to lead the group appointed to translate, copy, and consider the Scrolls of Tambryn. He found in the younger priest a man of trustworthy spirit. Although with the experience of years, both in his Office and in his life, the Archbishop sensed that there was something Renan was not saying, he was just as certain it was nothing that would put the Church, the kingdom, or the companions who trusted him at risk.

Renan hesitated to accept this commission from the Archbishop, again citing his duties to his parish—and to Selia and Lysandra—as the reasons for his refusal. When Renan was at last persuaded, the Archbishop knew it was more from Lysandra's words than from anything he said.

Renan was fortunate to have such a friend by his side, the Archbishop thought often. His eyes told him plainly of the affection and trust the two of them shared. Once, he might have been suspicious and censorious. But time had given him compassion with his experience, and as he listened to the voice of his own heart, he was just as certain that their affection had known no consummation. Neither Renan nor Lysandra was the kind to take his vows lightly enough to break them.

They each now had their duties. While Selia continued the studies Renan had, quite wisely in the Archbishop's opinion, set out for her—now under Lysandra's guidance—Renan went to work on translating the archaic language of Tambryn's Scrolls into the contemporary language of the kingdom so that they could be properly studied. The Archbishop was left to find something—anything—that might serve as the proof Selia needed.

It was not within Tambryn's Scroll; he had reread it five times now. The only other possibility he knew was the coronation texts. Those, like so many of the Church's ceremonies, had changed over the centuries, taking on new language and symbols to reflect the changes in the times and peoples they served. But the Church library still had copies of all the coronation texts, all the way back to Liam the Builder. He was a King with great, even legendary, foresight; the Archbishop hoped that now, all these centuries later, there might lie hidden in the coronation drafted by that first ruler the instructions to help the kingdom identify and crown the current one.

With this hope, Colm ApBeirne ordered the ancient coronation texts brought to him. Once more, a sleepless night of reading had come and gone without success. Several times in the earliest of the texts, the Archbishop came across a reference to something called The Heart of the Scepter. He had seen three Kings ascend to the throne, put the crown on the heads and the scepter in the hands of two of them, and yet try as he might, he could think of nothing that matched the description of King Liam's words. Whatever it was, it had been deleted from the coronation ceremony centuries ago.

With the dawn of yet another day, one morning closer to war, invasion, or both, Colm ApBeirne once more ordered his carriage. This time his destination was the Palace itself. Somewhere, amid the kingdom's crown jewels—perhaps among the oldest, such as King Liam's crown, which though still treasured were no longer used—he prayed that the answer to this puzzle was waiting.

It was his last hope; he could think of nowhere else to look.

The Palace, like the cathedral library, was not truly far from the Residence and on so fine a day the Archbishop entered his carriage with a little tinge of regret. In his younger years in this office, he had often waved away the mention of a carriage. He had walked to the Palace or the library, enjoying the beautiful, well-kept grounds of both places, and covering the distance in no more time than it required to harness the horses, prepare the carriage, and drive him to the Palace steps.

The difference, even then, was that by taking the carriage, he could work those extra minutes—and with over eight decades of life, and nearly as many of service, weighing on his bones, such long walks did not happen now. Regretfully.

He had ordered the open carriage today. After his long nights of worry, bent over the scrolls or the coronation texts, it was good to be out in the warm air. For the moment, he put all thoughts of work and of possible danger aside, content to so feel the comforting warmth of the early-summer sun, smell the rose garden as he rode past, see the waves and hear the calls of the people and the happy sound of children.

But the sense of respite did not last long. Tired as he was, Colm ApBeirne could not bring his mind to let go, to rest. It was especially the sight and sounds of the children that reminded him how quickly time was passing and how fragile the kingdom's peace had become.

Arriving at the High King's Palace, the Archbishop was helped from his carriage by a waiting footman. A moment later, the Palace steward, Gaithan, came hurrying down the outer steps toward him, wearing a look of harried concern.

"Good morning, Your Eminence," he said, giving the Archbishop a bow before offering an arm to help the old man to mount the steps.

They had come to know each other well through their mutual years of service, and the Archbishop was not offended by the offered support. Nor did he pretend to a strength he did not feel this morning. He was, in fact, grateful. Descending from the carriage, the Palace steps had looked very long indeed.

"I was surprised to receive your note," Gaithan continued as they slowly ascended. "It has been quite some time since anyone has made such a request. Everything is, of course, prepared. The guard who will meet you there is named Leyster. He has been told to give you whatever help you require."

"Thank you, Gaithan," the Archbishop said, as they reached the top of the steps. He took a moment to catch his breath, nodding his thanks to a liveried doorman who pulled open the heavy iron-hinged door and stood waiting for the men to enter.

"I knew I could count on you," the Archbishop continued.

"We all serve according to our gifts," Gaithan replied. "Mine happens to be organization."

"One we all need and too few possess," the Archbishop acknowledged with a smile, knowing that without his own stewards and secretaries he would be hopelessly lost.

"Thank you, Your Eminence," Gaithan said with another little bow. "What else do you require? Shall I call someone to escort you to the Jewel Treasury?"

The Archbishop shook his head. "I know the way," he said, "and while this visit is not secret, exactly, I would prefer to have as few people know of it as possible. These are unsettled times, Gaithan—times when dark hearts hide behind smiling faces and trust is a commodity to be given out with care."

"It is indeed, Your Eminence. Let us pray that the empty throne is soon filled, and with a ruler more worthy than the last."

"Amen," the Archbishop said with quiet fervency, knowing that Gaithan was one of those to whom trust could be given and who knew far more than most people just how much depravity had gone on in this Palace during the late King's time.

They had continued walking as they talked, and now the Archbishop reached the stairs that would take him down to the floor on which the Jewel Treasury was housed. With a tinge of regret he again dismissed Gaithan's offer of further assistance. He had meant his words about involving as few people as possible. He wished it were possible to exclude the guard, but the jewels of Aghamore were too precious to allow anyone completely private access. Even the King did not enter the Jewel Treasury unattended.

To the Archbishop's mind, it was more than the gold or precious gems that made the jewels important. Many were not of exceptional size or quality and could be easily replaced. Their true value, their irreplaceable quality, was in the history they represented. They were the physical sights and signs of Aghamore's past, and if that was lost or stolen, nothing could replace it.

Now, the Archbishop hoped, they were also the key to Aghamore's future.

With the help of the sturdy handrail, he slowly descended the stairs, then walked down the wide, tapestry-hung corridor toward the room he wanted. At the door, the waiting guard stood at attention. He did not have the keys to the room or to the cases inside. Only five people in the kingdom possessed those—the King, the Steward of the Palace, the head of the Palace Guards, the Chancellor of the kingdom, who was also the head of the Privy Council and so changed with each monarch, and the Archbishop himself. The guard was not there to provide entry; he was there to provide security.

As he neared the door, Colm ApBeirne withdrew the ring of keys he had been given the day after he took Office, from one of his deep side pockets. At the sound, the guard turned to fully face him, waiting. The Archbishop was struck by how very young, and how nervous, he looked.

Then he sighed. *Everyone looks young to me now,* he thought.

"Good morning," he said aloud. "Gaithan told me your name is Leyster—and you're to be my watchdog."

"It's . . . it's for form only, Your Eminence," the guard said with a quick, slight stammer. "No one thinks you would . . . I mean—"

"Peace, Leyster," the Archbishop said gently. "Such precautions are not misplaced, even with me. The words were meant as a jest not a jibe."

The Archbishop was surprised to see a slight flush creep into the guard's cheeks. *He is* truly *young,* he thought, understanding that this was Gaithan's way of making the required surveillance as unobtrusive as possible.

Hiding his smile so as not to further embarrass Leyster, the Archbishop unlocked the door. He let Leyster enter first and light the lamps, then stepped into the room. Inside, the large glass cases were filled with silver and gold, with jewels from different eras that all caught the light of the lamps and filled the room with sparkle. Even prepared for it, it was a breathtaking sight.

Leyster hung back by the door, turning so he could give the Archbishop as much privacy as possible. Colm ApBeirne appreciated the gesture as he walked slowly from case to case. In his mind, he named what he saw and placed them in their time, beginning with the first crown of King Liam— massive and heavy, with rough-cut stones set into each of the nine blunt points that formed its circle, one for each of the Provinces of Aghamore. The largest and front one, representing the central Province of Urlar, was set with a diamond the size and shape of a large walnut. There was something majestic in its lack of refinement, something that spoke of the honest strength of the man who had worn this crown.

Continuing through his first circuit of the room, the Archbishop at last came to the jewels with which the recent Kings had been crowned. By contrast to King Liam's crown, these jewels were in three bands of finely worked filigree, one of silver and two of gold, every other opening in the filigree filled with jewels. Larger stones, representing the Provinces, still encircled the crown, but they were no longer left in their raw form. They had been carefully cut to different shapes whose facets brought out the hidden fire at their hearts. Each of these stones was in turn encircled by tiny diamonds, while the large diamond at the forehead, easily the size of a hen's egg, was encircled by smaller versions of the colored gems that represented the Provinces.

It was almost too much opulence; the Archbishop found his eyes not quite wanting to focus, bedazzled by the color and shine. *Like the Kings themselves,* the Archbishop thought, *plenty of show and little substance.* Again, by contrast, his eyes were drawn back to King Liam's crown and all the solidity of both the man and the kingdom it established.

Not all of the ancient regalia had been abandoned for showier counterparts. Some, like the scepter, had come through time and use unaltered; other pieces, like the great Sword of Justice, had been refurbished and embellished, but not abandoned. These, along with the other articles of Coronation Regalia used by the last two Kings, rested in a glass case in the middle of the floor.

Using another of the keys on his chain, the Archbishop unlocked the case and carefully withdrew the scepter. As always, he was surprised by both the beauty and the weight of the thing. Although he had handled it during the coronations of both Kings Osaze and Anri, he had never examined it with the kind of close scrutiny he turned on it now. The Regalia of Coronation was a symbol of hope to the people, now as ever, glittering with a promise no less brilliant than the gold and jewels, of what the future *might* be.

Never was that hope and that promise more important, he thought as he continued examining the scepter. It was a rod about three feet long, made of long cords of gold and silver twisted together into a long spiral. At its base, a knob of gold was wrapped in a fine net of silver filigree. At the apex, a huge amethyst was held in a cage of thinnest gold—and this was topped by a single ruby. The stone was clear and flawless, the purest deep red. For the first time, he noticed that it was also slightly heart-shaped—and by natural design rather than the craftsman's touch.

Is this the "Heart of the Scepter"? he wondered, turning the rod so he could examine the ruby from every angle. But aside from its size and the rich clarity of its color, he could find nothing remarkable about it—or about the scepter itself. A beautiful piece of workmanship, certainly, but nothing that would help prove Selia's right to be Queen.

More disappointed than he realized he would be, the Archbishop put the scepter back in its accustomed place, locked the case, and turned away. He would have to keep searching—and hope that time did not run out.

"Well, Leyster," he said as he walked toward the door where the young man had waited as unobtrusively as possible, "you have guarded both me and the jewels faithfully. If you'll see to the lamps, I'll lock the door behind us."

"Are you sure you're finished, Your Eminence? I don't mind staying longer, if you need me."

"Quite sure," the Archbishop answered a little sadly. *And now what?* he asked himself as he waited for Leyster to make the required check of the locks on the cases and blow out the lamps. *What do I do next? Where do I look? What is it I'm missing?*

But the darkness filling the room gave him no answer. Once Leyster had stepped out into the hall, he firmly closed and locked the door, trying not to feel like he was locking away hope as well.

Elon, too, had spent much of the last few days locked away. Using Thomas to convey the message of illness to both household staff and visitor, he had used the time to search through nearly every text in his current possession. Frustration warred with desperation, and hopelessness nearly won . . . until this morning. In a tiny, almost overlooked volume, Elon finally found an answer. It was not the one for which he had been looking—it might be something much, much better.

He had hoped to find a way to force an increase of Thomas's visionary skills; it was something that would eventually happen on its own, but like any skill or talent it would take time and practice to develop. But time was a fleeting commodity, and the more patient he was, the closer both danger and defeat came.

Elon knew he no longer had time to wait.

What he had found now did not depend on Thomas—or on anyone other than Elon himself, his own skills and contacts. It was ancient, from a land whose identity had been swallowed up by the passage of time and forgotten by all but the few who studied, as he did, the dark arts that most of the world had abandoned.

This decoction, when combined with the skilled use of his voice, would break down any barriers of distrust the Archbishop was erecting. If he followed the recipe exactly, a few drops once a week would be all that was needed to ensure the old man's obedience.

With this discovery, Elon's need for Aurya and Giraldus ended. Wherever his daughter and her lover were now, Elon no longer cared. Whether they returned in a week, a year—or never—it no longer mattered. He would have what he wanted.

It would not be easy. The decoction called for some ingredients that were rare and must be handled exactly. But—Elon smiled as he put the tiny volume aside and drew a pen and paper to him—his years of passion for things arcane had given him contacts to procure such items. He would call upon all of them now.

Of course, the political situation in Aghamore could make

things difficult. Riders were constantly employed, so their services often required a wait, and the Armies of the Provinces now filled the roads. Elon knew it might take a little time—but he would get what he wanted.

He began to list the names and locations of various apothecaries, alchemists, and dealers of things arcane to whom he would send lists of his various needs. These were all people he knew he could trust. It was a trust built on more than time or past experience; every one of them knew that if they ever betrayed him, he had it in his power to destroy them.

As the list grew, Elon stopped and rethought his plan. He would *not* use the Riders to carry his letters or return with his packages. Riders were, for the most part, young men—and young men could be indiscreet. Furthermore, he *knew* none of them; they were nameless and faceless strangers who, with one casually dropped word in the wrong ears, could bring this new plan to a crashing and disastrous halt. No, Riders were one link in this chain he would forgo.

Thomas, Elon thought with a mental nod. Thomas could be his messenger. He had attended to such secret matters before, his face was already known to many of the people on Elon's list—and Thomas could be trusted. Completely.

A few of Elon's contacts were here in Ballinrigh and in little towns scattered throughout the Province of Urlar. But most were in Kilgarriff or just beyond. Two of them, who had been able to procure the most elusive objects of past searches, were just over the kingdom's border in the neighboring land of Salacar. They were, of necessity, very careful of their privacy . . . but they were also among those to whom Thomas was already known.

With a small, dark smile, Elon knew he had made the right decision. Each day that went by added to the danger of discovery, and although he would miss the company of the one person with whom he need keep up no pretenses, to whom he could speak his mind with at least moderate freedom, Thomas was his best hope of success.

In a way, Elon now thought Giraldus's continued absence was a boon. Even though the letters to summon the other bishops had been sent, it would take *time* to reconvene the College. It would take even more *time* to readdress the question of the succession and reach an agreement. It would also take *time* for the armies of the Provinces to reach Ballinrigh, for camps to be set, challenges issued and met, battles fought or even siege to be laid.

And it would take *time* for Thomas to complete this new mission.

Elon picked up his pen again, dipped it, and began to write, to finish the list so that Thomas could ride out. There were things to be done before he left—and much for Elon to do while he was gone. He must continue the work he had neglected during these last few days of feigned illness . . . he must continue to prove himself both contrite in the matter of proposing Giraldus as High King and indispensable to the Archbishop's needs. Only then, when Thomas returned and the decoction was finally ready, would he have the access to the Archbishop that he needed.

Time was now both an enemy and an ally.

Chapter Sixteen

The central Province of Urlar was the High King's Province; its Ruling House changed with each new branch of the succession. In times of war or invasion, every Province and its army, though governed and ordered by its own Baron, was at the King's command. Over the centuries, therefore, the Standing Army of Urlar, once King Liam's mighty conquering force, had become little more than traveling Peacekeepers. They rode throughout Urlar, chasing down bandits or responding to reports of trouble or need, ensuring that the King's Peace was upheld and the roads continued safe. It was a separate branch that maintained the law within Ballinrigh itself, and guarded both the Palace and the Archbishop's Residence.

There was one more, small select group who also guarded the King—and whose existence Colm ApBeirne had only just discovered. King Anri, it seemed, had devised a network of spies by which he had kept watch on the doings of the Barons. Now that there was no King, it was to the Archbishop that the infiltrator in Hueil's household had sent his secret report.

It was short and cryptic, saying only that there were secret stirrings within the household that were far more than just the Baron's preparation for the same civil war the other Barons were preparing to fight. Hueil, it was whispered, had been sending and receiving messages that were stamped with heraldic devices not found in Aghamore. The Baron spent hours closeted with two advisors, one whose expertise was military action. The other was said to actually be Hueil's Chief of Spies—and the tension in the Baron's household was mounting daily.

To the Archbishop, these words confirmed Lysandra's warning vision. He had been inclined to believe her from the start, and now all doubts, however unexpressed, vanished. With their passing, Colm ApBeirne found himself in a position he had never wanted and for which he felt himself ill suited.

Civil war was horrific enough, but with invasion coming that war became something even more terrifying. With no King—or Queen—to govern, Colm ApBeirne, Archbishop and servant of God, would be forced to make decisions that would send men to their deaths, in order to save the life of the kingdom.

It took the Riders many days to deliver their new orders to the scattered troops. But by the day of the Summer Solstice, the last of the men had entered the capital city. With their entry, and reluctantly, the Archbishop sent out one more order—to bar the city gates. Only the most urgent and well-documented travelers were to be allowed in or out, and the army was to man the gate towers and the walls against siege or invasion.

But these orders and actions, so necessary to the Archbishop's mind, had not proved popular with the people of Ballinrigh, and by afternoon there was a delegation of city wardens already at the Residence to deliver their complaints. There were too many to be heard in the Archbishop's study and so, dressed in full episcopal regalia, a very weary Colm ApBeirne sat in the ornate *cathedra,* the tall thronelike chair of the Archbishop, waiting to hear what the ever-outspoken people of Aghamore's largest city had to say.

The *cathedra,* usually off to the side within the sanctuary of the high altar so the Archbishop could sit at various times during the Mass or the daily Offices, had been moved to the center of the top step. It sat just outside the altar rail; the steps kept it elevated, as if on a dais, allowing the Archbishop to see—and be seen, a physical reminder to those present that he spoke today as both Archbishop, and as temporary Ruler of this land.

Colm tried not to shift under the weight of the robes and regalia he had worn for so many years. Today, however, the triple-crowned mitre felt cast out of lead rather than embellished gold, and the Chain of Regency that hung from his neck in addition to his pectoral cross kept threatening to pull his head to his chest. And it was hot beneath the fur-trimmed cope of purple silk and silver tissue that he wore over the sacerdotal garments of amice, alb, chasuble, and stole.

These latter were worn to show that he discharged a sacred duty here today. Though the matters discussed were of the kingdom and the city, not the Church, they were no less done in obedience to Divine Will. But they were also worn over the habitual cassock of the clergy, as was the correct and symbolic requirement, showing the white alb over the colored garment as the pure and purifying nature of redemption covering the impure nature of unredeemed humanity.

In the wintertime, in a cold, stone cathedral, the layers were welcome. On the day of the Summer Solstice, in a body already weary from too many nights of worry and too little sleep, they were more than a burden. Wrapped in their heat, the Archbishop found each moment more difficult not to let his mind drift and his eyes close.

". . . and closing the gates without give' us fair warnin' to prepare," the man before him was saying, his strident voice abruptly recalling the Archbishop's attention, "well—it creates a hardship, Your Eminence. It does indeed. How are my goods to arrive? I sell food—fruits and veg mostly—and they'll not keep forever outside. And how'm I to feed the people—m' family and m' regular customers who count on me—when there's so many soldiers claimin' the goods . . . and payin' too little?"

The Archbishop held up a hand. He had heard enough; every one of them was here to give the same complaints, with only minor variations. They did not like the orders to close the gates, they did not share the Archbishop's fear of what might yet be coming—and, above all, they did not want the entire Standing Army of Urlar roaming the city streets, refusing to stay where they were stationed or billeted. In essence, they wanted things to remain as they had always been.

Well so do I, Colm thought with a burst of irritation. *But they can't right now—and the city wardens have to make the best of it.*

He waited for the silence he wanted, complete silence without the shuffling and whispering that told him that the men before him were still more determined to be heard than to hear anything he had to say. The wait stretched on; seconds turned to minutes, and the Archbishop did not speak. Despite his discomfort, he knew he had more patience than they; it was a weapon granted by age, and he intended to use it.

Silence fell, stillness settled, deepened, and finally reached the cusp for which the Archbishop had been waiting. He closed his eyes for just one moment, then opened them again and let his gaze sweep across the assembly, drawing each of them in to what he had to say.

"I know," he began, "that the actions I have ordered require some sacrifice to the comfort of the people of this city. I wish it could be otherwise. But we are all in the midst of troubled times—far more so than ten years ago when King Osaze died without heir, or the following years, when King Anri was on the throne. It is a trouble that threatens the very existence of this kingdom.

"There are armies marching toward Ballinrigh right now, whose intent is war and blood. By Right of Arms, one of the Barons plans to claim the throne, and the price that may yet be paid in the blood of our people is more than has been shed in all of Aghamore's long history—"

"I don't believe it," one of the wardens said, pushing his way to the front of the group. "The Provinces, their Barons and armies, too, are all a part of Aghamore. I don't believe any of 'em'll harm us here in Ballinrigh."

"Then you are either deluded or a fool," the Archbishop snapped.

He instantly regretted his outburst; anger would do no one any good. But the patience he had called upon just a short time before was reaching its end. Looking down, he saw the shocked look on the man's face that his unexpected tone had caused. Then, with a sigh he ran a weary hand across his eyes and started again.

"It would be comforting to believe that our great city, the center of the kingdom, is rendered safe by the esteem in which it is held. But that would be more than foolish—it would be deadly. The hunger for power can turn friend into foe far too easily. The army is here for your protection. The gates are closed for the same protection—and not only from what lies without. The army must be free to range the city, to keep eyes and ears open for spies and saboteurs. I assure you that they *do* exist—and surely, a few days or weeks of such inconvenience is preferable to the armies of the Barons forcing their way into the city and fighting each other in our streets."

"And how do you know they'd do that? What's to say they'd not do their fightin' out on the open plain even if the gates be open?" another of the wardens asked. Loudly.

Again the Archbishop sighed. Why could they not see events as he did? They could not be that blind, that stupid, that . . .

"We don't know—but are you willing to take the risk? Are you willing to put not only this city, but your wives and children in harm's way just to keep the gates open? Commerce may be slowed while the people who wish to enter or leave are checked, true. But unless we are actually under siege, it will continue. Is that not a better choice than risking the battles taking place on your own doorstep? What will happen to you, or to your shops and homes and businesses then?"

The Archbishop was relieved to see his last points striking home. The men before him were beginning to realize that although they were not dealing with a King, neither were they dealing with someone unwise, unwary, unworldly—or uninformed.

At the back of the cathedral, the doors opened briefly, emitting a shaft of bright sunlight into the interior dimmed by size. A moment later, the Archbishop saw Renan enter from the narthex into the nave. If every issue had been dealt with—or at least as many as could be for now—it was time to conclude this meeting.

He drew himself up as straight and regally as his tired body would allow. "I ask you then," he said to the city wardens, "that you trust me a while longer. I ask this as your spiritual leader and, for the moment, as your secular one. There are matters I cannot yet disclose, but I say again that everything is being done for the protection of you and your families, for this city, and indeed, for this kingdom. May it please God, there will soon be a new Ruler upon the throne and peace again in Aghamore."

There was little the wardens could say to that. The Archbishop was trusted, and he knew it—which was why he had put his request in just such terms. Now he held up his hand and pronounced a blessing, making a large sign of the cross in the air. It was a signal that they all recognized, and if not completely satisfied with the way the meeting had gone, they were at least silent as they slowly filed back up the long central aisle toward the doors.

Once more, the Archbishop ran a hand across his too-tired eyes. Then he drew a deep breath, hoping it would give him a little more strength, as Renan approached.

The priest dropped to one knee quickly and touched his lips to the Archbishop's ring, then rose just as swiftly. The old man envied him the energy in that simple movement.

But what was more important, he found that Renan's presence made him feel a little less overwhelmed by his current burden. Here, the guiding voice of the Spirit told him, was someone he could truly trust, and that knowledge, amid all the present and mounting uncertainties, was like a balm to his heart.

"Come with me while I divest myself of all this," the Archbishop said with a slight wave of his hand to indicate his formal robes. "Then we'll go back to the Residence to talk. I need your help if we are to succeed in the matter before us."

Renan gave a little nod, then offered his arm to help the Archbishop rise and walk back into the vesting sacristy. With two attendants waiting, divesting was quickly done, and, within minutes, the Archbishop and Renan left by the little side door, outside beneath the wide stone walkway. A few yards from the door, the Archbishop finally stopped, closed his eyes, and breathed in the fresh, sweetly scented air.

"Are you all right, Your Eminence?" Renan immediately asked. Colm found himself touched by the concern in the younger priest's voice—because he knew it was genuine, and it was directed to the man, the *person,* not just the Office.

"Tired," he replied, "more tired than I have been in a very long time. But the fresh air helps clear the cobwebs, especially on a day as fine as this one."

"What can I do to help, Your Eminence?" Renan asked. "I know the news we brought has increased your burden, and I wish there had been another way. But—"

The Archbishop held up a hand to stop him. "The burden of this Office is one I accepted many years ago," he said. "I just pray God will give me the strength to see our people through this crisis and keep our kingdom strong and in peace. Then, younger hands and minds can take it up, and I can retire, to wait and rest until I am called to the Greater Rest that awaits."

"What can I do to help?" Renan asked again.

They resumed their slow walk toward the Residence. On the way, the Archbishop explained about the coronation texts, the Heart of the Scepter, and his failure to find it or any explanation of what it might be. Renan had shown that he had a great gift of discernment—shown it by his understanding of Tambryn's words and by his recognition of Lysandra as Prophecy's Hand and Selia as the Font of Wisdom. The Archbishop hoped that Renan's discernment would allow him to see something, some clue however small, that his own eyes had been missing.

"So you see, my son," the old man concluded, "I can find no other hope for our cause. We must *prove* Selia's right to the throne—her *predestined* right—or I fear the people will not accept her. I *know* the Barons will not. The only hope of proof I can find is in these oblique references to the Heart of the Scepter.

"I can no longer devote my entire time to the search, keeping myself locked away to read text after text. As you saw, there are other needs of the people I must address. If Lysandra's vision is true, and I believe it is, then those needs become more imperative with each passing hour, as danger draws ever nearer this city. Will you take up the search? I will set you up in a room at the Residence with its entire resources at your disposal."

Renan had stayed quiet while the Archbishop talked, keeping his head bowed in obvious thought. The old man did not want to push him into a burden he was not prepared to bear—and yet, Renan was one of the three who had found Selia, who had risked everything and done battle with evil, to get her here. This burden was already partly his to bear.

"I am not hesitating to help you, Your Eminence," Renan said, before the silence between them could grow uncom-

fortable. "I will, of course, do whatever I can. I'm just uncertain how much that will be. You are far more learned than
I, and if you can find nothing . . ." He let his voice trail off.

"Perhaps I am not the one meant to find it," the Archbishop replied. "We will see. But, successful or not, let me
thank you now. If we are able to avoid the bloodbath I fear is
coming, even in part, then it will be because of you and your
companions—and this kingdom will owe you all a greater
debt of gratitude than it yet understands."

They reached the Residence and entered through the door
that led into the Archbishop's private chapel. From there, one
could go to enter either the living or the working area. Every
muscle in Colm ApBeirne's body wanted to turn toward the
door behind the sacristy, to climb the small staircase and
open the door into his bedchamber.

But after all these years, duty was forever stronger than
inclination, so he turned up the aisle, toward the back of the
chapel, toward more work and not rest. Yet.

Soon, he silently promised his aching back and the slight
pounding that had tightened a vise around his forehead from
the weight of the triple-crowned mitre he had worn such a
short time ago. Tonight, he *would* sleep.

As they entered the bustle of the Residence's main area, the
Archbishop gestured at a passing aide and asked him to find
Brother Naal. "I'll see you settled in a room near my office,"
he told Renan. "The coronation texts, and anything else you
want or need, will be brought to you. Brother Naal is a fine and
most trustworthy young man. He is entirely at your disposal—
and, as much as possible, so am I. If you find anything—"

Renan nodded. "You will know almost as soon as I do,"
he said.

The Archbishop made a sign of the cross, blessing Renan,
as Brother Naal came hurrying down the hall toward them.

"Yes, Your Eminence," he said breathlessly. "Brother Cal-
lum said you needed me?"

"Not I, but Father Renan here," the Archbishop replied. "Please get him settled in the yellow-rose room and help him in any way he requires. *Anything* he needs, however large or small, is to be given him, and there is no place in the Residence that is off-limits to him. You are also to see to his comfort— food, drink, whatever. The work he will be doing is of the utmost importance, and I entrust you to see all is done to ease his burden."

"Yes, Your Eminence."

"And he is to have complete access to me—even if I am in the middle of a meeting. The work he is doing has my first attention, so you are to notify me immediately at his word. Is that clear as well?"

"Yes, Your Eminence."

The Archbishop turned his attention back to Renan, looking deeply into the priest's solemn hazel eyes. "God grant you guidance, my son," he said, "for both quick and clear insight. I will have the papers sent to you at once. All deference to your friend Lysandra and her wondrous companion, the wolf is at our gate and waits to consume us."

He could see that Renan understood exactly what he meant. Perhaps, he thought, Renan understood even better than he, for he did not miss the quick spurt of relief his words brought to the priest's eyes.

"I will leave you with Brother Naal, then," he said. "The duties and people I have put off these last few days will no longer wait. I fear it will be a long day ahead—for both of us."

Once more, Colm ApBeirne made the sign of the cross to bless Renan and his efforts, this time the gesture including Brother Naal, too. Then, turning away, he realized how much lighter he felt. Despite his biting fatigue, despite the crowd of people he knew would be waiting, and even despite the many threats he knew were fast approaching, Colm felt a sudden flood of Divine peace, the "peace which passeth understanding."

He did not question it or how long it might last. For this moment, he let himself embrace the bright hope that all would be well. Then, with that feeling to strengthen him, he headed for his office and the first of the many demands awaiting.

Chapter Seventeen

Back at Renan's parish, Lysandra was busy with Selia. While Lysandra continued her efforts to establish an herb garden for Renan, she had the younger woman sit on the nearby mourning bench and read aloud to her from one of the books Renan had set out for Selia to study.

At first, the younger woman had balked at the arrangement. She was tired of the dull outlines of history, law, court procedure and protocol, lineage records and the like. She had gotten over her initial fear of the city, and now she wanted to go out into it. Or, barring that, at least help Lysandra with her present and, Selia said emphatically, far more interesting task.

While inwardly, Lysandra agreed, she could not let Selia slack her own duties. But to ease the onus of them, she promised Selia that at the end of two hours more reading they would put aside the books and go into the city. It was time to look for material to make Selia some new clothes. She must have at least one new gown to wear when she stood before the Barons to claim her crown.

The promised two hours passed pleasantly, with each

woman concentrating on her task. Then, finally, Selia put the book aside.

"Can we go now?" she asked, and Lysandra could hear the new excitement in her voice.

She smiled, remembering herself at Selia's age—an adult, yes, but still near enough to childhood that the prospect of anything new or different was an adventure.

"Yes," Lysandra said to her question. "We can go—as soon as I've washed."

As Lysandra stood and walked toward the guesthouse, she knew that she felt none of her companion's excitement. But she was eager to give Selia some happiness. Today might be her only taste of freedom—and it would be little enough. She believed completely that Renan and the Archbishop would find the way to put Selia on the throne; they had all come too far and endured too much for her to believe otherwise—and surely, Tambryn's words would have warned them.

Or, if not Tambryn's, then the Cryf's, she thought as she headed out the door of the guesthouse, back into the sunshine, where Selia was waiting. *Perhaps they did, and no one told either Selia or me.*

However, even this thought brought a mental shake of her head. There was much—most—within the Cryf Holy Words she did not know ... but to have kept this from her would have been a betrayal of her trust, and that was something she would never believe of either Renan or the Cryf.

So sometime, and it *must* be soon for all of Aghamore's sake, Selia would have to face the restrictions that came under the guise of power. She would have servants and palaces, jewels and such clothing as would put to shame anything they might find today—but she would also have duties to fill her hours with the affairs of the kingdom and restoring its peaceful prosperity. People would do her homage, all the while wanting, needing, demanding. Her life would soon belong to Aghamore and to the people she was appointed to rule.

But today, at least for a few hours, her life would be her own.

Lysandra's money was in a small pouch tied around her neck and tucked beneath her clothes. She would, of course, go nowhere without Cloud-Dancer. For the sake of the people they would encounter, however, she had fashioned a collar and leash out of an old cassock of Renan's. It was too threadbare to be mended or worn any longer, but strong enough to be cut into strips and braided. Cloud-Dancer's well-trained obedience was not in question, but Lysandra wanted no trouble with shopkeepers to mar Selia's outing.

I'm sorry, boy, she told him silently as she slipped the collar over his head, then ran her hand lovingly through his fur. *It's just for a little while.*

He accepted the collar with more than his usual dignity, nor did he strain against the leash that Lysandra tied first to the collar and then around her waist. Standing, she put her hand on his head and twined her fingers down deeply into the thick, soft fur on the top of his head. This touch, and their mutual love, was his true control.

Contact between them thus established, Lysandra borrowed his vision. Her *Sight* might have shown her far more than Cloud-Dancer's eyes; the images he saw were not only of an altered perspective, with no true peripheral vision and a different type of focus than human eyes, but he saw only in sepia tones and soft pastels, like colors almost faded away with sun and rain. But her *Sight* might also show her too much.

She was learning to use and understand all that she now was, but it would take time. Her experience when she and Selia had twice gone with Renan to the Archbishop's Residence had taught her that amid the vast population of Ballinrigh, these new manifestations of her *Sight* could be overwhelming.

Perhaps, she sometimes thought, in another ten years she would learn to understand, even control, all these new manifestations of her *Sight*—the richer vision, the Far-Seeing, the prophecy, the occasional ability to *see* the truth in a person or situation, and whatever other gifts she had yet to discover. Before she met Selia, before she became Prophecy's Hand, she had learned to use the *Sight* as it had been before—so she would learn to use these new gifts, as well.

For now, however, here in Ballinrigh, she would not use her *Sight* unless it was truly needed. She was grateful anew for Cloud-Dancer and the freedom he gave her, as through their contact she saw with his vision. The muted colors and changed perspective were even more familiar than what her *Sight* might have shown, and Lysandra smiled as she and Selia walked through the iron gate that opened onto the crowded city streets.

The wolf walked serenely by her side, as if happy to be sharing his eyes once more. The bustle of the city—the noise of voices and traffic, of children and shopkeepers, animals and wagons—were a vivid reminder of how much the stone walls shielded Renan's churchyard and its contents.

Selia now seemed energized. She bounced forward, a step or two ahead, eyes wide with excitement as she tried to take in everything at once. As Lysandra and Cloud-Dancer followed, their pace steady but more sedate, she was happy to see Selia's joy; the younger woman *looked* seventeen now, looked like life was ahead of her and her pain was put in the past.

"Where do you think we should go?" Selia asked suddenly, her eyes brighter than Lysandra had ever seen them. "Renan said he'd take me around and show me the layout of the city. He said it was something I'd need to know. But he's been so busy with the Archbishop—"

Lysandra smiled a little at Selia's tone—politeness and an attempt at understanding only half covering the disappointment she did not want to admit. "We've all been busy," she said, "you, perhaps, most of all—though I know it's boring work. But it can't be too far. People in this part of the city wear clothes, too."

"But don't you want to go farther in, nearer the heart of the city? I'm sure there will be more and even better shops as we get closer to the Palace. We might even catch Renan coming home from the Archbishop's Residence."

Lysandra shook her head. "I don't think that's a good idea. We don't know our way around well enough—so we'd have to take a carriage, and that costs money. Until we see how much a dress or some fabric will cost, we're better off staying where we are. I'm sure the shops here will be fine. Once you're Queen, you'll see all there is of the Palace, the Residence—and the shops nearby."

Although this would do little to assuage Selia's curiosity about the city, Lysandra was glad that she accepted her word. While Selia stared, wide-eyed, at the sights around them, Lysandra withdrew her attention a little. There was something nagging at her, something she could not quite name but that had been growing ever since they set foot outside the churchyard.

Cautiously, almost fearfully, she lowered her guard a little to let some portion of the city's thoughts in. She had to protect herself from the full force of them . . . but she also needed to know what it was she was feeling—and from whom or where it came.

At first all she felt was a jumble, a wild pool that swirled with nothing clear or independent enough to identify. Then, slowly, thoughts separated. Lysandra felt the flow of the lives around her and, suddenly, she found she could float along it without being dragged down and drowned.

The life of this city had remained almost unchanged after King Anri's death. It had been protected from the callousness of the Barons and the growth of lawlessness such inattentive rule begat, by its size, centrality, and most of all, by the careful governance of the Archbishop.

But now Ballinrigh had become the focal point of all that the Provinces had been suffering, and it could no longer ignore what was coming. Lysandra sensed that growing fear of the people as realization of the kingdom's troubles finally dawned, made real to them by the closing of the city gates and the recalling of Urlar's small army to man the walls.

Yet, powerful as the people's new fears might be, they were not the source of the disturbance in Lysandra's mind. There was something else here, an undercurrent that ran through the nervousness and uncertainty of the people like a misplaced color in a tapestry. And as that single string would jar the eye, so this feeling tapped at Lysandra's awareness, almost daring her to find it.

Part of her knew she must face this new feeling—and she must give it a name. It was a foe, a threat, a harbinger of danger that she must identify so she could tell Renan. The war against the Darkness had not yet been won; the battle was approaching, and they must be prepared.

But another, and perhaps greater part of her, the part that had for ten years lived in solitude, not caring or wanting to know anything of the world away from her forest, wanted now to run back to the guesthouse that was her current home. There, protected by its sanctuary and thick stone walls, she could close the doors, close her mind, and welcome the comfort of ignorance.

But the days of such comfort were gone for her. Just as she could never go back to the innocence of her life before her blindness, she also could never go back to those years when her heart was as blind as her eyes. She had dwelt in the depths of darkness and been drawn forth into Light, to emerge irreparably changed.

She and Selia had now entered into one of the city's many market areas. Shops and stalls crowded the streets in a jumble of organized chaos. Bright summer clothing had replaced the heavy winter cloaks and somber hues, colors that seemed to shimmer like flowers in the sunlight. No less attractive were the displays in shop windows and those that hung from rafters or were laid out along the counters of the semipermanent stalls. They reminded Lysandra, briefly, of the main street of Scorda, the town of her childhood, where her father's dye shop had stood. Yet even on the busiest of market days, even at the yearly Harvest Faire, Scorda had never held such a vast array of wares.

Lysandra tightened her fingers in Cloud-Dancer's fur, deepening her touch for the comfort it gave her rather than any need for additional control. He showed no interest in moving from her side as they joined the jostling throng. Again, the sudden sense of discord swept through her. It came like a wave that crested, crashing in upon the rocks of her mind, her soul, then ebbing away again. Lysandra tried to follow the flow to its source, but it disappeared into the rippling ocean of people.

Selia's hand upon her arm recalled Lysandra's attention. "Are you all right?" the younger woman asked. "You haven't heard a word I've said."

"You're right," Lysandra said. "I'm sorry."

Selia looked at her quizzically, as if expecting more of an answer. Lysandra offered none; as yet, there was nothing she could explain. Finally, with the barest hint of a shrug, Selia said, "I said I saw a seamstress shop up ahead. Should we go there or keep looking?"

"It's a good place to start," Lysandra replied. If it was like the shop that had stood next door to her father's, there would be bolts of fabric as well as finished clothing. There would also be chairs where Lysandra could sit and, while Selia examined what the seamstress offered, try again to find out what she was feeling—and from whom.

They hurried now, past the remaining shops and stalls between them and where they were going. But as they passed a small apothecary's shop, half-hidden in the shadows between a tinker's stall and a cooper's display of barrels, a quick, sharp feeling of danger stabbed Lysandra's mind with a force that made her stop again.

Finger movements directing Cloud-Dancer, she looked around, using his vision to try to pinpoint the source of her disquiet. Then, again, the feeling disappeared, leaving only the lingering trace of its presence in her mind.

She hurried to catch up with Selia, who was just entering the seamstress shop. Lysandra suddenly knew it was imperative she get away from the bustle, however briefly, so she could find out what warning she was trying to receive.

The interior of the shop was cool and calm after the sunlight and crowds of the street. The proprietress came hurrying over as soon as they entered. Her step faltered briefly when she caught sight of Cloud-Dancer, but Lysandra was prepared.

She turned toward the approaching footsteps and let her sightless stare fix on the woman's face. Through Cloud-Dancer's eyes, she saw realization, and pity, spread across the shopkeeper's features—and now Lysandra would make use of the simple kindness those expressions revealed. It was not for her own sake or even for Selia's that she would feign a weakness she did not possess; it was for Aghamore's.

"Are there chairs here, Selia?" she asked softly.

It was not Selia who answered. Before the young woman could say anything, the shopkeeper quickened her step toward Lysandra.

"Yes," she said. "Please, let me show you. It is quite comfortable."

She took Lysandra's arm, careful to stay on the other side than Cloud-Dancer, and led her to a nearby seat. Lysandra continued to act out the blindness of her eyes as she felt along the chair's arm, locating the seat before turning and sitting down.

The shopkeeper now pointedly ignored Cloud-Dancer as she turned slightly to include Selia in her question. "How may

I help you?" she asked, either not seeing or misinterpreting the look of surprise the younger woman was giving Lysandra. "Is there something in particular you're looking for?"

"A dress," Lysandra said simply, "or fabric to make one."

"For yourself or the young lady?"

"It is for Selia."

"For a particular occasion?" The woman again turned her attention to include both customers.

"I . . . uh . . ." Selia began, obviously unsure how to answer.

"She has a special meeting coming soon," Lysandra supplied, "and must be dressed for it. We're looking for something fairly simple, where the quality is in the fabric and cut, not in piles of added ruffles and useless fluff."

"As the best things are. Have you a color in mind?"

"Something soft, I would think—perhaps in a sage green or a dusty rose. I will let you and Selia discuss it. But my father was a dyer, and I do know good cloth when I feel it."

"Yes, ma'am," the shopkeeper said. "If the young lady will come with me, we will see if we can find something that fits her needs. If you need anything while we're gone, you have only to call. We will not be far away."

The shopkeeper's voice said she was impressed enough for Lysandra to relax a little. All she needed now was some quiet. She listened to the footsteps go toward the back of the shop. Then, as their voices began discussing color, fabric, and cut, Lysandra closed her eyes. She disengaged her hand from Cloud-Dancer's head, not needing his vision for the moment, and felt the wolf lie down, putting his chin across the toe of her shoe.

Slowly, tentatively, Lysandra called upon her new gift of *Far-Seeing,* surprising herself when it came so easily at her command, and sent it out into the marketplace, to try to find the source of the Darkness she was feeling.

Her *Sight* slid over the population. Vendors and shopkeepers, mothers and children, couples old and young—all intent upon their own occupations and with no threat beyond. She was about to give up, to think she had imagined the feeling, when her *Sight* touched upon the apothecary stall.

But it could not penetrate the outer doors. Something kept turning her *Sight* away, like a mirror held up to block the sunlight.

Lysandra was not as familiar with magic as Renan; her only experiences with it had been along the quest to find and return with Selia. One of those contacts had nearly killed her—nearly trapped and smothered her *soul* while draining the life from her body. Her only other experience with magic had been to help Renan slow Aurya's pursuit. She had only stood with him, lending him such strength as she could; it was Renan who had focused and wielded the magic. With such limited knowledge, she was not completely certain it was magic shielding the apothecary's store—or something else, something darker and more dangerous.

What is magic? she suddenly found herself wondering. Her *Sight,* her visions in the garden, the Far-Seeing and prophecy, her connection with Cloud-Dancer, even the wondrous gift of true healing she experienced that once to save Eiddig's life—she did not think of these as magic, but might others? She believed them to be gifts from the Divine Hand that held and gave all gifts that fought the Darkness.

But what then was magic, she asked herself again, magic such as Renan's own? Was it not also an instrument against the Dark? Might it not, then, come from the same place, the same Divine Hand and Heart?

She had no answer to give—nor time to ponder it further. With her *Sight,* she now saw a man emerge from the apothecary's shop. There was nothing remarkable about his appearance . . . except to her. She *saw* the pouch he carried beneath his shirt which, although small of size, radiated a darkening sense of danger that grew the more she tried to penetrate its contents. It contained herbs, that much she could tell—but their names eluded her . . . and of their use, she could not guess.

Lysandra heard Selia's excited voice as she and the shop-keeper returned from the back of the store. Footsteps fast approaching, Lysandra recalled her *Sight*, to give the young woman her attention. Later, when they were back at the church, she would explain it all to Selia—her appearance of helplessness, her need for quiet—and she would try again, in the undisturbed serenity of that place, to find again the man she had just *seen*.

Perhaps, she thought, *if I can discover who he is, Renan will know what it means.*

"Oh, Lysandra," Selia said, with a skip in both her voice and her step, "we've found it, the right dress. It's beautiful. Here—feel this cloth."

Although with her *Sight,* she could *see* it well enough, Lysandra knew she must continue to play her blindness. After giving Cloud-Dancer a signal to stay, she stood and began to feel the cloth. And it was good cloth, a finely spun wool so soft that it could only be of a lamb's first shearing. Then, with her hands as guide, she walked around Selia, judging the fit to her shoulders, sleeves, waist—and having the girl describe it carefully.

The main body of the dress was pale yellow, like a newly hatched chick, but with a sprinkling of tiny flowers in the lightest shades of blue, pink, lavender, and green, all carefully and expertly embroidered. The center of each tiny flower held the smallest of pearls, giving the gown the sense of their soft luster. The sleeves were of good linen, softly white as the pearls. They belled out into long graceful tips that reached nearly to the dress's hem when her arms were lowered. The front of the dress's skirt softly draped open to reveal a front inset panel of the same linen as the sleeves, and both were trimmed with an embroidered band that repeated the tiny, pearl-studded flowers that covered the yellow wool.

It was not a practical dress for working in either home or garden, but it was a dress in which she could stand before the Barons.

Now came the important questions. "How much?" Lysandra asked, holding her breath and hoping the coins in her pouch would be enough.

"It is good cloth," the shopkeeper began her pitch, "and the detail work is very beautiful. It took many hours to do the fine stitches necessary, you understand. It is a fine choice, but not an inexpensive one."

Lysandra withdrew her hidden pouch, which made a satisfying chink as it moved. She saw the slight look of greed that swept across the shopkeeper's face when she heard it, and the renewed expression of deference to a paying customer that was part of her professional air.

"How much?" Lysandra repeated.

"Two silver sovereigns," the shopkeeper replied.

"And do you have any footwear?" Lysandra asked without a pause.

The shopkeeper was obviously surprised that Lysandra, in her own rustic and unimpressive attire, could accept such a sum with composure. "We, um, well . . . we do carry a few items," she said, quickly recovering herself. "There is a pair of doeskin slippers that would complement this dress well. They are not for outdoor wear, of course—but neither is the gown."

"How much?" Lysandra asked once more.

"Twelve silver pennies."

"Six," Lysandra said, knowing that if she did not haggle at all, the shopkeeper would think she was a fool. She should, in fact, haggle over the cost of the dress, but she did not have the time.

"Ten," the shopkeeper countered.

"Eight," Lysandra replied. They finally settled on nine,

but before Lysandra could open her pouch to pay the waiting woman, Selia threw her arms around Lysandra's neck.

"Oh, thank you," she said, her voice choked with all the unshed tears of a childhood filled with want and neglect. "I've never had anything so beautiful. I never thought I would."

It had been a long time since Lysandra had felt such an embrace; ten years, since the day her mother had been killed. She had forgotten the great joy such a simple act could give.

She quickly returned the gesture, then, after giving Selia's back a gentle pat, released her and focused her attention quickly on the money pouch in her hands, trying to hide the tears that had suddenly filled her eyes. By the time the shop keeper brought the slippers out, Lysandra had the coins counted and in hand, pleased that she still had a few left as she slipped her little pouch back into hiding.

The slippers fit well enough, and their soft hide would soon conform to Selia's feet exactly. Lysandra concluded her business with the shopkeeper while Selia changed from her new finery back into the gown and apron she had worn earlier. Then, packages filling Selia's hands and Lysandra once more holding firmly on to Cloud-Dancer, the women left the shop.

Lysandra had one more gift for Selia, one that she had brought with her this time from her cottage. When she had sold her mother's jewelry, she had kept the hair combs her mother had so often worn. She intended to give them to Selia on the day she at last stood before the Barons and the kingdom. True, Selia's hair was still short from its shorn time beneath the novitiate's veil—but it was growing rapidly, and the combs would shine in its rich brown.

But aside from one quick remembrance of them, Lysandra's thoughts were elsewhere as they walked back toward the little stone parish that was their city home. This time, though she kept her fingers buried again in Cloud-Dancer's fur, she did not borrow his vision. Instead, she let Selia chatter, mostly about her new dress and the others she had seen, hardly listening while she used her *Sight* to sweep across the people they passed.

She was still trying to find the man she had *seen* leaving the apothecary's shop. There was no sign of him—yet the feeling of Darkness remained. Perhaps, she thought briefly, she should go into the apothecary's shop herself and see what her *Sight* might reveal. Had Renan and not Selia been with her, she would have been tempted to do so, but she would take no chances with Selia's safety.

How much longer Renan would be with the Archbishop every day, she did not know; she hoped it would not be for too much longer. He needed to know what she had *seen,* and together they needed to decide what next to do. Aurya might be safely guarded by the Cryf, but the Darkness, it seemed, was still very present.

Thomas entered Elon's home in Ballinrigh by a side door in the servants' quarters, and after a brief greeting to the two maids he encountered, hurried to his master's bedroom. From there, he let himself through the hidden panel in the wall, into the secret study that held Elon's arcane hoard.

He carefully withdrew the pouch he had hidden beneath his shirt and put it next to three others on the little table by Elon's chair. Then he dipped a waiting pen into the inkwell and marked off the pouch's contents from the list Elon had made. There were only two more items to be collected—but that was proving difficult. With the city gates closed and the little traffic allowed through closely examined, Elon's sources within Ballinrigh had little of a more "exotic" nature to offer . . . nor had they any idea when—or if—his requests could be fulfilled.

Thomas had already volunteered once to ride to Kilgarriff, or beyond. Elon, however, preferred to keep him close. He said it was to monitor Thomas's progress with his studies, insisting they might well prove more important than any other factor in securing his succession to the Archbishop's Office.

Accepting Elon's word, Thomas applied himself all the more tenaciously to such books and exercises as Elon gave him. Lately, however, he had begun to wonder at the new fervor that seemed to have infected his master. Elon had always been restless, filled with an excitable energy when pursuing the avenues of true interest. Now that energy had turned to an obsession that sometimes made Thomas think he saw a glimmer of madness shining in Elon's dark eyes. He did not want to think what it might mean should Elon *not* be named as the next to wear the triple mitre.

Having delivered his package, Thomas was about to leave when he noticed a new book lying open in his habitual place. That meant Elon had left him something new to study. Beside it was a note. Thomas suppressed a sigh as he crossed over to it. To a large degree, he enjoyed the things he was learning and the feeling of awakening power they brought.

But, as with everything else about Elon lately, Thomas was being given no time to savor or master each new accomplishment. Every new exercise or step followed hard upon the last and, as interesting as he found his new studies, Thomas missed his time off. When Elon was gone and his regular duties were done, Thomas was used to a number of hours when his time was his own. Unlike Elon, *he* had never taken vows of celibacy, and over the years, both here and in Ummera, there were women with whom he had developed an . . . understanding.

Lately, he felt like he was living the life of a priest or monk—all duties and studies and no time for the pleasures of life. Today, he decided, he was tired of it; today, he would not see the note before him or open the book, and he would return into the city on an errand of his own.

I deserve it, he assured himself, trying to assuage the spurt of guilt he felt. *Even a bond-slave gets time off duty. I'll study later tonight, tomorrow . . . one afternoon won't harm anything. . . .*

With that thought, he let himself back out of the hidden room, back into Elon's private chamber. Then, after checking to be certain none of the vestments or other clothing needed his attention, he headed once more for the little side door of the servants' entrance. His step had a buoyancy it had been missing of late, and his thoughts of the afternoon's possible pleasures brought a smile to his usually controlled and taciturn face.

Chapter Eighteen

Elon, Bishop-ordinary of Kilgarriff, was one of the supplicants hoping for a bit of the Archbishop's time. Although his position within the Church did earn him some deference, today it was not enough, and he found himself waiting amid the too-little-washed masses.

Finally, he heard his name being spoken. He stood, straightened, and smoothed his already perfect attire, and stepped toward the door—only to be reminded by the rather officious monk who was the Archbishop's head secretary that His Eminence was a very busy man and so to keep his visit brief.

Elon could barely contain his fury as he swept past the man and into the Archbishop's study, swiftly crossing the room to genuflect and kiss the Archbishop's ring.

"How may I help you, Elon?" the Archbishop asked him

as he stood, waving toward the chairs on the other side of the desk.

"I've come to ask you the same thing, Your Eminence," Elon replied as he took note of how tired the old man looked, and of the weariness in his voice. "I know you bear a heavy burden. This Office is demanding enough, and with no King—" Elon spread his hands, letting his expression finish for him.

"The College of Bishops will soon reconvene," he then continued. "But while we wait for my brother bishops to arrive, I long to be of service. Please allow me to help ease things for you by taking some portion of the work from your shoulders. There are, I fear, things for which I must make recompense. Though they were mistakes made in all innocence, they were nonetheless mistakes—of faith in the faithless—and I beg of you to let me make such reparation as I can."

It was a good speech, one Elon had rehearsed several times, and he said it with his best, most humble and beguiling voice. Now to see if the old man would respond as Elon desired.

The Archbishop shifted a little on his chair, obviously weighing Elon's words. His face had softened a little; a good sign, Elon thought. He waiting silently, keeping his expression open, humble, even eager—again, as he had rehearsed.

"It is true," the Archbishop began at last, "that the long hours sometimes weigh heavily on my old bones. However, mine are not duties that are easily delegated to anyone, even to another bishop. Many, perhaps even most at this time, result from the fact that the throne still stands empty. The duties of acting as Regent must, by our laws, rest on my shoulders alone. So, although I thank you for your great offer and obvious concern, there is little you can do."

Elon was horrified by this response—and for a single instant, a sense of terror touched him as cries of "*he knows*" swept through his mind. But they were quickly subdued. The Archbishop might *suspect* his collusion with Giraldus and

Aurya, but he could *know* nothing. Suspicions could be allayed—with the correct amount of work and attention.

"Is there nothing, Your Eminence? No matter how humble a task, I am your willing servant. Truly, I feel I must do something. My duty to the Church and to this kingdom demands no less—and"—here Elon hung his head briefly, then raised it again and looked straight at the Archbishop—"I must do something to redeem myself in *your* eyes."

Elon saw a little of the guarded light fade from the old man's expression, and he silently congratulated himself on his excellent performance. Truly, the best lie was the half-spoken truth, properly delivered.

Again, the Archbishop shifted himself in his chair; again, Elon could see him weigh what he had heard and his personal inclination toward forgiveness, against the caution his instincts were urging. Which would win? Elon wondered. For the first time, he had no certain answer—and he found that carried its own type of excitement. He was gambling with stakes that those poor fools who risked only money or possessions would never understand. He was risking the only thing worth the game.

Everything.

"My son—Elon," the Archbishop began, and in those few words Elon realized that this hand was lost. "I believe you are sincere, and I do thank you—but for today, there is nothing you can do. The duties before me are, as I have said, ones I alone may discharge. Perhaps tomorrow that will change. If you truly feel uneasy of heart, then pray, my son, and seek your reparation there. You might also write your contrition to your brother bishops of Rathreagh and Camlough. Seek by this act to help mend the division that ended the College's last meeting and restore accord among us again. When you have done this, return to me, and perhaps then there will be further work you might do for the good of the Church."

Elon stood and again came around to kiss the Archbishop's ring, recognizing the dismissal he was receiving. While still on one knee, he raised his eyes to the old man's face.

"Thank you for your counsel, Your Eminence," he said. "I shall pray, and write—and then return, hoping that you have found other ways I may serve."

The Archbishop signed a cross in the air above him, blessing Elon's departure. The Bishop of Kilgarriff rose, bowed once, then left the room. But as he again stepped out into the waiting room with its clustered, needing humanity, he knew himself unwilling to accept defeat.

Today's hand went to the enemies of his chosen future— all and whomever they might be—but the *game* was far from over. Far, far from over. Even without Aurya, he had resources he had only begun to tap. Until the day someone else wore the triple-crowned mitre, he would not accept defeat.

Perhaps not even then. Accidents, illness, all sorts of dangers made up this mortal life . . . and as Elon walked back through the Residence, his thoughts were filled with their myriad possibilities. Commoners, Kings—even Archbishops —were just as mortal, just as vulnerable to one with the right skills. Those he did not possess he would find.

No, the game was definitely not over.

The carriage ride back through the city was one he passed with the shutters drawn. Elon did not care about the beauty of the summer day or about the sights of the people of Ballinrigh. He wanted to review his options in peace. By the time he returned to his house, and depending on what Thomas had been able to collect in the city today, there might well be some new tasks for his manservant to perform.

Elon would write to Rathreagh and Camlough, as the Archbishop had suggested. *Ordered,* he thought, *is the real word. A test. Well, I'll play the part better than he thinks. When I'm through, he'll believe me . . . they'll* all *believe me.*

Then, when trust has come and their guard is down once again, that's when I'll strike . . . and none of them will ever have the strength to doubt me again. Especially him, *the old man. His will, like his position, will soon be mine.*

The carriage rolled to a stop before his front steps, and a footman quickly came around to open the door. Elon did not spare the man a glance as he emerged from the carriage and swept into the house. He half expected Thomas to be waiting, silently conveying his success or failure with his expression. Frowning, Elon waved the servants away and headed for his chamber to change from the silk cassock he had worn to the Archbishop's, into a daily one of blended wool and linen. Surely, he thought, Thomas would be waiting there for him—or in the little room beyond, concentrating on the new exercises he had been left.

Not finding Thomas in his chamber, Elon forgot about changing and quickly let himself into his secret study. The greeting on his lips died, and his frown deepened when he saw that Thomas was nowhere within. The frown threatened to turn to fury when he saw the new packet on the table, the new scratch mark on the list—and that the book he had left for Thomas was untouched.

What's the man playing at? he wondered hotly. *He knows what's at stake. Why isn't he here working?*

But until Thomas returned there could be no answer. Elon picked up the list and examined it. Two more items . . . and he was out of contacts within this city. He was going to have to send to Kilgarriff. How, he wondered, and who? With the city gates closed and all traffic being well checked, his choices were limited. As Bishop of Kilgarriff, he could certainly send a messenger . . . but returning, carrying the items he needed, that were known to be poisons—that could be a problem.

A Rider, he thought suddenly. Although he had previously decided against them and he still disliked the idea of trusting so delicate a matter to a stranger, the Riders traveled the kingdom with impunity, even in such unsettled times as these—and a Rider would be less likely to be closely searched. Yes, it would have to be a Rider.

Elon quickly put down the list, sat and drew another piece of paper toward him. Then jotting out a note requesting that a Rider be sent to his house to undertake a service, Elon stood and went in search of a servant to deliver the message to Rider Headquarters. He would have to move quickly. Evening was fast approaching, and although on this day after the Summer Solstice true darkness was still a long ways off, the city bells would ring in under two hours to announce the night's closing of the gates. After that, not even a Rider would be allowed to leave until morning. Elon wanted *his* Rider to be on the road by then.

He sent the first servant he saw, then went into his study to write out the message the Rider would carry. It had to be worded very carefully; the supplier to whom he was writing must understand but, he hoped, no one else would. If the letter was intercepted and traced back to him, there must be nothing in it to further jeopardize his standing with the Archbishop.

After that letter was done, he would carry out the Archbishop's directive and write to the bishops of Rathreagh and Camlough, though he loathed both them and the idea. They, too, must be worded with the utmost care—he *knew* their contents would be reported. By the time they were done, Thomas should be back . . . with, Elon assumed, good explanation for his absence.

Whatever had taken him away, he had best return ready to work, Elon thought. From this time forth, there would be little rest for either of them.

In the port city of Owenasse, Baron Hueil of Rathreagh received his messenger in the town Hall, where he had set up his household. Not wanting to take any chances with the timing of his rendezvous, he had arrived in Owenasse three days ago—two days before the Summer Solstice. And he had come with a large retinue, far larger than the city wardens had prepared to house.

Of course, they could not know that Hueil was so lavishly attended to impress the King of Corbenica, not themselves. In fact, the only thing that the city wardens of Owenasse knew as cart after horse and row upon row of Hueil's household passed within the gates, was panic.

Hueil, however, soon set their minds to what ease he could. He, his daughter Margharite, their immediate advisors and servants, would all make their stay in the town Hall, Owenasse's largest building. There would, of course, be a certain number of their elite guards on duty at all times—but the rest of the retinue would camp outside the city walls.

The town Hall was quickly converted into such comfort and beauty as could be found. While it in no way rivaled his palace in Rathreagh's capital city, it was more than adequate for their short stay. Hueil took up residence with outward calm and good humor, delighting the inhabitants of the city by his availability.

For the next two days, Hueil spent most of his time sitting on a cushioned chair, on a quickly erected dais, in the Hall's great room while he listened to complaints, fears, petitions— and sometimes the praise—of the people. Then, on the longest day of the year, he officiated at the Summer Solstice Festival put on for his benefit, one that even included a fireworks display.

This was something about which the city was justly proud; it was one of the best exhibitions Hueil had ever seen. It had been planned and perfected ever since Hueil had announced Owenasse as his Summer Solstice destination this year. In the northernmost Province of the kingdom, where the hand of winter was ofttimes felt most keenly, the Solstice

Festival, with its promise of warmth to come, was celebrated with more exuberance than anywhere else in Aghamore.

All through today, the day after the Solstice, Hueil had been awaiting the message he now received: the square sails of the Corbenican fleet had been spotted, sailing out of the north. They were still distant, little more than dark specks upon the water, and it was impossible to tell their number. But with the experience of those who had lived and worked for generations upon the sea, the watchmen who manned Owenasse's tall towers knew it was large enough to be an invasion force—and that they would reach the harbor in the hour before sundown.

The messenger boy who now knelt before Hueil could not hide the fear this news caused him—any more than his surprise when the Baron smiled.

"At last," Hueil said as he stood.

Immediately the room grew still and silent. All the whispered conversations, the peripheral discussions of decisions passed or of petitions still to be heard, completely ceased. Everyone waited on their Baron's explanation of this unexpected event.

"People of Owenasse, of Rathreagh," he began loudly, his voice booming through the superb acoustics of the hall, "*my* people—I tell you there is nothing to fear. The Corbenicans do not come to destroy this time. They come, rather, in friendship and at Our invitation."

This caused an eruption of sound. The people of Rathreagh had, in centuries past, been the first ever to feel the strike of the Corbenicans' weapons and fury. The fear, and the hatred, of their northern neighbors ran deep.

Hueil held up his hands for silence. "My people," he said again, "the situation in our kingdom is a grave and a fearful one. Aghamore is near to civil war, with the strength of the Provinces so well matched that such a war could go on for months, even years. It could even completely destroy

Aghamore. At the very least, there will be deprivation, even starvation this winter, as whole fields of crops are trampled under the feet of marching armies or die from neglect, as those who tend them are forced to be soldiers not farmers.

"I have, therefore, called upon the aid of the Corbenicans to help *save* this kingdom, which is as dear to me as my own life's blood. With their help at my side, I will have the strength to end this war quickly, before it can overrun the entire kingdom."

"An' set yerself up as High King," came a voice.

"Yes," Hueil replied unrepentantly. "I will be High King—and will show this kingdom what it is like to have a King again who *cares* about their welfare."

This last statement raised a little cheer. It was not as great a one as Hueil would have wished—but it was a start, as the people here remembered the reign of the late King Anri.

"'Ow do we know the Corbenicans'll leave?" another voice, far in the back, shouted. "Once they're 'ere, well, they might like it."

"You have my word—and King Wirral's."

"An' 'oo can trust a Corbenican?" again a shout; the same voice.   '

"Trust *me*," Hueil returned, just as loudly. "Before the next day is out, you shall bear witness to the sacred and binding nature of our agreement with King Wirral. Have I ever let you down, my people? Trust me yet a while longer, and together we will bring both peace to this kingdom and the blood of Rathreagh's great House to the throne of Aghamore—and it will begin a new and great age for us all."

This time the cheer was much more to Hueil's liking. He knew how to win—and keep—the hearts of his people. He had meant every promise he had just made, and they knew it.

His only problem now was Margharite. He had not yet informed her of the part she had in this venture. Like her mother, Margharite had a temper he preferred to experience only when he must.

But she *was* his daughter, born to the role and duties of a Ruling House. Her future, including marriage, was preordained by that birth to be a matter of state not inclination. He had every faith that once the first fiery storm had passed, she would obey.

She was waiting for him. Messengers had also brought her the news of the sighted ships—and of Hueil's words to the people. Unlike so many of them, she guessed immediately what he had meant by a "sacred and binding" agreement.

Her.

When Hueil entered the rooms that had been rearranged to be her temporary chambers, he found her alone. She had even sent Braedwyn—who had been her nurse and was now her maid and companion—away. Such words as she would say to her father she wanted no one to overhear.

Margharite saw Hueil's nervousness grow when he noticed she was there alone—and she would have laughed had the situation been less grave. Hueil, Head of the Ninth Ruling House, Baron of Rathreagh and leader of men, was nervous facing a mere woman, his daughter, alone in her bedchamber. It was absurd; it was ludicrous; whether he admitted it or not, it was a sure sign of his guilt over what he was about to do.

The whole situation was ludicrous, she thought as she stood, hands on hips, staring at him and waiting for him to break the silence between them. Behind her, the windows were opened to catch the afternoon breeze. A gust of it lifted strands of her deep red hair, to blow it across her face.

"You look just like your mother, standing like that," Hueil said in a soft and fatherly voice. "I don't think I realized how much like her you've become until just now."

"And what would she have thought about what you're doing?" Margharite countered. She refused to let him defuse her anger. "If you think she would have approved, we remember a far different person."

"No doubt we do. You remember the mother. I remember the woman—who was both my wife and my partner as Ruler of the Province. And yes, she would have seen the necessity of this union, understood and approved.

"But come, Margharite—you're not a child to be cosseted any longer. Let us talk calmly, as adults. You'll see that what I'm doing is for the best."

"Best for whom?" Margharite asked. "For you, certainly. But for me or for Aghamore?"

"Yes—for both." Hueil was losing his temper, but Margharite did not care. She was not going to be bargained off so he could wear the crown. She opened her mouth to reply, but before she could speak he held up a hand to stop her.

"You've always known that as my daughter, the day would come when you would be called upon to marry for duty and the sake of the Province. You have also always known that *I* would make the choice of where that duty lies. Now, as both your father and your Baron, I command your obedience."

Margharite stared at him for a moment, appalled by the knowledge he had every legal right to such a demand. "And upon which marriage bed will you sacrifice my honor . . . *Father*?" she asked at last. "I hear King Wirral is without a wife at the moment. Am I to be broodmare to age or youth?"

"Margharite," Hueil said, softening his voice until it was almost pleading. He took a step toward her, one hand extended to take hers.

She turned her back on him.

"You will marry Wirral's son," Hueil then said, his voice harsh once more. "The betrothal *will* take place—tomorrow afternoon. You can either accept it, being glad I chose the son and *not* the father. You might, if you allow yourself, even like young Arnallt. Or you can let your own temper and your stubbornness keep you from even trying to find happiness. That is your choice—your *only* choice in this matter."

Margharite still did not turn back around. She waited until she heard Hueil's heavy footsteps and the closing of the door.

You're wrong, Father, she thought now that he was gone. *It is* not *my only choice—as you will soon learn.*

Margharite knew she would never marry any Corbenican, not even a Prince. As a child, the tales she had heard about Corbenica and its ways had been terrifying. She might have dismissed them as just tales, as stories to make children behave as were so many other morality tales and fables. But studies through the years had shown them to be true.

It was bad enough, to Margharite's mind, that by Corbenican law a woman was nothing more than chattel, a broodmare who could not own property, leave the house unescorted by a male, or speak in public—and she could be flogged for breaking these laws. But such attitudes were nothing compared to the tales of Corbenican cruelty in battle or toward prisoners.

The history books that Margharite had been made to read during her school years had been filled with Corbenican cruelty—attempted invasion of Aghamore, as well as other lands that had felt Corbenican wrath. They did not only kill their enemies, they beheaded them and tied their heads like trophies to their horses. In their camps, they used those disembodied heads like a child's toy, kicking it around for amusement, with no regard for the life it had once been.

When they took prisoners, they had devised terrible, torturous means for death. Some they impaled on long stakes, then left them to die slow, agonizing deaths. Others they hung, spread-eagled, and while still alive they cut them open and disemboweled them.

The captives that had become their slaves were better treated only in that they were left alive. Women were raped into submission—through shock if no other way—and flogged if they showed any spirit. Men were castrated with a hot knife, so that it cauterized while it cut.

And these were the . . . creatures . . . with whom her father had joined himself. Margharite was so appalled that for a moment she was sure her heart would quit beating. Then, suddenly, she drew a painful breath as the word nagging at the back of her thoughts finally took form.

Treason, she thought, trying out the word. *My father is a traitor.* Putting the word to the action somehow made it even more terrible, and she shivered with it. For the first time in the three years since her mother had died, Margharite was glad that she was not here. She knew her mother would never have approved, despite what her father had just said, and would have fought against this action—as Margharite herself intended to do.

How? She thought as she began to pace the room. *How can I get away . . . and where will I go?*

The door connecting this room with the next one opened, and Braedwyn poked her head around. "M'lady?" she said.

"Oh, Braedy," Margharite cried, reverting to the childhood name she had given her nurse.

The woman quickly entered the room and opened her arms. Margharite rushed into them, allowing herself to be enfolded in the comfort of Braedwyn's middle-aged softness.

"Hush now, poppet. Braedy's here," her nurse cooed, stroking her hair like the distressed child she felt. "Come tell me what's wrong, though I can guess like as not."

Margharite kept her head on her nurse's shoulder as they went and sat together on the bed. She then told Braedwyn everything that had passed between herself and her father.

"I have to get away, Braedy," she concluded. "I won't marry Arnallt. Even if he proves to be handsome and virtuous, or any of the things I believe his father is not—the things I *used* to believe my father was—I'll not betray this Province or this kingdom."

"Of course ye must," Braedwyn said. "Now, let me think a bit and perhaps an idea'll come."

They sat in silence for a few minutes, each running possibilities through her mind. The breeze through the window picked up. It blew in from the water, bringing the Corbenicans—and her fate, one way or the other—ever closer.

Chapter Nineteen

King Wirral of Corbenica stood at the tall prow of his ship as it led the way into the harbor of Owenasse. Behind him, his fleet—twenty ships in all, each carrying two hundred men—kept in as close a formation as their long oars would permit. The square, painted sails had been furled for the approach into the harbor, where their flat-bottomed ships would find easy anchorage at the long quays.

The quickly lowering sun struck the long rows of shields that hung suspended along the sides of the ships, sending shafts of brightness reflecting back into the water. These shields were far more than decoration. Like links of an iron chain, they armored the ship against attack. On days like today, their brightly polished and painted surfaces also bedazzled, even blinded the eyes of their foes. They, as much as battle-axes or battering rams, were weapons of war.

Everything about the Corbenican invasion force was focused on that single purpose. They were a people of war. Their songs and epics, their religion, their festivals and celebrations were all founded in the wars that had made them strong and given them the identity to which they clung with such ferocity.

And they had no respect for those who did not think the same way.

Wirral's alliance with Hueil of Rathreagh was grounded in the fact that the Baron was willing to do what he must to succeed. He wanted the crown of Aghamore; that was something Wirral could both respect and understand. It was a worthy aim for a warrior. What was more important to Wirral, the marriage of his second son, Arnallt, to Hueil's only child and therefore heir, would give him a prize long coveted by the Kings of Corbenica. Soon, one of Corbenican royal blood—*his* blood—would sit upon the throne of Aghamore.

Even if, by law, Arnallt was crowned only as Prince Consort—and Aghamorian law was something about which Wirral knew little and cared less—his *grandson* would be King in full right and power. Then would come a new day in both Corbenican and Aghamorian history. By their law, *his* law, it was the father who controlled the way a son was raised. Wirral had no doubt that Arnallt would make certain his sons learned the Corbenican beliefs and way of life. That being true, Corbenica would soon rule Aghamore, in fact if not in name.

Yes, it would be a new day indeed . . . and if the Aghamorian woman who would be his grandson's mother objected—Corbenican men knew how to control their women.

These thoughts played through Wirral's mind, as they often had during the sea journey to Aghamore. His scarred visage made his smile appear like the grimace of a death mask, like those worn by the dead before they were buried. These masks frightened away the demons who waited to steal a warrior's soul before it could take its final journey to the Hall of Many Feasts.

It was the goal of every warrior to spend eternity in that great Hall. There, those whose lives had honored Doenaar the Mighty, god of strength and war, would have eternity to fight and drink, to feast and celebrate their deeds.

The Hall of Many Feasts was only open to those who had honored the god with the blood of many enemies. And it was there that Wirral intended to spend his afterlife. Nor would he go unarmed—he would go from this world with a weapon in his hand and the cry of battle on his lips and in his heart.

Wirral intended to make certain of that, however he must. This God whom the Aghamorians worshiped, of whom he had learned from the representatives of this Church who had dared try to corrupt his land with that tale—and had met their deaths for doing so at his own hands—would not be allowed to soften either his son or grandson. The alliance with Hueil had, so far, made no mention of how any children would be raised. But Wirral knew his son, and he knew that Arnallt would not dishonor either him or Doenaar.

Hueil and his entourage were gathered on the banks at the head of the quay. Wirrul let his eyes sweep over the assembly, noting the fine clothing and jewels in which they had bedecked themselves. It was not warrior's clothing, but he would accept this display of wealth as an act to do him honor, a welcome rather than the affront it would have been from a Corbenican. From one of his own, to be greeted without a show of strength would have said he was considered too weak to be a threat.

But these were Aghamorians, not Corbenicans, he reminded himself, and they valued wealth above battle. At least no women were present; this was the business of men, and Wirral was glad to see that Hueil understood that, too. To have been greeted by women, even Hueil's daughter who was his heir, would have been an insult beyond what Wirral would bear.

He motioned to his son, who stood a few paces away, and Arnallt stepped quickly to his side. "Your kingdom awaits, my son," he said. "It is a sign of how Doenaar favors us, that both my sons shall rule."

"It is, Father," Arnallt agreed.

"There will be those in this land who will not like that a Corbenican sits on the throne. When she who will be your wife follows her father to the high status we shall win for him, many in this land will loudly protest."

"I care nothing for their objections," Arnallt replied, "only for their obedience. They will obey her—by their own laws—and she will obey *me*, by ours. Aghamore will be Corbenican, Father. In that you may trust. Doenaar has, by this alliance, decreed it."

"See that you do not waver in your resolve, my son," Wirral said. "Or in your obedience to the ways of Doenaar. The might of his arm is great, and what has been given can be taken away."

"I know my duty, father," Arnallt replied. "I shall not fail. Not you, not Doenaar, and not Corbenica."

Oars shipped, they were sliding up to the quay. Men scrambled over the sides, quickly slipping lines around pilings to secure the vessel in place. As its motion neared a standstill, Wirral and Arnallt jumped from the side onto the long wooden dock, then, each raising a weaponless right arm in peaceful greeting, they strode together toward where Hueil stood waiting.

"I have come at the time arranged," Wirral said, "prepared to do battle in your aid and for the future of our children. My son stands here, ready for the betrothal that shall unite our people into one."

Wirral watched as an uneasy expression darted across Hueil's face, and the Corbenican King's eyes narrowed.

What game, he wondered, was Hueil playing? Was it a lie that had brought him here? If so, then the men at his back would begin their slaughter of Aghamorians here—starting with Hueil.

"Your arrival is most timely, and we welcome you in friendship," Hueil began, his words doing nothing so far to allay Wirral's sudden doubts. "But the betrothal to seal our families' joining cannot yet take place."

"What?" Wirral roared. "What deceit is this?"

"No deceit," Hueil quickly countered. "My daughter—a woman and thus a weak creature—is overexcited and suffers a headache for it. The betrothal is but postponed so that she may rest this night and greet her future husband at dawn, unburdened by such pain as would otherwise rob her of the joy of this occasion. It is her wish to present an untroubled face to him always, and especially on this their first meeting."

Wirral considered these words. His first wife had sometimes suffered from such headaches—yet she had been a worthy mate, strong of both back and spirit, who had given him three sons and four daughters. He decided to accept Hueil's words. For now.

"At dawn, then," he said.

Hueil broke into a grin, the relief on his face obvious even in the quickly deepening dusk. "Come," he said to Wirral and Arnallt, "there is food and drink within the Hall. A feast of welcome, if not yet of betrothal—and here is my hand on it, to carry our new friendship through until dawn can finish the bond."

Wirral looked at the proffered right hand and for a few seconds considered not accepting it. But a handshake would mean nothing if there was treachery awaiting. So, forearm to forearm, he clasped the hand of peace with Hueil.

Before he went with his host toward the large town Hall, he turned to Arnallt. "Pass the word along to the other ships," he told his son, speaking quickly and quietly in their own tongue. "Have them wait one more night aboard, and have them anchor in the harbor but away from the docks—keeping good watch. If there is treachery here, I'll not have us caught unprepared. When all is done, come join me."

While Arnallt nodded and turned to do as Wirral ordered, the King of Corbenica turned a seemingly trusting face back to the Baron of Rathreagh.

"Lead on, then," he said, "and let us raise a cup as the brothers we are soon to be."

Keeping his death-mask grin firmly on his face, Wirral walked with Hueil up from the quay. The people of Owenasse, who had gathered in silence to watch the exchange, fell back at their approach, parting to create a wide path before them. Children, feeling the thick tension in the air, hid behind their mothers' skirts; one child—*a girl,* Wirral thought with disdain—screamed when he glanced her way.

In Corbenica, such scars as puckered his left cheek, gained in honorable battle, were worn and looked on with pride. The child's scream was to him yet further proof of Aghamorian weakness.

They reached the Hall, where tables had been set out in the great room, covered with platters of food and pitchers of ale. Musicians were already playing sprightly tunes when they entered. It was a festive air that did nothing to reassure Wirral of the Baron's sincerity.

Many a lie has been hidden in fair-seeming words, he thought, *and perfidy in celebration. If that be your game, you'll find I'm not so easily fooled. Nor is my son.*

But, just as lies could hide in words, they could also be masked by smiles, and Wirral let his match his host's as Hueil himself poured them ale and made the first toast. Then, with a wave of his hand, the Baron summoned a great paper brought forth.

Wirral looked down at the scratches of ink upon the page. Among his people, such documents meant nothing. Paper was easily burned and words destroyed or ignored. It was a man's *deeds* that counted, and the strength of his arm. A man, a warrior, kept faith because of his *honor,* not because of marks on paper. *More Aghamorian weakness,* he thought.

"King Wirral," the Baron began, "I have had the terms of our alliance set down so that all within both our lands may see the esteem in which we hold the union of our Houses. This document will hold a place of honor here in Rathreagh and a copy shall go with me to Ballinrigh, so that when I am King, all of Aghamore can see the great foundation upon which our union is built. Then they will understand that a new day has dawned for both our kingdoms.

"I had planned to present this treaty and its copies in the celebration after the betrothal. But though illness prevents Margharite from joining us tonight, I hoped we might still conclude the business of men in this matter, and give further cause to this celebration."

Wirral stared again at the paper set on the table before him. Some fine hand had bordered it with designs of wondrous beauty. Stylized wildlife mixed with equally elaborate scenes of nature, all entrapped by intricate lines that flowed into knotwork. It bedazzled the eye until one could not see where tree or bird and twisting knots separated. The vivid colors were like liquid jewels painted on paper, highlighted with brightest gold and silver leaf.

It was truly a masterpiece—*that* Wirral would not deny—but he would not sign it until every word on it had been read to him, and he had given his approval. Again his thoughts whispered of the lies that could be hidden within beauty.

"I am unfamiliar with the writing of your people," he told Hueil, not bothering to keep the edge of menace from his voice.

"Then I shall read it to you, and happily," Hueil replied expansively, trying to hide the burst of unease Wirral had seen flash through his eyes, behind a loud and jubilant voice.

But Wirral shook his head. "My son reads," he said, "and shall soon join us. He shall examine your paper for me. Only then will I put down my mark."

"Fine, fine," Hueil replied. "He shall tell you I am a man of my word and find only that which we have already agreed. But let us be merry while we wait. This night marks a new beginning for our people. Let us therefore drink to the bright future ahead."

Arnallt entered the Hall as Hueil was refilling their cups. Wirral quickly motioned him over, momentarily ignoring Hueil's toast. Then, as Arnallt set to work, the King of Corbenica raised his cup to meet the Baron's.

"To the future," he reiterated Hueil's words—wondering if they truly meant the same thing.

Soon he would know . . . and then either alliance or vengeance would greet the dawn.

In her room, Margharite heard the festivities below and did not wonder what words were being said. The men were, she was certain, drinking toasts to the marriage she was determined would never take place.

Traitor; that word, a word that only a day ago she would with her life have denied could ever apply to one of her blood, now was her father's undeniable title. *Traitor;* it whispered itself in her ear, her breath, the beat of her heart.

Traitor.

Now she would not accept it as her own. Never. Born of the Ruling House of Rathreagh, bred and raised to duty, she would run, even die now, rather than obey. Her higher duty was to Aghamore—and her obedience was something her father had forfeited by his traitorous act.

Braedwyn entered her chamber softly, coming through the same connecting door she had used earlier. This time she was not alone. Glynna, Margharite's dear friend, was with her.

Glynna rushed forward and embraced Margharite. "I've

heard—Braedy told me what your father wants you to do," she said with a sympathetic shudder. Then she brightened. "But you don't have to worry any more—I have a *plan*."

The word, and the way Glynna said it, brought a welcome smile to Margharite's lips. Over the years Glynna had produced dozens of plans—some as simple as how to skip their lessons or get out of some onerous task, and some so elaborate that they sounded like a farce performed by a group of players to entertain the court.

But now was not the time. The situation Margharite faced was deadly serious, and she had to think of how to get away.

She glanced at Braedy. "'Tis all right, poppet," the nurse said. "The girl's plan just might work for ye—and I've no thought better."

Margharite searched first Braedwyn's face, then Glynna's. They were both so eager that Margharite sighed, then gave a very slight smile at her friends.

"All right," she said, "what do I do?"

"Stand here," Glynna said, pointing to a place by her side. Once Margharite was there, Braedy stared at them intently, and Margharite began to understand what they had in mind.

She and Glynna were often teased by their families for being so much alike. But there were differences. Glynna's hair was red like Margharite's, but it was a darker shade. She was also more buxom that Margharite, and an inch or so shorter.

Could these differences be hidden long enough for Margharite to get away? And if she did, then what? Where should she go and how?

Margharite turned and looked at her friends again. They might offer her answers, but could she let them take this risk?

"Are you sure, Glynna?" Margharite asked her directly. "Father will be furious if he finds out. But . . . oh, Glynna, this is dangerous, to me now and possibly later, if you're caught. You don't have to do this."

"Yes," Glynna said firmly. "Of course I want to do this.

It's my idea, Margharite, and I believe that I've—that we've, for Braedy helped me—thought of everything this time."

The nurse came over and put a fond arm around Glynna's shoulders. "Go on, lass," she said, "tell her. Ye've a fine head on yer shoulders. I've always said so, and it just might be the savin' o' us all."

"It's true, Glynna," Margharite agreed. "And if this works, you may have just saved Aghamore, as well."

The girl blushed. "I don't know about that," she said, lowering her eyes, "but I'm glad to save *you* from such a terrible marriage. I wouldn't want to be forced to marry someone I didn't even know—and a Corbenican. I hope—"

She stopped, but Margharite understood. Glynna had already given her heart, and quite probably her father had no idea or would not approve. It did not surprise Margharite that Glynna should keep such a secret from her father, but it did surprise her that Glynna had not told *her*.

"I promise," Margharite told her, "that when this business is through, I'll do what I can to help you, too."

The smile Glynna gave her was brilliant, telling Margharite she had guessed correctly. And she would keep her promise, to the full extent of her power; from this day forward, Margharite intended to make certain that none of her ladies were ever married off against their will, be it by the authority of father, brother, Baron—or the King himself.

"Now, Glynna," she said, "tell me your plan. The night is passing far too swiftly, and we will have much to do. . . ."

It was a good plan, full of imagination and intelligence, and backed by a good knowledge of Rathreagh's history and laws. It was also practical in application. For much of it, Margharite would be already absent; the future of Rathreagh—and Aghamore—would be in Braedwyn's and Glynna's hands.

Margharite trusted that, trusted them, more than she now did her own father. Such a thought would have saddened her had she allowed herself to dwell upon it. Instead she threw herself into such preparations as could be made, while waiting for the sounds of the revelry below to die down.

But two hours later, the noise of music and laughter was still loud, perhaps even greater with the loudness of drink. Glynna had left Margharite's rooms to make arrangements, and had not returned to say that all was ready.

Margharite was ready, too. She had changed her fine clothes for an old and somewhat stained wool skirt of faded green and an equally nondescript blouse Braedwyn had filched somewhere among the servants. Her bright, flame-colored hair she had braided and bound beneath a green kerchief, hiding it as much as possible.

But her disguise did not end there. Using ashes from the fireplace, she darkened what hair could still be seen around her face, dulling its brilliant color to a more mousy shade. She also rubbed the wood ash into the skin of her face, neck, arms, and hands, making them appear both darker and covered in long-standing, unwashed filth, paying close attention to her hands and putting dirt around and under her fingernails. Using charcoal, she also darkened her eyebrows and lashes.

As a final touch, Braedwyn made a thick paste of the charcoal and painted a mole on Margharite's chin, adding the tiny ends of three of her own hairs. Then she turned Margharite toward the mirror. At the sight, her heart took a sudden soar of hope; the woman who looked back at her bore no resemblance to the easily recognizable daughter of the Baron.

When Glynna returned, Margharite had just finished replacing her soft kidskin slippers with stout but worn boots, easily visible beneath the barely ankle-length skirt. She then stood and looked at her fellow conspirators, turning slowly so that they could not only get the full effect, but see anything she might have missed.

"Gor . . ." Glynna let the commoners' expression escape in

her breath. "I'd have never guessed. But—one thing—" Taking a ribbon from her own hair, she folded Margharite's long braid back in on itself and tied it up, so that her hair looked far shorter and not so much of the color difference could be seen.

"There," she said, satisfied as she stepped back again. "I've just made a walk through the Hall," she then continued, "saying good night to my father. The feast continues, and from the look of them, they've no mind to end it soon. You'd best go now, while they're occupied, than chance waiting any longer for them to sleep."

Margharite nodded, grabbing the short wool cape— equally old and dirty as the skirt—from the foot of her bed. She grimaced a little at its smell of cooking fires, old food, and unwashed body, as she tied it around her shoulders. But, she reminded herself, such odors were one more thing to keep her from being recognized.

"Durkin will be waiting by the fountain in the square," Glynna continued, naming the boy to whom she had already given her heart—without her father's consent or knowledge. "He'll have two horses and some provisions. There wasn't time to gather much, but if you ride hard, it should only take you a few days to reach Ballinrigh."

"I *must* do this," Margharite said, "but Durkin need only give me the horse. There's no need for him to endanger himself. Nor you, Glynna. When the dawn comes and the betrothal is called for, if you decide it is too much, I'll not think less of you. Remember that. I'd not have this chance now, if not for your help already, and both my gratitude and esteem are without measure. Nothing more is called for."

Again Glynna blushed at Margharite's kind words. "Durkin wants to go with you," she told Margharite. "He hates the Corbenicans. They killed his grandfather—and he's eager to do what he can to stop them. Besides, he says he'll not let you or any woman make such a ride unprotected. He's very brave, and kind. He's a good man, even if he's not one of what my father would call 'good family.' His family is honest and decent . . . they're hardworking people who raised their son into a man to be proud of. To me, that's the only 'good family' that counts."

Glynna's voice had taken on a bit of an edge. Margharite suppressed a smile at her fervency, thinking that Glynna had no doubt had more than one argument with her father on the subject.

"And *your* father raised a brave and loyal daughter," she told her dear friend. "It seems to me like a fine match."

"Poppet," Braedwyn said softly, "ye'd best away whilst ye can. We'll see to the rest here."

Margharite drew a breath. "Yes," she said. She took Glynna's hands into her own, lightly, mindful of the dirt disguising her skin. "Thank you," she said, then leaned forward and kissed the girl's cheek.

Then Margharite went to Braedwyn. She wanted to embrace her nurse — for love, comfort, for reassurance — but again mindful of the ashes covering her, she restrained herself. Instead, she also kissed Braedwyn's cheeks, trying not to notice the worried tears in her nurse's eyes . . . nor let her own respond in kind.

"Be careful — both of you," she said. "Do not risk anything you don't have to, either with my father's anger or the Corbenicans'. I'll return as quickly as I can."

Margharite turned quickly away. If she did not go at once, she would not be able to control the too-close tears any longer.

Closing the door, she stood in the corridor, trying to remember the layout of the building and how she might get away, being seen by the fewest number of people. She must try to avoid them all — servants, cooks, anyone who might remember the passing of an out-of-place, unrecognized woman.

Margharite drew a deep breath, and moving carefully, she headed out of her hiding place in the shadows. As she walked, she silently prayed. She prayed in gratitude for such dear friends as Braedwyn and Glynna, asking for Divine protection to guard them during the days and trials ahead.

She also prayed for her own protection and guidance— now and on the road. The corridor ahead looked so very long, the distance to freedom felt immeasurably far, and the chances for danger in between were incalculable. Without the help for which she now prayed, Margharite was certain she would never make it.

Slowly, slowly, each passed. She reached the back stairs, the ones used by servants, that led down to the kitchen and other places her father would never go. Still hugging the shadowed wall, she descended, listening for any step coming her way and still praying she would hear none.

As she neared the kitchen, her heart was beating so hard that Margharite had to stop on the bottom step and waited until the pain of it had passed and she could breathe again. From where she was on the stairwell, she could hear both the servants in the kitchen and the celebration in the main Hall.

The noise there was just as Glynna had described—loud, jovial, and giving no indication of winding down. It made Margharite feel a little more confident. This plan might work after all.

Now, if she could make it to the side door used by the servants, she would be on her way.

But to reach that door, she had to pass by the kitchen. Once more she took a breath; if she did not move now, she would never have the courage to go.

The first few steps were fine. But before she could reach the door, and her freedom, one of the cooks noticed her and called out.

"You, girl," she yelled, "come 'ere."

Margharite lowered her head as she complied, keeping her face turned down and away from a clear view. She also slumped her shoulders and slightly dragged one foot.

"Aye, mum," she said, making her voice raspy, so that it, too, would be less recognizable.

The cook turned and gave Margharite a stare, looking her up and down. The girl held her breath a moment, waiting.

"Ye dunna work in my kitchen," the cook said, "nor in the scullery—no' in that state o' filth. I'll no' have filthy hands nor clothes in 'ere."

"Nay, mum," Margharite said. All these years of listening to Braedwyn were about to save everything. "'Twas m' day t' scrub th' hearths and such. 'Tis long an' dirty work."

"Oh aye—ye be just leavin' then?"

"Aye, mum. I come 'ere afore dawn and me Ma'll be keepin' supper 'til I be 'ome."

The cook glared at her for a moment, then waved her beefy arm toward the door. "Off w' ye, then," she said, "an' see ye be on time in th' morn. Things'll be startin' right early, w' all th' fancy doin's what be comin'. An be ye clean to-morrow, girl."

"Aye, mum—that I'll be. Good night, an' thank ye, mum."

Margharite added a bit of a curtsy, keeping it clumsy and unpolished. Then she turned away.

It was only by strong control that she walked rather than fled toward her escape. And it was only after she was out the door and a few steps away, that Margharite allowed herself to straighten up and breathe easily again.

Before going any farther, she looked up toward where her chamber window would be. She saw the two figures watching. Margharite raised a hand in final farewell, then turned and dashed into the shadows. She was on her way.

Margharite hurried the few blocks toward the town square. Durkin was waiting, as Glynna said he would be, dressing in clothing as old and dirty as her own. He looked up at her approach, but did not recognize her until she said his name.

"My . . . m'lady," he said, jumping to his feet. "Glynna said ye'd be disguised, but I'd have never known ye."

"Let us hope everyone else sees the same thing," Margharite replied in a whisper. "And I'm not m'lady or Margharite—until we're far from here." She thought for a moment. "What is your mother's name?"

"Mairie, m'—" He stopped himself.

"Fine . . . a good name. And your father's?"

"Rholland."

"Then for now I am Mairie, and you are Rholland—should anyone ask. Ready?"

"Aye, m'—Mairie. The horses are already outside the gate. I thought it best that we're not seen riding 'em. Dressed as we are, some'un might think we'd stole 'em."

Clever, Margharite thought with a nod. *As bright as Glynna. I think they'll make a good pair.*

She stepped up to Durkin and slipped her arm through his. "Best play the part," she answered his startled expression.

Arm in arm, they began to hurry through the streets. At first they saw no one. Then, as they neared the city gates, they saw two of the town guards making their rounds. Margharite quickly pulled Durkin into a half-shadowed area, not quite hiding but neither in plain view.

She put arms around his neck and moved closer. "We're servants out for a few stolen moments," she said into his ear. "Careful now—they're coming this way."

The sound of heavy-booted steps clicked on the pavement. "Hey—you there," a gruff voice called. "What are ye doin' about this time o' night?"

Durkin stepped back a bit from Margharite so that some of the moonlight fell on her. "We're, uh, we're just trying for a bit o' privacy," Durkin said, turning his speech into the broad sounds of the lower workers, as befitted their clothing. "'Tis hard enou' t' get with the mistress always a'watching, like."

The guards exchanged glances, and one gave Durkin a knowing smile. "'Oo are ye, then, and 'oo yer mistress?"

"I be Rholland, Rholland DeSur—and this be Mairie, m'intended, if we can get permission. I works for ol' Bobson at the docks, and Mairie 'ere is scullery for 'is missus."

"Well, Rholland, these streets be'ent no private parlor, see, so ye'd best be off a'fore the midnight bell and curfew."

"We will—but just a bit more time, eh? The mistress don't let us see much o' each other—and we's 'oping to be wed as soon as we can get permission from hisself."

The guard chuckled and nudged his companion. "Right," he said, "but th' bell'll ring within th'hour. If yer caught out, we'll have t' fine yer household—and that'll not get ye in good graces. 'Specially with the Baron 'ere—and that new lot 'e's with, though why 'e'd truck with *them*, I'd not like to say. But the way of 'em what's tasted power be strange, and that's truth. But with 'im 'ere, we daren't let the law go unminded."

"We'll not miss th' bell," Durkin assured him.

With a nod, the guards finally moved off, and Margharite blew out a slow breath. "Brilliant," she said in a whisper. "You were brilliant."

"Oh, they be'ent bad lads," Durkin replied with equal softness. "They're just doin' their jobs, as with most folks here—and it'll be a good hour before they make it back this way. By then, they'll be glad to see that Rholland and Mairie are gone. We'll give 'em a few more minutes to be far enough away not to hear the gatehouse door, then we'd best hurry. Are ye sure ye'll not be missed afore then? One alarm, and we're lost."

"I doubt they'll look for me until morning," Margharite said. "For the moment, my father and his new friends are all too busy congratulating themselves for their well-planned treachery to bother about me."

Durkin nodded, then took a step back and leaned out of the shadow. "The guards have just turned a corner. Are ye ready?"

Margharite gave a nod. Durkin took her hand firmly in his own, and, staying as much as possible still within the shadows, they again began their escape.

It felt like hours and miles of quick dashes from one building's shadow to the next, but Margharite knew it was only a few minutes. Then the gatehouse was up ahead—across an open, shadowless road. The moon was shining brightly on the area, only a few nights from full; there could be no more hiding, only speed.

Durkin checked around one more time. "It's now," he said.

With that, they sprinted across the open and to the door of the gatehouse, where Durkin withdrew a key from the pocket of the stained work apron he wore. Margharite could only wonder how he came to possess it—but she did not ask. Not yet. If they were caught, she did not want to know the names of those who had helped them. What she did not know, she could not be forced to betray.

Again, the time seemed slowed as she waited for the sound of the lock clicking open. Finally, she heard it, loud within the silence of the night; finally, the door moved, and Durkin all but pushed her inside, following just as quickly.

He locked the door behind them, then led the way through the gatehouse to the little door leading outside the walls. The same key opened this one, too. Once they were out, he again locked everything.

"That'll baffle 'em a bit and make 'em look for ye within the city a bit longer," he said. "The horses are still a ways off. Do ye think ye can run some more?"

"I can," Margharite assured him. "I may be a Baron's daughter, but I've legs, same as you—and to my father's disapproval, I *like* to run."

"Now's yer chance, then," Durkin said, and in the moonlight, Margharite could see him smiling.

The expression changed his rather average face into

something akin to handsome, and as they began to dash toward where their mounts were waiting, she again understood what Glynna saw in him. Once more she promised herself that if they eluded capture and made it to Ballinrigh with their warning, she would return and repay both Glynna and Durkin for their bravery by ensuring their marriage.

They reached the thicket where the horses were hidden. Mounting, Margharite knew there would be many people in Owenasse to whom both she and this kingdom would owe a debt. They had proved their loyalty by the clothes she now wore, by the key once more in Durkin's pocket, by the horses on which they sat . . . perhaps even the story he told the guards had been prearranged.

It pleased her to know that the people of Rathreagh had more loyalty than its Baron—and she would make certain the Archbishop knew it, she vowed as she and Durkin began their long ride toward the kingdom's capital.

Chapter Twenty

Lysandra tossed upon her bed, caught in a sleep of more trouble than rest. The night had begun peacefully enough, showing Renan the dress they had bought for Selia and hearing his news from the Residence. Then, while Selia was hanging the gown away, Lysandra told Renan about the Darkness she had felt from the apothecary's shop and the man she had *seen* leave it.

For now though, there was nothing they could do. Their first concern must be getting Selia on the throne. Only after that was accomplished could they turn their attention to expelling the Darkness from Aghamore's borders.

The triumph of Light over Darkness was the very reason for Selia's reign.

After dinner and an evening of soothing tea and conversation, Lysandra had been glad to slip beneath the warm covers of her bed and seek the comfort of slumber. With Cloud-Dancer curled next to her feet and the bed beneath her now almost as familiar to her body as the one in her own cottage, sleep had come easily.

But not now. It was as if the moonlight shining through her window carried messages her mind must hear.

Within her dream she saw a harbor city, also bathed in the soft glow of the moon. Like an eagle riding the thermals, Lysandra felt that she was hovering over that city, seeing it all, both land and water. But it shone not on a sleepy harbor; this one was filled with a forest made of the masts of a large anchored fleet.

Her *Sight* was suddenly drawn to the large town Hall. Just as suddenly, she was inside. Here she saw men drinking, feasting, and singing songs of battles and of the sea. Up at the High Table presided two men in earnest conversation. One had the scarred visage she recognized from her past vision of the Corbenican invasion. This, she knew, was their King.

Beside him sat Hueil, Baron of Rathreagh. Although Lysandra had never before seen him, she knew who he was in the same prophetic way she knew the Corbenican's identity, the same way she knew this was a true vision of treachery unfolding.

But she also knew that the Baron's actions were not those of his people. She could feel the tension within the place, and her vision was drawn to an upper room where three women were gathered. Lysandra *saw* one of them, disguised, escape through a side door and dash into the shadowed street. Her *Sight* followed the woman as she met up with a man and they began to run through the town, eventually reaching the gate and escaping into the night.

They found horses, mounted and rode, and again Lysandra *knew*. This was not a prophecy of what was to come, but a true *Far-Seeing* of what was now. And with this knowledge, Lysandra was filled with all the sense of fear and desperation the riders themselves were feeling.

They *must* reach Ballinrigh—she knew it as clearly as did they. What they did not know was the allies that here awaited. They would find the way already prepared.

Lysandra awoke in a blaze of Sight and certainty. She had to go to the Archbishop—now, not waiting for the dawn. Sliding quickly from her bed, she hastily changed out of her nightclothes. She then reached over and lightly shook Selia's shoulder.

"I must go to the Archbishop," she told the younger woman. "Stay here. I'll be back as soon as I can."

She was answered by a mumbled "all right," which told her Selia had at least half heard her. Then, with Cloud-Dancer as always beside her, Lysandra went to awaken Renan. She doubted that she would be allowed access to the Archbishop alone, especially at this time of night; even taking a carriage, it would be well past midnight before they knocked on the Residence door. But Renan already had the old man's ear and trust, and he was known at the Residence. Lysandra prayed that all the hours he was spending there would benefit them now.

Renan came quickly to Lysandra's call and dressed even more quickly at her words. Within minutes they were leaving the churchyard and walking toward the Residence, while they kept an eye open for a carriage to hail.

This time of night, they did not roll along the streets in search of fares. But when at last she sat back in the padded seat, Lysandra could not relax. The fear from her vision, which the young woman and her companion still felt as they made their escape, filled her with an urgency that pounded in every thought and filled every second with the whispered need to hurry.

She did not realize how much of her tension she was broadcasting until Renan took her hand. "It will be all right," he told her softly. "The Archbishop believes you already. He'll know this is true, too, and he'll know what to do about it."

Lysandra nodded, hoping it would be as easy as Renan obviously believed. Even if it was, even if the Archbishop did listen, believe, and act upon her words, the Corbenicans were still in Aghamore. With the threat of civil war growing closer every day, on whom could the Archbishop call to drive off this new danger?

To this, Lysandra found no answer . . . and the question added to her distress as the carriage rolled on through the night.

Wilham Tybourne was at the Riders Headquarters when the summons came. He had only been back in Ballinrigh two days, and he had slept less than an hour. But the summons asked for him by name—and it was from the Archbishop himself. Such a call could not be put off, regardless of his lack of sleep or the amount of ale he had consumed earlier.

Wilham dressed as quickly as he could, claimed and saddled his favorite mount from the stables, and within the hour was being shown into the private study of the Primus of Aghamore. The whole situation was unusual, surprising—especially when he found Father Renan already there.

It did explain why he was named in the summons, Wilham thought as he looked around at the faces in the room when he entered. Most surprising of all was the woman, standing a little ways off from the others, her hand entwined deeply into the fur of a large silver-and-white wolf. Wilham's initial reaction was to turn and run, but neither Father Renan nor the Archbishop seemed concerned about the animal's presence, so Wilham stood his ground and waited.

It was Father Renan who welcomed Wilham and Father Renan who explained the reason for requesting Wilham's presence. As the young Rider listened, he could not keep the surprise off his face. Had it been anyone else telling the tale, he would have thought himself on the receiving end of a hoax, perhaps being played on him by his fellow Riders— not an unknown occurrence.

But this *was* Father Renan—and it was the Archbishop himself—and so, despite the odd nature of the mission, Wilham would undertake it seriously. He was to ride toward Rathreagh, by the route this woman would tell him, and meet two people hurrying here. It would be a young man and woman, dressing in old and dirty clothing but riding good horses that were far above the station their clothes proclaimed. Wilham was to find them and bring them here, to the Archbishop, with all possible speed and safety.

These people's identity, especially the woman's, was something he was told he did not need to know—for now. Times in Aghamore being what they were, Wilham accepted that without comment. He was far too amazed at what followed to wonder about what he was now being told.

The woman and her wolf stepped to Father Renan's side. Wilham, who had seen wild wolves many times in his travels, had to force himself not to start edging toward the door when the beast neared. Then he saw its eyes.

They were blue—the same blue, he suddenly realized, as the eyes of the woman who stood beside him. They fixed on Wilham, and the Rider could see that still buried deep within them was the wildness of his kind, but that wildness had been overlaid by something else. It was not domesticity, as one might see in a family pet; it was devotion, pure and unwavering, to the woman under whose touch he sat so quietly. With her present, all was well—but Wilham knew he would not want to be the person who threatened this woman's safety.

Then the woman spoke to Father Renan. He listened intently, then made some marks on a map. Her words were too soft for Wilham to hear, so instead he watched her, trying to give a name to the odd way she held herself, staring straight ahead instead of truly looking at anyone or anything in the room.

She's blind, he thought suddenly. Then, just as quickly, he realized that she must see in visions and prophecy. He found himself wanting to kneel, that he should be in the presence of and witness to such a miraculous moment. *It's no wonder the wolf sits so quietly by her side,* he thought. *Even the Archbishop and Father Renan listen to her. She must have God's hand upon her.*

When Wilham looked away, he found that the Archbishop was not watching and listening to Lysandra, not this time. He was watching Wilham. While the blind woman—Lysandra, he remembered the name he had heard when he entered—and Father Renan continued to work on a map for him, the old man motioned him over.

"You look troubled, my son," the Archbishop said softly. "You need not be."

"Not troubled exactly, Your Eminence, but—" Wilham did not know how to go on.

The old man nodded, understanding the unspoken. "But it is not easy to be in the presence of one whose gifts exceed our understanding—perhaps even our belief," he said. "Nevertheless, her gifts are very real, and they are nothing to be feared. I believe that she feared them more than any of us ever can. But they exist and have been granted to us through her, so that we may better serve the Truth. Do you understand, my son?"

"Not completely, Your Eminence," Wilham answered

truthfully. "But I know that Father Renan would never serve anything else. If he—and you—trust her, then so will I."

"Good lad. Remember that faith is the hope of things not seen, not understood. Understanding will come later—and if not in this life, then in the life to come."

Wilham bowed his head, accepting the Archbishop's words and the comfort they offered. "I won't let you down, Your Eminence," he said, "not any of you. I will find the ones you need and bring them here. I promise that nothing will stop me."

"Father Renan said you have a trustworthy heart. I see he was correct."

The Archbishop put a hand on Wilham's head and spoke a blessing. The touch and the prayer made Wilham feel filled with light and a new strength; all vestiges of his late night were vanquished by the sudden awed excitement he felt for the mission ahead. He was ready.

So was his map. Father Renan called to him and, with a nod that was a bow to the Archbishop, the young man sprang to his feet.

"Here," Renan said, "this is the route Lysandra sees them taking. I'm sorry that for now we cannot tell you more. But it is imperative that no one else gets their hands on the woman."

"I understand," Wilham replied, looking at the map now in his hands. "You can trust me."

"I know," Renan replied, putting a hand on Wilham's shoulder. "I would not have called for you otherwise—and I can think of no one else I'd have in your place."

Father Renan's words made Wilham stand a little taller. He smiled at the priest who, over the last two years, had become his friend. Then, as he left, Wilham had an idea that might well ensure the safety of his charges, once he found them. With that in mind, he headed back toward Rider Headquarters for one brief stop before he was truly on his way.

* * *

Dawn was just breaking when a knock came on the door of what had been Margharite's chambers. Inside, Braedwyn was just putting the finishing touches on the veil that, they hoped, would adequately disguise Glynna for a while longer. Every moment gave Margharite and Durkin an added chance of success.

Under the heavy veil, Glynna was sweating—and only partly from the many layers of cloth and lace. Most of what she was feeling came from the fear of what would happen if she were discovered. She and Braedwyn had a story all worked out; they would claim the ancient Aghamorian custom of betrothal by proxy, that the couple did not physically meet or touch until they were properly wed.

Although this practice not been used for centuries, it was in accordance with Aghamorian law. Their best hope was that Glynna's—and Margharite's—duplicity would not be discovered until after the betrothal vows had been said. Even then, everything rested on Hueil's reaction. As Baron, and especially as Margharite's father, he had the right to demand her presence; it was the *parents* of the bride or groom who arranged the betrothal by proxy, as they arranged the betrothal and marriage itself.

What the women hoped was that rather than chance a scene before the King and warriors of Corbenica, Hueil would accept the betrothal as if he had planned it this way—and deal with his errant daughter in private. By the time the ceremony and celebration were concluded, Margharite would be a few hours closer to Ballinrigh, a few more miles away from capture.

Their best hope, though neither woman dared breathe it aloud, was that Hueil would be too embarrassed—or too fearful of Corbenican wrath—to admit to any discovered deceit. If he did not tell them otherwise, Wirral and Arnallt would never know it was not Margharite who stood beside them until it was time to meet the bride for the wedding . . . after Hueil had won the crown. And, if Margharite was successful now, it was a wedding that would never take place.

It was a great many "ifs" on which to hang their hopes, but it was the only hope they had.

The knock came again, followed by Hueil's voice calling for his daughter.

"Are ye ready, lass?" Braedwyn whispered.

Glynna took a deep breath. "Ready—and may God and his angels grant us aid."

"Amen," Braedwyn said, softly but fervently.

Glynna could hardly see through the multiple layers of lace as Braedwyn went to the door and opened it. Baron Hueil stood framed in the archway, dressed in his finest of fur-edged robes and bedecked with jewels. Behind him, an honor guard waited.

Hueil strode into the room, hardly glancing at Braedwyn except to mutter his displeasure at being kept waiting. Glynna held her breath while he walked around her twice, looking her up and down as if judging the gown and veil she had chosen.

The veil, three layers of cream-colored lace, was topped by a chaplet of rosebuds. When Hueil made a move to raise the lace, Braedwyn came rushing over to stop him.

"Nay, m'lord," she said quickly. "The roses are but freshly picked and pinned. There wasna' time t' weave 'em proper. If ye move th' veil, they'll come undone, sure as sunrise."

It was for this very reason the chaplet had been chosen, and Braedwyn's words stopped Hueil's hand . . . but not his frown.

"The veil's too thick," he told the women. "She can't be seen. What are you playing at, Margharite? King Wirral and his son will think we've something to hide."

Glynna said nothing. This, too, had been rehearsed, and she had to rely on Braedwyn's words—hoping that Hueil would not think there was time to argue with them.

"She'll not speak t' ye," Braedwyn told him. "She vowed she'd speak only at t' betrothal and only when she must. But neither before nor after, t' ye or t' th' others. She be terrible angry wi' ye, m'lord."

"Humph," Hueil grunted. "She can be as silent as she wishes now—as long as she's obedient when the time comes. Do you hear me, daughter, or has this veil stopped your ears along with your tongue?"

Glynna bowed her head slightly, as if to acquiesce. Again, Hueil grunted.

"Come, then," he ordered, "and let's get this over with. Wirral and Arnallt are already below. They won't agree to enter the church and say the betrothal before the altar. But they have agreed to the porch of the church as a midway point between their faith and ours."

Glynna was relieved, as she followed Hueil from the room, to know she would not have to speak her lies before the altar and the Presence within the tabernacle. It did not matter that betrothal by proxy was a lawful act or that the ruse was being played for the salvation of the kingdom. Nor did it matter that she was acting in obedience to her mistress and that she was certain of absolution when the time came. The words she spoke, even on Margharite's behalf, would be lies—her lies and Margharite's—and she would just as soon not be within a church to say them.

King Wirral and Prince Arnallt were waiting for them, as Hueil had said. Although both had made the effort to dress regally, no amount of finery could soften Wirral's terrible visage. Glynna felt herself start to tremble beneath his scrutiny. She found herself pitying the women truly marrying into his family.

Prince Arnallt, however, was not so fearsome. He was as tall as his father, but lacked both his father's barrel chest and his battle scars. Arnallt's hair was a darker blond and his eyes a richer, warmer blue. But most of all, they lacked the expression of cruelty and distrust that tainted King Wirral's gaze, as if he looked on everything—whether family or stranger, homeland or distant shore—as an enemy to be conquered . . . or killed.

Arnallt on his own, Glynna thought, might be worthy of her mistress's attention, even her favor. But Arnallt, King Wirral's son . . . *never*.

As Hueil had done, Wirral now walked around Glynna, looking her over as if judging an animal for barter. "Why is she so covered?" he demanded. "Is she deformed? If she's to be the mother of my grandsons, she must have no imperfections."

"My daughter is known for her beauty," Hueil answered haughtily. "You may ask anyone in the kingdom. But it is our custom that, as a virgin, she remain veiled until properly wed. Only then, when the laws of marriage protect her honor and virtue, may her husband gaze upon her beauty . . . and then he may see *all* of it," Hueil added with a knowing grin to soften his words.

That satisfied Wirral, and, seeing that, Glynna breathed a little easier. The words Hueil had given the Corbenicans were true, though they were rarely practiced any longer. They came from the same time as the betrothal by proxy. Hueil had played his unwitting part well. The women had counted on his pride and his desire to prove himself in the eyes of his new allies and—*Thanks be to God,* Glynna thought—he had lived up to their expectations.

Keeping her head demurely bowed, Glynna laid the hand now bedecked with Margharite's rings on Hueil's proffered arm. They walked two steps ahead of the groom and his father out of the town Hall, across the square, and to the porch of the church for the betrothal to take place.

Margharite and Durkin rode through the night, stopping only when the tiring of their horses demanded it. Scant moments for rest, water, and food, other times at a walk or easy canter instead of a gallop; they could afford to give neither themselves nor their horses more than these.

When dawn arrived, Margharite said a silent prayer—for Glynna, for Braedwyn, for them all and the protection of their undertaking. She could see, too, that the swiftly growing light brought the fear out in Durkin's expression. But, like hers, she knew that his fear was not for either of them.

"We must believe all will be well," she told him, understanding. "She is very brave to have done this—and so are you. My father, for all his misguided judgment of late, is not a cruel man. If he punishes anyone when this is over, it will be me, not Glynna. Have faith, Durkin—and, please God, we'll see this through long before *any* punishment can be rendered."

"Aye, m'lady," Durkin said. Yet Margharite saw that the fear he felt for the woman he loved did not fade from his eyes. Nor would it, she knew, until they were together again.

Glynna is very lucky, she thought, a touch wistfully. *I hope that someday I will have someone who loves me so very much.*

Chapter Twenty-one

While Margharite and Durkin rode toward Ballinrigh and Wilham rode toward Rathreagh in the hope of finding them, while Glynna kept her voice to a whisper as she murmured betrothal vows she did not mean, Aurya, Giraldus, and Maelik were just rising for their day's work in the Realm of the Cryf. For many days now they had been secreting away bits of food—crusty bread, dried fish, and fruit—so that they would have enough to attempt their escape. By silent agreement, they all knew the time had come.

It would be tonight.

Despite the thought of their impending freedom, Aurya could hardly drag herself from bed. For the last week or more, she had been fighting a growing lethargy that seemed to fill every moment of her day. The smell of food had begun to sicken her, especially in the mornings. At first she had attributed the lack of energy to the depression she felt over her captivity, her sickness from the loss of her magic. Now, however, she feared it was something else, something far more mundane.

But, in the hope she was mistaken, she had said nothing to Giraldus. Nor would she—not until she must. She would let nothing interfere with their plans for tonight.

Tonight, she thought as she followed their ever-present guards toward her daily workstation. *Tonight you will all feel the first taste of vengeance . . . and it will be but the first. Once we are free and Giraldus is King, we will return. We will come with an army—and we will not stop until every one of you is dead.*

This thought seemed to banish the morning's feelings of illness and imbue Aurya with a sense of strength she had not felt in far too long. Her fingers, now toughened by weeks of this work, were quick and nimble as they began separating the plant fibers that were turned to so many uses by the Cryf.

The city of Ballinrigh awoke to a sight that chilled the hearts of its citizenry. Now, even those who had grumbled the loudest were glad that the Archbishop had recalled Urlar's small Standing Army and closed the city gates.

Sometime in the hours near dawn, the armies of the

Provinces had begun to arrive. Their camps dotted the level plain from which the central Province drew its name, and the sounds of men and animals in the thousands could be heard all through the city, drowning out the more ordinary and peaceful sounds to which the people were accustomed.

Despite whatever hope anyone might have held, Ballinrigh was now under siege. Civil war for the throne of Aghamore had begun.

The Archbishop knew that for the moment they played a waiting game. There was little more he could do than was being done. Wilham had left the city shortly after midnight. If he stopped to change horses at each station along his route, as was usual on rides that demanded speed, he could be halfway to Rathreagh by now. Father Renan was, at the Archbishop's behest, busily at work trying to find something, anything, in the historical texts to help them put Selia on the throne.

The bishops were beginning to arrive for the reconvening of the College, to discuss the succession once again—and not even the armies now camped outside the city gates dared to stop them. So far, however, only four of them—including Elon—were in Ballinrigh. The Archbishop was not, therefore, honor-bound to begin the meetings he no longer believed were needed. In his mind, the question of the succession was settled; he only had to convince the rest of the kingdom.

And there was Elon. What to do, what to think about this particular bishop who was still a thorn in the Archbishop's side. Every day he was back here at the Residence, offering his services and all but begging to be of use. He said all the right words, did all the right things—and yet, something in the Archbishop's heart whispered not to trust him.

But the feeling was there, and he could no longer deny it. In his continued contact with Renan, Lysandra, and Selia, it was as if a veil, dropped over his eyes by the years of complacency and routine, was being lifted. He felt as if he saw and discerned things more clearly than he had in decades— perhaps than ever before.

This feeling, so clear in some areas, did not help him find the way to prove Selia's ascendancy to the throne. For that revelation, all the Archbishop could do was rely on Renan's eyes and insight, keep busy with the many other affairs of the kingdom, pray . . . and wait.

Colm ApBeirne, Archbishop and Primus of the Church in Aghamore, was discovering how very much he hated to wait.

Elon, too, was playing something of a waiting game. He could no longer doubt the change of attitude he had perceived in the Archbishop; he was no longer the favored successor for the triple-crowned mitre.

Until the Rider he had sent to Kilgarriff returned with the final two elements Elon needed, the bishop of Kilgarriff had to rely upon the other weapons in his arsenal—intelligence, determination, cunning, and prevarication. Luckily for him, they were talents he possessed in abundance.

The darkest area of uncertainty was still Aurya and Giraldus. Where were they? Elon could think of no explanation short of their deaths that could account for their continued and prolonged absence. But surely, after all this time, the death of the Baron of Kilgarriff would have been discovered.

Yet, his mind kept asking, if they were not dead, then where *were* they?

And where was the child they had gone to find? With the armies of the Provinces now camped outside the city, these questions took on an even greater importance. Because of Thomas, Elon had a window, albeit a still sporadic and cloudy one, into the plans and happenings on the Urlar plain. He knew, as he doubted did the Archbishop or anyone else within the city walls, who was working in alliance and who was battling in their own cause. He also knew that opening challenges had been issued and answered. By the time the sun rose to its zenith in the summer sky, the clash of swords and the sounds of battle would bring their unique thunder crashing through the clear day.

Thomas was, in fact, the only bright spot in Elon's world right now, a world that had become troubled by the deepening darkness of growing doubts and dashed hopes. Plans, so clearly and carefully laid a few weeks ago, lay in ashes from which he was attempting to raise his own phoenix. The wings of that phoenix were, for now, made of Thomas's still-burgeoning powers—and Elon's own control over them.

His household had barely risen. He still had at least an hour before he was expected to ring for a servant, appear to lead the household in Morning Prayer—a duty he found more and more onerous—and then breakfast before truly beginning his day. But both he and Thomas had been awake for quite some time, in Elon's secret study. Thomas sat, focusing on the flame of a lamp while Elon stood behind him, hands on his shoulders, using his voice to guide Thomas's current efforts.

They had found that a larger flame than a candlewick gave Thomas a clearer picture. This morning, not wanting to take the time to build a fire, they were trying the lamp. So far, it was working better than Elon had hoped.

"The first battle will be soon," Thomas spoke in the slightly monotone voice of the entranced. "The horses are being readied. Men are strapping on swords. Archers are stringing their bows, counting arrows. Camlough has sent out the first challenge and is awaiting reply."

Camlough, Elon thought. *But where is Rathreagh?* Their bishops so often moved in tandem that it was hard for him to believe the Barons would not do the same.

He posed the question to Thomas. His servant was silent for several minutes, as if struggling with this change of focus.

"Baron Hueil is angry," he said at last. "He has discovered deceit among his own. But he must hide it. He must pretend all is as he planned. This makes him more angry."

"What deceit?" Elon asked. "Where is he?"

"In Rathreagh," Thomas answered, "in a city with a great harbor. It is filled with ships. There is an army with him, but they are not all his men, and he is afraid of them. That is why he must pretend. He must not anger them before they begin their march toward Ballinrigh."

"Whose army is it?" Elon asked eagerly, possibilities swirling through his mind.

But Thomas shook his head. "I see only that they come with blood on their minds. Their goal is destruction, far more than the Baron knows."

Thomas was tiring; Elon heard it in his voice, saw it in the way he held his head. Soon it would be time to let him rest.

"Only a few more minutes, Thomas," he said. "You have done very well, and your powers are growing. Now I want you to look toward Kilgarriff. Can you see what is happening there? Where is the Rider we sent and what is Lord Iain doing?"

Again the pause as Thomas changed the direction of his vision. "The Rider is on the move," he said slowly. "But not toward here. He has nothing to bring you yet." Once more the pause, then, "Lord Iain is doing . . . nothing. Sleeping. His army is sleeping. Kilgarriff is peaceful."

Thomas's voice was growing softer, slower, as if each word was a challenge. This was the most Elon had ever called upon him to do. It was proof of how well the exercises were working; not only had Thomas been able to maintain this trance for far longer than Elon expected, but the focus of his vision was becoming clearer and more easily directed.

"One final try, Thomas, and then you may rest," Elon told him. "Where is Lady Aurya? Try, Thomas—try to find her now."

The room grew silent. Beneath his hands, Elon could feel Thomas's shoulders tense with his effort to obey. Elon waited, hoping, almost praying . . . almost.

Still the silence continued. Through the connections beneath his fingers, Elon could feel Thomas's strength waning ever further. Much more, and Thomas would be of no use for hours, perhaps days. Elon knew that, entranced and obedient as he was, his servant would keep trying until the last reserves in his body and mind were used up. Perhaps, even, to the point of death.

While Elon might use others in such a reckless way, Thomas was too valuable. "It's all right, Thomas," he said. "You may stop the search now."

"I'm sorry, Your Grace," he said. "I find nowhere in Aghamore that harbors the Lady Aurya. There is only emptiness that I cannot fill."

"Rest now, Thomas," Elon replied. "Look no more. I want you to close your eyes, blocking the sight of the flame. Close your eyes and take a deep breath."

Elon waited while Thomas obeyed. He felt the tension slowly releasing from the shoulders beneath his hands.

"Very good, Thomas," he said. "Now you will sleep for one hour. It will be a deep sleep of rest and peace. When you awaken, you will feel strong once more. All right, Thomas, sleep now."

Elon heard the change in Thomas's breathing, signaling the man's sudden and complete slumber. All the muscles in his shoulders had gone limp, and his head slumped forward a little toward his chest. Elon lifted his hands, breaking the contact between them. He wished someone could give him the same sleep of complete peace he had just given Thomas.

Instead, his servant's last words kept repeating themselves in Elon's mind. *"There is only emptiness,"* he had said. Not death—emptiness.

What did it mean?

* * *

Hueil of Rathreagh was furious—and trying to hide his fury as he sat at the betrothal banquet next to his daughter's imposter. He knew it, though Wirral and Arnallt did not.

Hueil was doing his best to keep it that way.

The betrothal ceremony had gone well and quickly, with the couple standing on the porch of the town's largest church and the rest of the company, including their fathers, on the steps below them. Much of the city population had turned out to fill the town square and watch.

The intended bride, covered still with her layers of lace and crowned with the chaplet of early white roses, had spoken her words softly, as was not unexpected from a maid. Unexpected, though, was the way she had prefaced each vow by saying, "on the authority of Hueil, Baron of Rathreagh, Head of the Ninth House of Aghamore . . ."

King Wirral and Prince Arnallt, unfamiliar with the traditions of this kingdom, had not questioned such odd phrasing —assuming, Hueil thought, it was a sign of the girl's obedience to her father's will, something right and proper in the Corbenican mind. But Hueil knew these were no ordinary vows, nor was Margharite given to mindless obedience.

When the vows were over, rings exchanged as symbols of intent, the erstwhile bride excused herself from the following festivities by pleading a continuance of the headache that had kept her to her bed last night. Hueil had seen Wirral and Arnallt settled in the seats of honor at the high table, where a grand breakfast was waiting, then also excused himself to check on his daughter.

He entered the chamber without knocking, in time to see Braedwyn removing the last layer of lace from . . .

Hueil closed the door quickly and crossed the room, glaring. Both women met his expression with looks of fear. *As well they should,* he thought furiously.

"Who are you, girl?" he asked through clenched teeth. He

kept his voice low, but it was all the more dreadful for its lack of volume.

" 'Tis Glynna, m'lord."

Hueil should have known; who else would dare? "What game are you playing, you and Braedwyn? Where is my daughter?"

"I don't know, m'lord," Glynna answered, looking Hueil in the eye. He could see she told the truth—or at least some of it.

He turned from her to the nurse. "Braedwyn," he ordered, "I see your hand in this. Tell me where Margharite is."

"Not so, m'lord," Braedwyn told him. " 'Twas the lass's doin' and right enough, too. She fled during the night rather than pledge herself t' wed where her heart denied. All we've done this mornin' has been for yer lordship's sake—and for the safety of our people from them dogs wi' what ye'd join us. 'Struth, we could think of naught else t' save us, nor ye."

They were ready words—and Hueil did not believe her. But he knew that nothing short of torture would force anything more from Braedwyn that she did not want to say—and for Margharite's sake, perhaps not even then. Hueil had no choice but to try and salvage what he could from this situation.

"You—Glynna," he said. "You'll continue your role a while longer. I'll not take the risk of Wirral's rage here in Owenasse. I need him too much for what's ahead. So, you'll put some of that lace back on, and you'll come downstairs with me, where you'll continue your part as my obedient daughter. God help you both if anything goes wrong. I swear I'll disavow all knowledge of this and let Wirral deal with you for your lies, if he finds them out."

By the horror that washed across their faces, he was pleased to see that they took his threat seriously. Quickly, Braedwyn put the first layer of lace over Glynna's head. Through it, hints of long red hair could be seen, close enough in color for everyone to recognize as Margharite's. When Braedwyn reached for the second layer, he stopped her.

"That's enough," he said. "Now pin those blasted flowers so it'll not come off and be quick. I've left the Corbenicans too long already."

Hueil tapped his foot with impatience as, with shaking fingers now, Braedwyn carried out his instructions. Once the chaplet of roses was firmly enough in place, he grabbed Glynna by the wrist and pulled her with him from the room.

"You will be modest, obedient—and as silent as possible," Hueil said firmly, again speaking softly through clenched teeth, which this time were part of a set but forced smile. "You will do and say *nothing* to arouse suspicion. Your father will be informed of your actions later. I'll let him deal with you, and *I'll* deal with Margharite—when I find her."

King Wirral did not stand, but Prince Arnallt came to meet them as Hueil brought Glynna down the stairs.

"Here we are, Prince Arnallt," Hueil said in a great voice, filled with an exuberance he did not feel. "My daughter has been persuaded to join us again. Perhaps the good food and better company can chase her headache away, eh? I've often said that joy is a far better medicine that all the possets in a healer's cupboard."

"I agree, m'lord Baron," Arnallt said solemnly, his eyes searching through the lace for any glimpse of the woman before him, whom he thought was to be his wife.

"Let us be formal no longer," Hueil said, still speaking expansively to hide his nerves as he watched Arnallt's close scrutiny of Glynna. Hueil silently gave thanks that Braedwyn, for whatever part she had played in his daughter's disappearance, had shown the good sense to choose someone with near enough hair color.

"You are to be a son of my House," he continued, putting

Glynna's hand into Arnallt's, "and, God willing, father to my grandchildren. Let us speak as family as well as allies now."

The young man merely gave Hueil a brief nod, his attention fixed all the more on the woman whose hand he now held. Hueil stepped away quickly and went to sit next to King Wirral, as Arnallt led his betrothed to the central seats.

"They'll make a fine couple," Hueil said as he sat down. But Wirral glared at him.

"I like not that your daughter remains so covered, even from the eyes of the one who shall be her husband. From anyone else, I would think it an insult. But, as you did suggest, I asked all those I chanced upon—servants, guards, the people of the town—of your daughter's looks. Each one swore of her beauty—and they spoke of her hair, saying it shone like rubies in the sun. This, I can see, even through the veil she wears. I will, therefore, believe you. Today. But if I find it is not so, or if, with these headaches such as she claims, she proves unable to breed, our alliance will be dissolved—as would any based on falsehoods. Be warned. I dislike lies and will avenge any that I discover."

Hueil took a quick sip of the sweet spiced wine before him to cover the nervous tic he felt developing beneath his left eye. Tales of Corbenican vengeance were legendary and fearsome.

Swallowing half the goblet in two large gulps, he gave a well-practiced smile to Wirral. "There is no need for such words between us," he said. "My daughter will breed, and give us many grandchildren to seal the partnership of our lands. Had her mother not died of sickness, she would have given me many more heirs—of that I'm certain. My own mother bore nine sons and three daughters. Margharite comes from good breeding stock—and a headache such as this one comes but rarely to her. A result of traveling and so much excitement, no doubt."

Wirral again seemed satisfied by Hueil's words, and the

Baron of Rathreagh breathed a little easier. But in his mind, he rained down several curses on the head of his stubborn, self-willed, and disobedient daughter. Once this required banquet was over, he would put Glynna's own father in charge of the search for Margharite. If she could not be found . . .

No, Hueil would not think on that, not today. If need be, some plan would be devised—but *after* he had won the crown. Once he was High King, there would be nowhere in Aghamore that Margharite could hide from him—and no lawful justification for her disobedience.

Looking past Wirral, he saw Arnallt whisper something to Glynna, then raise a handful of her loose-flowing hair to his lips. That brought a true smile to Hueil; at least one aspect of this farce was going well.

He turned again to Corbenica's King. "While our children speak of softer matters, let us speak of the battles to come, eh?" he said. "The day is marching on and we must soon with it. Are your men ready?'

Wirral nodded. "I have already given the order for them to finish unloading the ships. By the time we have concluded our meal, they shall be waiting."

"Then let us break our fast quickly," Hueil said. He signaled to the ready servants to begin bringing their platters forward. Before the sun had risen to noon, he would finally be on the road to Ballinrigh   and to the throne of Aghamore.

Chapter Twenty-two

Lysandra had felt uneasy all day. It interfered with everything she tried, everything she did. She had trouble concentrating when Selia asked for help with her studies. Food had no taste—no tea or herbal infusion either calmed or satisfied her. Not even gardening brought her any satisfaction today.

At first, she thought it was nothing more than the way she was missing Renan. From the time they had met until recently, they had spent nearly every day together. She had come to rely upon his presence—his thoughts, his voice, the way his mind worked, and how his laughter filled the empty spaces in her heart.

But now he was so busy at the Archbishop's Residence that she rarely saw him. He was there in the morning to say Mass for his parishioners, and he came home each night for dinner. After that, they had little time for conversation before Renan fell into the sleep of an exhausted mind—so that come the next day, he could do it all again.

The tedium of absence and separation was wearing on Lysandra. Yet, she reminded herself, this was only a foretaste of life to come. Soon, somehow, they would find the way to put Selia on the throne, and then they would all return to their lives of before . . . lives apart. Renan would resume his life as a parish priest, here in this little stone church where the people loved and relied on him—and, perhaps, as one of Selia's advisors.

And she would go back to the forest, to her cottage and her quiet, solitary life as a healer. The thought both attracted and repelled her. She loved her home, her life, the quiet beauty of her garden and the healing work she did. But now, that solitude would be changed to loneliness, forever empty of Renan's company.

She had survived loneliness before, she told herself, and come out the other side. She would do so again. The words sounded hollow even as she thought them, yet she clung to them as her only light in the darkness of her future.

Today, however, try as she might, she could not bring her thoughts to focus on anything else. It was not until evening brought Renan's return that she realized there was something more behind her feelings. Yes, she would still have to face and accept the loneliness she dreaded, but there was something else her mind was trying to tell her, something that was terribly, terribly wrong.

Renan noticed her quiet when they all gathered for their evening meal. "What is it, Lysandra?" he asked, gently laying a hand atop hers. His touch warmed her skin, warmed the icy feeling that gripped her heart.

"I wish I knew," she told him. "I have a feeling that something is about to happen, something far worse than what is already happening on the plain outside the city. War has begun, Renan. We've heard the sounds of it all day. But it is not the worst thing in the kingdom. I just wish I knew what it was."

"Your *Sight*, your *Far-seeing*, shows you nothing?"

Lysandra shook her head. "Nothing," she replied. "It's all dark, empty when I try. It is as if something I don't understand has placed an impenetrable veil over my visions."

"Aurya?" Renan asked. But again Lysandra shook her head.

"I thought of that," she said, "but I would know the *feel* of her magic. This is something else. Besides, she and Giraldus are with the Cryf. We're safe from them."

Renan patted her hand. They both fell silent, wrapped in their own thoughts. Now that he had mentioned it, Aurya's name hung in the air between them. She was with the Cryf, Lysandra's thoughts said again, safely guarded and away.

But, her thoughts continued, the Realm of the Cryf was the one place her *Sight* could not penetrate. Perhaps . . .

No, it could not be. It could not . . .

It was the sleep period for Aurya, Giraldus, and Maelik. All throughout the Realm, things had quieted. As was the usual pattern, their guards had changed from their daytime companions to the ones who would spend the night sitting quietly outside the two sleeping caves occupied by the Up-worlders. If all went tonight as every other night in the past weeks, in a few hours they would relax their vigilance and then, when they were sure the prisoners slept, begin to doze themselves. Or they might become involved in one of the games they played with a board and colored stones; Aurya had seen them sit for hours, hunched over the board, aware of little else.

It had not been that way in the beginning. When Aurya and the others were first here and the memory of the battle had been fresh, the watch under which they were kept, day and night, had been both fierce and unflinching. But days became weeks in which the pattern never varied and the prisoners made no trouble; vigilance slowly faded into routine.

Aurya had feigned sleep often enough to know the guards' pattern almost down to the minute. Ever since Giraldus had first mentioned the possibility of escape, she had found sleep to be of far less importance. What was more, with the changes taking place in her body, there were nights when not even the nesting material on their sleeping shelf was enough to make her comfortable. It was easy on those nights to stay awake and watch.

Tonight—in soft-spoken, cryptic words, they had agreed to make their move exactly five minutes after the guards brought out their board game or began to doze. The latter would make for a long wait, but if the guards were half-asleep, they would be all the more easily overcome.

Even so, Aurya was not sure she could wait the extra time. From the moment their plan was set, through the rest of the meal, every minute felt as if time had come to a stop and was refusing to move.

They finished eating, and Maelik went back to his cave; Aurya and Giraldus had gone to bed as usual. At first, it had been easy for them all to stay awake. But the minutes had felt like hours and the hours seemed like days as they waited . . .

. . . and waited . . .

She could tell by his breathing that Giraldus had fallen into a light doze by the time she saw the Cryf guards finally move from their station and the cave's opening.

So, tonight it's the game, she thought.

Soon she heard the rattle and click of stones as the game began. Then came quiet laughter punctuating the semiwhispered sentences, spoken in the odd language that was the Cryf's own. Tonight Aurya did not try to understand it. She merely listened to its cadence, its intensity, counting off the seconds and waiting for the moment when the time was right.

Finally, she gave Giraldus a nudge, and he came instantly awake. She saw his dark eyes reflecting the soft shimmer of the luminous stones that lit the front part of the cave. The expression in them was hard and determined, the look of a soldier prepared for battle.

It was a look she had rarely seen from her lover; his eyes were usually soft when they looked at her. But at this moment, the sight thrilled her. It excited her to think of his strength fighting on her behalf, for her freedom. She reached up, pulled his head to hers, and kissed him.

"Ready?" she whispered against his lips and felt him nod. It was time.

Giraldus slid softly from their bed, keeping low as he slowly made his way forward. Aurya followed a few seconds behind, gathering up the bundle of food they had secreted and the other that was their own clothing.

She saw Giraldus pick up one of the luminous stones. She saw his muscles tense, ready to spring—and she hoped that in the next cave Maelik was doing the same.

Giraldus stood, half ran—half jumped out of the cave. He was on the guards before they had time to do more than look up. Maelik sprang at almost the same instant. Aurya saw their arms rise and come down. She heard the dull thud and crack as stones met skulls—and not even the Cryf were strong enough to withstand the desperate strength in their prisoners' arms.

Blood spurted; bodies fell in a heap. It was over with a speed that Aurya would not have believed possible. For a silent second, she felt rooted to the ground.

Then Giraldus dropped his bloodstained stone. It hit the ground, the sound breaking the sense of unreality that had gripped Aurya. When he turned to motion to her, she was already on the move. Their guards might be dead, but they were not free yet.

Without a word, the three of them began to run, traveling along passages that had become familiar. Giraldus led the way to where the Cryf kept their boats stored. Even with the lateness of the hour and the regular habits of Cryf life, they moved as silently as possible, constantly aware of what would happen should they be caught.

It would be far worse than captivity this time. With their guards lying dead in their own blood, Aurya was certain that the Cryf would no longer be gentle keepers. She had seen them fight; she knew that they were well aware of how to use the tools they carried as weapons.

She, Giraldus, and Maelik had no weapons to carry, nothing but their own hands, whatever stones they might find . . . and their determination to get free. She did not even have her magic to help them.

She was free now, she thought as she ran, and she would remain free—even if it was the freedom of death.

Aurya kept expecting to hear a cry, an alarm of some kind, warning of their escape. But all continued silent. By the time they reached the boats, she actually dared to allow herself a breath of hope.

"Hope" . . . it was a word with which Aurya had not had much experience. Anger, certainly, determination, selfish focus on her own intentions—but never hope, pure and complete of itself. At first, she did not recognize it; when she did, she was not certain what to do with it.

While Giraldus and Maelik wrestled one of the boats free, Aurya searched for anything she could find that might serve them. She found two small knives, a three-pronged hook, and a barbed pike. Those, she gathered, not stopping to admire the beauty of the workmanship in the carved wooden handles of the pike and hook, or the gem-encrusted handles of the knives.

The knives went quickly into one of the bundles. The pike and hook, she handed to Maelik as he helped her join Giraldus in the boat. Then, almost suddenly, the men were using their oars to push them off, into the current, and they were on their way.

Free.

They did not just ride the current, content to travel at the speed of the river. From the first instant, Giraldus and Maelik put their full strength to the oars. They picked up speed with each stroke, going faster and faster until Aurya felt as if they were flying rather than riding the water. It was a heady feeling, almost as much as the thought of what awaited her.

Soon there would be open air . . . open sky . . . and *magic*.

The thought of her magic returning was enough for her to do anything, risk anything. She cared nothing for the dead Cryf they had left behind—or anyone else who might lie dead before all this was over. She cared only that soon she would feel the fire of magic flowing through her blood, her muscles, sinews, and bones, filling her very soul with power.

She would finally be whole again.

An hour passed, two, while the men kept paddling. Still there was no sound of alarm or pursuit. Only as Aurya began to believe they might indeed make it did she realize how much she had expected death to be her only path to freedom again.

Now her mind turned to the future—and to revenge. She *would* have it. Nothing would stop her now. First would be the ones who had left her here in this underground prison, especially that one who dared call herself the Font of Wisdom.

She'll find out just how un*wise she was to leave me alive,* Aurya thought, some of her old fire returning.

But Selia would be only the beginning. There were so many others, and they would all feel her wrath. Aurya began naming them in her mind:

There was the priest. He would go somehow; she would find a fitting way. Yes, he had magic, and she would have to be wary of the spell she used. But once her own powers returned, she knew she would find the way to strike him when and where he was the most vulnerable. *Perhaps,* she thought, *a spell of poison on the wine he consumes at Mass . . .*

In her mind's eye, she could see him drinking the wine and falling dead at the altar, right before his congregation. It was an image that Aurya enjoyed . . . but sacramental wine, once consecrated, had a power all its own and to overcome that was something Aurya was not certain she knew how to do.

Yet . . . but she would find the way . . . *somehow . . .*

Then there were the blind healer and her wolf. *The wolf*

first, Aurya thought, *so the healer knows it and suffers. But how? Shall I summon the fire that took Kizzie?*

She could imagine the wolf howling in agony as arcane fire burned through fur, flesh, and finally bone, until he was completely consumed. She imagined Lysandra trying to save the animal, unable to get near it because of the flames.

Or, Aurya now thought, *perhaps the flames won't stop her and she'll be consumed by them, too.*

Above all, there were the Cryf. When her magic had ensured Giraldus the crown and subdued the kingdom to *her* will, then she would return. Armies would destroy the Realm and its inhabitants . . . but Fiddig and Talog would be hers. Magic would not work against them, that much she now knew. But a sword would pierce their flesh as easily as it killed a human—and this time there would be no healer to save them . . .

The thought brought something akin to a smile to her face, a dark and twisted smile that had nothing to do with joy. It had nothing to do with anything but hate.

In the last two months, this hate had become so much a part of her that the last fragments of other emotions had begun to fray within her. Now, as she spent the silent hours in the boat, watching the men paddle with all their strength toward the hope of freedom, those fragments coalesced into one brief and final instant of life—then dissolved into nothing. All Aurya had left was hatred . . . and revenge.

It was all she wanted.

In the guesthouse of Saint Anne's Parish in Ballinrigh, Lysandra tossed upon her bed. The feeling that all day had refused to focus had turned into a wave of terror that crashed through her sleep. There were no images, nothing to tell her who or why. There was only the terror.

It turned and crested again. It built and drove itself

through every corner of her mind. It filled her soul as she tossed and moaned. It became sweat that drenched her body.

Terror became a torrent that would not ebb, would not cease. It became fire. Sleep burned away in a blinding flash, and she bolted upright, awake . . .

Screaming . . .

At the same instant, Cloud-Dancer raised his head and let loose a long, plaintive howl. It joined Lysandra's scream. The sounds filled the room, echoing off the walls.

Selia, too, came awake, jerked from her sleep by the terror filling the room. It was in the sounds; it was in the air. It was everywhere.

Her arm went around Lysandra's shaking shoulders, but the healer hardly felt it. All she knew was the terror that even now would not let her go, and the image of fire that came with it.

Her mind heard a door open and slam, and suddenly Renan was there. With Selia, he held her. She could hear that they were speaking, but she could not make out their words. Their voices were a jumble that meant nothing. She could not answer them.

Suddenly, Cloud-Dancer howled again. He came from the foot of the bed, where he had been sleeping, and put his head beneath Lysandra's hand. His touch, Renan's and Selia's, shattered whatever force held Lysandra. The terror fled, leaving her breathless and clutching her head.

Finally, she was free.

"Lysandra," Renan said, and this time she could understand him, "tell me what's wrong. What did you *see*?"

"It's . . . it's not *Sight,* Renan," she answered, though the words were still difficult to form. "It's something else. Oh, Renan—something has happened, and I don't know what it is. But there's a danger that . . . I don't know. I can't explain—but I'm suddenly afraid, for us all. Renan, we must be more careful than ever before."

"We will be, Lysandra," he said, tightening his arms around her. "Whatever comes, we'll be ready."

"It will be all right, Lysandra," Selia added. "As long as we're all together, nothing can truly harm us. We've already proved that."

Selia's words, like Renan's, were meant to give her comfort—but Lysandra felt none. All she felt was the continued whisper of danger all around them. It had receded, but not disappeared—and she knew there was nothing she could say or do so that these people, the ones who mattered most in the world to her, would understand.

And, for all their assurances, she was uncertain they could ever be ready. All they could do was wait ... and hope ... and pray ...

Chapter Twenty-three

In the Province of Kilgarriff, Rhys Llewitt was also sleepless. The rest of the army, especially the conscripts who had been forced from their homes and families, were counting the days until Lord Iain's promise would be fulfilled. Because of that promise, the whole atmosphere among the troops had changed. Gone was the angry boredom, the hopeless apathy. The men no longer went into the city—with or without permission—to work off those emotions by drinking, fighting, destroying property in the same way their own lives had been destroyed.

Discipline problems in the camp had ceased as well. The professional soldiers who counted their service, ahead or behind, in years rather than weeks or months, suddenly had more patience with the men who would soon be gone. They no longer had to train them, knowing their lives would depend on how well a farmer had learned to wield a sword.

It was almost over; that feeling, unsaid, seemed to hang in the air, infusing everything with a sense of expectancy.

Except for Rhys. Despite what Dafid had said about following orders, despite the disciplinary action he would face for what he was about to do, Rhys had made his decision. He must return to Rathreagh, to try to find Lady Aurya.

He would seek Baron Giraldus and Sergeant Maelik, too, of course—but they were an afterthought in his plan. Finding Aurya was the only thing that he truly cared about and the only reason he was willing to risk the anger of his superiors . . . from Lord Iain on down.

He would have to steal three horses—one for himself and one for each of the men. Lady Aurya would have to ride pillioned behind them, but he did not think he could handle more than two extra horses and maintain any speed while he traveled. Of course, Lady Aurya would probably ride behind Baron Giraldus—but if she took turns, then he might also be favored.

That thought alone was worth any danger to Rhys. To have those few hours when she rode with him, her arms around his waist, her body pressed softly against his, was the only ensorcellment he needed to ensure all of his effort.

With that thought to drive him, Rhys rose three hours before the camp would be called to reveille. He dressed quickly, made a bedroll from the extra blanket in his foot locker and the one on his bunk, thankful it was summer and the nights would be warm enough that with a fire, little else would be needed.

Moving as silently as possible, he left his barracks and

headed for the camp kitchen, to steal a few days' food. After it was gone, there would be wild berries and such to supply his food.

The whole camp was asleep. Now that Lord Iain had taken them off battle readiness, the night watch had been reduced to only two sentries walking the outer perimeter of the campground, and they were easily avoided. He only had to time his movements and keep to the shadows.

The one difficult part would be getting the horses away. But once he was mounted and riding, it would not much matter if a sentry heard him. Even if they gave an alarm or raised a pursuit, given the majority of the soldiers' current preoccupation with ending their own service, he doubted that any group who followed him would do so with much determination.

It took Rhys nearly an hour of moving with extra care and silence to gather supplies, load and saddle three horses, and be ready to leave. Reins in hand, he waited inside the stable, door ajar the merest crack, until he saw the sentries meet at the gate, exchange a few words, then start their circuit again.

He continued waiting, giving them time to get out of earshot, counting the steps and seconds. Finally, his impatience could stand no more. He led the horses out, still walking in shadows until the time came to cross the final open space between the last building and the barred gate ahead.

Rhys had never disobeyed before. He had been an easy child to rear, an easy soldier to train. He did not question or grumble over the orders he was given or the duties he pulled. Now, his heart was pounding with what he was attempting.

He stood in the shadows and stared at the barred gate. For one brief moment he considered turning around, taking the horses back to the stables, and returning to his bed before he was caught. Then, the memory of Aurya grew like a vision before him. He remembered how she had looked that night in Rathreagh when she sat beside him, moonlight making her glow like some ethereal creature, too lovely for earthly bounds. He remembered, too, how she had said that she would rely on him and on his help.

He saw again the shining darkness of her hair cascading unbound down her back and across her arms, the rich blue of her eyes, which shone like sapphires in the soft silver light of the moon. He remembered the warmth of her scent, of her nearness—and all reasonable thought left him. He had been reasonable all of his life; now, for her sake, he would be daring.

It would take two men to lift the bar and open the main gate to the compound—but there was also a smaller, seldom-used entry to the side. That he could do alone. The only danger was that, because of its size, he could take only one horse through at a time. That meant three trips—with the sentries getting nearer all the time.

But he had to try . . . he had to *succeed,* he told himself; Lady Aurya was relying on him.

The gate, though little used, was well maintained, and it opened silently for him. He placed the wooden slat on the other side, so it would not catch a passing eye when the sentries made their return.

The horses were sufficiently well trained to give him no trouble as he took the first two through the small opening. With their reins looped over a bush on the other side, they were content to wait as long as he needed. Rhys then returned for the third horse, his final trip back into the compound.

He put his hand on its soft muzzle, to keep it quiet as, walking backward, he started toward the little gate. Then he heard the scuff of a footstep. Rhys's heart felt as if it were suddenly in his throat, choking him, as he realized the sentries were nearing. *Are they close enough to see me?* His thoughts pounded as he now tugged on the reins, heedless of the extra noise.

He got the horse through the opening and pulled the gate shut, then did not move again while he prayed that the darkness, the late hour, and familiar, uneventful routine would make them not notice that the closed gate lacked its bar. Then he held his breath, afraid to breathe while he listened.

Footsteps neared, matching each other's cadence in the trained steps of a soldier. Voices mingled in soft, unexcited tones. With one hand, Rhys kept his grip on the gate, continuing to hold it closed. But all of his muscles remained tensed and ready to spring onto the back of the horse whose reins he still held.

Finally, the sentries parted and began their routes again. Rhys heard footsteps go past the gate . . . and he kept waiting. Once more he counted off the seconds that were footsteps, wanting to be certain they had plenty of time to be on their way before he moved. Once he did release his hold on the gate, if it moved inward even a little and a sentry saw it . . .

Seconds became minutes . . . he counted three, four, five, before he finally considered himself safe. Then he let go of the gate and took the horse he was leading over to the others. He still would not ride, not yet, not until he was certain he was out of earshot. But once he was mounted, a good gallop would give him enough distance to ease the tight ball into which his stomach had constricted.

Don't worry, m'lady, he thought into the still thick darkness. *Wherever ye be, I'll find ye. I'm coming . . . .*

With that, Rhys finally mounted his own horse and, holding tightly to the reins of the others, began his ride toward Rathreagh.

Margharite was tired. She and Durkin had ridden through a night and a day with too few stops and too little sleep, and now it was night again. She wanted a warm fire, a good meal—and to sleep all the way till morning.

But she hesitated to say anything. Durkin must be as tired as she was, yet he made no complaints. This was not his mission, yet he had accepted the danger and discomfort of it without hesitation. She would make no complaint that might make her seem ungrateful for all he had done.

At the moment, they were riding at a walk. The horses held their heads at a droop, showing that they shared their riders' fatigue. Suddenly, Durkin's horse stumbled. He reined it to a stop and slid from his back, then ran a practiced hand down its foreleg.

"I'm sorry, m'lady," he said. "I know that speed be important, but if we dunna' gi' the horses some proper rest, they'll soon be lame, and speed will no be possible."

Then he looked at her, scrutinizing her condition with the same practiced eye. "I think we could all use the rest," he said. "Ye'll see, m'lady, we'll make better time and cover greater distance by restin' now than by tryin' to keep goin' when we've no strength in us."

Margharite nodded, gratefully. "Do you think it's safe to chance a fire?" she asked. "A hot meal and a mug of tea would be nothing less than heavenly fare right now."

"If we find a sheltered spot," Durkin agreed. " 'Tis my guess that if we was bein' chased, we'd know by now. If Glynna was found out, then please God, it wasna' until mornin' and yer father had too many other concerns to take after a daughter runnin' away from a betrothal for which she had no mind. 'Tis not unknown — and I doubt he'd be thinkin' ye'd go all the way t' Ballinrigh. T' send riders after ye would mean tellin' th' Corbenicans and riskin' their wrath."

Margharite nodded, weariness sapping most of the enthusiasm from her action. Durkin's words were full of encouragement and hope — but the only thing she could think of was a fire and a night of rest.

It did not take them long to find a stand of trees whose leaves would give them shelter. A little stream trickled nearby, from which Durkin brought water for them before taking the horses down to drink.

When he returned, she watched in true appreciation as he

started a fire from seemingly nothing and soon had a cheery—and nearly smokeless—flame going.

"How did you do that so quickly?" she asked.

"Oh, m' Da was a great one for woodland trips—not that there be trees as grand as these in Rathreagh, 'cept by th' river. But we thought they was grand enough when we was kids, m' sister an' me."

Durkin's hands were busy the whole time he talked. His tone was so light and ordinary that Margharite was briefly able to forget the terrible reason they were on the road. She smiled, picturing him as a child camping with his family. Once more, she thought how very lucky Glynna was in the man who had won her heart.

It seemed miraculously little time when Durkin held a platter and a steaming mug in her direction. She had not thought about supplies when they fled, and, until now, their meals had been bread, cheese or some dried meat, maybe some fruit—all things eaten easily in the saddle. Now, somehow, Durkin had combined the meat and water, brought a few roots out of his saddlebags, and created a stew that made her mouth water with its aroma.

The mug contained a tea with a sharp, tangy flavor that, when she sipped it, seemed to fill all the tired places with warmth. She looked up and gave Durkin a surprised smile.

"'Tis rose hips and red clover blossoms," he told her. "Me Ma was a big believer in rose hips and red clover. Said they'd cure many an ill by cheerin' th' heart. A happy taste, she called it."

"And she was right," Margharite replied. "Sounds like your mother is a wise woman."

"Aye, she was. She passed on two years ago come Michaelmas, an' I still miss her every day."

"I'm sorry," Margharite said softly. There was nothing to add, so she turned her attention to the stew and began to eat.

As with the tea, the flavor delighted her and made her fully realize how hungry she was.

Companionable silence fell as they ate. Too soon, Margharite found herself mopping up the last of the gravy with a hunk of bread—an action never seen at her father's table and something she would have never considered doing before—and enjoying every bite of it. Eyes closed, she smiled again, this time with satisfaction.

"Wonderful," she said. "Thank you."

"My pleasure, m'lady," Durkin replied, reaching out to take her platter. "Now a quick wash and then sleep—and tomorrow's ride should be all th' easier for it."

"Durkin," Margharite said, as he stood. "Do you think you could stop calling me 'm'lady'? I'd be pleased if you'd call me by my given name."

"But that wouldna' be proper, with ye bein' th' Baron's daughter."

"Well, perhaps not under normal circumstances . . . but these are hardly normal, are they, with us traveling alone together? And if anyone has earned the right, it's you—and Glynna. Without both of you, I'd be—"

She shuddered, not wanting to finish the thought. "So please, Durkin," she said, "call me Margharite."

"Aye, then, m—Margharite. As ye say."

While he went to wash their few dishes, Margharite retrieved blankets from the saddles. Within minutes, she was stretched out next to the fire, glad of its warmth and the solid ground beneath her. Sleep would not be long coming . . .

She awoke with a start she did not know how much later, awakened with Durkin's hand across her mouth.

"Shh," she heard him say next to her ear. "There be some'un near."

She nodded, and he lifted his hand away. "Who?" she said just as softly.

"Don't know. Stay 'ere."

Again she nodded, and Durkin slipped silently into the darkness.

Margharite's heart began to pound so hard she felt as if her whole body was shaking with it. It was hard to lie there silently; the fire had burned low, and suddenly the darkness felt thick and ominous.

She wanted to get up and run, to scream at whomever was in the dark to go away and leave her alone. But she did not dare move. Durkin had told her to stay, and she would do nothing that might increase his danger.

The time felt endless. Then, suddenly, there were sounds from the trees, footsteps not even trying to hide their approach. That frightened her all the more. She jumped to her feet and began to run.

It was hard to run in the darkness, amid the trees. She had only made it a few yards when she heard Durkin's voice calling to her.

"M'lady . . . Margharite . . . 'tis all right. Come back— 'tis help arrived."

Margharite could hardly believe her ears. Help—how and from whom? But she trusted Durkin. Turning back around, she headed toward the soft glow of the campfire.

When she neared, she saw another young man standing with Durkin. He held the reins of a slightly lathered horse and wore the badge of a Rider. He also had a broad smile on his otherwise plain face, a face that showed signs of the same weariness she and Durkin felt.

"M'lady Margharite," the Rider said, as she stepped into the light, "am I glad to see you. I've come from the Archbishop, and I'm t' bring you back t' Ballinrigh under his protection. You need fear no more, m'lady."

"The Archbishop?" Margharite felt even more stunned. "How did he—?"

"I know not, m'lady," the Rider answered. "But 'twas His

Eminence himself sent me t' find you and keep you safe. I know you've both been traveling hard to have come so far, but we'd best be riding again by dawn. I've a feeling there's more danger about than we know."

By dawn, Margharite thought. It seemed that her sleep was not to be as long as she had hoped.

"By dawn, then," was all she could think to say, still too stunned by the Rider's appearance to care about being quick-witted.

She looked over at Durkin. His expression said that he was relieved not to have sole responsibility for her protection anymore. The look on his face also told her that she would continue as "m'lady." She was sorry for the loss; she had always been surrounded by formality and far too little friendship.

But it was the role to which she had been born. She assumed the title, so close to being shed, however briefly, once again. It was there in her stance, her look, her voice, and clothed her far more surely than the borrowed, tattered garments she still wore.

"Have you eaten?" she asked the Rider, as if welcoming him to her home.

"Aye, m'lady," he said with a bow. "I'm fine. Now I think we'd best get what sleep we can—and come morning, I've brought something that'll make the rest of the ride easier."

"And what would that be?" Durkin asked him, a little defensively. "M'lady's been safe enough wi' me."

Margharite could hear the hurt pride in Durkin's voice. She stepped over and quickly laid a hand on his arm.

"More than safe," she assured him. "Without your help and guidance, I would never have gotten away. Your quick wits and strong arm have saved not only me but, God willing, Rathreagh, too.

"But now—" She looked askance at the Rider.

"Wilham," he supplied.

"Wilham can help us both. You have done a great service to Aghamore, to Rathreagh—and to me—and I will never forget or disvalue it."

"Thank ye, m'lady," Durkin said with proud humility, looking straight at Wilham. There was a bit of challenge in the gaze.

"Aye," Wilham said, "and the Archbishop'll wish to thank you, too."

Margharite was grateful for the Rider's obvious understanding. Durkin, born of solid working-class parents, had crossed over, however briefly, into the heroic. He saw Wilham as a threat, a denial of that service—as if those in authority were saying he was either unable or unworthy to take care of a Baron's daughter.

Male pride, she thought, shaking her head slightly as she turned away. It was here now, pulsating in the air; it was coursing through the armies that surrounded Ballinrigh—and it was why her father had become a traitor.

She was tired of pride—male or otherwise—being the driving force in the decisions that governed the people. There were other, better choices. Compassion, justice, truth . . . these, and so many more, were far better than *pride*.

"So, what is it you've brought, Wilham?" she said as she again lowered herself onto her blanket.

Wilham smiled again as he turned back toward his horse. From out of the saddlebags he withdrew two tunics. They each bore the same badge he wore upon sleeves and breast.

"I've two more with me," he said. "I did not know with whom or how many you'd be riding, so I brought all I own. There are trousers and pouches, too. With all the Riders travelin' about these days, I figured it'd be the easiest—and safest—way t' get you into Ballinrigh and to the Archbishop. No one'll be lookin' at more Riders goin' through the gates."

Durkin walked over and fingered the tunics. "'Tis a good plan, m'lady," he said to her. "And a chance t' change off these filthy clothes. If ye care t' wash afore ye don it, I'll heat ye water and hang ye a blanket fer privacy."

"Thank you, Durkin," Margharite said, smiling at the thought of washing away the ash and dirt darkening her skin and hair. "You are *Sir* Durkin, with your gallantry — in heart if not in fact. *Yet.*" She lifted her chin regally, her smile broadening. "But you shall be, Durkin. Recognized for your service, you shall be a husband Glynna's father will be proud to welcome."

That assurance made Durkin stand a little taller and swell his chest. Margharite lay down, and waited for the hot water. And she smiled; she was pleased she could give Durkin such a promise.

And it was one she intended to see kept. She did not know exactly what her father's treachery would mean for her future, but Durkin deserved the reward she had just promised, and she would do everything within her power to be certain he received it. If she could not do that, then what did being "m'lady" truly mean, after all?

Chapter Twenty-four

The wail and cry that went through the Realm of the Cryf was unlike anything heard there before. There had been deaths in the battle with Giraldus's soldiers — but there had never before been cold-blooded murder.

Now there were the cries raised by the dead guards' families, wails of loss and pain. There were also the cries of anger, of rage and vengeance that built like the rumbling of a cave-in and swept through the Cryf with the same uncontrollable swiftness. Eiddig saw it happening to his people, and even while he understood it, it broke his heart. For one brief moment, he felt the same thing Talog had felt during his journey Up-world. Briefly, he questioned the wisdom of the Holy Words that said the Cryf and the Up-worlders would and must unite.

But the Holy Words were given of the Divine, and Eiddig's doubts did not last long. The Up-worlders had brought pain and sorrow to his people—but they had also brought the Healer and the Font of Wisdom. Eiddig was willing to continue trusting that the Divine Hand had a purpose in all It gave, good and bad.

He was Guide to his people; he must continue to trust so that they could.

But that did not mean he would do nothing about these . . . abominations that had hurt his people. The Cryf had tried to be kind, even as guards and captors. It had been Eiddig's hope—as, he knew, it had been Selia's—that this kindness would bear like fruit and change the hearts of their prisoners. Only such a change could truly set them free from the evil they followed.

Instead, he now saw that evil had festered while it waited. Like a pustule under the skin, it had now burst its poison fort—and must be washed clean before it infected the whole body.

Eiddig ordered a search. While Cryf scattered through the various passages and tunnels, he went with the Healers, to pray over the bodies while they cleaned them and prepared them for burial.

He did not try to hide his tears while he prayed. These had been good and dutiful followers of the Divine, proud in their service to their people. They, like Eiddig, had believed that the Up-worlders could be persuaded from the path of Darkness by the continuing contact of kindness. They had, therefore, kept their touch light, gentle, giving the prisoners as much privacy and freedom as possible.

Kindness had been repaid with death, and the tears in Eiddig's eyes were for more than the lives cut short. They were because Eiddig feared that life within the Realm of the Cryf could never be the same.

Hours passed without the Up-worlders being found. They had to be *somewhere,* Eiddig kept telling himself as he left the Healer's cave and went into the Great Cavern to wait.

Some of the Cryf had already assembled there, knowing their Guide would soon appear. They were looking to him for the words of wisdom he did not feel he had to give. But somehow, he must find them; his people needed him.

Slowly, he made his way through the cavern. Hands reached out to touch him as he passed, both drawing and giving comfort, as was the way of the Cryf. Nothing was ever done only for oneself; always the welfare of the rest was considered. The gestures touched more than Eiddig's body. They helped his heart hope again. By the love and kindness of the Divine that had filled the Cryf for so long, he now saw that his people would heal.

Eiddig made his way up the slope to the first level of ledges that encircled the cavern. From here, all the Cryf below could see and hear him. Then he raised his staff high above his head, a gesture they all recognized, and the gentle murmuring of the Cryf language ceased. The only sound that remained was the soft sobbing of the bereaved.

The ancient Guide looked over all the faces now turned to him, expecting wisdom and explanation. How could he give them something that all his long years—almost a century and a quarter—had not prepared him to face? All he could do was give them his love . . . and his faith.

"My people—my children," he began, "today hath great

Darkness touched us. Yet we, whom the Divine didst name The Strong, shalt not waver. Long and perfectly hath the Divine guided us. Though we understand not this path, yet shalt we be unwavering in our trust unto all the Divine Hand doth give, be it joy or sorrow. We know that we art cherished within the Divine Heart and that such Love shalt heal even such wounds as we have this day received."

The sound of grief reached him anew. He spotted the young mate of one of the dead, newly joined and in the first bloom of pregnancy. She was held in the comforting arms of her dead love's mother. Nor were theirs the only tears. The other guard, too, had a life-mate—and a mother, and two children. The children looked bewildered, too young to truly understand but frightened by the grief around them.

The grieving families were in the center of circles of comfort, of love that was the Cryf custom. Eiddig struggled again, trying to find the words to say. He wished Selia were here; surely the Font of Wisdom would be able to fill the silences as he was failing to do.

He had never felt himself a failure before. *Mayhap,* he thought, *my time hath passed. If this be the new life my people must face, mayhap they needeth one to guide them who hath walked among the Up-worlders and knoweth more of their ways.*

Even as he thought this, Talog came running into the cavern. "Eiddig-Sant," he said breathlessly, as if he had run across half of the Realm. "The Up-worlders hath stolen a boat and rideth upon the Great River."

The Great River, the heart's blood of the Realm; it fell as a great waterfall from the high peaks where no man, Upworlder or Cryf, walked and returned to the Up-world in a beautiful ribbon that twisted, pure and clean, through passages lined with bright veins of gold and silver, quartz and colored crystal. Pockets of gems shone back the light from the luminous stones, their colors shimmering on the surface of the water.

The Great River was holy to the Cryf—and Eiddig felt as if it had been defiled by the Up-worlders' touch. He had not felt so about Renan, Lysandra, Cloud-Dancer, and Selia—but Aurya, Giraldus, and Maelik . . . they were different. They were the Darkness against which the Holy Words spoke.

The murdered guards had been dead several hours by the time they were found and more hours had passed while the Realm was searched. Eiddig realized they would not be recaptured here. Furthermore, the Great River must be purified, the Realm—and the lives—of the Cryf cleansed again. To do that, Eiddig suddenly understood what must be done.

He must go Up-world.

He motioned to Talog. The younger Cryf hurried over, and they conferred, speaking in voices too low for anyone else to hear. After a few minutes, Eiddig nodded. With each word of Talog's, Eiddig had become more and more certain. The Divine Hand was still upon him after all.

This thought brought him comfort. It was with a lighter heart that he turned back toward his people and raised his staff again overhead. Once he had their attention, he began to speak so that they would also know and be comforted by the Divine guidance he had received.

Aurya had felt the first whisper of air upon her cheeks before the gray light of dawn reached into the underground. With its touch, she felt faint but unmistakable stirrings deep within. It was the one thing she wanted, the only thing she had been waiting to feel.

Magic.

She took a breath, drawing the freshening air deeply in and holding it there until her lungs burned. The breath went out in a gush, and she did it again. With each breath, the stirring grew, like embers being fanned.

Slowly, faintly at first, came the awakening of a remembered sound as the birds who inhabited the hollow columns at the Realm's entrance began to greet the spreading light. Free, Aurya thought, they—she—were nearly free . . .

Light changed from gray to golden rose, promising a beautiful day. After seeing nothing but the luminous stones all these weeks, sunlight was brilliant, even at this early hour. But even more brilliant was the fire Aurya was beginning to feel coursing through her veins.

It burned like golden heat, sweetly, exquisitely painful. It was the pain of rebirth into herself, welcomed and glorious. With it, she felt *alive* again.

The boats sped on, past the columns, past the great maw of an opening. Each second the feeling within Aurya grew. It spread out through her muscles, it filled her breath, her head, her thoughts.

"Hurry," she said to Giraldus. "To the bank."

With a nod, he switched his oar to the other side, the same side as Maelik's, and the boat turned. It took only a few more minutes, a few long strokes, and the boat hit the bank. Maelik jumped out and held the boat steady as Giraldus helped Aurya to shore.

She could see they were near exhaustion from the hours of paddling. Although her powers were not yet complete, Aurya was still certain she could help. She went over to Giraldus and took his face in her hands. Then she closed her eyes and let her magic come.

She gave some of herself to Giraldus and some to Maelik, just enough for them to travel a little while longer. There was something strange in the way the power filled and flowed from her, but she said nothing. She gave the men what she could, and they moved on. She would keep the rest to herself.

"How did . . . ?" Giraldus said, the words an effort as they ran.

"It's back, or coming back," she told him. "Soon I'll be strong enough to pay them back. You will *still* be King."

Giraldus only grunted as they kept going. Aurya glanced at Maelik and saw a fierce smile on his face, telling Aurya that he, too, had been thinking of revenge.

They kept going for the better part of an hour, scrambling through undergrowth and over the uneven ground. They were already on the Tievebrack side of the Great River, trying to find a way around the mountains that were the southern border between Rathreagh and Urlar, and under which the Realm of the Cryf existed.

Going through Tievebrack was their true option. They knew they could not cross the mountains on foot—and in Tievebrack their faces would be less immediately recognized. All was going well now . . . or almost all. There was a different feel to her returning magic, something Aurya still could not name, and it worried her.

She said nothing to the men. Once they were asleep, she would find out what was happening and why. And if her captivity within the Realm of the Cryf, where no magic could exist, had somehow damaged her connection to the powers she had felt all her life, then the death she planned for them would be all the more horrible in recompense.

They found a sheltered thicket in which to sleep. Although Aurya lay down next to Giraldus, she did not close her eyes for more than a few minutes, only until the men's breathing deepened into the soft snores of exhaustion.

She eased herself out from beneath Giraldus's arm, moving carefully so that she made no noise that might awaken them. Then, coming to her knees, she held out her hands. It was time to test the feel of her magic once again.

She closed her eyes and waited until the sensation of

power welled. This would be only a little spell, but she needed it for what she had in mind; she needed to know that Giraldus and Maelik would keep sleeping. If all went well, they would sleep even after she removed the spell, a natural sleep that would only end when their own bodies awakened them, and they would never know anything else.

"Essence of the night just passed," she chanted,
"Time of darkness, time of rest,
Cast thy veil, firm thy grasp
And on these sleepers let thy breath
Into their minds and bodies go
Draw them down in shaded deep;
Not to awake or conscious grow
Until my words release their sleep."

The spell worked—yet again Aurya felt that change she could not name. But now that she was certain she would not be disturbed, she would find out the reason and, she hoped, the cure.

She walked out of the thicket and away from where the men lay. A few yards back they had passed a clearing and she headed for it now. She needed to be somewhere she could move freely—and she still craved the feeling of open air.

Once in the open, she raised her arms as if to embrace the sky. She could not believe the beauty of such a simple sight. She felt she could go on looking at it forever . . .

Then she closed her eyes. She must focus on what she had come here to do, not give in to the distraction of pleasure.

Her voice started low, calling for her inner self—or the only self that truly mattered to her:

"Fire of Power, Power of Life
Power of Earth and Air and Stone;
Power in blood, Power in bone;

My voice hear and my voice heed;
I summon all, my power to feed;
Power to feel, Power to name;
Power to wield, Power I claim."

With each word her voice grew stronger, louder; with each word she felt the stirring, the building of her magic. With these last words, it erupted in a wave that pulsed through her body and flew out the tips of her upraised fingers. It whirled all around her until she felt as if she were caught up in a whirlwind of the arcane.

But then, again, came the difference, the sense of something changed. She began to search through the sensations, going deeper and deeper into the well from which her power sprang, down into the core of her being. It was a place she had visited only once before, in the early days of her magic under old Kizzie's guidance. She had never needed to visit it again.

This place, this core was something far different than her habitual retreat from outward distractions to which she went to summon forth her powers. It was a place far deeper, like diving into a well rather than drawing water from an ever-flowing stream. It was the core of her magic, but it was also much, much more. It was the place that held the spark, the shining thread that was her very life, and to reach it took an act of power itself.

Under Kizzie's guidance, she had found it once, and that had released her powers so that she could call upon them at will. But she had never thought to make this inner journey again—alone. She had no one to anchor her in the outer world.

But the possible peril was not as great to her as her need to know what was happening to her magic. Nothing else mattered . . . *nothing.*

Aurya closed her eyes. She began breathing slowly,

deeply. Soon she felt the familiar sensations grow; her magic was there, as ever, ready for her use. Instead of calling it forth, she let her breath carry her down, into the magic.

Entering it was like entering living fire. Each breath that filled her now made her feel as if the air was made of living flame that heated but did not burn, that turned with a multitude of colors she felt upon on her skin and erupted behind her eyes. With each breath, she rode the swirling power backward, down deeper, farther and farther . . .

Finally, she touched it . . . and she *knew.* The change *was* within her. It was the child she carried, conceived in the Realm of the Cryf, where her magic could no longer prevent it.

With pregnancy, everything changed.

Everything.

She lowered her arms and sat upon the ground to think. She realized that part of her had suspected what she now knew. The knowing took her determination to a new level, a depth she had never known before or suspected the lack.

Giraldus's child—*her* child—must have the throne, must rule this land. *Her* child must have everything. There was nothing, no twist of fate, no unrelenting foe, *nothing* that would stop her now.

But her magic had changed. She did not know how much greater that change would become as her pregnancy progressed. For now, she would say nothing. There was a chance, a good chance, that by continuing to use her magic she would ensure that some of it entered her child and created a life of power—a life like hers . . . or, perhaps, greater.

She closed her eyes and, using the still-swirling magic, she touched the new life she carried. Her child—her *son*—must know from the beginning who and what he was. She would teach him, as her own mother had never taught, never cared for, never cherished or fought for her. She would be all to her son that she had been denied.

Together, mother and son, creatures of magic both, they

would rule; they would conquer and they would own Aghamore—and anything beyond that they desired.

Aghamore was only the beginning.

But it must start with Giraldus becoming High King. For that, they must reach Ballinrigh. Once more, Aurya stood. Once more, she raised her arms in supplication to the great realm of power and magic. Whether or not the goddess whom Kizzie had served truly dwelt there, Aurya did not know or care. Whatever the source, Aurya would use it as she used all else . . . and through it, she would get what she wanted.

For her *son*.

Power welled and built, ready at her call. When she felt the new twisting path it took through her, this time she smiled.

Soon, my son, her thoughts caressed him. Then she sent her thoughts, borne on the wings of magic, to discover whatever she could about what was happening in Aghamore so she would then know the next, the best, move she needed to make.

After a night of sleep, the ride to Ballinrigh felt far less arduous to Margharite than the ride of the days before. Wilham's tunic was too large, of course, although its counterpart fitted Durkin reasonably well, but riding in trousers was certainly more comfortable than in any dress.

Although Urlar meant "the level place," the foothills of the mountains curved around its borders to the north and east. Those foothills changed into smaller hills, undulating more and more softly until finally becoming the great plain from which the Province took its name.

Cresting one of those hills, Margharite reined her horse abruptly to a halt. It was hard to hide her shock when she saw the armies camped around the great walled city of Ballinrigh. She sat, staring, overwhelmed.

The noise coming from them was like low thunder that

did not stop. It rose and fell with outbreaks of skirmishes, challenges issued and answered in charges and retreats. She had been feeling the noise as a rumbling in her bones long before she knew what it was. She wished she did not know now.

Which was worse, she asked herself, the sight before her of the kingdom's capital under siege—or the sight behind, of her own father in alliance with her kingdom's sworn enemy?

Both were horrible. Both must be stopped. With a look at Wilham and Durkin that said everything necessary, she put her heels to her horse's sides, and they all galloped forward.

The noise grew as they neared. Terrible as it had been from a distance, closing in on it, hearing the clash of swords, the sudden scream of shying horses, or the wail of men in agony, all amplified by the smell of blood and death, was like entering a nightmare. Margharite could hardly believe that such sounds existed in the true and waking world—or that men would seek them willingly.

She was increasingly grateful to Wilham's foresight as they rode on unchallenged. She saw other Riders amid the chaos, carrying messages between the Barons or to and from the city, and she understood that without Wilham's plan, she and Durkin would probably not have made it this far, let alone into the city and to the Archbishop.

Wilham was obviously known to the gatekeeper. It took him no more than a wave for them to be admitted. Margharite was glad when the heavy gates closed behind them, blocking out enough of the terrible noise that she could think again.

She had been in Ballinrigh a few times with her father, and once again she was dismayed by the sights before her. The beautiful, peaceful city that held the kingdom's greatest cathedral, libraries, and palace, parks and graceful buildings, now had armed troops in the streets and fear on the people's faces.

She reined in her horse. Immediately, Wilham was on one

side of her, Durkin on the other. Both men looked at her with concerned expressions, though Durkin's held a trace of understanding.

"M'lady?" Wilham said.

"You did not tell me it would be like this," she said to him. "How long has Ballinrigh been a center for war?"

"Not long, m'lady," he said gently. "But come, if it is not to continue longer and become much worse, we must hurry to the Archbishop's Residence. His Eminence is waiting."

Margharite turned to Durkin. She gave him a true, if slightly pained smile. "So, my gallant companions, are we— am I—ready to go and betray the people we love?"

"Better 'em than t' whole kingdom, m'lady," he said softly, understanding on his face and in his voice.

It was good to hear him say the words—ones she knew, ones she believed. But it was still good to hear them.

"Lead on then, Wilham," she said to the Rider.

The Archbishop was indeed waiting. He received them quickly and listened to her words, his face growing grave but revealing no true surprise. That shocked Margharite almost as much as her father's actions had done. How could the Archbishop not be surprised? she wondered. Had he suspected, seen the ambition that she had missed all her life, lurking in her father, only awaiting a chance to thrive and drive him forward into action?

Or was there something else?

She waited, but he gave her no explanation. Instead, he called for his secretary and dictated a quick letter, which he handed to Wilham. When the Rider left again, the Archbishop came over and sat by her, taking her hand. Margharite found that there was great comfort in his touch.

"I know, my daughter," he said, "that this has not been an easy choice for you to make. Yet you have done a great thing. We shall both pray that your father, for all the mistakes he is currently making, is not beyond salvation. There may yet be a way for him to redeem himself."

Although it was not a hope she held highly at this moment, the Archbishop's words brought her even greater comfort than his fatherly touch. She understood why he was so beloved of the people.

"You need worry no longer, my child," he continued. "Rooms have been made ready for you and your companion. You may rest now at ease and believe that you have helped more than you know."

"Thank ye, Yer Eminence," Durkin said, quickly coming to his feet. "But I must get back. Glynna'll be worryin'."

"I'm sorry, my son." The Archbishop stopped him. "But leaving is impossible for now. Few people are allowed in or out of the gates, not while the armies remain, nor would they be likely to let you pass through unharmed.

"But the letter I have just sent will, I pray, help speed an end to all this . . . and we are not alone in our efforts to bring a quick and peaceful end to our troubles."

"Who —?" Margharite asked.

But the Archbishop merely smiled. "You shall know soon enough, if all goes well. For now, I think you should both rest. There are accommodations for both and clean clothes waiting."

The Archbishop rose slowly. Margharite could not help but think how difficult and tiring all of this must be for him. She suddenly felt very sorry to have added to his troubles.

"Your Eminence," she said. "If I can help—"

"You already have, my child," he said, again giving her his soft smile. The door opened and a young monk entered. "If you will go with Brother Naal now, I have things I must do."

Margharite rose, and she and Durkin began to follow the monk. Then on an impulse, she turned back around. She went quickly to the Archbishop and kissed his cheek.

"Thank you, Your Eminence," she said softly.

"Bless you, my child," he said just as softly, patting her shoulder.

Then she turned and hurried with the others from the room. As she left, she was suddenly afraid, as she had not been during her escape or their long ride here. She was afraid for the old, frail man on whose shoulders the future of the kingdom rested—and for all the others who might yet die before this was over.

Chapter Twenty-five

Rhys had been riding for nearly two days straight. When he had left the army camp and for the first days of his journey, finding Aurya had been a need that whispered constantly in his mind, perhaps in his soul. But it was like a half-remembered dream—compelling but indistinct.

He had left Kilgarriff and was making his way across the northern plain of Urlar. He was heading for the place where he had seen Aurya, Giraldus, and the others go underground, hoping to reach it by the day after tomorrow. As of yet, he had no other goal; he hoped that there, somehow, he would find some clue to tell him where he must go next.

Rhys realized that his errand was a journey of hope, with no real promise that he would find anything at its end. And yet, with every mile, the whisper in his mind grew stronger.

So far there had been no pursuit, at least none that he had

seen. But he rested little and never eased his vigil. He kept moving, always moving; he would let nothing turn him away from his goal of finding and saving Lady Aurya. The thought of her gratitude, which began as a passing daydream during long hours in the saddle, had taken on the grandeur of an epic event as might be told by a gifted storyteller in the Baron's employ.

The sun was still climbing when he felt it. The whisper became a shout, awakening all the buried connection Aurya had left there. Suddenly Rhys *knew* where he must go. Aurya was calling; she would be waiting.

She needed him.

He changed his direction slightly. It was into Tievebrack, not Rathreagh, he must go—and that was closer. With no mountains to cross, he might be there by evening.

I'm coming, m'lady, he thought. And, in the same way he was certain Aurya was calling to him, he knew his thought was heard.

Elon was again at the Residence. He went there every day with the same appearance of contrite humility and the same offer to help. Occasionally, some little task was given to him through one of the Archbishop's secretaries, but he rarely glimpsed the old man himself. And he knew that these tasks were only busy work, assignments to keep him away while the Archbishop did whatever he was hiding from Elon. Now that the other bishops had arrived in Ballinrigh, the chances to see the Archbishop alone grew fewer every day.

Today, when he arrived, there was a message awaiting—and it was from the Archbishop. It was a hopeful sign, and Elon opened the folded pages eagerly, trying to hide his dismay as he read the words asking him to celebrate the daily Mass and lead his brother bishops in prayers for the kingdom's peace.

Giving the secretary a forced smile, Elon turned away and

crumpled the note in disgust. Oh, he would do what he was asked, playing the part he still needed to maintain—but he was growing heartily sick of it. If only the Rider he had sent to Kilgarriff would return, he could complete his own work, and then the Archbishop would be performing the tasks *he* set. In the meantime . . .

Tossing the crumpled paper aside, he left the outer office of the Archbishop's study. His steps were hard, his thoughts on what he planned for the future, as he strode down the corridors toward the arched exit that would take him to the cloistered walk connecting the Residence and the cathedral. He paid no attention to the people already gathering everywhere, hoping for an audience with the Primus. He did not even see the monk, his arms laden with a tray, until he walked into him.

The dishes on the tray flew everywhere, several shattering as they hit the floor. Elon started to shout at the monk for his clumsiness—but suddenly a door flew open and a priest, drawn by the commotion, looked out.

The priest was vaguely familiar, but that was not what stopped Elon's words or what made him take an involuntary step toward the door. It was what lay behind the priest.

Several lamps were lit, brightly illuminating the room. A large table was at the center. It was covered with papers—some in piles, some scattered and falling onto the floor in a patchwork of wood and white. But at the center of the table, spread out and held open by two of the lamps, was the Thirteenth Scroll of Tambryn.

Elon had studied it often enough that there was no doubt or question in his mind. That glimpse was enough . . . and if it was being studied here, then the Archbishop had read it, too.

But what does the old man know? Elon's thoughts erupted in questions and possibilities. Too many possibilities—none of which boded well for *him*.

He took another step, trying to see a little better over the priest's shoulders. The Scroll of Tambryn was not the only text on the table. There were other scrolls, some still rolled, both in and out of ornate, jeweled tubes that shone within the bright light of the room. Other texts were in book form; their pages, too, were bound and covered by jewel-encrusted cases. They were obviously important—and Elon recognized none of them.

The priest looked straight at him, and for a few seconds their eyes locked. A sudden shiver shot through Elon. In those hazel eyes, he thought he caught a glimpse of his own defeat, perhaps his own death.

Then, just as suddenly, the priest stepped back and shut the door. Elon would see no more, but he had seen enough. Leaving the monk to deal with the broken dishes and spilled food, Elon turned on his heel and strode away. Forgotten were his duties at the cathedral. He had to get back to his own House and Thomas; he had to know what was happening with the Rider he had sent forth.

He had to get the Archbishop under his control immediately, before everything toward which he had worked and planned was lost. If the Archbishop knew about the scroll, then time was running out.

Elon took his carriage home, each moment growing more annoyed by the traffic, the people, the delays. He wished, not for the first time, that he possessed the power to speak a spell and clear the obstacles from his way. If only Aurya were here . . .

A Rider's horse was tied to the post near his front entrance. Forgetting all decorum, Elon nearly leapt from the carriage when he saw it. His eyes were wide and wild enough when he rushed through his front door that his own servants backed away. Elon did not care. He cared for nothing but that the one for whom he had been waiting had finally returned.

A few steps and he was at the door of his study. When he

slammed it open, the Rider jumped to his feet and turned. His face, too, filled with fear when he caught sight of the look on Elon's face. Again, the bishop did not care . . . he cared only that the man had completed his task.

Elon threw the door closed and in three steps was at the Rider's side. "Well?" he demanded, holding out his hand. "Give them to me."

The Rider hung his head. "I'm sorry, Your Grace," he said, "but I've nothing to give you."

"Nothing?" Elon could not believe the word. "Nothing at all?"

"No, Your Grace. I tried, honest. I went to every name you'd given me, but no one had aught of your request. But here," he reached into his pouch and withdrew a letter. "The woman who lives outside Laisca sent you this."

Elon snatched the letter and turned away. He went to the window, breaking the wax seal as he walked. Then, with the sunlight on the words, he started to read.

His face grew more and more grave with each second. Mathelda was a source who had never failed him before, and she said the herbs he wanted could not be found anywhere but in Phrygia, a place Elon was not sure existed any longer outside of the magical texts he had read. Even if it did, it would take months, perhaps years to find it, acquire what he needed, and return.

Elon crumpled the paper and held it in his fist. He wanted to strike out, to put that fist through the nearby wall—or better yet, through the Archbishop's face. At that moment, he felt that he could take the old man apart with his bare hands . . . him and whoever else got in his way.

Swallowing hard, he turned back around. "Thank you," he told the Rider through clenched teeth. "See my secretary and you'll be paid. You may go now."

"Yes, Your Grace. Thank you." The Rider gave a bow,

then left, his eagerness to be away in every line and movement as he sped toward the door.

Elon stood still only a moment longer. Then he, too, went to the door.

"Thomas," he yelled.

The manservant appeared almost immediately. "Your Grace?" he said calmly. His tone quieted Elon a little, reminding him of all the watching eyes and listening ears around him.

Elon cleared his throat, bringing himself back under control "Thomas," he said again, his voice much more normal, "I have work to do and *cannot* be disturbed. See to it, then send my apologies to the Archbishop. I must return to Kilgarriff. *We* must return. Have our horses saddled. I'll see to my own packing."

"Yes, Your Grace," Thomas said as he bowed.

He understood, as Elon knew he would. *Perhaps,* the bishop thought, *he already knew what was going to happen today.*

Elon wished he had known. He wished he knew something, *anything* for certain. But since he did not, he would return to Ummera and the secret library. Perhaps there, in all that he had left behind, he would find a new way to still make his plans come true.

Baron Hueil of Rathreagh was beginning to regret his alliance with the Corbenicans. Wirral was crude and cruel, the army of Corbenica lacking in formal discipline. They wanted to burn and destroy as they marched south toward Ballinrigh. Hueil felt as if he was already trapped on a battleground as time and again he argued with Wirral about keeping his men under control.

They were not here, he kept reminding the King of Corbenica, to sweep through the countryside as conquerors, not if they wanted the ultimate prize—the crown of the High

King. But the Corbenicans were never persuaded for long. It was their way of warfare, their way of religion and life, to take what they wanted. It proved their strength and their worthiness in the afterlife.

Their version of heaven was a great warrior's feast. There would be food—meat and drink and delicacies in plenty—music, stories, dancing. Warriors would wrestle and battle each other in games of skill and strength, and if wounded, they would heal so they could give battle again.

But in the kingdom of Aghamore, Corbenican ways had to be kept in check. Hueil's men, instead of finding allies with whom they could raise a cup or share a tale, had to become watchdogs to keep mothers, sisters, and daughters from being raped, towns from being fired, crops destroyed.

They complained to Hueil, who complained to Wirral. Again. By the time the combined troops crossed into the Province of Urlar, Hueil of Rathreagh knew he was near an insurrection. He had to do something . . . but what? He was trapped by his own ambition.

He now knew that Margharite had the right of it. He hoped she had made it to Ballinrigh. In that act, which he had once seen as her betrayal, might well lie his chance of salvation.

The sun was low in the sky, but at this time of year, when darkness was short, it was still two hours from setting. Rhys had slowed his horses to a walk, directed by the sense that had become his internal guide. He felt that his goal was near. Even so, he was unprepared for the sight of Lady Aurya standing in the middle of the little road, hands on her hips, her dark hair shining in the touch of the evening sun.

The sight took his breath away. He pulled his horse up short and stared. She was more beautiful than he remembered or imagined—so beautiful that he had trouble believing she was real.

Aurya suddenly laughed and strode toward him. It was then, and only then, that the reality hit him.

He had truly found her.

Found *them,* Rhys thought, as Giraldus and Maelik stepped from the trees. For a moment, Rhys was terrified, remembering Dafid's warning of what the sergeant would do about his disobedience. But they were smiling, too, slowly easing Rhys's fears.

"So, my young guide," Aurya said as she neared him, "you've come to show us the way to freedom."

"More than freedom," Giraldus said in the booming voice Rhys knew, respected, and had occasionally feared. "He's here to lead us to victory. What do you think, Maelik?"

"I think he's a good soldier who knows when t' obey— and when t' think for hisself. It's good t' see ye, lad. Better'n ye know."

All these words, this unexpected welcome, made Rhys feel light-headed. Quickly, he slid from the back of his horse and went down on one knee in front of Aurya—and the others.

"M'lady," he said, his voice choked with the joy of seeing her. "M'lord Baron, Sergeant—I . . . I couldna' stay and wait in Adaraith any longer. I don't know what led me here—I planned t' go back t' the river where ye built the barges. It must o' been God's own Hand what directed me here."

Then he looked around. "Where be th' others?" he asked. "Be ye all what survived . . . wherever ye've been?"

Giraldus's eyes grew cold. "Yes, lad," he said. "We're all. But that's another story, and a long one. Stand up, lad, and tell me everything that has happened. How are my men? Has their training continued, as I ordered? Are they ready to march on Ballinrigh?"

Rhys had been dreading this moment. He looked from Giraldus's face to the others, seeing them all growing wary at his silence.

"Nay, m'lord Baron," he said softly. "Th' army no longer drills. Th' Archbishop . . . he gave yer title t' yer cousin, and Lord Iain has promised t' dismiss th' army a week from now."

The words came out in a rush. He was afraid and ashamed to meet the Baron's—to meet Aurya's—eyes, to be the bearer of this news. When at last he did look up, the expression in Giraldus's eyes was pure fury.

But Aurya's eyes were something that reached past the fog of adoration through which he beheld her, and filled Rhys with true terror. He took a step backward and lowered his eyes again.

"How dare he," Giraldus suddenly roared. "I'll kill him for this outrage—he and Iain, both."

"Do that, and you'll have the whole kingdom against you," Aurya said just as sharply.

Giraldus whirled on her. "Am I just to stand by, then, while another takes what's rightfully mine? *I* am the Head of the Third House—not my cousin."

"And if you're patient, smart, and stick to our plan, you'll be much more than that."

"She's right, m'lord," Maelik said quietly.

Giraldus heaved a great sigh, then, clenching and unclenching his fists, he turned and walked off a little ways. Rhys, who had felt his stomach knot as tightly as Giraldus's fists, breathed a little easier with the distance. Anger radiated from the Baron in waves that were almost visible and were certainly palpable to anyone near.

"What shall we do, m'lady?" he asked Aurya, glad that she had taken his news calmly. "I've brought horses—"

"*I'll* tell you what we'll do," Giraldus said, whirling around again. "Rhys, you're to take her ladyship back to Adaraith, where she'll be safe. Maelik, you and I are going to Ballinrigh."

"But Giraldus—" Aurya began.

The Baron cut her off with a gesture. "Not this time, Aurya. I'm going to Ballinrigh, and the Archbishop *will* give me whatever writ necessary to restore my birthright."

His voice was lower, but his eyes glinted like a finely honed sword, sharp and hard. He walked back to Aurya and gently touched one hand to her cheek.

"Go to Kilgarriff and wait for me. I'll join you as soon as I have what's mine. Go there and stop Iain from dismissing my army. I'll need them when I return, and I need someone I trust holding them for me."

"I will hold them for *us*," Aurya told him, "and I'll be waiting."

She turned and smiled at Rhys. All other thoughts in his head melted in the brilliance of that smile.

"Well, Rhys," she said, "it seems you are to be my guide and my companion once again. I can think of no one more pleasant or trustworthy for the task."

Rhys felt the blush starting at his neck, rising up to stain his freckled cheeks until they were nearly as bright a red as his hair. "I am your servant, m'lady," he said softly, "in this and always."

"I know you are, Rhys," Aurya replied, giving him a strange look that sent another shiver down Rhys's back and raised the hairs on the base of his neck. "I know you are."

Up in Adaraith, Lord Iain received Wilham in the great Hall of the Baron's Fortress. When Wilham gave him the Archbishop's letter, he opened it and scanned the contents quickly.

"Do you know what's in here?" he asked the Rider.

"Aye, m'lord. I was there when it was writ."

"Then you know the truth of these words? They're more than suspicions or unfounded fears and rumors—the Corbenicans are truly in Aghamore and marching under the banner of Rathreagh?"

"Aye, m'lord—they're here. His Eminence is depending on you, more than on any of the others. He's *hoping* for their aid and obedience—but he's relying on yours."

"And he shall have it," Iain said firmly. He walked to the wall by the dais and pulled the bell cord, tapping his foot while he waited.

Wilham watched the set of Iain's shoulders as he stood there. Many men, probably the other Barons, would have been gratified, even excited, by the duty to which the Archbishop had just called Iain. He was to be the leader of the forces sent to stop the Corbenicans, forces that would begin with the army of Kilgarriff. But, if the other Barons heeded the Archbishop's call, more armies would soon follow, and Lord Iain was to command them as well.

But as a Rider, Wilham met all types of people in all stations of life. He had learned to read people well. In Lord Iain now was no exultation, no thirst for battle, glory, or recognition. He saw nothing but sadness.

Here was the kind of man the troops would follow not because they feared his wrath, Wilham thought, but because they respected—perhaps even loved—the man. The Archbishop had made a wise choice, both for Kilgarriff and for Aghamore.

Giraldus and Maelik took the two extra horses and galloped off toward Ballinrigh, leaving Aurya to ride behind Rhys. She took the time to change from the Cryf clothing into her own, relishing the feel of silk and leather, the fine cloth and stout boots that told her she was herself again. Then, swinging up behind Rhys, they set off at a much easier pace toward Kilgarriff.

Aurya did not miss Rhys's shiver when she slipped her arms around his waist, and she smiled. It was almost as good to feel the return of this power as it had been to feel her magic again. *Almost.*

"Tell me what Lord Iain has done in Kilgarriff," she said

to him, "and tell me what's happening about the succession. I need to know everything before we reach Adaraith."

"I already told th' Baron," Rhys replied. "'Tis not much more. They say th' armies are gathered 'round Ballinrigh, but I've heard naught else, m'lady. Lord Iain isna' interested in th' throne—only in rulin' th' Province."

Not interested in the throne, she thought, amazed. Every other Baron in the kingdom coveted the throne, the crown, the power . . . .

She suddenly realized Giraldus was on the wrong errand. Iain *should* be left to rule Kilgarriff—Giraldus would soon be busy elsewhere. He would be ruling Aghamore.

"Rhys," she said, "we have to go to Ballinrigh. We have to stop the Baron."

"Nay, m'lady," he said. "I canna' disobey his orders. It be not safe about the capital, w' all th' armies there. Ye must be safe."

Aurya thought for a moment more. "Then take me to Ummera, to the bishop. Elon will get Giraldus to listen. He must come back to Adaraith *before* he sees the Archbishop. Yes, that's it—take me to Ummera."

To this, Rhys nodded. He put his heels to his horse's sides, and the animal sprang from a walk to a canter. By riding into the night tonight and by dawn tomorrow, they could be in Ummera by tomorrow night. Aurya hoped that would be soon enough.

Then, she was certain, she and Elon together would be able to ensure that their plan, altered to fit the current necessities, still went forward. When it was over, Giraldus would be High King, Elon would be Archbishop . . .

And *she* would rule.

What about the child within her? a little voice whispered. Her child—her son, she told it, would rule with her. He would ensure Giraldus's compliance every bit as much as would her magic.

She smiled against Rhys's back. Everything was back exactly as it should be. Soon she would have both the mundane and the arcane power she craved. And then she would have her revenge . . .

All of it.

Chapter Twenty-six

With Margharite's confirmation of Lysandra's vision, the Archbishop had not been idle. It was not that he had disbelieved Lysandra, but he knew that the Barons, intent upon their battles for power, would demand more than a blind woman's *Sight* to convince them to put aside their challenges and dreams of glory and to join together for a greater good.

Now that Margharite had come, he had that voice to make them listen.

He sent Riders to each of the Barons and told them, on threat to their immortal souls, to gather at the Eastgate an hour after dawn. Then, all through the night, he prayed for the right words to say. When dawn came, he was not certain he was ready—but he was out of time.

Margharite went with him as his carriage took them to the gate, then gave her arm to help him mount the long steps to the wall's ramparts. Each step felt as if it took more out of him. The weariness was more of the soul than of the body, though that was real enough, too. This morning, the day of his retirement felt as if it was still a lifetime distant.

But his true weariness came from knowing that war was already within Aghamore's borders, and not only was there nothing he could do to prevent it, but he must now encourage it. He must ask the men below to go north, to fight and some of them die, in the name of peace. It was something his scholar's heart had never thought to do.

The Barons were waiting just as he had asked, though they were all mounted, armed, and looking eager to return to their fray.

"We're here, Your Eminence," one of them called—Oran of Camlough, the Archbishop thought—"but unless you've the way to name one of us King, and prove the right, then your words, and our time, will be wasted."

The Archbishop shielded his eyes as he looked over the Barons. They all wore the same expressions of stubborn agreement, as their voices began to rise.

The old man held up his hands. "Silence," he ordered in the voice he had once used to preach to a full cathedral. It carried out across the plain, surprising them all—including himself. The shocked Barons immediately complied.

"It is neither the crown nor your personal glory I have come to discuss," he continued, his voice lowered only slightly, "but something more dire than either. Beside me stands Margharite, daughter and heir of Baron Hueil of Rathreagh. "

"Where is Hueil?" another voice—Mago of Tieve-brack—interrupted. "Is he inside with you? If you've named him as King without our agreement, I swear that I'll not be stopped—"

"Silence, I said," the Archbishop shouted again, close to true anger. "Hear me out before you speak again, any of you."

The old man was satisfied that they would obey. Once more he lowered his voice before he continued.

"Hueil is *not* within these walls," he told them. "He is even now marching from the north—and he does not come alone. Hear me now and understand—Hueil of Rathreagh has been joined by King Wirral of Corbenica, who has brought an army to our shores."

There was an immediate cry from the assembled Barons. Shock and horror that one of their own could do such a thing, anger that held both belief and disbelief in equal proportions.

"It is time to put aside your challenges and battles, and to face the common foe," the Archbishop continued. "Only together do we stand a chance of saving our kingdom."

"And who's to command?" another shout came from below. "We've no King to lead us—who's to be your voice in the battle?"

"I have sent to the one Baron who does not seek the crown and will, therefore, lead without the aim of personal glory. *He* will be my voice and speak fairly to all.

"Even now, Lord Iain of Kilgarriff, cousin to Giraldus and governing by my orders in the Baron's absence, is leading his army toward the north. I now charge all of you to join together and march to meet him. Hueil—and his Corbenican allies—must be stopped before they reach Ballinrigh. At noon today I will return to this place and bless your armies as you march north. Do I have your agreement, your obedience?"

To a man, the Barons raised their arms and their voices. They would march at noon.

The Archbishop turned away and, leaning even more heavily on Margharite's arm, again descended the steps, hoping he had time for a little rest before noon. Even more, he prayed he would have the strength to see this through until the end. Today, his strength felt in very short supply.

* * *

At noon, when the Archbishop stood again on the rampart, his hands and voice raised as he blessed the assembled armies, two hooded figures were creeping around the far side of the city walls. Although it was difficult this time of day, they lingered in what shadow they could find, trying to stay away from the painful brilliance of the sun.

They were also trying to hide from the eyes of the soldiers, not daring to think what such armed men might do if they noticed the Cryf.

Luckily — although Eiddig did not believe in luck and preferred to think of it as the continued care of the Divine — both the soldiers outside and the city watch manning the walls were too busy to notice two more people in nondescript, hooded capes.

As Talog had done before, they were both dressed in the Up-worlder fashion of trousers, shirt, and shoes, disguising much of their strangeness. The rest was covered by the hoods that also protected their sensitive eyes.

They had traveled by night as much as possible. But at dusk the city gates would be locked; they had to find a way inside before that happened. Talog spotted a pocket of deep shadow where a section of wall jutted out decoratively, a carved angel perched on top whose outstretched wings provided shade. He led Eiddig there, and the old one sank to the ground, giving a relieved sigh.

Talog sat beside him. "Hast thou seen a way to enter?" he asked.

Eiddig shook his head. "Patience," he said in a weary voice. "The Divine shalt provide."

With a nod almost as tired as Eiddig's voice, Talog accepted his teacher's reminder and settled himself to wait, repeating the words in his mind and heart like a meditation.

The Divine shalt provide . . .

* * *

Inside the city, Lysandra and Selia were just sitting down to their midday meal. Lysandra picked up her cup of tea and inhaled; she had been looking forward to this moment for the last busy hour.

Suddenly, her hands started to shake. Hot tea spilled across her fingertips. A second later, she dropped her cup.

"Lysandra?" Selia's voice was sharp with worry.

"We have to go," Lysandra said, standing. She put out her hand for Cloud-Dancer. She wanted both her *Sight* and his vision available. She was not certain why they had to go, only that they must.

"Go where?" Selia said, also standing. "To the Archbishop's? Is it Renan—is something wrong?"

"No, not there." Lysandra shook her head, then stood very still, listening to whatever was directing her.

"To the Southgate," she said finally, "and we must hurry."

She slipped the braided lead she had made over Cloud-Dancer's head. People reacted with less fear when they saw him thus—and right now there was enough fear raging through Ballinrigh, and in the great plain beyond.

They hurried toward the Southgate. Renan's parish was only a few blocks away, and he was well-known to the gatekeeper. Through him, now so were Lysandra, Cloud-Dancer, and Selia. The noise built, seemingly with every step they took in that direction—men, horses, voices shouting, wagons beginning to roll. It was the sound of a kingdom at war, and it was more horrific the closer they drew.

At least there are no dying men—today, Lysandra thought, *no screams of agony, no smell of blood or taste of terror thickening the air. Today . . .*

The air was, in fact, filled with excitement, even eagerness, as the armies joined forces to march against their common foe. It was so intense, Lysandra needed no special gifts to feel it. But it was not what drew her on. There was something—or someone, she suddenly knew—outside the gate.

She felt again that they must hurry. She waved at the gate-keeper, who was up on the ramparts watching the spectacle. The gate itself was closed, as it had been for many days, but the little side door was unlocked.

"'Tis not safe outside," he called down to her. "Does Father Renan know you be here?"

"He sent us," Lysandra lied, knowing that Renan would have done so had he known. "We've friends of his to meet here."

"Then pass through," he called back. "But be careful. I've no wish to explain your death to the priest."

"We will," she promised him, waving back.

With a nod at Selia, Lysandra and Cloud-Dancer led the way through the door. It was only big enough for one man and, maybe, a horse to get through — but there was plenty of room for a woman and a wolf. Once on the other side, Lysandra sent her *Sight* searching. It almost passed by the pocket of shadow where the Cryf were resting. Then it was drawn back, suddenly, like a thread stretched and snapped. Lysandra *saw* the huddled figures and began to rush their way.

They rose as she drew close. "Eiddig," she called with delight. "Talog — you're . . . you're here."

Beside her, Selia gave a gasp and ran forward. Soon, the four of them were embracing with their gladness.

"Come," Lysandra said as the first moment passed. "We'll talk inside. But hurry, it's not safe out here."

With one hand still holding Cloud-Dancer, she put her other arm around Eiddig to help the old one toward the gate.

"Ah, Healer," he said, "the Divine hath been kind again, and as ever hath directed thy footsteps. I am pleased to see thee, and grateful thou didst find us so quickly."

Lysandra tightened her arm briefly in another embrace. "I am glad to see both of you, too. But — why have you come Up-world?"

"We bring thee dire news," Eiddig said, solemnly.

"Let it wait until we reach home," she told him. "There we may speak more freely."

A half hour later, Lysandra sat in stunned silence; Aurya and Giraldus were *free*. She now understood the reason for her dream—and her screams—the other night.

She had to get to Renan. Not alone—she must take Eiddig and Talog to the Archbishop. He had heard their tale and knew of the Cryf. She did not fear the Archbishop's reception of Eiddig and Talog; the news they brought, however, was fearful enough to affect everything they were doing or hoping to do.

There was one thing she needed to do first; she would send a message ahead so that the Cryf would not have to chance a delay in the waiting room. But how? she wondered. It would take too long to summon a Rider . . .

The only one to send was Selia. Lysandra went into the bedroom, into the small chest that held her few belongings while she stayed in the guesthouse. It took only a few seconds to find and withdraw two of her remaining coins; she still had a few more, some of which she would spend today to get herself, Cloud-Dancer, and the Cryf to the Residence. These two were for Selia to take a carriage ahead of them, for speed was now the only weapon they had.

"Take this," Lysandra told Selia once she returned to the main room, "and go to Renan. He'll know what to do. We'll follow in one hour. Tell him to be certain everything is ready—this cannot wait. Are you sure you'll be all right alone?"

"Of course—I'll be fine," Selia said, and Lysandra could hear the eagerness in her voice. "I'm nearly eighteen, and if you expect me to rule a kingdom, you can certainly trust me to take a carriage."

She was right, of course. Lysandra knew it, but she still felt a trifle uneasy letting the girl go out alone into the city. So much could happen . . . in an instant, all of life could be changed. Lysandra could not help but think of the day, ten years ago, when she had left her house. Nothing was going to happen to her, either. She was only going to the stables.

But everything had changed that day. Lysandra had to stop herself from calling Selia back . . . but she knew she could not; this was part of why she was born, and what Lysandra and Renan had been training her to do.

Lysandra turned to Eiddig and Talog and smiled. "While we're waiting," she said, "let me get you some food and tea. You've traveled a long way—and I think we're about to have a long day ahead."

The Archbishop was delighted to meet the Cryf. Like so much else, they were a myth made real, a legend in flesh and blood, sitting across from him in his study. Meeting Lysandra with her *Sight* and her visions, Selia who was the ancient prophecy come to life, the Font of Wisdom who would save the kingdom, and the scrolls themselves—those had been miraculous enough. But meeting the Cryf left Colm Ap-Beirne feeling as if he were walking through a maze. It was confusing, bewildering, and behind each new twist was something more amazing.

But as they talked, one bright hope emerged. Until Aurya and Giraldus showed themselves, there was nothing to be done about them, either here or in Kilgarriff. The armies were on their way to stop Hueil and his allies; that, too, was out of the Archbishop's control for now.

The problem still to be solved was how to prove Selia's right to the throne—with proof that could be seen by all. So far, they were at an impasse in the search. But as Renan and the Archbishop told Eiddig about the coronation texts and the reference to the "Heart of the Scepter," the old Guide got a strange look on his lined and ancient face.

"What is it, Eiddig?" Renan asked. But the Cryf shook his head.

"I must see this thing of which thou speakest," he said.

"Do you know what it means?" the Archbishop asked, trying not to let too much hope overtake him.

"Mayhap," Eiddig said softly. "Mayhap."

They waited until it was fully dark, when the Cryf could travel with ease—and be less recognizable. The Archbishop had sent word ahead to the Palace, and once more Leyster was standing guard, staying back as far out of the way as his duty would allow.

The Archbishop unlocked the case that held the scepter that had come down through the ages. As he withdrew it, he saw how the design of twisted ropes of gold and silver that created the long rod matched the massive Necklace of Office Eiddig wore.

"Is . . . is this of Cryf design?" he asked, incredulous. Here was yet another of those unexpected twists in the maze.

Eiddig nodded. "The hand of Dewi-Sant didst make this, even as he didst make this symbol all Guides do wear; as we honoreth his name and memory, keeping all that he didst teach us in the Holy Words given of the Divine." His hand went to the beautiful coils of gold and silver around his neck. "Unto the hands of thy first King wast this given, to be kept unto the day when its full glory wouldst be fulfilled. Now hast that time arrived."

The Archbishop looked astonished, felt even more so. "Are there other things here made by your people?" he asked.

Eiddig walked slowly around the Jewel Treasury, looking over the cases. He leaned upon a carved and beautiful wooden staff. It was not the one Renan had described once to the Archbishop, and in a way the old man was glad the Cryf had not carried it here. Although Colm would have loved to see more of the Cryf workmanship, to have carried a staff wound with such gold and silver would have been a terrible danger.

But it seemed he was to see Cryf workmanship after all. Eiddig stopped and raised a hand toward the case in which all the ancient regalia were displayed, including the Crown of King Liam.

"All here wast made by Cryf hands," he said. "Yea, by the hands of Dewi-Sant."

"But how would King Liam have gotten them?" the Archbishop asked.

Eiddig smiled and put both hands to his staff as he stared at the regalia. "The great Dewi-Sant wast the first Guide unto the Cryf and unto his heart didst the Voice of the Divine ever speak. Sixteen great Showings didst he receive of the Divine and didst he write as the Holy Words, to guide us always unto the path the Divine didst call the Cryf to walk.

"But the Voice of the Divine didst direct Dewi-Sant in all things, and in a vision didst he see that he wast to make these which thou seest before thee. With his own hands didst he free the gold, silver, and the bright stone from the land of the Realm, and took them unto the fire. There, working alone, didst he purify the metal, fashion it as thou seest it now, and set within it the stones, doing all as the Divine didst ordain.

"Then, too, didst he make the chain and staff that all Guides hath worn since that day, and also those worn by the Elders of the Fourteen Clans, all fashioned unto the same manner. By this, didst he know that when the time appointed didst arrive, all wouldst see the unity of our peoples, as it wast intended by the Divine."

"But how did King Liam get them?" Renan asked again. "I've never heard that anyone, even King Liam, knew of the Cryf."

"He didn't," the Archbishop answered before Eiddig could speak. "We, too, have our legends, Renan, and this one says that on the night before King Liam was to be crowned, he came into the cathedral to keep his vigil. At that time, there was only a plain gold circlet for a crown and his sword to serve as a scepter. He entered the cathedral, which was also much smaller then, and knelt to pray. It is said that his prayers were so fervent that he saw and heard nothing until finally he looked at the altar. Upon it, he found this regalia, resting there as if God's own hand had so placed it as a sign of His blessing upon Liam's sovereignty. In all these centuries, there has never been another explanation—until now."

He turned back to the Cryf Guide. "If all this was made by the Cryf, do you know what is meant by the 'Heart of the Scepter'?" he asked eagerly.

Again the old Cryf nodded, and he smiled. "Yea—and even now it is in thy possession."

"What is it—is it here?"

"Nay—not here. She for whom it wast intended keepeth it safe, though she knoweth it not."

"Then we're ready," Renan said, a touch of ferocity in both his voice and his eyes.

"Yea and verily," Eiddig agreed. "The time of fulfillment hath indeed arrived."

"And may God have mercy on us all," the Archbishop added.

Chapter Twenty-seven

At the urging of the Archbishop's letter, Lord Iain immediately called for the troops to be assembled. When they heard of Baron Hueil's betrayal, of the Corbenicans' invasion, and of the Archbishop's plea for their assistance, they had been eager to serve their kingdom. Iain had offered a release from service to any man who wished, but few chose to accept it. With this new threat, even the conscripts had a reason, and were now willing, to fight for their homeland.

With such an impetus, it took little time for the army to be ready to march. Most of the preparations had already been made and had only to be loaded onto the wagons and horses, while the men collected their gear and weapons, also in standing readiness. Before the day was out, the army of Kilgarriff was on the move.

They made only eight miles the first day, but nearly twenty the next. They had made camp and were settling down for the night, when Iain heard the sound of galloping horses. He grabbed his sword, ready to march out and lead his men, when one of the watch burst through the flap of his tent.

"M'lord Iain," the man gasped out, "it's . . ."

He got no further before the flap was pushed aside and Giraldus strode through, shoving the soldier out of his way. He was covered with sweat and road grime, obviously tired, but his eyes burned with a fury that almost made Iain take a step backward.

But he stood his ground. He was here under the direction and authority of the Archbishop himself, and until the Archbishop decreed otherwise, *he* was the Baron of Kilgarriff and head of the army.

"Where have you been, Giraldus, and what are you doing here now?" Iain asked sternly.

"The question, my dear cousin, is just what *you* are doing here."

"I am here serving my kingdom and, by obedience to the Archbishop, serving God Himself—something about which you would know little. And the men whom you forced to leave their homes and families are here doing the same—but willingly this time. Of course, having men follow you willingly, because the cause is right, again seems to be something you know little about."

"Why you—" Giraldus took a step forward.

But Iain again stood his ground. He raised his sword just a little, just enough.

"No, Giraldus," he said, "not this time. I'm not the little boy you used to bully. I don't back down when I'm right. Not anymore. Until this is over and the Archbishop says otherwise, if he does, *I* am the Baron of Kilgarriff. You gave up the right when you abandoned your people."

After all these years, it felt so good to tell Giraldus off that Iain nearly laughed aloud.

Once more, Giraldus started to step forward, but the man next to him, a man Iain did not recognize and who was just as covered with the dirt of the road, put a restraining hand on his arm.

"Perhaps, m'lord," he said evenly, "we should ride on to Ballinrigh after all."

"Oh, we shall, Maelik," Giraldus said, still not taking his

eyes from Iain's face, waiting for him to flinch. But Iain did not, knew he would not.

"This is not over, Cousin," Giraldus said harshly. "I'll go to Ballinrigh—and then I'll be back. We'll see just who is Baron then."

Giraldus turned on his heel and strode back through the tent flap. Slowly, Iain lowered his sword and, one by one, unclenched his fingers from the hilt. They ached from the force of his grip.

Finally, the anger he had been using as a shield began to pass, and the glee he had been holding back set in. He had done it—the thing he had dreamed of since he was a child, what he had wanted to do each time his cousin took what was his, beat him at play or in games, then teased and berated him in front of others—he had stood up to Giraldus. He had not backed down . . . and he had won.

Suddenly, Iain raised his sword high over his head and laughed his triumph into the night, a sound to follow his cousin on his way. Despite the Archbishop's decree and all he had done since receiving it, despite the brave words he had given Giraldus, *this* was the moment when Iain knew himself to truly be the Baron of Kilgarriff.

Rhys and Aurya traveled somewhat more slowly than Giraldus and Maelik, but not as slowly as Rhys would have liked. For him, the ride could have gone on forever. But Aurya was not content to take it easy or stop for rest unless the horse required it.

By forcing themselves onward, they reached Ummera near evening of the second day. Rhys tried to tell Aurya that the bishop might not be there; all the bishops, it was said, were in Ballinrigh, to address the question of the succession once again. But Aurya would not listen. She *knew* where Elon was to be found.

He was in Ummera, as she had said—but only just. When

they reached the bishop's Residence, Elon was preparing to ride to Ballinrigh again. When Aurya arrived, he was standing beside his horse and about to mount. His expression when the horse carrying Rhys and Aurya drew near was one Aurya found hard to read. Surprise and anger combined with hope and excitement—and something else Aurya could not quite name.

He strode immediately over to Aurya. "Where the hell have you been?" he demanded as he walked. "I'd begun to believe you must be dead."

"It is a very long story," Aurya told him, as he reached out to help her dismount. "But it is one you must hear."

"And there are things you must know, as well," Elon replied, "many things. It's a precarious place we're in right now—in danger of losing everything."

Aurya turned to Rhys. "See to the horse, then get yourself some food," she ordered, softening her words with a smile. "After that, get some rest—you've earned it. His Grace and I will be busy for quite a while, I think."

"Yes, m'lady," Rhys said. "But I'll be near, if ye need t' call me."

Aurya again gave Rhys a smile, then she turned back to Elon again. The bishop nodded and led the way toward where they could speak without fear of being overheard.

An hour passed as Elon listened to what Aurya told him, and all the while his mind was calculating, planning. Even with his presence in Ummera, he had been unable to procure the things he needed for his plot against the Archbishop—or to find a new device to accomplish what he wanted. At least, not one that would work in the time he had. With all of the other bishops gathered in Ballinrigh and the battles for the crown having already begun, he was out of time. If it was not something that would work immediately, it was of no use to him.

His saddlebags were stuffed with more books that he hoped might offer him something, anything, he had yet to find—but he planned to study them after he returned to Ballinrigh. He needed to be present there to protect his interests. He was more determined than ever to claim the status, the power, toward which he had worked all his life.

Now that Aurya had returned, it was within his grasp once more.

With Aurya's tale, he now understood the identity of the priest he had seen with the Scroll at the Residence—and he also understood the threat that represented. Alone, Elon realized that he might well have never succeeded in controlling the Archbishop, no matter what he tried. But now that Aurya was here . . .

It was Elon's turn to talk now. He told Aurya all that had happened in her absence. He also told her what he wanted, what he believed he needed, to do. A strange look passed across her face when he spoke of her magic.

Elon leaned forward. "What is it?" he asked quickly. "Did these—Cryf—change you? Do you no longer want Giraldus to be High King? Well, I still will be Archbishop. If you can't or won't help me, then I'll—"

"No," Aurya stopped him. "Giraldus *must* become King, now more than ever. Whatever strength or power I have is only for that purpose—that and revenge. For you to become Archbishop is part of it.

"But I am tired and must rest before I travel again. Then, you're right—we need to be in Ballinrigh."

"And your man—will he return to the army or come with us? Can he be trusted?"

"Rhys will come with us, and he will do whatever I ask of him."

"How much rest do you require, Aurya?" Elon asked. "We must get to Ballinrigh as quickly as possible. I took a chance just coming here—but I could think of no other way to get what I needed."

"A few hours—three or four—and some food. Then I'll be able to ride again. Oh, stop for now, Elon," her voice again grew sharp and impatient. "Enough for now."

He could not miss how tired she looked or the pallor to her skin, and he wondered what she was hiding. But he pressed her no further—for now. As long as it did not threaten their still mutual goal, she could keep whatever secret she liked. He, certainly, had plenty of his own.

He rang for a servant and ordered Aurya shown to a guest room and provided with whatever she needed. "Three hours, Aurya," he said as she stood to leave. "No more. That's all the time we have."

"Three hours," she agreed. "Don't worry, Elon. After what I've been through, nothing will stop me now. *Nothing*. That's why I'm here."

Elon nodded and let her go. There was a different tone to her determination. Fierce, she had always been, and stronger of both will and mind than any other woman—almost than any man—he had ever known. But he had never before heard the hint of desperation that was part of her now. It was quiet, but for those who knew how to listen, it was unmistakably present.

Again he wondered just what had happened to her in that Realm of the Cryf of which she spoke with such hatred. Well, hatred was a weapon he could—and would—use.

The kingdom of Aghamore seemed to be holding its breath with fear and anticipation.

While the Armies of the Provinces marched north, Lord Iain brought the army of Kilgarriff across the plain of Urlar to meet them; Giraldus and Maelik rode with all speed toward Ballinrigh, with Aurya, Elon, and Rhys not far behind; the Archbishop, the Cryf, Renan, and Lysandra finally began preparations for Selia's coronation. Deep inside, everyone could feel that now was the moment of silence before the storm exploded in fury.

Margharite stayed within the bounds of the Residence, sometimes walking the gardens, but most often in her rooms—and she fumed. Part of her worried about Braedwyn and Glynna. She had no doubt that her father had discovered Glynna's impersonation—but had he done so before or after the betrothal ceremony, and what had happened when the deception was discovered?

But, as concerned as she was about her friends, there was a greater question that kept Margharite from any possible peace of mind. Had she arrived soon enough, had her warning given the armies of Aghamore enough time to stand a chance of turning back the invasion?

Her own father . . . she still could not believe this had happened. And what was going to happen to him now? To all of them—the entire Ninth House? How much would they be punished for *his* treason?

These questions ate at her until she could hardly eat or sleep. Despite all he had done, Hueil was still her father, and she loved him. Right now, with this partnership with the Corbenicans he had forged, she did not *like* him much. Still, she worried about him as much—or more—than she was worried about the others. She did not trust the Corbenicans, no matter what pledge of peaceful alliance they made. She feared they would turn and be a knife in his back.

A knife at his back, a war awaiting him—knives, swords, death everywhere . . . one of whom could be her father.

Durkin, Margharite thought suddenly. He had been uneasy here, too, chafing to return to Owenasse and Glynna. She could not send him there, not against the Archbishop's word—but she did have an idea he might like. She still had the Rider's tunic Wilham had lent her. Wearing that, Durkin would be able to leave the city, ride north, and spy on what was happening with the armies . . . with her father.

The thought lifted a cloud from Margharite's heart. An hour later, after walking the grounds, she finally found Durkin in the stables, helping the grooms clean the stalls and curry the horses.

"M'lady," he said, surprised when she walked in. "I . . . I thought I'd try t' be useful, as I be here and all. Might as well be doin' summut. I canna' stand t' be just sittin' and worryin'."

She motioned him aside. "That's what I came to talk to you about," she said softly, conscious of being overheard. "I have an idea, one that I think will suit us both. Walk with me, Durkin, where we can speak freely."

Durkin put the currycombs aside and quickly followed her from the stables. "What be it, m'lady? Ye know I'll do whatever ye need o' me."

"I think this is something we both need," Margharite answered as they walked. Then, quietly, she explained her plan.

Durkin accepted it eagerly. Like Margharite, he still had the Rider's uniform. That would lend him anonymity as he rode, protecting him as well, or better, than anything else she could offer.

"How soon can you ride?" she asked finally.

"Now," Durkin said, starting to turn back toward the stables.

Margharite laid a hand on his arm, stopping him. "Wait," she said. "Take a moment to think. I know you're eager to do something, but you'll need to change, and you'll need some supplies. I've no idea whether it will be hours or days before you will be able to return."

Durkin sighed. "Aye, m'lady," he said. "But every minute's a delay that eats at m' heart."

"I know, Durkin," she said softly. "I know. You go to the

stables and order the horse you'll need, then go get changed. I'll go to the kitchen, then meet you back at my room."

"Aye, m'lady," Durkin said again. "I'll be there quick as I can."

He hurried away. Margharite noticed that her own step was lighter as she, too, hurried back toward the inside and the task she had set herself.

Giraldus and Maelik reached the Westgate of Ballinrigh. In their present disheveled condition, it was difficult to convince the gatekeeper to admit them. But finally one of the watch set to man the city ramparts recognized Giraldus.

"M'lord Baron," he called down. "Admit him, you fool," he said to the gatekeeper, "and be quick. You've kept Baron Giraldus of Kilgarriff waiting long enough."

"Baron Gir—" The gatekeeper's face first flushed, then drained with the burst of fear the name brought him. Everyone in Aghamore knew tales, true and apocryphal, of the Baron who had a sorceress for a consort.

The man hurried to open the gate, his eyes darting all around. Giraldus knew he was looking for Aurya. Even though she was not there, her reputation rode with him and brought the speed of fear to the gatekeeper's actions.

Once the gate swung wide enough, Giraldus charged through, with Maelik right behind him. He had decided to go straight to the Archbishop's Residence without stopping at his own house to clean up and change. The old man would take him as he was—and give Giraldus back what was his or, by whatever means necessary, Giraldus would begin exacting his revenge here and now.

He paid little heed to the people in the streets, feeling a spurt of satisfaction as he watched them scurry from his path. It had been too long since he saw the effects of his place and his power in the kingdom.

The old man who has dared to give my title away will

scurry, too, Giraldus thought as they finally neared the Residence grounds. *I* will *have back what is mine.*

He and Maelik rode their horses straight up to the great steps. Grooms came rushing from the stables to take the reins. Giraldus barely spared them a glance as he dismounted and stormed up the steps like a general entering the battle. It was a battle to him, and one he intended to win.

But not in this skirmish, it seemed. Giraldus found his intentions thwarted by a statement so commonplace, it was almost laughable.

"I'm sorry, m'lord Baron," he was told, "but His Eminence is not here."

"Not here? What do you mean, not here? Where would the old f—where is he, man?"

His voice was hard, impatient, and the young monk, who was one of the Archbishop's outer secretaries, blanched at the sound and the look in Giraldus's eyes.

"I . . . I don't know, m'lord. He left with another priest, with Father Renan, and they told no one where they were going—or when they'd return."

Giraldus whirled away, anger and frustration mounting, combining with an odd feeling that the mention of Renan's name evoked. Giraldus suddenly felt as if the walls of the Realm of the Cryf were around him again, closing in, threatening to crush him. He suddenly had to get outside, into the open air once more.

He did not spare a word or a backward glance as he strode down the hallways and out the front door. Maelik was at his side, as ever, and only when they had again grabbed their reins and mounted did Giraldus look at him.

"We'll be back," was all he said. Together then, they headed for the only place in Ballinrigh left to go—to the house Giraldus kept here in the city. They were not expecting him, and the house would not be prepared, but for once Giraldus did not care. After how he had lived for the past month, it would be luxurious whatever its condition and supplies.

Yes, we'll return, he thought as he wheeled his horse back toward the gate of the Residence grounds. *You, old man, will give me what I want—but you, priest, you will learn what true wrath is. Whatever hell you've preached, whatever hell you've feared, this will be worse. I promise you that.*

Chapter Twenty-eight

L ord Iain knew he was driving the men hard. If the cause had been less desperate he would not have demanded twenty miles a day. But there was no choice. The men knew it and responded, giving him all he wanted and more. Nor did Iain let himself be constrained to the roadways and Province boundaries. The only thing that mattered was joining the other armies so they could stop the Corbenicans from reaching Ballinrigh.

When, at last, the dust rising from the men, horses, and wagons could be seen, Iain sent a messenger on a swift horse, galloping ahead with news of their approach. By that night, Iain would meet with the other Barons to form a battle plan to be used against Hueil and his allies.

It seemed to Iain that the combined armies marched with renewed vigor. They made better time than he had hoped, and the sun was still two hours from setting when Iain was finally able to give the order to make camp. He had the Archbishop's letter to grant him authority—and he had, he hoped, a plan of action that would bring them victory. His greatest hope was that it could be accomplished with minimal loss of life—on either side.

Once more he sent the messenger out. Then, as soon as his tent was erected, he sent his aides away so he could have a private hour for prayer. The deaths that were an inevitable part of the coming confrontation tore at his heart and ate a hole into his soul.

Was he fit to be a Baron? he had wondered as they rode. Could he do what was necessary, give the orders for men to die? Over these questions he now prayed. They were not easy prayers, like those said in the comforting quiet of chapel or bedchamber, his wife kneeling by his side. These were tortured prayers of Iain's private Gethsemane, faced with the same need for resolution.

Slowly the answers came. He did not want war, did not seek battle—but he would protect this kingdom and these people he loved however he must. This war would save lives, and save the *life* he lived, loved, and honored within these borders, despite the deaths ahead. It was his regret over them that made him fit to bear the title that the Archbishop had bestowed.

If he rode into battle with only the thought of glory for himself, and none for the suffering of his men or their families, then he would be no better than all he had despised in Giraldus. His doubts and questions made him strong enough to be Baron, not too weak to bear either the title or the duty.

He heard the sounds of the men setting camp—shouting, talking, even singing and laughing. His heart reached out to them all, tonight not thinking of them as soldiers, but as fathers, sons, brothers, husbands—the same as he—and with his heart he saluted them. Their bravery and sacrifice was an inspiration, something Iain intended to keep in his memory to guide him, not only tonight and tomorrow, but for as long as he was granted the privilege of being Baron of Kilgarriff. He was more determined than ever to use that position to serve the people of that Province—and these men, in their willing service to the kingdom, even in the face of probable death, were his teachers.

He rose from his knees, aware again that the other Barons would soon arrive. Quickly now, he went to the tent flap and asked his aides to prepare his tent and set out a supper for their guests. Then he waited, trying to ready himself for the arguments and objections to his presence that were sure to come.

One by one, the Barons rode in: Phelan Gradaigh of Tievebrack, Curran OhUigio of Dromkeen, Oran Keogh of Camlough, Ardal Mulconry of Sylaun, Thady Cathain of Farnagh, and Einar Maille of Lininch. Soon Iain's tent was filled with their noise and energy; they seemed to feel none of the doubts of either worthiness or ability that had so plagued him.

Iain stood a little apart, watching them as they greeted each other with an affability that belied the fact they had been battling each other so short a time before. Their eyes then were only on the prize of the crown, but now the prize was something far different, and in the difference lay the change of attitude Iain was witnessing.

Wine began to flow; although Iain's stomach had squeezed too tight with nerves to eat, the other Barons had filled their hands and platters with chunks of meat and bread and fruit. They ate and laughed—and waited for Iain's words. Finally, it was Thady Cathain of Farnagh who spoke directly to him.

"Well, Iain," his voice boomed over the din. "You're not Giraldus, but we're here as ye asked. What have ye to say and why should we listen?"

It was the opening Iain needed. He produced the Archbishop's letter and passed it to them.

"As you can see," he said while the letter made the rounds, "His Eminence has named me Baron of Kilgarriff in Giraldus's continued absence, and he has placed me in command of our combined armies."

"Why should we listen t' you, for all the Archbishop's words on paper," Curran of Dromkeen demanded, tossing the writ aside. "I've no objection t' you in Giraldus's place—he was a pompous ass and I'm not sorry t' see the back o' him." There were murmurs of agreement around the table.

"But," Dromkeen continued, "why should we trust you as our leader when we've never even heard o' you bearin' a sword?"

Iain took up the writ from where it had fallen to the floor. "'Tis true, you do know little of me," he said without rancor, "and it is not I who asks your forbearance. But you do owe your obedience to His Eminence, and I call you to that now. Our enemies approach quickly. If the information given to the Archbishop is correct —and it comes, at least in part, from an eyewitness to their landing—they come with nearly twelve thousand men at their backs. These are Rathreagh— and Corbenican—forces. Therefore, we cannot take the chance of defeat."

"No Corbenican will defeat the true men of Aghamore," Oran of Camlough said angrily, coming to his feet. "They're all bloodthirsty curs."

"True enough," Iain agreed, his voice gaining confidence at last. "But they are *united*—which we are not. *That* is the reason His Eminence has sent me. I, alone, of all of you do not seek the throne. I have no thirst for glory. My only thought is for Aghamore's survival."

To that, the Barons had no immediate retort. They heard both the implications, and the truth, in Iain's words.

"Have ye a plan, then?" Tievebrack spoke.

Iain smiled softly. "I have indeed," he said, "and if you do not think it worthwhile, then I shall bow to your greater experience."

With that, Iain took up the long tube containing the map of Aghamore and began to unroll it, ready to show them what he had in mind.

It was nearing midnight when Elon and Aurya approached the Westgate of Ballinrigh. It was only because Elon rode in his ecclesiastical robes and was known to the gatekeeper that they were admitted.

They then went straight to Elon's house, Aurya trying to hide her exhaustion. Elon, for all their hours on the road, appeared energized. Aurya knew that once she would have felt the same way. Tired though she was, she could not let Elon see it—not yet. After her work was done and Giraldus mounted the dais to be crowned, then it would not matter if her pregnancy was revealed. Until then, it would be a distraction that would endanger their success, and *that* she would not allow.

She and Elon had formed a plan, and she was prepared to do her part, only hoping she had the strength to complete it tonight. Everything now depended on timing.

Elon said little to the servants, except to order that they not be disturbed. Then he led Aurya up the stairs and into the secret room, where Thomas was waiting. Aurya was surprised to see him, but Elon quite obviously was not.

There was something going on with Thomas, she thought, something Elon had not mentioned. *Yet,* she thought again. *I will know it all before this is over. I will not have secrets kept from me, not if I am going to use my magic for Elon's purposes as well as my own.*

Thomas had something waiting on the table. As Aurya drew closer, throwing off her traveling cloak, she saw it was an ornate box, carved and gilded, a true masterwork. Thomas then opened the box for her—and Aurya gasped.

Inside was a beautiful pectoral cross of yellow gold, with bands of white gold inlaid in an intricate knotwork design. Down the rows of knots shone the deep crimson of garnets, and at the center of the cross was an almond-shaped diamond ringed around with tear-shaped amethyst. It was one of the most beautiful pieces of its kind Aurya had ever seen. Soon, if all went as planned, it would also be one of the most deadly.

"Can you do it?" Elon asked her.

"It will hold the spell," she said.

"But can you do it?" he asked her again.

Aurya looked him straight in the eyes. "You doubt my abilities, my powers? Then why did you ever come to me in the first place? Why bring me the scroll and enlist Giraldus and me in your partnership if you doubt we can do our parts? I'll set the spell, Elon. The rest is up to you. Can *you* do *your* part?"

Elon laughed. "Give the Archbishop a gift? With the way I've been all but licking his boots lately, it will be expected."

Aurya nodded yet again, then she looked at Thomas. "How much can he be trusted?" she asked.

"Thomas? Completely."

"Good. Can I use him?"

She saw Thomas glance up at Elon. The bishop gave him a little nod, a gesture of trust and to trust. Then Thomas turned to her.

"What can I do, m'lady?"

Aurya was grateful the servant was so well trained in his compliance. He could provide the strength she was lacking.

Aurya put her hands on the cross. Closing her eyes, she waited, letting each heartbeat bring up her magic. She rode the silence down into her center, down into that core where magic had been absent and now was filled again.

Then she rode her power up again, up and out to be molded into the course and shape she desired. She raised her hands off the cross. The magic was there, it was hers, filling all the empty places with power and fire.

She felt the difference within it once again. The new life in her womb, tiny though it was, moved as the magic flowed into it and gave it strength before its time. Aurya pushed the sensation from her thoughts; she could not let it distract her. Later, when this was done, and she was alone, then she would try to discover what it meant.

Aurya had Thomas step behind her and put his hands on her shoulders. Then she let the magic weave a connection between them. It took shape quickly and she understood why he was here and why Elon trusted him. Thomas, too, had power. It was budding, still in need of training—as Kizzie had once recognized in her—but it was undeniable.

At the moment, there was no way to tell exactly what final form Thomas's power would take or how much stronger he could become. But for the moment, it was only his physical strength in which Aurya was interested. She let the connection grow stronger, into tendrils of current that would not cease now until she gave the command.

Before she began, she thought again of exactly what they wanted. Setting this spell was a delicate thing. Too much, and the Archbishop would be so changed no one would accept or believe him. The Barons, the bishops, even the people, would think the old man had been too old for all the pressure and had lost his sense of reason. The change had to be subtle, gradual—and something she and Elon controlled.

> *"Gold that glitters, gold that shines*
> *Stones of color and diamond bright,*
> *Hear my words that magic binds*
> *Now into thy beauteous light;*
> *Power is mine and power I send*

Deep into thy brilliant core,
Power controlled, power I bind,
Power hold and power store."

The cross began to emit a soft glow as Aurya's magic touched and entered it. Again there was that sensation of power slightly twisted, slightly altered. But again, she pushed the feeling aside to continue.

"Upon my voice does magic flow
And my command releases all;
Magic set and magic goes
And once released no one can stall.
The wearer of this cross shall be
A captive tool, no will his own;
From the first touch until death frees
His life by magic now is owned."

Aurya stopped to gather strength, drawing even more intensely from Thomas's energy flowing beneath his hands. Her own strength was failing fast, even with Thomas's aid, and she was not used to such a feeling. Striving to hide it from Elon, she pulled herself up straighter, ready for the final part of the incantation.

She looked down. By now, she expected to see arcane light glowing in the garnets, streaming out from the central diamond. But the stones held no more brilliance than the last time she looked. Power was present, but it lacked intensity. It—she—lacked the strength that would normally be hers and mark anything that she did.

Again, however, she refused to let Elon know that anything was wrong. She forced a smile to her lips, ready to begin again. With these final words she would seal the Archbishop's fate; once he put on this cross, nothing would save him.

"By gold of yellow, gold of white
That from the grip of stone was drawn,
By gems of color and diamond bright
Is wearer turned to magic's pawn.
Elon shall now thy master be
None other power of heaven or earth
Shalt wearer hear or wearer see;
To wear this cross is magic's birth.
By magic's touch is soul now brand,
Mind and heart are turned to dust
And formed again by magic's hand
Into the shape that magic trusts.
None may break this bond of power
But that it cause unending pain
To mind and heart and soul; most dour
Suffering builds 'til wearer's slain.
Only shall the wearer's death
End the power that holds him fast;
Only with death's final breath
Shall magic flee and free at last."

Aurya now stepped back. It took everything within her to remain upright; it was only her pride that kept her from crumpling to the floor and not moving again until the rest of the night had passed.

Trying her best to minimize the action, she let her hand stray to the back of a chair, as if in a casual movement. But then her fingers gripped the cloth-covered wood like a lifeline.

"Is that all?" Elon asked her. "There's still much of our purpose left unsaid."

"It is enough," Aurya assured him. "Too much, and we give ourselves away. Once the Archbishop puts this on, he will have no choice but to give you both his support and his complete obedience. I've made sure of that. You can do the rest once Giraldus is King and you finally wear the triple-crowned mitre you covet so much."

"True enough. But—"

"Enough, Elon. Magic comes at a price, even for me."

"As I see. Your face has gone very white, Aurya. Are you unwell?"

"Not unwell—merely tired. Show me to a room, Elon, and let me alone for a while. The spell is set, and you may have it delivered in the morning—or deliver it yourself, if you've a mind. But the ride was long, and I've had far too little rest for far too long."

Elon was looking at her oddly, but he nodded and spoke a few quick words to Thomas. The man rose, the perfect willing servant.

"This way, m'lady," he said—seeming unaffected by the energy Aurya had siphoned from him.

They left Elon gloating over his gift for the Archbishop. Thomas led her out from the secret room, down the corridor and to a ready guest chamber. Aurya dismissed him with a murmured "thank you," to which he silently bowed as he closed the door.

Aurya did not bother to undress. She merely fell on the bed and hugged her belly. Once more, she felt the life growing there. It was only a month old; there should have been no awareness, no sensation—for mother or child. But she was no ordinary woman, and her magic had touched her child— *her son*—and decided otherwise.

All through the setting of the spell, she felt the child. Again and again, it distracted her, pulling a part of her away from her magic and down deep within her own body. That part of her, of which she had always thought herself devoid, wanted nothing more than to touch, explore . . . did she really want to cherish? . . . that newly growing life.

She wrapped her arms even more tightly around herself as

she felt sleep rapidly closing in. Whatever differences the child would bring, she would face them after she had rested.

And what about you, Giraldus? she thought, darkness coming closer. *Where are you right now? This child is your son, but I will never let you use him to change me. He is* my *son, too, and he shall be as* I *choose.*

With that thought, sleep refused to be held away. Its thick blanket enveloped her and she thought no more.

Still in his private study, Elon waited for Thomas to return. He stared down at the pectoral cross he would take to the Archbishop tomorrow, thinking and worrying.

There was something very different about Aurya. Whatever she claimed, it was more than fatigue, more than long travel and lack of sleep. The change was something deeper, something more fundamental than that.

Perhaps being with those creatures, those ... Cryf ... left more of a mark on her than she knows, he thought. *Or, perhaps having her magic flood back after so long an absence, as she said, takes an adjustment I can't understand.*

It was this latter he both wanted and chose to believe. To do otherwise would mean everything was in jeopardy. He walked over and stared at the fire.

No, he thought, *Aurya would know if something was not right. Her magic was strong as ever—I could feel it filling the room. It was as if the air itself was alive.*

Envy welled up inside him, and he slammed his fist against the mantel. He *wanted* that power himself. He hated that others possessed what he did not, even his own daughter. For one brief instant, he hated her.

Then, as he heard Thomas returning, he drew himself up straighter. Aurya had magic, yes—but of *his* making. She was his tool, and he would continue to use her.

And he would make certain he found the means to control her, too. He would wait and watch and find out exactly what change he sensed. Then he would use it to be certain she never turned on him. Without him, she would be nothing— she would not even exist. Perhaps someday soon he would tell her that.

Thomas entered and gave him a small nod. "She is sleeping," he said.

"Tell me, Thomas," Elon said, "what did you sense when she touched you? Was her magic real?"

"And strong," Thomas said. "But—"

"Go on," Elon said sharply. "Everything . . . I need to know."

"After she backed away, I caught a look—a glimpse only—of what might await. There is danger, Your Grace, and death. I could not see for whom . . . but it is there."

If Thomas had glimpsed the future without the aid of fire and trance, then either his powers had grown or contact with Aurya's magic had triggered them. Either way, Elon took his words seriously.

"Yes, Thomas, there will be death," he said. "But not ours. Death awaits those who oppose us."

The look on Thomas's face said he had meant something else entirely.

Chapter Twenty-nine

Morning dawned over the kingdom of Aghamore. Through the night, the combined armies of Hueil of

Rathreagh and Wirral of Corbenica had taken position on the northern plains of Urlar facing the Armies of the Provinces.

Hueil had slept little. It was not fear that kept him awake to hear the tramping of the sentries' feet walking the perimeter of the camp, the jingle of tackle as horses were unloaded, fed, curried, and corralled, the sounds of troops—the laughter of the Corbenicans, the restlessness of his own men as each prepared himself for the morning's battle.

What kept Hueil from sleep was regret and conscience. He had entered this alliance to gain the crown, and he still might. But tonight he felt as if he had lost everything of true importance. He had lost his daughter—her respect and, perhaps, even her love. He had also lost his self-respect, and that hurt almost as much.

As he lay within his tent, on the only relative comfort of a camp bed, trying to catch the sleep that kept eluding him, the losses seemed to far outweigh anything he might yet gain. Without Margharite, what did the crown matter?

And the Corbenicans; Hueil's mind shuddered at the thought of them. This partnership was the worst folly of his life.

They could not be trusted, no matter what he said or how often he complained to Wirral. The men were out of control. Their objective was supposed to be Ballinrigh, and they were supposed to be fighting for the crown, the good of the kingdom.

Yet Hueil could not stop the Corbenicans from leaving formation whenever the desire struck them and dashing off in looting raids. And he had seen their handiwork, passing through the remains of a town some of Wirral's men had visited the night before, when they were supposed to be asleep.

Hueil tossed again upon his camp bed, uncomfortable with the memory, trying to deny any culpability. Yet the memory and the dead—the burned, the tortured, the raped—all cried out their accusation.

He closed his eyes, grinding the heel of his palms into them, trying to hold back the tears of shame and rage that he felt. Even that could not erase the memory. The visions built, swirled, would not be denied; Hueil groaned at the horror in his mind . . .

The place was still a smoldering pile of ash and rubble, sending a gray veil over what had once been the town of Antara. But it seemed to accentuate, rather than hide, the horror as Hueil rode slowly through.

The smell of blood was almost as thick as the smoke. Bodies lay scattered and crumpled amid the ruins. They were the lucky ones. As Hueil rode forward through the smoke, he passed a sight that nearly made him retch.

Tied to trees were the spread-eagled bodies of both men and women. They had been cut open from throat to groin. All of their innards—hearts, lungs, entrails—had been cut out and piled on the ground at their feet, then set on fire as an offering to the Corbenican god of war.

An old woman stumbled out from behind the rubble of one of the fired buildings. Dried blood still plastered her head and lay encrusted on face, hands, and stained her clothing. She pointed a filthy, gnarled finger in his direction. Her eyes filled with hatred, and finally she spoke.

"Yer fault," she said, her voice slowly taking power with each step she took toward Hueil. "Ye see what they did, them demons what be with ye? Demons, I tell ye. Nothin' else 'ud do such things to another livin' soul. Ye shouda' heard th' screams. Dyin' was a blessin'.

"An' do ye know what they did t 'others? Those what they didna' rape, they beat—as they did me, ol' woman what I am and no threat to 'um. An' it be *yer* fault. Ye did this—t' yer own people. *Ye* did this."

She spit on the ground, then she turned her back on Hueil

and slowly, painfully, walked away. Beside him, Wirral laughed. Behind him, Hueil could hear his own men growling their anger while the Corbenican men joined their leader's laughter.

That laughter, like the pointed finger and accusing words, filled Hueil's mind until he could not stand it. He bolted upright in his cot. Hanging his head, he cradled it in his hands, shaking it slowly side to side.

He had made a horrible mistake; he had known it, a thought that lingered unacknowledged and unsaid, from the moment he had faced his daughter. Now, the realization refused to be denied. It pounded in every heartbeat, accusing him as surely as had that old woman.

But what could he do about it? The question ran circles in his mind, darting in and out of possibilities. But none of them provided the answer Hueil needed, and he knew he was trapped. He was left only with his wishes — that he had never contacted the Corbenicans, that he had never coveted the throne — that he had possessed the same courage as his daughter.

With a sigh that seemed to rise from somewhere deep inside his weariness, Hueil lay back down. He was no closer to finding a way to the freedom that he knew he needed. In the darkness, he felt that there would never be such an answer — and the dawn was many long hours away.

The night wore slowly but inexorably on. Darkness deepened, and silence just as slowly spread as the men, Rathreagh and Corbenican, fell to sleep. Hueil dozed and woke and dozed again. Each time he awoke, it felt as if he was a little closer to . . . something. It was nagging somewhere just beyond conscious thought, but it was not until daylight neared that it finally moved from the hidden realms into something usable.

Moving as quietly as he could, he rose and wrapped a

blanket around himself. He must get a message to his men, but without the Corbenicans—without *Wirral*—suspecting.

His aide was sleeping just outside the tent flap. Hueil knelt and softly touched the man, quickly motioning for silence when he jerked awake. Then Hueil whispered quickly and directly into the young man's ear.

He gave a single nod and began crawling off in the direction of Hueil's generals. Hueil watched him go, a sense of rightness slowly replacing the regret that had been gnawing at him these last days. What he was doing now was dangerous. If even one of his generals did not agree and took the news to the Corbenicans, Hueil knew he would be dead before the battle even began.

He had already prepared a story, should Wirral receive news of the meeting he was convening. It was customary before a battle, he would tell the Corbenican King, for the generals to meet for prayer, which was not far from the truth . . . and Wirral would know no difference. Had their cause been more righteous, Hueil would have a priest or two traveling with them, and the troops would receive the Sacrament at dawn.

For this campaign, however, Hueil had no priest. There had been no blessing upon their departure, no spiritual comfort and direction given to strengthen their hearts or guide their purpose each day. For that purpose, he had known from the beginning, he could neither ask a blessing nor expect the Church's sanction.

But again, Wirral would know nothing of this, and that would buy Hueil the time he needed. By tomorrow night, he hoped he could again seek solace in the sacraments. *Especially,* he thought as he waited, *in Absolution.* He was desperately in need of forgiveness.

It was something he hoped he would earn in the next few hours.

*   *   *

Hueil was not the only Baron awake before dawn. Iain of Kilgarriff, too, was aware of the soft lightening of the sky, where deep blue-blackness became violet, then brushed with the first streaks of palest gold.

It would have been a beautiful morning had he not known that for too many here it was the last they would ever experience.

The meeting last night had gone far better than he expected. The other Barons had, of course, been reluctant to accept his leadership—whatever the Archbishop's writ decreed—and he understood their reluctance. He had no illusions about himself or his standing in their eyes.

Yet, as the evening progressed, he had seen reluctance give way to dawning respect as he laid his plan out before them. What was to come would have to be a joint effort to succeed. The other Barons had greater experience and training, and he was relying heavily on their knowledge—but *he* was the unifying factor. That, too, had its importance. He knew it, as had the Archbishop—as did the Barons . . . finally. The long meeting last night had produced an accord that, if all went well, could easily be the salvation of the kingdom.

Everything depended on timing, and on not letting the Corbenicans see the placement of the troops. The army of Kilgarriff had taken up the central position. Four armies had reshuffled and fanned out, making it look as if there were six—with two generals impersonating the absent Barons. Then, under the cover of night, the missing Barons had led unmounted troops silently up into the hills behind the enemy, to await the signal and close in, surrounding the traitor and the invaders in a pincer action.

It was, in Iain's mind, the best chance they had to succeed. Together, the Armies of the Provinces outnumbered the Corbenicans—but the savagery of the northerners was something legendary; he doubted any Aghamorian could equal it. And, in battling the army of Rathreagh, the Aghamorians would be fighting their own, when instinct told them that all of their energy should be turned against the Corbenicans. This, Iain knew, was making the troops uneasy—it might well stay their arm at too crucial a moment.

The Armies of the Provinces received a blessing and the Sacrament before they broke their fast. Then they took up their appointed positions and waited.

The sun rose higher. The northern plain of Urlar lost its places of shadow and became an expectant killing field. Iain raised his sword arm high, ready to give the signal. But he kept it there, waiting. He could feel the anticipation. It was an equal mixture of eagerness and dread, adrenaline and fear—but it was also the feeling of strength flowing into the sword arm of every man behind him.

Across the field, the Corbenicans stared back defiantly. Their ranks were uneven, as if barely held back, and many of them waved their weapons eagerly. Their joy in the thought of the upcoming battle was obvious.

By contrast, the men of Rathreagh stood straight. Each bore the symbol of the House—the wild tusked boar on a field of red—on a large, diamond-shaped patch sewn to their left breast. Iain's men wore the same patch, but with the black griffin of Kilgarriff on its silver field, cut in a shape of a shield.

All the Armies of the Provinces wore the color and emblem of the House for which they fought.

Iain's eyes sought out the leaders—they were not hard to find. Wirral of Corbenica was wrapped in his white fur, glaring with even more hatred than his men. Next to him sat Hueil, mounted on his gray stallion. The wild boar of Rathreagh on its brilliant ruby field was emblazoned over the entire front of the surcoat that covered Hueil's chain mail.

Beside Hueil stood a man whose sole duty was to keep Hueil's standard, the flag of Rathreagh, raised by the Baron's side. As long as the standard was raised, the men knew their Baron lived, and they would go on fighting.

Wirral had no such device, no standard-bearer. His men lived for the fight, with or without him.

Iain squinted to better see in the distance. Hueil sat slumped in his saddle, and even from the distance Iain could see that the fire was not there. Iain wished there were time to send a message, to call for a parley before the battle and give Hueil a chance to end this peacefully.

But even as he thought this, King Wirral gave a cry that made the hair on Iain's neck and arms stand up and his stomach knot into a ball so tight that he felt momentarily ill.

The sound grew as other Corbenicans joined their voices. Then, suddenly, the world erupted.

The battle for Aghamore began.

In Ballinrigh, Elon approached the Archbishop's Residence. He came today in full splendor—his finest carriage, his cassock of watermarked silk with the gold buttons and piping. In his arms he carried the ornately carved box that contained the pectoral cross. It had been even more beautiful when he looked at it this morning; surely, he thought, the Archbishop would be unable to resist at least putting it on. Once he did, the spell would take effect.

He would be theirs . . . Aghamore would be theirs.

Aurya had not yet awakened when Elon left his house. He did not begrudge her the sleep, but he did worry a little. He still could not shake the feeling that there was something altered about her.

He pushed his concerns aside and prepared himself for the face that he must show to the Archbishop. The humble and contrite façade must not only be maintained, but also built upon so that this gift would be accepted.

It was early, and the Residence did not officially open to the public for half an hour. But the doorman readily admitted Elon; now that the last of the other bishops had arrived in Ballinrigh for the reconvening of the College—presently postponed—the coming and going of the episcopal body of the Church was expected at the Residence.

"His Eminence is currently engaged," he was told by the grumbling, stern-faced monk he had seen there often before. "But I shall announce your arrival."

Elon smiled graciously, even while inside he was fuming. The man's tone was dismissive and arrogant, as if he looked upon Elon as no better than a street beggar and unworthy of both his and the Archbishop's attention.

I'll show you soon just how unimportant I am, Elon thought to the monk's retreating back. *Soon you'll not dare speak to me in such a tone, however gracious-sounding your words. Soon, I will be master here, and you will treat me as such.*

He waited, pacing, his hands itching to open the box and look at the cross again. He knew it was the magic pulling at him. It was a wonderful sign; if he, who knew of the magic's existence, was finding it so difficult, the Archbishop should find it impossible not to put the cross immediately on.

I won't doubt you again, Aurya, Elon thought. *Whatever this change is in you, your magic is still strong.*

The inner door opened again, and the monk returned. His face told Elon all that was needed, but he waited politely, careful of his current persona.

"I'm sorry, Your Grace," the monk said, in a tone totally without the regret his words professed, "but His Eminence cannot be disturbed at the moment. He says that he will see you at Mass, when you and the other bishops gather to pray for the great cause our armies are facing."

Elon realized that he had been partly expecting this,

though he had hoped beyond that expectation. No matter; he did not need to be present for the spell to work. He had wanted to be present to witness the change that came over the old fool when he put the cross around his neck, and Aurya's spell slowly but inexorably took charge of him, mind and soul.

But he would have the result, and that was all that really mattered. He accepted the monk's words with full-seeming graciousness as he gave a somber smile.

"Yes," he said, "and may God grant them both strength and guidance this day. But, before I go, perhaps . . . I realize how very busy His Eminence must be at a time like this. I only came to deliver this gift from the people of my Province. It was fashioned by some of our finest craftsmen. If you could, perhaps, present it on my behalf? It is but a token of the gratitude the people of Kilgarriff feel for all that the Archbishop did for them by the elevation of Lord Iain."

The monk's long face had softened and taken on a look of understanding as Elon spoke. "Certainly, Your Grace," he now said. "I'm sure His Eminence will be touched by the gift and its meaning. I know that the welfare of your Province has been greatly on his mind."

Elon picked up the box and placed it in the monk's outstretched hands. The man accepted it with a little bow and a placid smile, replacing his earlier scowl. His face reminded the bishop of the look worn by sheep—which was all that this monk, and his kind, meant to Elon.

Elon watched the monk turn away to deliver the package from the only true wolf within their fold. *You understand nothing,* the bishop's thoughts followed him as he disappeared behind the closed door. *None of you have any idea what is truly happening or truly at stake—here and on the northern plain. Let the armies all kill each other . . . and I hope that fool, Iain, is among those slain. But the* true *battle*

*for the throne is won the moment "His Eminence" puts on
that cross.*

For the first time all morning, Elon gave a true smile. But
it was not a look that contained either comfort or joy. It was
a look of pure, ferocious avarice, the look of a predator about
to bring down his prey.

The Archbishop was not alone. He had been rarely alone,
except to sleep, these last several days. Ever since the Cryf
had arrived, bringing the secret of the Heart of the Scepter,
he and the others had been busy secretly preparing for Selia's
coronation.

It could now take place, of that Colm ApBeirne was certain. There was so much to do, and without a staff, that his
every waking thought was taken up with it. And now he had
the College of Bishops with which to contend.

Again, he wished he had a trusted successor on whose
shoulders he could place some of these duties. Once he had
thought that would be Elon. It almost had been, and the realization of how near he had come to unwittingly handing the
kingdom over to the Darkness, appalled him anew each time
it crossed his mind.

Now, however, the possibility was gone—and the Archbishop could think of no one within the College about whom
he felt any spiritual direction to appoint. Occasionally he
thought that Renan might be the leader this kingdom needed.
He had certainly earned the trust of the Archbishop. But they
had never broached the subject.

Even if he could persuade Renan to accept the position, it
would mean he must first be consecrated from priest to
bishop. Then he would have to be trained—and that would
take two, three, possibly several more years. Colm ApBeirne
felt his retirement slipping further and further away.

Already this morning, Renan and the Cryf, Selia, Lysandra, and Cloud-Dancer had been in his office for the last

hour, planning and discussing what still needed to be done and how long it might take to accomplish. When the second knock came, interrupting them yet again, the Archbishop gave a nod for Renan to answer it.

He returned a moment later with a box in his arms . . . and a worried look on his face.

"What is it, Renan?" the old man asked.

Renan shook his head. "A gift," he said, "from Elon—and, he says, from the people of Kilgarriff as a symbol of their love and gratitude. But—"

"Yes?" the Archbishop prompted when he hesitated.

"Your Eminence—there is something here. I don't trust it . . . and I don't think you should, either."

The Archbishop looked at the other faces. The Cryf expressions he still found hard to read beneath the hair that covered their faces, though their eyes were grave enough. Selia, too, looked somber. But it was Lysandra's expression that truly stopped him.

"What is it, daughter?" he asked her gently.

She started, as if she had forgotten where she was or that she was not alone, forgotten everything except what she was experiencing. She blinked her sightless eyes, staring at the box still in Renan's hands. The Archbishop realized that her *Sight* was showing her something beyond his understanding.

"Speak, Healer," the ancient Cryf said to her. "Tell us what the Divine showeth thee."

She shook her head slowly from side to side. "Renan," she said sharply, suddenly, "put it down. Get away from it. It is Darkness. Oh, Renan, I recognize it . . . I *know* the feel of it. She's here—and it's from *her*."

No one had to ask whom she meant. Renan put the carved box on a little table far from the Archbishop's desk and backed away. The last lingering, hopeful doubts about Elon's affiliation now left the Archbishop's mind.

He wanted to leave the box untouched until he could think of its proper disposal—but Eiddig slowly rose from his chair and crossed the room. With a gesture, he waved Renan away.

"Eiddig," the Archbishop began, rising himself.

"Nay," Eiddig said, "stay and approach not. Neither fear, for the Divine hast given unto the Cryf a strength for to fight such Darkness. Yea, I seeth now that for such hath we been sent unto thy company. Trusteth the Divine and be at peace. All shalt be well."

Slowly, Colm sat back down. An unsaid prayer rose from his heart as he watched the Cryf's hands touch the lid of the box. His eyes were closed as he ran his gnarled fingers over the ornate carvings.

Then, suddenly, he threw the lid open. The Archbishop heard Lysandra gasp. His glance flew to her, and he saw that all the color had drained from her face. She looked filled and torn by an inner pain.

Renan and Selia must have heard it, too. They both came to her side, comforting her with their touch.

"Yea," Eiddig said, "great be the Darkness herein. And yet . . ." He stopped and picked up the large cross, holding it in one hand and the chain on which it hung in the other.

The Archbishop watched, fascinated. It was truly amazing —Lysandra could feel the dark magic so strongly, even from across the room, that it caused her physical pain . . . and yet Eiddig could hold and handle it with impunity.

Of what else, he wondered, *are these Cryf capable? How much have we here in the "Up-world"*—he almost smiled at the Cryf term—*been missing these centuries because of our own blindness?*

After a moment, Eiddig put the cross back in the box and closed the lid. The look on Lysandra's face eased a little; even the atmosphere in the room changed, lighted by locking that . . . thing . . . away. The old Cryf then turned and came back to the chairs in which everyone else still sat.

"Well," the Archbishop said after a moment of tense silence, "what now? Elon has finally revealed his hand—how much do we reveal of ours?"

The silence held while everyone considered the question and the outcomes of the various answers. Finally, it was Eiddig who spoke.

"Healer," he said to Lysandra, "as thou hast felt, it is the work of she who hath touched thee with darkness afore, and though the wound of that touch hath healed, always shalt thou beareth a scar. Unto this doth the Darkness here reach out. And yea, though our enemies be at hand, our cause still standeth strong and we art all held within the Hand of the Divine. Therefore, shalt we prevail, even against this."

He looked at the Archbishop, and as their eyes met, Colm ApBeirne felt a deep connection with this Guide of the Cryf. He nodded, silently urging Eiddig to continue.

"If thou wearest not this ill-given gift," he said, "the giver shalt too soon know that his deceit hath been discovered."

"No," Lysandra cried. She gripped Cloud-Dancer as if only by his touch could she feel safe. "You can't . . . you don't know what it's like to be buried in and beneath that Darkness. It suffocates the soul. It—"

"Peace, Healer," Talog said to her very softly. "Eiddig wouldst not ask such."

His hand was on Lysandra's arm. She looked at him, her sightless eyes somehow appearing to see all the more. Then she turned them on Eiddig and the Archbishop. Colm found himself giving a little shiver, trying not to imagine the horror in that Darkness she had just described.

She gave a little nod, and Eiddig continued. "We needeth yet time," he said, "and thus must our enemies believe their fearful trick hath known success. Thou must, then, weareth this foul thing . . . yet not as it doth now exist.

"Magic, dark and heavy, hath here been set, yet its hold be not strong. Talog and I shalt, by the Help of the Divine, breaketh it free unto the beauty of its forming again. Then thou mayest wear it without danger unto soul or body."

"Can you do that?" the Archbishop asked, once more amazed by the hidden strengths of these beings.

"Yea, by the Hand of the Divine," Eiddig answered. "Such gifts hath the Divine given unto us."

"What do you need?" Colm now asked. "Whatever it is, it is yours. What can we do to help you?"

"We needeth little, save a place of silence, of safety and solitude. For thy safety, thou must not be beside us as we releaseth the Darkness and banish it again unto the abyss from whence it was summoned."

The Archbishop rose. "Come with me," he said.

He led the way out of the study and into a small antechamber. It was not much of a room, merely a small prayer closet to which he sometimes retreated from the pressures of his duties. It contained a small altar, with candles and crucifix, and a padded kneeler on which he prayed when he was here.

"Will this do?" he asked Eiddig.

The Cryf Guide nodded. He motioned for Talog to put the box on the altar, then looked at Colm solemnly.

"Thou and the others must pray," he said, "that the Darkness findeth no place to rest until it be full banished. Then, only, shalt all be safe again."

"Very well," the Archbishop said "And Eiddig—thank you. Your presence here truly is a gift of the Divine."

"Thank not me, but the Divine whose Hand hath brought us unto this place and at the time appointed, that we may best be of service unto thee, unto She-Who-Is-Wisdom, and unto the Heart and Purpose of the Divine."

Again the Archbishop nodded. He turned away, closing the door behind him and leaving Eiddig and Talog to their work. Then he rejoined Lysandra, Renan, and Selia.

Raising his hand in the gesture he had made over half his

life, he began. *"In nomine a Pater, et Filii, Et Spiritus Sancti . . .*

"Let us pray. . . ."

Chapter Thirty

Eiddig stood, silent and still, staring at the box Talog was placing on the little holy table of the Up-world Guide. *Archbishop*, he thought the word. It was strange to him, but he understood the meaning. This man was the Guide of his people, helping to keep their feet on the Path of Light—as Eiddig did for the Cryf. They understood each other, as much by the unsaid as by the words that passed between them.

"Art thou ready, Son of my Path?" he asked Talog, speaking in their own language and using the name of fondness he had given him long ago.

"Ready and at thy side, Father of our Way. Dost thou truly believe thou canst banish the evil from this . . . thing?"

"Have faith, little Guide. It shalt not be I, but the Divine who worketh here. Standeth by my side and giveth me of thy strength, then shalt all be well."

Eiddig walked over to the altar and threw back the lid of the box. It opened with a dull clang. Inside, the two golds, the deep blood red of the garnets, and silver-purple of amethyst caught and glittered in the light of the candles that were kept lit in this place.

But it was the diamond at the cross's heart that drew Eiddig's eyes. It was smaller, but just as flawless as the diamond at the heart of the Guide's necklace he had worn these last eighty years. Now, it held the light of the candles in its heart as if the flame had entered and become part of it.

Within it also burned the core of Darkness that had been placed upon this once-beautiful work of art and holiness.

It shalt be beautiful again, he thought, *and again given unto holiness, as wast the intention of its maker. That intention shalt soon be honored.*

He took the cross out of the box and laid it on the altar. Then he placed atop it his old and twisted hands, hands filled with a lifetime of service to his people and to the Divine. Then he closed his eyes.

The dark power within the cross throbbed, but it could not truly touch him. *Unto this moment, O Divine, hast thou created and hath thy hand placed me,* his prayer began. *Let thy Strength, against which naught mayeth stand, flood me now unto this great purpose. Mine heart and life hath ever been unto thy keeping. I standeth open now and ready for the battle against thine, and our, enemies.*

Eiddig waited. Under his hands, the ill-set spell on the cross beat harder, as if in response to the threat it felt from his prayer. But Eiddig felt something more. He felt a great warmth welling up from deep within him, filling him like a fire that had been banked and smoldering throughout his lifetime but had suddenly erupted into flame.

Power met power in a silent and bitter battle. The room, tiny as it was, reverberated as the powers pounded and clashed off the walls, flew from ceiling to floor and back again, surrounded the Cryf in the confrontation of Darkness and Light. Eiddig could see it all through his closed eyes; he could see it with the eyes of his soul, and for the first time he understood the *Sight* of Lysandra.

He felt, too, the weariness and weight of his years. His time on this world had already been long, and although it had been lived mostly in the peaceful Realm of the Cryf, that did not stay time's passage. He was the Guide of the Strong; he prayed he would now have the strength to continue this most important of battles.

Talog suddenly placed his hands on top of Eiddig's, youth covering age. It was a fitting reversal of universal reality, for age inevitably lays its blanket over the youth that remains always alive, though sometimes sleeping, within every living heart. Now, however, youth covered age, and Eiddig nodded at the rightness of the act.

With Talog's touch, with the prayers that Eiddig knew were rising from his protégé's heart, the power on the cross began to wither. If the Archbishop had put this thing on, Eiddig knew with certainty, the twisted Darkness would have gripped his mind and slowly shattered it. The evil here would not have controlled him—it would have killed him.

But not Eiddig and not Talog. Under the strength of their united faith, the battle began to abate. Little by little, the eyes of Eiddig's soul beheld the twisting core of Darkness change from black, to violet, to gray. It became smoke, then mist, insubstantial and impermanent.

Suddenly, Light erupted. It filled and poured from Eiddig, into the stones, and back outward again, freeing the cross from the Darkness that entrapped it. Eiddig kept praying, kept centering that Light deeply into all the places where Darkness had just existed, cleaning away any vestiges of evil that might remain to catch the unwary.

Then, when he was finally certain all was done, he raised his hands and spread his arms wide, as if to embrace the room. His gift, his power, was not magic—not as the others claimed it, not as this cross had already known. Eiddig's power was faith, and in it he felt as if the Light, in which he had walked his long path of life, was now pouring from his fingertips. The room, into which Darkness had fled, provided it no haven now. Like a hunted animal, it sought the corners and shadows and found no place where Light did not follow it.

Eiddig opened his eyes and found that what he was feeling and seeing internally was fact such as he had never thought to witness. His hands *were* fountains of Light. Talog's too, as he stood facing his teacher, were ablaze.

The Light was golden white, yet it also contained all the colors of Creation, colors felt more than seen. It was brilliant, warm, but it did not burn. It soothed both body and soul merely to gaze upon it. It replenished within Eiddig all that the battle with Darkness had drained from him, and more, until he felt stronger than he had for many a year.

Slowly, the Light abated. It did not go away, Eiddig understood that; instead it stayed within him, where it would and always had remained.

Talog smiled at him, and softly Eiddig returned the expression. He saw the astonishment in the younger Cryf's eyes. There was so much he wanted to say to Talog—things he had never truly understood until this moment.

But now was not the time. There was still much work ahead of them, and Eiddig knew that before he tried to explain what he had come to experience and know today, he must spend some time in quiet communion with his own heart, and with the Divine.

There was, however, time for gratitude. He spoke a prayer praising and thanking the Divine for the Light that had protected them and made them strong. Then he took up the cross again and headed back to where the others were waiting . . . and praying, too.

When Eiddig opened the door, the Archbishop ceased his prayers and came hurrying over.

"It is finished," Eiddig told him, "and all is well. True beauty hath been restored, that this"—he held the cross out to the Archbishop—"mayeth be again used unto the purpose for which it was intended. Thou mayest now wear it without fear."

"What?" Renan asked sharply as he came to his feet and rushed over. "Your Eminence, you can't honestly intend—"

The Archbishop held up a hand, stopping him from speaking further. He and Eiddig stared at each other silently over the cross still in Eiddig's hand. Finally, the Archbishop reached out and took it. The Cryf Guide gave a small nod, knowing he had understood.

"He's right, Renan," the Archbishop said.

"But—"

"Peace, Renan. Have faith."

"Our enemies must yet thinketh themselves safe," Eiddig said, still watching the Archbishop's face. He understood all of Renan's concern for the safety of this one who was Guide of his people and their faith.

The power that had been set upon the cross had been dark and far more dangerous than Eiddig had thought possible. Even for him, who was immune to its imprint, the memory of that Darkness was not one he cared to remember—or would ever forget. Again he thought of what might have happened to this gentle old man, and gave silent thanks to the Divine that he and Talog had been here to prevent it.

But the Archbishop would have to touch and wear the cross in order to play a part and buy them the final time necessary. Renan must accept and understand.

"Time," the Archbishop said as if he had heard Eiddig's thought, turning to meet Renan's eyes. "Time is what we need—and have too little of. But we must provide all that we can. If that means I must wear this . . . thing . . . then I will. Our friends say it is safe, and I trust them."

In a sudden, decisive movement, the Archbishop put the cross around his neck. Eiddig held his breath as, he was sure, did everyone else.

Then the old man smiled. "I'm fine," he said. "Everything

is fine. If anything, I feel better, lighter and stronger some-how."

"Ah," Eiddig, too, smiled then. "The Touch of the Divine still resteth upon it."

There was a discreet knock on the door, and a moment later Brother Naal opened it. "Excuse me, Your Eminence," he said, "but you wanted to be told when the bishops were assembled. They are awaiting you in the cathedral now."

"Thank you, Naal," the Archbishop said, turning toward the young monk. "I shall be there presently."

Once the door had again closed, he turned back to Eiddig. "I shall get us the time we need. And you—"

"Shalt prepare all as thou hast devised," Eiddig assured him.

"God be with us all, then," the Archbishop said, turning away.

Eiddig watched him as he walked toward the door, stop-ping to give his blessing to each one of them he passed. Eid-dig could not hear what was said with his ears—but his heart and his spirit knew, and joined in the quiet prayers.

After the door had closed behind the Archbishop's back, he also breathed a blessing. "And the Divine go with thee, keep thee strong, and grant thee grace in what now must come," he said. He did not think anyone heard him, except the Divine, who heard all.

But Renan did. "Amen," he said fervently . . . and the word was echoed around the room.

Elon sat among his brother bishops, endeavoring to ap-pear gracious and unconcerned. Inside, however, his stomach was churning as he waited for the old man to appear. What would happen? his thoughts kept repeating the question. Had he put on the cross? Had Aurya's spell worked?

Finally, the door of the vestry opened, and the Archbishop came out, attended by the Dean of the Cathedral, a deacon, and the two acolytes who had helped him robe and who would assist at the Mass. After that, the bishops would continue here in prayer for the safety and success of those in battle on the plain to the north. This would be their only meeting today. They would not assemble to debate the succession until after the outcome of the battle was known.

The Archbishop spoke to one of the acolytes, and the young man gave a little bow before he left the sanctuary of the altar and approached Elon. The Bishop of Kilgarriff tried not to appear concerned or anxious, covering the way his heart was now pounding by flipping through the pages of his breviary, as if looking for the prayers for safety that were soon to come.

Yet, out of the corner of his eye, he watched the young man closely. The boy's face, though fittingly solemn, was untroubled. He was focused on his errand, yet he did not look as if it was something unpleasant or to be feared.

He could be going to retrieve something from the back of the cathedral or from the narthex, or any of a dozen other things, Elon knew. He could be . . .

But he stopped at Elon's aisle and motioned to the bishop. This was it; this was the moment of crux, when he would know what his future would hold. He stood and went to the acolyte, stopping first to properly genuflect as he entered the aisle, all show of piety intact.

"His Eminence asks you to join him in leading the upcoming prayer service," the young man whispered. "He begs your forgiveness for the short notice and no time for preparation, but says that fatigue lies heavily upon him today, and he needs your aid."

Elon inclined his head, again careful of his show of humility. "Tell His Eminence that I shall be honored to aid him in any way I can, today as always."

The acolyte gave Elon a formal bow then returned to the altar. Elon resumed his place in the pew. Now, instead of nervousness, he strove to hide his elation. It had *worked;* Aurya's spell, all their plans . . . they had *worked.*

He looked up and found the Archbishop looking at him. The old man wore an odd expression, one that Elon could not exactly read. But he did not need to do so. Not anymore—he was certain he knew what the old man was feeling. The magic was weaving its tendrils through his mind, down into his soul, and taking possession of him.

The Archbishop—and the kingdom—now belonged to them.

The Archbishop raised his arms in the long-recognized opening gesture. "I will go unto the altar of God."

"Even the God of my joy and gladness," Elon's rich voice joined the response.

The Archbishop went through the opening salutation and invocation to prayer, chanting the language in his unimpressive voice. Elon thought of how that would change when he stood at the altar. *His* voice would fill the place. The people of Ballinrigh, of Aghamore, might never love him as they did Colm ApBeirne, but they would admire him. He would impress, beguile—perhaps with the power of his voice, the one power he had cultivated all these years, he would even entrance them.

It was more than enough, he thought. It was all he had wanted and dreamed of these long years past.

He hardly noticed the rest of the Mass, going through the familiar words and motions mindlessly. They had no meaning for him anymore, except as the means to an end. The end was all he cared about.

The Mass finally moved into the prayer part of the service. Once more Elon struggled to hide his elation as, with a nod from the Archbishop, he stepped from his pew. Nor did he miss the quickly silenced gasps as he walked toward the altar to take his place beside the Primus. Elon knew then that the others read this action as he did, as he and Aurya had intended in the setting of the spell.

Once more, the Archbishop was publicly acknowledging Elon as his chosen successor. Soon Baron Giraldus would come to Ballinrigh, riding at the head of the army that he had gone to reclaim. Then, with the Archbishop properly controlled, Elon was certain that the bishops could be brought back into line.

He did not care if Rathreagh and Camlough again stormed out, refusing to give Giraldus—or himself—their support. Once *he* was Archbishop, they would be called to discipline for their lack of obedience—something the old man either did not have the memory, energy, or inclination to do. After which, Elon would see that they were replaced with far more malleable counterparts.

Elon intended to see that all his enemies were replaced . . . in ways so they could never return.

These thoughts kept going through his mind as the gathered bishops of Aghamore prayed for the men of the armies fighting for their lives—and the life of the kingdom—on the northern plain of Urlar.

Chapter Thirty-one

The Province of Urlar was the "great plain" its name defined. It was bordered to the east with foothills and mountains that ranged north from Farnagh and Lininch, then turned when they reached Rathreagh, like a hand cupping the central Province. To the northwest and west, there were the cliffs of Tievebrack and the rugged hills of Kilgarriff. By Dromkeen, the land gentled into farms and the beginnings of the Great Forest that covered much of Camlough. Then, finally, there were the rivers and farmland of Sylaun, which slowly became the foothills of the mountains once again.

Ballinrigh sat at the center of the Province, the heart of the kingdom both emotionally and literally. It was on the northern plain, halfway between Ballinrigh and the northern mountains, that the armies met.

Each of the seven Outer Provinces who were still loyal had brought between four and five thousand men to the defense of Aghamore. Lord Iain thus found himself a combined army of over thirty-three thousand. By contrast, the army of Rathreagh and Corbenica stood at only twelve thousand— with four thousand of those being the Corbenicans.

But it was said that one Corbenican fought like five men from anywhere else. Perhaps, Lord Iain had thought as he faced them across the field, it was because the Corbenicans did not fear death. They served and worshiped it; and you could see the eagerness for battle the same way you could see how some men craved the drink. And that meant that the soldiers of Aghamore had more than men and weapons to fight— they must also overcome their own fear.

It was the most formidable enemy on the field.

A single war cry began the fray. But soon, the bedlam of forces— the thunder of horses, the pounding of thousands of feet, the shouts and battle cries, the clash of swords and shields, the screams of the wounded or dying— was thunderous, chaotic, nearly deafening to those in the midst of it. Only the magnitude of the task, on both sides, kept the soldiers to their charge.

This noise in all its horror, this cacophony of death, filled the plain. It was picked up on the wind and carried still farther. As the armies fought on, the sounds of battle crescendoed.

The day was beautiful, bright and warm with summer sun. It was the kind of day that should have sent farmers to their fields, families and children to the nearest pond for a day of picnics and swimming.

But not in Urlar. Especially in the city of Ballinrigh, where the sounds of the battle were carried on the breeze, over the walls and to the people below. They were not as distinct as some would have liked, and no one could tell who was winning.

Dogs barked at the unexpected noise that came in the waves of attack and retreat. Horses whinnied, adults grew nervous, and children, sensing the fear that was spreading everywhere, whined and became short-tempered. They did not understand why their mothers were pulling them from their play and their fathers paced in unexplained agitation.

The city guard watched along the ramparts, straining their eyes for any signs of defeats and victories, and the people within the walls waited on news of the same. The Archbishop, though his prayers were with the armies and all the men were going through, had other concerns that demanded his greater attention at the moment. He continued his charade of compliant acquiescence to Elon, buying the others the time they needed to complete the preparations for Selia's coronation.

And they were putting it to good use. Renan, Talog, and Eiddig, along with Gaithan, the Steward at the High King's Palace, were all working together. Gaithan was the only person at the Palace whom the Archbishop had taken into his confidence—and only as much as necessary—but they needed his help for access to the Coronation Regalia.

Quietly, secretly, the men were moving the Regalia from the Jewel Treasury into one of the side sacristies of the cathedral. There, at least one of them would guard it at all times until the moment it was brought forth on Selia's behalf. The Archbishop himself had rewritten the coronation ceremony, blending back into it many of the ancient elements that the centuries had seen slowly deleted and forgotten. Each member of the company—even the Cryf—would have an important part to play.

While the men were thus occupied, Lysandra was busy with Selia, helping the young woman prepare in both body and mind. She had bathed and washed her hair, purifying her body, and from the Archbishop's own hand, she had received both absolution and the Sacrament, purifying her soul. Now she was dressed in the white linen shift over which her new gown would go. Finally, over her dress, would be fastened a simple robe of pure and unspotted white silk.

It, too, had been among the Regalia, worn at the coronation of one of Aghamore's Queens over a hundred years ago and very carefully preserved. It hung now on the back of the door of Selia's chamber, shimmering in the glow of the lamps and the small fire, giving the deceptively endurant fabric a softly golden sheen.

Selia kept going over to stand before it, staring at it as if it could tell her all the secrets of ruling she imagined were better known by the one who had worn it before. But Lysandra knew there were no secrets to be told and that Selia was as well—or better—prepared as anyone who had previously accepted the crown.

How long it would take for the men to finish their tasks, neither woman knew. Nor could they guess how long the battle would continue; it could be hours . . . or days. They knew they had to be ready when the Archbishop sent the word, and while they waited, it had become a time of nerves, and faith—and friendship.

Selia's hair, freshly washed and freed from beneath the kerchief she habitually wore, now curled softly around her face. To Lysandra's *Sight,* it made her look even more young, more innocent, and yet stronger and more vibrant.

"Selia," Lysandra said to the younger woman, who had begun pacing the room, "come and sit beside me. I have something for you."

Selia came quickly over. Cloud-Dancer, curled at Lysandra's feet, looked up eagerly, as if giving her his encouragement, too. Selia stopped and smiled, then dropped to one knee to pet him. The touch seemed to soothe her; Lysandra smiled and waited, understanding.

After a moment, Selia looked up at her friend, though she did not release her touch on Cloud-Dancer's fur. "You should try to rest," Lysandra told her, knowing it was an unlikely occurrence but suggesting it all the same. "There may be little opportunity soon."

"How can I rest?" Selia asked. "Everyone else is *doing* something, and here I sit, waiting. There is so much that could go wrong. What if Eiddig was mistaken about that cross?" she said with a sudden shiver. "Or what if Hueil and the Corbenicans prevail? The cross had Aurya's magic on it—you said so. Are she and Giraldus here in Ballinrigh? What if they—"

"Selia," Lysandra stopped her, "life is full of what-ifs. We cannot live by them. We must believe we are here on a true purpose that by faith, guidance, and walking in the Light, we shall accomplish. All of the prophecies in both Tambryn's Scrolls and in the Holy Words of the Cryf, have led us to this moment. Now we must stay true to our goal, trust in the Divine's purpose—and, unfortunately, wait."

Selia gave Cloud-Dancer's head one last caress. Then she stood, and with a sigh, turned and plopped down on the divan next to Lysandra. Both the sigh and the movement carried a sense of weariness, of frustrated energy, that Lysandra felt . . . and silently shared.

Her lips twitched in a quick, unnoticed smile, then she

reached into the pocket of the apron she was wearing. Her fingers found and wrapped around the small package she had been saving for this moment. Slowly, she brought it out and handed it to Selia.

The younger woman did not take it at once. She looked into Lysandra's face as if trying to tell by her expression what the gift might be.

"Well," Lysandra said, giving a little laugh. "Take it, open it."

Selia reached out, her fingers moving with slight hesitation until at last, she took the gift into her own lap and unfolded the handkerchief in which it was wrapped. The handkerchief, like its contents, was not new. It was made of once-white linen that the years had softened, both in feel and color. The linen was embroidered with tiny flowers everywhere and trimmed in hand-tatted lace of palest yellow—a perfect complement to Selia's new gown.

On the handkerchief rested two sets of hair combs. One was narrow, with three long tines, obviously meant to hold up longer hair. Cut from the bone of deer antler, their white had mellowed with years and use into soft ivory. They were high-arched on top, carved with vines and sprays of roses that were deceptively simple in their execution—but on closer look, simplicity became true elegance.

The other pair was silver and shone with freshly polished brightness. They were broader, shorter, but they had several more tines and were more decorative than practical. The tops were inch-wide bands of finely formed filigree work that made Selia run a finger along the tops, as if feeling would reveal even more than her vision. Lysandra could remember often doing the same when she was a child, and she gave a soft smile of remembrance.

"These are . . . beautiful," Selia said in breathless wonder.

"They were my mother's," Lysandra replied. Her tone was quiet, matter-of-fact . . . and full of memories.

"I can't take these," Selia said. "You should keep them—

you must. You've done so much and given me so much already—and they're all you have of hers."

"No, what I have from my mother is far more than this."

"But if you have a daughter, you'll want to give these to her."

Again Lysandra smiled softly, though this time it was tinged with what she hoped was a well-hidden sadness. The possibility of such an event was more than unlikely. The man she loved, the *only* man with whom she might have joined her life and had children, was a priest. Selia was, in many ways, the daughter Lysandra knew she would never have.

"No," Lysandra said again. "These are for you. I brought them from my cottage for this day. Please, Selia, take them, keep them—with my love, and my mother's."

Selia slowly folded the linen back over the combs. Tears filled her eyes and began to spill over and run down her cheeks. She turned and embraced Lysandra. Silently, thought to thought, Lysandra felt Selia's heart thanking her for having given her more love and being more of a mother to her than her real mother had ever been.

Lysandra's own eyes filled with tears; she, too, was grateful for the love she had learned both to give and to receive—and for learning that it was love that gave life its meaning.

At Elon's house in Ballinrigh, Aurya was also waiting impatiently. But unlike the soft joy Selia was feeling amid her impatience, Aurya was muttering and cursing under her breath. This morning her body was churning with discomfort, with increased nausea and headache from her exertion last night. Pouring her magic into that cross, although necessary, had exacted a greater physical price than she had expected.

She hated the weakness and, as another wave of sickness crested through her, she briefly hated the pregnancy that held her captive. The prospect of all the months ahead felt unbearable. But she also felt strangely protective of the child she carried—and the dichotomy of feelings only fueled her impatience with this day . . . and with her life.

Suddenly, there was a pounding on the front door. Although Aurya knew Elon's household staff was well trained and would take care of whatever was necessary, she felt compelled to go see for herself—if only to give herself a break in this interminable waiting. As the pounding came again, she hurried from her room. This was no polite knocking, but the demanding call of someone whose impatience matched her own.

She was coming down the stairs just as the doors were being opened. There, on the front step, stood Giraldus. Framed by the doorway and imbued with Aurya's sudden and unexpected joy at the sight of him, Giraldus seemed bigger, broader, more muscular and commanding than she had ever seen. She found herself wanting to rush forward and throw herself into his arms.

Instead, she forced herself to stillness. She would not change the persona she had so carefully and calculatingly built all these years—not for Giraldus, for her unborn child, or even for her own momentary satisfaction.

Giraldus, however, had no such hesitation. He strode through the door, ignoring the servant, and headed straight for her.

"Aurya," he boomed, "why are you here? I thought you safe in Kilgarriff—as I commanded."

"Since when am *I* subject to your commands?" she said in the quiet voice he would recognize as the prelude to her anger. "It is here, in Ballinrigh, that I am needed. Why are you here and not with the army?"

"That fool of a cousin that the Archbishop appointed in my place would not step aside—as was his duty. He said that the Archbishop himself gave the Writ of Elevation, and only by the Archbishop's word would he return my rightful place to me. I am here to demand it be done. *Now.* This cannot wait—but they refuse to let me see the old fool. They—"

Aurya held up a hand. Giraldus's voice was getting louder, as heedless here of the servants' ears as he was at home. But these were not his servants and could not be trusted in the same way.

She turned her attention to the man still standing by the door, and for the first time she noticed Maelik standing beside him. She gave a nod to the sergeant. Although she felt closer to him, she knew—as he did—they would never truly *like* each other.

But that did not negate the trust she had in him. What she and Giraldus must discuss, Maelik could hear—but it was not for the casual hearing of servants or for their gossip in the kitchens.

"Gareth," she said to the servant, "bring some food for the Baron and Sergeant Maelik. We shall be in the blue parlor."

"Yes, m'lady . . . and for yourself?"

"Nothing. No, wait—I'll have some mint tea," she corrected, vaguely remembering that mint was reputed to be good for a queasy stomach.

She started down the steps as the servant began to leave. Then Aurya called to him again.

"Gareth, do you know where Rhys is—the young soldier who accompanied me here?"

"I believe he is in the stables, m'lady."

"Please have him found and sent to us."

"Yes, m'lady."

Only when the servant had again started away did Aurya finish approaching Giraldus. She still had to keep a tight rein on her reactions, especially when she saw the light that came into his eyes as she neared. She laid a hand on his arm.

"In here," she said softly. "There are things you must know. But patience, Giraldus," she counseled, using the old familiar word that had passed so often between them. "We will talk after the servant has come and gone with the food."

With that, she turned and led the way into the blue parlor. The men had no choice but to accept her words and follow.

Giraldus's impatience filled the room. It was even greater—or at least less controlled—than Aurya's own. To curb it, she questioned him about his meeting with Iain. Even should the servants walk in, it was not a conversation they could not hear. Indeed, she was certain at least half of them knew about it already.

She listened, hearing his anger as well as his words and letting him vent the former. He would listen better when she chose to speak if he had spoken his mind already. Two servants arrived carrying trays of food. They put them down and departed as Aurya began to sip on the mint tea. She was pleasantly surprised to find that it lived up to its reputation. As each sip soothed her stomach a little more, her patience returned bit by bit.

Finally, they were alone, and Giraldus had finished his tale. He piled meat and cheese on bread and motioned for Maelik to do the same. Then, sitting in one of the nearby wing-backed chairs, he turned his full attention to Aurya.

"Well," he said around a mouthful of food, "tell me, Aurya, why you are here instead of where I wanted you to be—and what is preventing me from getting the Archbishop to reverse his blasted elevation of my cousin."

"Let Iain have the Barony," she said.

"What?" Giraldus roared, coming up out of his seat. "Did our time underground addle your wits, woman?"

"Sit down, Giraldus," Aurya said quietly, again using the tone she knew Giraldus would recognize. "Let Iain have the Barony," she said again, "because you will not need it. You will soon be High King—Elon and I have seen to that . . . and *that* is why I am in Ballinrigh and not in Kilgar-riff."

"What do you mean?" he asked, eyes narrowing slightly.

"Elon was in Ummera when I arrived," she began, "and he had the means to accomplish our mutual goals after all. If everything has gone as we anticipated, the Archbishop is even now growing more and more under our control."

"Tell me," Giraldus said, now easing himself back in his chair. "Tell me everything."

Aurya gave him a small, triumphant smile. Then she began the tale of her work in the night just past.

On the field to the north of the city, the fighting continued. Clods of earth, turned to mud with the blood of the wounded and slain, were churned beneath the great iron-shod hooves of the warhorses. Arrows still flew occasionally, though their main volleys had long since been expended. By now, most of the fighting was hand-to-hand.

The cries of the men—war cries, wails of agony and shouts of triumph, orders shouted across the din—were deafening. The thunder of the battle gave no evidence of letting up. The noise was maddening. The sights were like a scene from a tortured nightmare or a madman's prophecy.

Men slashed at each other, their swords covered with blood. By now, there was so much blood that it ran past the guard and over the hilt. There was blood everywhere—on their hands and faces, running up their arms, splattered onto the shirts and surcoats until it often obscured the device of their House so that no one could tell who was fighting whom. It was even soaked through their chain mail and into the protective jerkin beneath.

Some of the men had the difficult and onerous job of trying to dash between the fighting and drag the wounded from the field. As the battle moved over and around them, the corpses were often trampled underfoot of the advancing Corbenicans, who would give no break in the fighting—such as civilized combatants allow—to clear the field of the honored dead.

So the men battled on. At their feet were the bodies of the fallen, were the severed hands and arms, the broken trampled-off legs, the heads that rolled like a child's ball—but were being kicked by booted feet trying to keep from falling.

All through the morning, they had fought. The accursed Corbenicans, with their mad cries, their wild, unregimented manner of battle, and their unholy welcome of death, were somehow winning the day, even against the greater numbers.

At this moment, the outcome did not look good for Aghamore.

Iain had deployed all the troops along the lines agreed in his meeting with the other Barons. But the Corbenicans did not seem human. The Aghamorians were not cowards, but life was precious in their beliefs, and they would not willingly throw themselves on the enemies' swords, to break the line and let their forces through. That—and worse—the Corbenicans had done time and again.

Iain was at a loss to know how to inspire his men in the face of such horror and death. Yet, they must continue fighting —and dying. However slim, it was Aghamore's only chance to survive.

The same prayer had been in his heart all day. He did not pray with words, only with his faith and with the silent desperation of command. He feared that without some gift from the Divine Hand, the day would soon be lost . . . and with it, would go all of Aghamore's hope.

A rider approached. He wore the uniform of Rathreagh, but he also had a white rag tied somewhat inconspicuously around the horn of his saddle. There had been a few others who rode behind the lines so marked, defectors from their Baron's alliance. But they were far too few to truly help the armies of Aghamore.

Iain had given orders that those who wished to join their forces were to be accepted and this rider, too, was let through unharmed. This one, however, continued straight toward

Lord Iain—and he came holding out a written message so that the guards who surrounded the Baron could see his intent.

The man quickly reined in his horse and slid off. He gave a quick genuflect of obeisance, then handed his missive out to Iain.

"From Baron Hueil," he said, breathless and obviously tired.

"M'lord, 'tis a trick," one of the nearby guards cried.

But Iain held up a hand. He searched the kneeling soldier's face. There were no signs of fear or treachery—only of hope.

Iain took the folded paper. He quickly opened it . . . and with it, the Divine Hand also unfolded, giving his prayer the answer for which he had silently cried out all day.

He folded the letter and turned to his men. "Call for the other Barons," he ordered. "Get them now, and hurry. This cannot wait."

He then looked at the still-waiting soldier. "Can you get back to Hueil without being noticed?" he asked.

"I believe so, m'lord."

"Then go, and tell him—yes."

The man nodded, remounted, wheeled his horse, and rode away, carrying Iain's renewed hope for victory with him.

Chapter Thirty-two

Baron Hueil waited anxiously for the messenger to return. His men were fighting—and dying—under his orders, but he could see that they hated fighting beside the Corbenicans and killing soldiers of their own kingdom. They were Aghamorians all . . . and with Corbenicans in their midst, it did not feel right to any of them to be at war with their own. Hueil understood and did not begrudge the occasional defection that he witnessed. It had been what solidified his idea to contact the other Barons.

This idea had been growing in him unawares for these last days of their march. Ambition had temporarily blinded him, as he gazed from afar on the glittering prize of a golden, bejeweled crown. That crown had grown in his thoughts and in his internal vision until he could not see the truth behind it.

But now that truth had become more real to him than anything else, and, with it, he realized the dilemma that his ambition had forced upon his men. The blood and the death had dulled the gold and jewels, robbed that ambition, and promise of its fulfillment, of any sweetness. Hueil saw himself as the other Barons and the rest of Aghamore—including his own daughter—must see him. In the revelation, he felt sullied and ashamed.

And shame was not a foundation upon which to build a dynasty . . . not in Rathreagh and not in Ballinrigh.

If the other Barons accepted the plan he had sent them—if they were willing to believe and accept anything from his hand—then he would have taken the first step to his redemption.

His stomach churned as the battle continued; he fought his conscience. But, too deeply committed, he had to keep to his course until he knew what the Barons of Aghamore had to say.

The messenger he had sent finally rode through the lines and came straight toward Hueil. The white flag was gone, carefully hidden away so that no Corbenican might see it and guess at its purpose. Hueil, also mounted, rode out to meet him. His heart felt like it was pounding louder than the horse's hooves; he was both eager and terrified to find out what the Barons had said.

The messenger delivered his one-word message, the look on his face begging the Baron to move quickly while the Corbenicans suspected nothing. But Hueil hardly noticed. With that single word, Hueil's soul soared.

He would soon be whole again, Aghamorian again . . . *himself* again.

And the punishment? a part of him whispered. It told him to fight on—once he was King there could be no punishment. He shook his head in defiance. If he did not do this thing now, every day of his future would be a punishment. Whatever he might be asked to endure in its place was nothing by comparison.

He gave a quick nod to the messenger. Word would now be carried to his troops. But his new orders must be given cautiously, mouth-to-ear, so that none of the Corbenican troops could overhear and warn their King—until it was too late.

Hueil did not worry about how his new plan would be received among his own men. Their loyalty had led them into this place—but loyalty and conscience could be reunited, for them as it was for Hueil. The thought made him smile, quickly hidden, as he wheeled his horse around. He passed two of his generals with a silent nod. They were privy to his plan and accepted the signal. Then they, too, slowly changed direction, going to station themselves where their new goal required.

It would take time for his men to be notified and positioned. That worried Hueil. He was afraid that King Wirral might have time to realize what was happening. If that happened, Hueil had no doubt that the Corbenican army would turn and attack—and his new allies would be too far away to save them.

Suddenly, the Armies of the Provinces charged, shrieking war cries that sent a chill through Hueil. Worse yet was the howl with which the Corbenicans met it. The tide of battle, which broke in waves as men charged or retreated, attacked or fell back to regroup, now crested again—but this time it moved with more energy and was longer than at any time since that first emphatic clash of the day.

Hueil realized that the other Barons were giving him the time and the distraction he needed to get his men into place. Each new crash of metal, sword upon sword, each new wail of pain, struck deeply into the core of his soul and his guilt. Men were dying so that the kingdom might live.

He would not fail them.

The moment had come. The Aghamorians had kept up their attack, meeting the Corbenicans' ferocity with such determination that the forces from the north were finally beginning to give ground.

Hueil knew that now was the time.

He raised his sword and gave the loud cry of his House, the cry his men would recognize and to which they would rally. As Hueil struck his heels to his mount and began to gallop down the line, the voices of his army joined him. They were like one mighty voice raised in unity and in defiance.

Then, without warning, they turned on the Corbenicans by their sides. For too brief a moment, confusion reigned. Then, realizing what was happening, the army of King Wirral fought back.

Hueil parried attacks as he searched for the Corbenican ruler. He and Prince Arnallt were in the thick of a knot of battle, arms rising and falling as they fought. Blood flew from Arnallt's sword and from Wirral's great axe; their faces were twisted with effort and hate.

Wirral saw Hueil. The sound that erupted from him was bestial, bearing no sense of humanity to Hueil's ears. Then Wirral charged, and Hueil prepared himself for the hardest battle of his life . . . and, possibly, for his death.

Then Wirral's arm was grabbed from behind. Arnallt began pulling his father away, toward a path of escape that his men were keeping open for him—at tremendous cost. Bodies were piling; death was everywhere.

Death . . . and victory. For the first time, Hueil felt he might succeed.

The men of both armies saw it, too. The Corbenicans, still fighting fiercely, were now trying to follow and cover the escape of their King. Neither their onetime allies nor the closing Armies of the Provinces were giving them quarter.

The Corbenican army fought with a frenzy now, fed by an anger that was terrifying to see. Over and over, as their swords and axes slashed—too often meeting flesh—their horrific war cry wailed. Some men were following their King, others made no attempt to flee. Their lives belonged to their King, and they gave them willingly for his escape.

Both Hueil's men and those of the armies now joining him fought just as hard, determined that some would get through and—if they could not kill him—chase King Wirral from the kingdom.

Bodies fell on both sides. But though they fought like madmen, the reduced number of Corbenicans could not stand against the increased army of Aghamore. They stood, fought on until the last man, still swinging his battle-axe, fell dead of a sword thrust in his neck that cut silent the cry of defiance he shouted.

The way clear, Hueil's men led men from every Province as they joined the chase, obeying orders to give no quarter until the Corbenicans were gone—or dead. The men of Rathreagh had seen what the Corbenicans could do on the march south. They feared what King Wirral would do if he had time to unleash his wrath. He must be kept on the run.

Hueil wanted to follow them. All the feelings of disgust, with himself and with the Corbenicans, which he had been suppressing ever since Wirral's ships had landed, boiled violently inside him now. He wanted to be at the fore as they chased them back to Owenasse. He wanted to be there first, to burn those ships and meet the Corbenicans on the shores with drawn swords and death.

But what happened now was in someone else's hands. Hueil had another duty to perform.

His men kept fighting, but he now turned and rode toward the back of the troops, where the Barons were awaiting him. His mood was an odd mix of dread and elation. What he was doing was not easy—but it was *right*.

Hueil found Lord Iain's standard, the black griffin of Kilgarriff, and rode toward it. Then, coming to a halt in front of the Baron, he slid from his horse and silently offered up his sword.

On a rise of land away from the battle, a lone horseman sat. He wore the borrowed, slightly ill-fitting uniform of a Rider, which had given his presence both protection and acceptance.

Durkin had fought a battle of his own as he sat astride his horse, watching the soldiers below giving their blood for the life of this land. He had many friends upon that field. He wanted to charge down among them and add his sword to the fray.

But Lady Margharite's orders were specific — and she was waiting. Now Durkin had something hopeful to tell her. The sight of her father leading his troops *against* the Corbenicans had almost made him turn back to Ballinrigh then, eager to bring her the news that he knew would ease the sorrow and pain she was feeling.

Yet he did not leave. He kept watching, his own need to see the outcome keeping him in place. He had no sense of time; each minute of watching, of seeing and hearing the death below, seemed endless.

But then he saw the line moving forward, little by little pressing the enemy back. His heart gave a glad leap. He leaned forward, eager for every hopeful sight. The movement was slow, but each moment brought Durkin more certainty.

It was then he saw Hueil leave the field, leave his men. Given the fickleness of Hueil's actions of late, Durkin did not know what to expect — and he was relieved as he watched the Baron ride over and surrender to the authority of his peers. For Baron Hueil of Rathreagh, the battle was over.

Finally, Durkin had witnessed all he needed. He turned and began the ride back to the capital. Margharite was not the only one who would want this news.

He entered a city gate two hours later, again the Rider uniform gaining him unquestioned admittance. He headed straight for the Residence, and Margharite.

Although it was nearing evening and the sounds of the battle no longer wafted over the city walls, all remained preternaturally quiet. The population was still holding its figurative breath, waiting.

Durkin knew the Barons, including Hueil as their prisoner, would not be far behind him—but he did not want to wait for their arrival. *He* wanted to be the one who carried the news to Margharite. She had been through so much, risked so much to get away, he was sure she would want to be there when her father surrendered to the Archbishop and formally rejoined this kingdom.

She must have been watching for him, because Durkin had not yet dismounted before she was already there. Her face was so eager, so hopeful, that he was grateful to have good news.

"They are coming," he said, gulping in air to fuel his words as he spoke, almost as eager to get them out as he imagined she was to hear them. "The tide is turned, and Wirral is vanquished—and, m'lady, 'twas yer father what saved the field."

"God be praised," Margharite said. It was not said loudly, but Durkin heard the fervency in it more clearly than if she had shouted. The hand she placed on his arm trembled ever so slightly, making Durkin wonder if it was with relief, with eagerness for more news . . . or with something else entirely.

"Tell me, Durkin," she said, "everything you saw of him. Please."

"Aye, m'lady—but t' ye and His Eminence both—if'n ye know where t' find him. There be news he must have, too."

"Yes, of course. Come," she said, keeping her hand on his arm as she led the way back into the Residence and down the corridors toward the Archbishop's inner waiting room.

Brother Naal was at his desk in the room usually filled with people. Today, however, it was empty. It made Durkin realize that the people of Ballinrigh were as anxious for news of the battle as Margharite had been. And, if their reasons were somewhat different, it made the tension in the city no less intense.

The monk looked up, surprised, when he heard them enter, his frown deepening when he saw how Durkin was dressed.

"M'lady Margharite," he said, coming to his feet, "and ... uh ... Durkin, isn't it? His Eminence is accepting no petitions today. There's too much—"

"We must see him right away," Margharite said over the monk's words. Durkin eased himself back a pace, silently reminding the secretary that he spoke to no commoner.

Brother Naal had the sense to look a little flustered. He knew his duty to the Archbishop and the Church, but he was also Aghamorian-raised, and the status of the Houses was deeply ingrained. Durkin waited, a little amused at the man's quandary. He had no doubt which would win. Lady Margharite, he had learned, though outwardly soft and gentle, had a core of will as strong as any tempered blade.

She stepped closer to the monk. Though she gave him a slight smile, her voice held the edge of command to which she had grown up accustomed.

"We need to see him," she said again. "Now. Durkin has brought news from the field that His Eminence must hear ... and he *will* want to hear this, Brother."

The monk hesitated only a few brief seconds more. "Wait here," he said at last. Then he hurried toward the study door and walked through without a knock, an act that told Durkin that the Archbishop was somewhere else.

They waited. Seconds became minutes; half an hour passed in silent tension. Lady Margharite began to pace, and Durkin watched her. He could only imagine how important this moment must be for her. Despite her anger with her father, Durkin also knew how much she loved him and what her disobedience and flight had cost her emotionally.

He had left Glynna to play a part, and he would worry for

her safety until he held her once again. But Margharite had left much more behind. She had left her home, her identity, and the only family she had, all for the sake of personal convictions of right and wrong. It was an act that took far more formidable courage than facing the physical dangers of the escape itself.

Even in that, she had never complained, accepting whatever discomfort was required—and Durkin admired her more than he could say. The only part of the whole ordeal about which she did not try to keep her feelings hidden or put on a brave front . . . was the waiting.

Finally, Brother Naal returned, the Archbishop on his heels. Although they had not been in Ballinrigh very long, Durkin had seen the Archbishop celebrating Mass—and occasionally had passed him in the corridors. Right now the old man looked more tired than Durkin had ever seen him.

Still, he was gracious and appeared quite eager for the news. When both Margharite and Durkin made to genuflect, preparing to kiss his great ring of Office, he quickly caught Margharite's elbows and raised her up.

"There is no need or time for that," he said. "Come with me, both of you. There are others who need your news as much as I." Then he looked at Brother Naal. "No one else is to be admitted until I tell you," he said in an emphatic tone that had an unexpected harshness, almost an anger, to it. "Tell them whatever you like, but keep them away."

Durkin was sure that the look of surprise on Brother Naal's face was also on his own. With all of the bishops assembled in Ballinrigh, Durkin would have expected the Primus of the Church to be surrounded, to *want* to be surrounded by them.

"Yes, Your Eminence," Brother Naal said solemnly, giving the Archbishop a small bow. "Should I expect them?"

The old man gave a shrug, a gesture that somehow imparted much more than an uncertainty over schedules. "The prayers continue in the cathedral, and shall until I send word. But I expect that soon some of them will try to gain a private moment to . . . discuss . . . their own vision of what I should do next. So remember, Naal—no one is to be admitted."

"Yes, Your Eminence."

The force with which this last order was spoken surprised Durkin. He had always thought of the Archbishop as a gentle, and patient, spiritual leader, someone of kindness and compassion, someone with his eyes fixed on the rewards of heaven. He knew that most of the kingdom thought the same of the old man.

But for a moment, Durkin caught a glimpse of the formidable side of Colm ApBeirne. It was this side that allowed him to keep order in the great body of the Church—and, for Aghamore's sake, to keep the kingdom together even though the throne sat empty.

Durkin smiled a little to himself as he realized how much Margharite and the Archbishop were alike—and his Glynna, too. They all appeared soft, gentle, easily ruled . . . until they were angered or crossed. When that happened, you found that the gentle appearance covered a will of iron and a backbone of steel.

They followed the Archbishop through his public study, into and through a small prayer closet, and into a more private parlor. There were others gathered here in an odd assembly that surprised, even shocked, Durkin.

A priest, older than he though not yet middle-aged, stood near two . . . *men,* he thought for lack of knowing what else to call them. They were quite unlike anything else he had ever seen. The room was darkened, with the shades drawn against the sun and the lamps in the room turned down quite low. They burned only in the corners. But even the dim light and the common clothing that covered them, could not disguise the strangeness of the priest's two companions.

The long hair of their bodies escaped from cuffs, neckline, and around the bottoms of their trouser legs. The hair on their faces was far different from normal beards. It was finer, like the hair of a child, and it grew up until it joined with their thick eyebrows, surrounding their eyes like the frame around a picture.

Their eyes were even more different . . . fascinating, compelling. They were easily twice as large as any eyes Durkin had ever seen, and although their color was dark, they also seemed to glow. Durkin felt as if he could see all the way through them—and as if they looked all the way into the depths of his soul. He knew that if he had anything to hide or of which he was ashamed, these eyes would frighten him.

Could these be the creatures of myth, of the stories told to children, somehow real before him? Most of those stories said they lived in a realm of both wonder—and terror. Some said they lived beneath the mountains, others said in deep, deep caves. He had always assumed they were told to keep children from dangerous explorations—and the stories did not portray the underground beings in very favorable light. Yet, as they looked at him now with those wondrous eyes, any sense of fear left him.

The younger one's face was less hirsute, his eyes easier to see, but it was the older one's attention that truly drew Durkin. His long white hair, drawn back and bound, seemed to make the huge darkness of his eyes into saucers of soft welcome, encouragement, faith, and hope; they were a place of beauty untainted by the touch of hatred, ambition, or greed. And with the feeling that they looked deeply into Durkin's soul, they gave him the promise of a better world to come.

He blinked, breaking the hold that he then realized had

been but a few heartbeats long. He heard the Archbishop making introductions and turned to see Margharite as wonder-struck as he had just been.

"Now," the Primus said to them, "tell us your news, and leave nothing you saw or heard from your tale. This is more important than you can realize."

"Durkin—" Margharite said gently, encouraging him to speak.

Durkin took a deep breath. He was not used to so exalted a company, or to so many eyes upon him. He would have been far more comfortable telling his tale to the Archbishop's secretary than to the Primus himself—but he would not fail Lady Margharite, or Glynna, waiting and counting on him.

"Well, Your Eminence, sir," he began nervously, " 'twas m'lady Margharite's idea. We still had these tunics what t' Rider loaned us, see, and so she thought 'twould be a good idea . . ."

The Archbishop heard Durkin's tale with satisfaction. He watched the others while they all listened; only Eiddig seemed unsurprised, as if this answer to his unbending faith was inevitable. When Lady Margharite's servant concluded, the Cryf Guide smiled.

"The Hand and Heart of the Divine hath opened unto us all this day," he said. "Our way hath been cleared of all save the darkest, and even unto those shalt the Divine show us Light."

"Amen," the Archbishop said. All the hows and whens of necessity suddenly coalesced. He turned quickly to Renan.

"Your friend the Rider, the one who led Margharite and Durkin here," he said, "do you know where he is today?"

"I told him to stay close in case—"

"He's at the stables, waitin'," Durkin supplied.

"Good," the Archbishop said, his voice now full of energy. "Durkin, can you bring him here? We'll need him—

and you in that uniform—one more time today. And Renan, if you'll find paper, there are letters to prepare quickly."

Durkin gave a quick nod, then dashed off to do the Archbishop's bidding. Colm watched the door close. While Renan went to retrieve paper, pen, and ink from the study, the Archbishop went to Margharite and enfolded her in a gentle, fatherly hug, happy for the girl at this news of her father's redemption.

"It shall be well, my child," he told her, "and you shall have a part in the great events now to come."

He could see that she did not understand—but he did, and with a smile he turned away.

Renan returned, sat down, and waited. With a nod, the Archbishop began to dictate:

"To Iain, Baron of Kilgarriff, unto whom God hath shown favor with victory this day, from Colm Ap-Beirne, Primus of the Church in Aghamore, and to the Barons of the Ruling Houses of the Provinces, hear now Our decree:

"None, save Hueil of Rathreagh, shall enter yet into this city. Hueil must be escorted into Our presence by such messengers as We have now sent, that he be held in the charge of his crime. But of you all, We crave patience until the morrow.

"The Westgate alone shall be opened tomorrow, at ten o'clock in the morning, in order to allow each Baron to enter Ballinrigh . . . IN PEACE. Each Baron may bring no more than ten men, to serve as personal guard and retinue. At the hour of eleven you must be gathered at the cathedral. It is then you shall hear and witness the great future God in His mercy has decreed for our kingdom.

"Of this, We charge and command your obedience."

"Is that all?" Renan asked when he stopped.

The Archbishop stopped. He frowned for a moment, while he thought if he should say more. "Prepare one for each Baron," he said at last, "then bring Iain's to me before they go out. I've a message to add for his eyes alone, and under my private seal. But quickly, Renan. The evening is approaching, and we have much, much more work to do before our hour arrives."

That said, Colm ApBeirne smiled. The weariness of months, perhaps of years, suddenly, happily, gone.

Chapter Thirty-three

Lord Iain drew himself up straight and proud, determined not to show his fatigue as the galloping hooves of two approaching Riders pounded toward him in the gathering dusk. They rode straight through the lines of the newly re-united Armies of the Provinces, armies that had been gathered to battle each other and now called each other comrade. This was, to Iain's mind, the best of what had happened on this field today; in the vanquishing of their common foe, Aghamore had become a united kingdom once again.

What will happen now? he could not help but wonder, however. *Has His Eminence found the way to keep this unity strong?* Iain hoped that the other Barons had seen enough of blood and death this day to allow the Archbishop to find a peaceful settlement to the question of the empty throne.

The Riders expertly wheeled their horses to a standstill in front of him. Although one remained mounted, the other slid from his saddle into a quick bow of respect, then stepped toward Iain, holding out a folded and sealed letter.

Iain saw that this was the same Rider who had brought him news before. "What is your name, lad?" he asked.

"Wilham, m'lord. Wilham Tybourne."

"Well, Wilham," Iain said, taking the letter from him, "let us hope that this message is as fortuitous as the others you have brought me."

The Rider smiled at him in an odd way, but he did not reply. Iain broke the seal and scanned the bold, official words summoning himself and the others to the cathedral in the morning. Then he looked at the addendum. It was a personal message written in the Archbishop's own hand and imprinted with the small seal-ring the Primus always wore.

The handwriting was thin and not nearly as easily read as the official lettering of whatever scribe had done the other. But, though its tone was more casual, its message was more important. Iain was asked to retain the command of the armies a while longer and to be certain that factions did not split once more. He was also asked, when he and the other Barons entered the city, to ride at their fore and to continue his command over such retinue as they brought, keeping their number to the size requested. Finally, the Archbishop asked Iain to come into the sacristy upon his arrival—but to come alone. What was then to happen was for his eyes and ears only.

All this, Iain could and would do—though the letter had more piqued than satisfied his curiosity.

"Have you a reply, m'lord?" the Rider asked. "We must find the other Barons before we return with Baron Hueil, and the sun is droppin' fast."

"Only that you tell His Eminence that I am his servant, in this as in all things. I will do as he requests as best I can."

The Rider nodded and turned to remount. Before he could ride away, however, Iain stopped him.

"I think," he said somewhat dryly, "you'll need not look for the Barons. They have come to find you."

The Heads of the Ruling Houses of Aghamore were indeed fast approaching, as if afraid Iain was being granted knowledge—or power and glory—denied to them. Again, the Rider turned that odd and knowing smile upon the Baron of Kilgarriff, and Iain wondered what was being prepared for them all in Ballinrigh.

The Baron of Camlough reached them first. "What news?" he demanded.

Iain gestured to the Rider, who, quickly rifling through the letters in his pouch, held one out to Oran of Camlough. While he broke the seal and scanned the contents, his mouth silently forming each word in an old unconscious habit, the other Barons also rode up. Each received his message in turn, and for a moment all was silent while they read.

"What does he mean we're not to enter the city until tomorrow?" Ardal of Sylaun demanded. "By God, I've earned the right this day to—"

"Peace," Iain said sharply, cutting him off before his quarrelsome attitude could affect the others.

The command in his voice surprised them to silence. Iain knew he had always been seen as merely his cousin's shadow, as having little in either strength or personality of his own. But to Iain's mind, it was high time the other Barons realized that strength did not have to be belligerent or personality grandiose. His was a quieter way than his cousin's, but when needed, strength, strategy, understanding—perhaps, occasionally, even wisdom—were his to command.

"His Eminence has made a request of us which, in our duty to him as Regent and our obedience as sons of the Church, we *shall* obey," he said firmly.

"And who are you to decide what I obey?" Camlough countered.

"By the authority of the Primus—who until the throne is again occupied, is the head of *both* the temporal and spiritual body of this kingdom—I am the one who commands this *united* army of Aghamore . . . including its leaders," Iain said in a stern and unyielding voice, reminding them again of their duty of obedience. Then he softened his tone. "Division almost destroyed this kingdom, and only by our unity did we win this day. Let us hold to that unity a while longer—and trust that the Archbishop has a purpose in his words. He has never failed this kingdom before, and I believe he will not fail it now."

Slowly the tension that had been mounting around him began to abate. For this one night, there would be peace on the plain of Urlar, though the armies would again surround the capital city. Tomorrow? Whatever awaited them in the cathedral tomorrow morning must give answer to the succession, or the civil war would erupt again—and this time there would be no mutual threat to stop it. They had one night's grace, and he prayed that, with whatever the Archbishop had planned, it would be enough.

Once more, Iain saw the strange smile, one tinged this time with satisfaction, on the face of the Rider. Then, with another little bow, the young man returned to his horse and mounted.

"We are to bring the Baron of Rathreagh back with us," he reminded Iain.

The Baron of Kilgarriff gave a gesture, and in a moment the prisoner was brought forth. "Guard him well," Iain said. "Though he has made no move to escape, there are many here who have no love for Rathreagh this night."

"And within the city. But His Eminence knows what he is doing."

"I hope so, lad," Iain said . . . and as the two Riders rode off with the traitor Baron between them, he repeated it softly under his breath.

"I hope so—or we are all lost." Then, pulling himself up straight, he turned to his peers. "Let us eat together this night, as the brothers we are meant to be, so that our men may see the peace between us and be at ease."

At least for tonight, Iain thought but did not say. *And tomorrow will come of its own . . . .*

Baron Hueil of Rathreagh had said nothing as he was brought forward. As he had passed through, from among the ranks rose the jeers of men calling him traitor. Some had been quickly silenced—but not all. He endured them; he was, he had been, a traitor.

And he would face his punishment without evasion, he told himself. He knew that, by law, the other Barons and the Archbishop could call for his death. Even that, he would accept. His one, his only true hope now was that Margharite would forgive him for what he had tried to do to her.

He was as grateful for her disobedience as he had once been angry. She had always been willful and headstrong, given to action instead of decorum. He had often considered it the bane of his parental duties and joy. Yet he did not think that way now. She had seen more clearly than he, acted with more courage and honor than he. She was a credit to her proud lineage—and he was grateful.

Would he get the chance to tell her so? That was the only question that truly mattered, he now knew. Kingdoms and crowns meant nothing compared to the simple reality that he had possibly—probably—lost his daughter.

The weight of these thoughts had kept his tongue silent and his head bowed as he sat, mounted, before Iain and the other Barons, hearing of his summons to Ballinrigh, and kept him silent as, under guard, he was herded in the city. Despite the objections of the other Barons, Iain had not subjected him to the indignity of having his hands bound to his saddle. Though it seemed a small service, Hueil was grateful for the trust in his renewed honor that it represented, and he made no move to betray it.

Twilight was turning to darkness by the time the designated city gate opened to admit them. Rumors of his treachery had obviously reached the inhabitants, for here again he was met with jeers and raised fists from within the crowd that gathered to view his passing. Hueil endured them, his shame mounting as they rode on toward the heart of the city and the Residence of the Archbishop.

Once there, he was taken to a bedchamber to wait upon his sentencing. It was not the grandest or most sumptuously appointed of rooms. It was, in fact, a monk's room, with nothing more than a bed, small standing wardrobe, a table and two chairs, a stand with a ewer and basin, a kneeler and lamp, and a small hearth for warmth. But it was also not the dungeon cell that he would have received had some of the Barons—and many of the people—had their way.

"His Eminence will send for you when he is ready," Hueil was told. "Do not try to leave. The guards are armed."

Hueil gave the Rider a sad smile of acknowledgment. These were the first words, save a tersely spoken "come," that either this Rider or his companion had uttered. Again, it was no more than Hueil knew he deserved.

"Wait," he said when the Rider began to close the door. "My daughter—does she know I'm here? I'd like . . . would she be allowed to come see me?"

"She knows," the Rider said. "She has permission to speak with you—but whether she will . . ." The man gave an eloquent shrug. The gesture said far too little—and it said everything, and Hueil made no further sound as the Rider again turned away and closed the door.

The Baron of Rathreagh was alone.

* * *

Giraldus was tired. Yet, as much as he wanted to sleep, there was something else he wanted more. He wanted Aurya to trust him and tell him whatever secret she was holding back.

She had told him all about meeting with Elon, and about the magic and the cross sent to the Archbishop. When Elon had returned from the cathedral with triumphant news of the old man's public acknowledgments, Giraldus waited for Aurya to confide the rest.

Nothing more had been forthcoming. But now that they were alone in their chamber, he did not intend that they should go to sleep with secrets between them. The days when he would accept such things were past.

All through the supper they had shared with the bishop, Giraldus had kept quiet. He let Aurya and Elon talk, especially Elon, and they were effusive in their self-congratulations. They were now certain that the tide of events had turned in their favor, and several times during the evening, Aurya had told him that the crown would soon be on his head.

But Giraldus was not so confident. There were forces in play he could feel but not name. Something within him still whispered a warning—but the one time he had tried to tell Aurya, the look on her face had silenced him. She would not listen then, and, as they sat in the bedchamber Elon had supplied, he knew she would not listen now.

Yet Giraldus did not miss the desperate edge to her enthusiasm. All her assurances, though directed at him, made Giraldus feel that it was herself she was truly trying to convince. He kept coming back to the question of *why*? What was it she was not telling him? What was making her usual confidence so precarious that she felt the necessity of displaying continuous—and possibly false—bravado?

Nor was her restlessness confined to her words. She had begun to pace the room like a caged animal, and she moved as if unaware she was doing it. These last days had been exhausting, even for him—the adrenaline of escape, the forced rides, the meeting with his cousin, and the anger that still filled him to know that Iain bore *his* title. All this, and now Aurya's incessant pacing, made Giraldus too tired to watch her. He wanted a good night's sleep in a bed, not on a Cryf sleeping shelf or on the bedroll of a soldier.

Like every soldier, he knew that lack of sleep, fatigue of both body and mind, could be as much of an enemy as an attacking army. But until Aurya wound down or at least faced what was troubling her, neither of them would get the rest they needed.

"Aurya," Giraldus said firmly, as she started yet another circuit around the room. "Come—sit."

"No," she said. "You don't understand . . . there's still so much—"

"Aurya," his voice changed into a command, "come and sit down."

Her steps were reluctant, but for a change she obeyed. She sat on the edge of the bed, far from relaxed, but at least Giraldus could take her hands into his own.

"Well," he said, his voice softer but not relenting, "are you going to tell me—or are you going to make me drag it out?"

"I don't know what you mean."

"Of course you do. After nearly ten years together, do you think I'm blind? Do you imagine that I've been so distracted by all we've been through not to see the changes in you—the change in you now? Losing your powers, getting them back . . . I can only guess what that must be like. But this is something more. I know it—tell me what it is."

She stared at him for a long moment. In the silence and stillness, Giraldus saw again the woman she had always been—until now. The restraint, the strength, and the control that had both grounded and guided him throughout their life together were still there. Yet right now, she was filled with other forces that made her seem like a barely contained whirlwind.

The restlessness built and spilled over again. Giraldus realized it was filled with anger that he could feel pounding like great waves of heat. But, after the enthusiasm she had displayed at dinner, he did not understand it. At whom was it directed . . . at herself? At him?

"Tell me," he commanded. He was trying to be gentle, but he would not give up.

Aurya tried to pull her hands away, but when Giraldus would not let them go either, she stared at him with slightly narrowed eyes. A month ago, perhaps even a week ago, he might have accepted the unspoken warning in this expression and let the subject drop. But not now; he met her gaze unflinchingly, with a wordless warning of his own.

Aurya must have seen it, for her eyes widened. "Giraldus," she began.

But he shook his head. Too many times she had used that tone to wheedle and coax him into the mood she wanted.

"Enough, Aurya," he said in a voice he rarely used with her, one he kept for the times with his troops or in the Judgment Hall.

She recognized it and stopped trying to pull away. Her face took on the strange expression Giraldus had seen several times since his arrival. Once more, he drew a breath and waited.

"I'm pregnant," the words finally exploded from her. She spoke as if she hated the sound of them. "I'm pregnant—and that changes everything."

"Pregnant," Giraldus repeated softly, wonder filling the word. Whatever he had thought or suspected, this was something he would never have dreamed. He could hardly believe the word now.

But Aurya had said it . . . she was *pregnant* . . . and she was right, it did change everything. The small part of him that might have been willing to accept defeat, to reclaim his place as Head of the Third House and Baron of Kilgarriff and return to his home in peace, now vanished. *His child* . . . for that, he would continue the fight for the crown, however long it took.

"Do you know, can you tell . . . I mean . . . what . . . ?"

"It is a son," Aurya said simply, and with the word, Giraldus felt a great swelling in his chest.

A son . . . *his* son . . .

Aurya was looking at him strangely again. "You're pleased," she said.

"Pleased?" He could not understand her question. "Of course I'm pleased. A child, an heir . . . you know how long I've wanted this. I assumed, after all these years, there could never be a child between us.

"But now my son . . . *our son* . . . will be King. I promise you that, Aurya. Tomorrow, we'll go to the cathedral with the other Barons and, by God, I'll find a way to stop whatever the old man has planned. Tomorrow, nothing will stop us."

He pulled her into his arms, wanting to hold her and yet almost afraid that he might hurt her with the embrace. "Oh, Aurya . . . Aurya," he said softly, resting his cheek against the top of her head, "you shall have everything—you and my son. Everything."

She allowed him to hold her, but she did not relax. In spite of his joy, he heard a little voice inside that whispered another warning. There was still something she was holding back. Whatever it was, he thought, he would get it from her after tomorrow.

Tomorrow, he told himself, they would confront the Archbishop together; tomorrow, they would stand side by side to claim the crown that they had worked so hard to obtain. Tomorrow she would realize how much closer their union would become through the new life they had created . . . together. *Tomorrow*, he told himself again, everything between them would be different, better; it would be all that he had always wanted it to be.

With a child in her womb and the crown on my head, he thought with sudden glee, *Aurya will marry me. She'll see that she must—for my son's sake, if not her own.*

Aurya was finally beginning to relax in his arms. Her body softly molded itself to his in the familiar way that always filled him with the desire to give her . . . everything. That desire had grown a hundredfold with these last minutes and the news of her pregnancy until, at this moment, Giraldus felt as if there could be nothing in his life, his reign, or in all the future might hold, of equal importance.

Yes, even as he bent to kiss her, wanting to put all of his joy, all of his love and hope and determination for her happiness into that kiss, the feeling that danger waited whispered again. For one brief instant Giraldus heeded it.

Then he looked into the deep sapphire of Aurya's eyes, and the importance of everything but her faded away.

Margharite knew her father was in the Residence. She had, in fact, watched from a second-story window, glad when her own eyes confirmed that he had suffered no true harm during the battle.

But she would not see him. Despite her relief at his safety, she was ashamed of his actions and far too angry with him yet to seek his presence. Instead, she paced her own room. Soon it became too small, and she knew she must escape from it—at least for a little while.

An undercurrent of tension and expectation ran through the Residence. True night, which came so late this time of year, had finally fallen, bringing a rich, deep darkness, in which she knew she should be sleeping. But sleep refused to come, and the beautiful grounds of the Residence were no longer an inviting place in which to walk off the restlessness she was feeling.

Margharite thought about trying to find Durkin again, but decided against it. Anything he might tell her about the retrieval of her father would carry its own kind of darkness, every bit as black as the night outside.

Instead, she began to wander the hallways. Somewhere in this maze of rooms and corridors, the future of Aghamore was being decided and prepared, but it was her future—and that of her father—that filled her thoughts and her heart tonight.

During the day, people—servants, clergy, Religious, as well as petitioners and supplicants of all sorts—were everywhere. Tonight, the quiet emptiness made the Residence seem even more immense . . . and made Margharite feel ever more small, insignificant, and lonely. She did see a few scurrying servants, two of whom stopped to ask after her needs, but she quickly dismissed them. They could not provide what she wanted.

She wanted Braedwyn. She wanted to go home—and she wanted her father back, as he had been before and not as this creature of ambition, greed, and treachery into which he had changed this last year.

Margharite finally found herself in one of the four chapels of the Residence. There was a large one on the ground floor, always open to the public and in which the Hours were chanted, daily Mass celebrated for the household and whomever else wished to attend. The Archbishop himself had two private chapels, one attached to his study and the other part of his personal apartments.

But the one Margharite now entered was something between. On the second floor of the Residence, where so many guest chambers were located, it was warm, intimate, and welcoming. It contained a small altar, the white of the fair linen gleaming softly in the glow of the lit candles and the tiny but beautifully fashioned Presence Lamp. Hanging on its brass chain in a corner of the sanctuary, it announced by its flame that consecrated Elements filled the little tabernacle.

As she slid silently into one of the eight pews, four to a side, which filled the area to near capacity, she wondered why the chapel stood in such obvious preparation. But there was so much happening in Aghamore right now, currents of perhaps drastic change churning just below the observable surface, that her mind refused to guess.

A side door opened and through it came that wonderous being she had only met once. He was covered with hair that shone like silken mahogany in the candlelight. The hair on his head was pulled back and bound into a straight fall that was at least as long as her own. She could tell that the hair continued over his body by the way it flowed out from collar, cuffs, and around the ankles of his bare, hair-covered feet.

He carried something long and of white cloth that she could not quite make out, moving with a strange silence as he carefully draped it over the altar rail. Then, as he turned to leave again, he saw her even in the gloom. He turned and looked straight at her and she saw that his face, too, was covered with hair that was more than a man's beard, but quite unlike the fur-covered features of an animal. There was nothing about that face that spoke of other than intelligence— and compassion.

Especially from his eyes. These were remarkable, and Margharite found herself gazing into what seemed like pools of living kindness. They made her breath catch in her throat so that she could not speak.

This being—was he a creature, a man . . . an angel?— walked toward her in a silent, slightly rolling gait. A part of her wanted to run from something so strange . . . and yet, the kindness of those eyes made him somehow ethereal, other-worldly, and kept Margharite where she was.

"Thou needest not fear," he said softly. "Tell me thy name."

"Margharite," she managed to whisper.

"Margharite," he repeated slowly, as if trying it out, his tongue rolling the r's and giving a breath to the center sounds. "She-Who-Is-Wisdom hath spoken of thee. I am Talog, second Guide unto the Cryf and servant of the Divine. How camest thou hither, Margharite, and what troublest thou?"

She shook her head. "I am not troubled," she said—she lied, not knowing this Talog or what he meant by the Cryf.

But he stared even more deeply into her eyes, then shook his head, too. "The pain riseth from thy heart unto thy face," he said gently. "Hide it not, that the Divine who seeth all, mayeth give thee healing."

His voice held a rise and fall, like a melody spoken rather than sung. It made Margharite think of the monks chanting Benediction in their haunting harmonies.

This being—*Talog,* she thought his name—kept watching her. Again she felt the kindness pouring from his gaze. It vanquished the final traces of her fear and encouraged her to speak.

"It's my father," she began, "Baron Hueil . . . I don't know what to do or how I feel about him any longer . . ."

Little by little, she let out her fears and feelings, of some of which she was unaware until she spoke them aloud. All the while, Talog kept watching her with his eyes of living kindness, which kept encouraging her and never once looked at her with judgment or condemnation, no matter what she said.

When she was finished, Margharite felt cleansed. Gone was her anger at her mother, buried under duty and sadness and never before admitted—anger that she had died and left Margharite without a female parent to soften her father's understanding. Gone, too, was much of the loneliness that loss had left and the unrealized guilt she felt over her anger.

Margharite also found herself cleansed of the anger she had felt toward her father and her shame at what he had done. She could forgive now—the man, if not the action; there could be reconciliation.

Talog sat back, nodding gently. "She-Who-Is-Wisdom hath chosen thee well," he said.

Margharite was confused. "Chosen for what?" she asked. "Who is this 'She-Who-Is-Wisdom'? Please, tell me what is going on?"

But this strange creature merely smiled a strange smile. "Thou shalt know when the time cometh for thee to know," he said. "Thou shalt then understand that all is as it must be."

"But—"

Talog shook his head. "Thou must leave this place now, for what is to come in the hours hence must be done in solitude. But thou must also prepare thy heart. With the dawn cometh great things—unto this Up-world land which thou dost love, and unto thy own life, also."

"Prepare? For what?"

Once more Talog shook his head. "Trust thy way unto the Divine, and thy path shalt be ever straight, ever clear— even though thou knowest it not. Of tomorrow, I mayeth tell thee naught, save that thou hast been prepared by the Hand of the Divine and art more worthy than thou dost yet realize."

With these words, the Cryf stood. He placed his hand on Margharite's forehead in a strange gesture of blessing, palm flat and fingers pointing upward. Then he stepped from the pew and walked with his quick, silent steps back to the altar.

Margharite stood, too. He had said that she must leave, and she would accept his words. But as she walked toward the door at the back of the chapel, she knew she had just as many questions in her heart—different, though just as unsettling—as when she entered.

Tomorrow had never felt so far away.

Chapter Thirty-four

I t was a night of vigils, of sleepless hours, of worry and prayer. It was a night of contemplation and resolution. For some, it was a night of remorse; for others it was a night of anticipation.

Then, into the long darkness, came the first wakening hint of dawn. Blackness slowly softened into violet shadow and to the east, gray gave way to the promise of golden light. Criers of the Watch announced day's advent to the city, as they did every morning.

But today was not like every morning, as many of those who, awake throughout the night, heard the Criers and understood. This was a day of beginnings and endings, both; a day of fulfillments bound in patterns of dark and bright.

Today was the true battle for the future of Aghamore . . . fought not with weapons, but with faith. The city held an air of expectancy; everyone knew that some great event awaited within the cathedral. Around the morning hearth, mothers and fathers speculated, while shopkeepers opened their shops and stalls to the shared music of gossip. Everyone had an idea—and no one knew anything for certain.

The Archbishop had ordered the city gates to remain closed; only the Westgate was to be opened and not until his word arrived. At ten o'clock Wilham was sent out bearing the instruction that at ten-thirty the gate was to be opened and the Barons admitted. Each Baron was allowed a retinue of ten men, and they could carry no more arms than a single ceremonial sword and dagger. If any Baron refused to obey these orders, they were to be refused admittance . . . and the Archbishop promised that the army of Urlar, who were still within the city as guards of safety and peace, would be on hand to enforce these orders if necessary.

The forward pews of the nave, just down from the transept and quire, had been reserved for the Barons and their companies; behind those, the rest of the huge cathedral would be open to as many from the city population as could squeeze themselves inside. It was important that as many people as possible witness what was about to happen. It was important today, and it would be important to the lasting peace in the years to come.

The Archbishop had also sent messages to the bishops. Wilham had delivered those shortly after dawn, summoning each of the prelates, save Elon, to assemble at ten-thirty in the quire of the cathedral, robed in their white copes and vestments of celebration. There was no other explanation given, only a call of their obedience.

To Elon, another handwritten summons had been sent. He, too, was to come to the cathedral with his white vestments—but unlike the others, he was to wait in the side vestry next to the Lady Chapel until he was called forth. The Archbishop and Renan had worked together on the letter to Elon, carefully wording it in a way to touch his vanity. They needed him to assume he was waiting in isolation so that he could be brought out into the public acclaim he craved.

There had been no direct confrontation from Aurya and Giraldus. The only indication they were here at all, had been the dark magic on the cross sent to the Archbishop—and that had come from Elon. It was vital that he continue to think the plan had worked, so that Aurya and Giraldus would think the same long enough for Selia to be crowned. After that . . . well, as Eiddig would say, after that all was in the Hand of the Divine.

Selia had kept her requisite Vigil of Purification in the little chapel of the Residence that the Cryf had prepared for her, rather than in the cathedral, as had past rulers on the eve of their coronation. They had prayed and contemplated the role they were assuming, while keeping watch over the Regalia of Coronation. In those prayers, it was their duty to try to discern the lessons symbolized by orb and scepter, crown and sword, robes, throne, slippers, canopy, ring, and seal.

For Selia's vigil, the regalia had been under careful guard at the cathedral, watched over by Renan and Talog while she passed her hours in mostly solitary prayer. Each one of her friends had visited her once, to pray with her and to give their encouragement. The Archbishop, busy with preparations, had been able to give her little time, but Eiddig had spent over two hours with her, giving Selia such guidance as his years could impart.

But now all that was past. Preparations were in place, the messages had all long been delivered, and the gates were finally opened. At the same time, the largest of the cathedral bells began a slow, steady, and solitary peal, the sound carrying over the city to summon the people. And inside the cathedral, the coals in the great, ceiling-hung thurible were lit, preparing them for the incense that would soon billow forth.

The Archbishop had met Elon when he arrived, and being careful to exude the expected air of welcome at the Bishop of Kilgarriff's presence, had personally shown him into the room where he was to wait. It had been an exercise in self-control for the Archbishop, to smile and pretend he was happy at the sight of Elon, to offer his ring to be kissed and to give Elon a blessing. What he wanted was to call the guards and have the bishop taken into custody, stripped of his vestments before the assembled company, then thrown into the most isolated cell in the kingdom and left there for the rest of his days.

Secret orders had been given, and after the other bishops arrived, there would be guards placed outside Elon's door. When the time was right, Elon would be brought forth—not to the honor he expected, but to the fate he deserved.

Colm ApBeirne, Primus of the Church in Aghamore, stood in front of the altar, facing the long nave that was slowly filling up with people. He was dressed in the most ornate and sumptuous cope and vestments of his Office. The cope, chasuble, stole, and maniple were all made of white silk woven with gold thread. The chasuble orphreys, and the banding on the stole and maniple, were of gold, studded with sprays of tiny diamonds that made him look like a heavenly being, too bright for earthly habitation. The Chi-Rho on the back of the cope were created out of garnets, and more garnets studded the edge of both garments all the way around.

On his head rested the triple-crowned mitre. It, too, was white, and the crowns, gold studded with jewels. In his hand he held the great crozier, the Shepherd's Crook, of the Archbishop. It was of ancient design, its long staff wound with twisted bands of gold and silver, and the center of its curved head set with a diamond the size and shape of a walnut.

He stood absolutely still as the people poured in. The bishops of the Provinces, also vested though none so amazingly, filled the quire. Their white vestments also shimmered in the light of the myriad candles and the sun that was just beginning to shine through the many colored windows. It was easy to imagine that the heavenly host had come down to stand between the altar and the pews.

The Barons arrived amid their personal pomp, striding

forward through the gathering throng to find their places in the front. The Archbishop watched them closely. All but Iain's face wore the same expression of puzzled arrogance. This pose was habitual, held firmly in place this morning as if to remind the people—and each other—of their mutual rights as Heads of the Ruling Houses of Aghamore.

But none of them knew why they were here or what the Archbishop had planned. They were each aware that the succession remained unsettled and that their armies still stood in battle readiness outside the gates. Their expressions said that they had not completely dismissed the idea of using them again.

Lord Iain, by contrast, looked confident and peaceful. He bobbed his head in an informal bow to the Archbishop before entering his assigned pew. Then he knelt in prayer. The Archbishop, watching him, gave a mental nod; he knew that the appointment he had awaiting Iain was both well deserved and the best possible choice for the welfare of the kingdom.

People were filing in from the city, too, a host of humanity that came in a jostling mass of bodies and voices. They came full of curiosity—but they also came full of confidence in the Archbishop and ready to accept whatever he was about to do. It rang in their laughter and shone from their faces as they filled in the pews, the side aisles, the narthex, and spilled out onto the porch.

Shortly before eleven o'clock, the sound of the bells changed. For a few brief moments all eight of the bells pealed . . . then, as the hour arrived, fell silent. The sudden lack of sound was startling.

All eyes were fastened on the Archbishop as he slowly mounted the long steps to the elevated pulpit, where he could be seen and heard by everyone.

"People of Aghamore," he began, "our kingdom has been through a time of darkness and great sadness that touched each of our lives. This current darkness did not begin last week or last month—or even last year. It began when we, as a kingdom, left aside humility and gratitude and began to be convinced of our own infallibility. This attitude led to the reign of such a King as Anri, whose selfishness and depravity over the welfare of his people infected all those in power, and with his death has taken Aghamore to the brink of civil war—and beyond, opening the door for our great enemy to enter. It is only by Divine Mercy that this kingdom has survived."

Below him, in the front pews of the cathedral, the Barons shifted and would not meet his eyes, uncomfortable now in both their seats and their conscience. The Archbishop stood in silence for a moment, letting them feel the full impact of their shame before he continued.

"But long ago," he continued, "King Liam the Builder, first High King of our beloved land, made provisions for the situation in which we now find ourselves. Hear then, the words written by King Liam himself as they speak to us across the centuries:

" *. . . And if thus there comes a time when the throne stands empty, and all the branches of the tree that is Aghamore are of like strength, so that none stands alone of the courage and wisdom of heart that befits the ruler over all, but each is equal unto all; if into this time no one name is spoken by the Barons, known by the common consensus, judged by the Church, and acknowledged even before pronouncement, as the right and perfect King . . . even then shall the Heart of the Scepter decide.*

"By the Hand of the Almighty was the Heart of the Scepter fashioned and So shall that Hand, which ever holds and guides Aghamore's way, deliver the Heart of the Scepter unto the one Divinely chosen to fill the empty throne. By Divine Right shall the one who bears

*the Heart of the Scepter rule, and no earthly power
shall deny this right.*

*"This do I, Liam I, High King of Aghamore, decree
and make law, from this day forward unto the end of
ages of man."*

The Archbishop ceased reading. All shuffling within the
cathedral had ceased, and the great building was filled with
an eerie quiet while everyone waited for the Primus to explain what he had just read.

But he said nothing. Instead, at his signal, the door of the
side chapel dedicated to St. Michael the Archangel, Patron of
the great cathedral and of Aghamore, opened. Renan stepped
out. He was vested only in a long white rochetta over his
black cassock, the bottom half of which had been hand-tatted
to echo the Chi-Rho pattern on the Archbishop's cope and
chasuble.

In his hands he carried two items, held straight out and at
arm's length so that none could say he was hiding anything
in the fold of arm or clothing. In his left hand he carried a
scroll which, after a bow of reverence, he placed upon the
altar.

In his right hand he carried the great and ancient scepter
of the Coronation Regalia. Many in the room had seen it at
the coronation of King Anri, ten years ago, and some at the
coronation of King Osaze ten years before that. But it had
been one piece among many, buried amid the grand pomp of
the day and few, if any, had looked at it closely.

Renan held the scepter at arm's length as he walked down
the middle of the quire, under the intent gaze of the bishops.
Finally, he stood at the top of the nave, still holding the
scepter out for all to see. The beauty of it was obvious, with
its long wand wrapped in twisted ropes of gold and silver,
with jewels at the top and bottom. The top, the large amethyst
held in a cage of golden wire, glittered in the light of the can-

dles, drawing everyone's eyes. The Archbishop could almost hear their thoughts, wondering about the words that the Primus had just read as they stared at the scepter and tried to see its "Heart."

That was what he had intended, and he looked directly at the Barons. "Each of you," he said, "was so filled with your own greed for power that you came to Ballinrigh ready to shed the blood of fellow Aghamorians. But the words of King Liam have given us a better way. He foretold that the Heart of the Scepter would reveal the next true ruler of this land. I, therefore, call each of you forward to take the scepter in your own hands. Show us the Heart of the Scepter and you will wear the crown."

The Barons shifted uneasily in their seats, uncertain what to do. "Come," the Archbishop ordered, gesturing them forward. "There is nothing to fear. Come, and let none say that he was denied a fair chance."

The Baron of Camlough was the first to stand, then Dromkeen, then Sylaun; one by one, the others followed. Together, they stepped out into the central aisle and marched up the nave, a tiny army of men still bent on gaining the throne. Of the Barons, only Iain remained seated.

As he approached, Renan held the scepter out to the Baron of Camlough, willingly relinquishing his hold into the Baron's hand. Oran Keogh of Camlough, Head of the Fifth Ruling House, the House of Nuinseann, and Baron of the Province of Camlough, took it confidently. He turned it over and over, the expression on his face not wavering as he examined every part of it. He tried twisting the jewels at the top and bottom, attempted to open the golden cage that held the amethyst, tried to find a way to remove the slightly heart-shaped ruby that crowned it.

Slowly, his expression was changing. It went from confidence, to defiance, to anger—and finally to defeat as he passed it on to the next of his peers. He then stepped back, folding his arms across his barrel chest as he waited, as if daring the next man to do better.

One by one, the others did the same—with as little effect or success as the Baron of Camlough. Finally the last in line—Baron Einar Maille, Head second branch of the House of Baoghil, Baron of the Eighth Province of Lininch—handed the scepter back to Renan. They all looked up at the Archbishop, awaiting his next words.

"Are you satisfied?" he asked them. "If you are not, then take up the scepter and try again. Try as many times as you need to believe there is no trick."

None of the Barons reached for the scepter. After a moment, they turned and collectively returned to their places. Before he entered his pew, however, Camlough again turned to the Archbishop.

"*We* are the Ruling Houses of Aghamore," he said. "If we cannot find this Heart of the Scepter, then who can? *We* are the branches of the tree, as said the words you read—what other branches are there?"

"You shall soon have your answers," the Archbishop assured him.

He gave a signal to Renan. The younger priest turned, marched back to the altar, and placed the scepter there. Then he took up the scroll and crossed to the lectern.

Without waiting, he unrolled the scroll, cleared his throat, and began to read. While the people turned their attention to Renan, the Archbishop watched each of the Barons closely; confusion, expected, but any threat must be caught and dealt with immediately.

"*. . . Though the ravening beasts of the north have been chased from the shores, the hold of Darkness is yet not vanquished. Fear still existeth and shall until the Font of Wisdom standeth before all. Only by Wis-*

*dom's hand shall that which is closed be opened and
that which is empty be filled.*

*"From obscurity shall the Font of Wisdom come,
from tears and sorrows rise, an innocent who knoweth
not the ways of the world. Yet, in the heart that knoweth
not the paths walked by those called 'Mighty,' by their
own, resideth the untapped wealth of Truth.*

*"Only the Font of Wisdom hath the power to stop
the Darkness and set Aghamore free. In the reign of the
Font of Wisdom, both Light and Truth shall again
strengthen Aghamore, and her enemies shall be vanquished into the ages. . . ."*

The Scroll went on to describe where and how the Font of
Wisdom was to be found—the many passages that had
guided Renan and the others in their quest to find Selia. But
in the planning of this coronation, they had all agreed that
nothing more needed to be read. Looking at the confusion on
the faces below him, Colm ApBeirne hoped it had been the
right decision. The next hour would tell.

Over to the side, the door of Saint Michael's chapel
opened again. This time, Selia stepped out. She came forward alone, dressed in her new gown and looking every bit
the innocent of whom the scroll had just spoken.

She walked down through the center aisle of the quire that
filled the chancel, each step taken under the scrutiny of the
bishops, finally reaching the rood arch, where Renan stood
with the scroll. The Archbishop came down the steps of the
tall pulpit. Bishops, Barons, people—everyone had begun to
whisper, the noise mounting while the Archbishop walked to
the altar, where he again took up the scepter.

Outside, the sun was moving toward the zenith of noon,
sending even more colored light streaming from the stained
glass, and especially from the great rose window at the back
of the cathedral. At noon, the sun would shine directly

through its center, sending a great beacon toward the sanctuary of the altar.

The Archbishop came forward to stand with the others. Then he held up his hands for silence. "Our kingdom has indeed faced Darkness," he began, "and faces it still. But the words you have just heard, from a prophecy of promise, have told us the way to defeat that Darkness, and bring the Light to fill Aghamore once again. That way stands before you, in the person of this young woman. *She* is the Font of Wisdom, promised and now fulfilled."

Once more it was Baron Oran of Camlough who spoke out. He sprang to his feet, pointing an accusatory finger in Selia's direction.

"The Font of Wisdom—this . . . girl?" he shouted. "She's hardly more than a child. You can't mean to crown this girl and have us accept her. Why should I, why should any of us, accept the words of some prophecy we've never heard of before?"

"Do you accept the Laws of King Liam?" the Archbishop countered. "It is by those laws that you govern Camlough."

The light was getting brighter. The Archbishop held the scepter high.

"By King Liam's own words, this scepter—once held in his own hands—shall answer and proclaim the truth in the prophecy you denounce. Each of you has held it. You have felt its weight, tried to find its Heart. But you have failed—because it was not meant for you. Nor do I know its secret. Let us learn the truth . . . and stand together for the future of this land."

Oran of Camlough stared back at him a moment longer. Then, finally, he nodded and sat back down, folding his arms across his massive chest. The Archbishop turned and handed the scepter to Selia.

The young woman's fingers were trembling slightly as she accepted it. She looked deeply into the Archbishop's eyes. He wanted to comfort her, to tell her that everything would be all right—but whatever happened now was out of his control.

The Archbishop stepped back a little. Selia stood alone, vulnerable, as she turned the scepter over and over in her hands. Her actions were no different than the Barons'. Then, just as her hand went to the top, a tiny shaft of light from the rose window hit the amethyst in the Cryf necklace she always wore. It refracted through the stone and bounced back to touch the scepter. No one in the cathedral could miss the single chime that rang through the air, and, with the sound, the golden cage holding the scepter's crowning jewel opened.

The great amethyst was hollow. Moving as if guided by something outside herself, Selia lifted the stone of her necklace and slid it into the hollow place. It filled and fitted, a perfect and complete match.

The Heart of the Scepter.

Light poured from the union of gems, and with it came a sound sweet, high, and clear, a chime of ringing crystal as brilliant and beautiful as the light itself. Throughout the cathedral, people gasped. Some fell to their knees, crossing themselves in wonder. Even the face of Oran of Camlough had lost its belligerence.

From the back of the cathedral, a procession began. People crowded in the narthex parted to let them through—one more wonder in this morning of wonders.

First came Talog, the beautiful robe of the monarch draped over his arms. This robe, woven in the deep blue that was King Liam's color, was trimmed in white fur with a clasp of gold, diamonds, rubies, and sapphires at its throat.

Behind Talog came Lysandra and Cloud-Dancer. Although she was not touching him, the wolf walked sedately by her side, freeing Lysandra's hands to hold the great orb, a golden ball jeweled and set with clusters of stones representing the Provinces. It was topped with a golden cross that had a perfect diamond at its heart to represent the Divine Mercy by which the Kings governed and which was to be the guiding force throughout their reign.

Finally came Eiddig. The Cryf Guide wore his own great necklace of Office and carried the Crown of King Liam in his gnarled hands. This ancient crown—like the scepter, like the crozier of the Archbishop, and like Eiddig's own necklace—was made of ropes of both gold and silver that twisted around each other in glimmering strength and beauty. Again, the crown was set with eight large stones, each one a different color, to represent the Eight Outer Provinces, and had a large diamond set above the brow to signify Urlar, the King's Province.

Cries of surprise followed the appearance of the Cryf. But the sounds died back to whispered murmurs as the people looked with eagerness to see what would happen next. The people, if not the Barons, trusted the Archbishop and knew he would do only what he knew to be best for them.

The Archbishop was beginning to think that the dangers were under control, if not completely over, and that they would get through Selia's coronation after all. He allowed himself to relax just a little. Then, as the Cryf joined the rest of the procession where it waited halfway down the nave, another commotion began.

Aurya stepped out into the aisle, eyes burning with hatred. "No," she shouted, her voice cutting through the sounds around her.

The Archbishop saw Selia start, and he put a comforting hand on her shoulder. Talog, Lysandra, and Eiddig turned. Recognizing Aurya, they hurried the rest of the way toward Selia. Then, Renan also joining them, they turned to face the foe together.

The Archbishop stepped in front of the others. "Guards," he called, "take that woman—"

But even as he spoke, Aurya started forward, pointing an accusatory finger and chanting as she walked. The Archbishop knew that the final battle for Aghamore's future was about to begin — and he prayed that they were strong enough to win.

Chapter Thirty-five

Before they had left Elon's house, Aurya made both Rhys and Maelik remove every insignia and article of clothing that bespoke either the army or the Province of Kilgarriff. She then had Thomas find hooded cloaks for herself and Giraldus, procured from among the other servants' belongings. Only when she was certain they would be faceless among the crowd did they join the throng heading toward the cathedral.

Although they were unarmed, Giraldus and Maelik were still imposing figures, and Aurya let them force their way forward, making certain they would be seated and not among those standing, straining to see and hear from the narthex or porch. But when they did reach a pew, Aurya would not accept Giraldus's attempt to place her on the inside, for her protection. She insisted on being nearest the aisle. She told Giraldus that after their long captivity by the Cryf, she could no longer stand to be closed in, even by other bodies.

She knew, however, that she had another reason for wanting to be seated where she could move freely. Giraldus did not argue with her—but the look in his eyes told her that he knew it, too.

Once they were seated, Aurya searched for a glimpse of Elon. At first, his absence did not worry her; with so many things happening, there were a number of reasons why he might be somewhere other than in plain sight. However, once the Archbishop appeared *not* wearing the cross they had sent him, she knew their plan had failed.

All during the time the Archbishop had stood on the elevated pulpit, Aurya had tried to think of what to do. Whatever the changes to her magic that pregnancy was causing, she was still a creature of power.

She was still to be feared.

While the Barons spent their futile efforts on the scepter, Aurya closed her eyes. She sent her thoughts searching, down deeper and deeper, past the reality of who she was now, of who with her pregnancy she had become. She needed to find the core of who—and what—she had always been before.

It was becoming harder to find. Almost hour by hour, her pregnancy altered the internal pathways she was used to following, and the magic she had already felt changing was altered still further. Nothing within her felt as it should.

Once again, she silently cursed the Cryf, their Realm, and all those who had been responsible for her captivity there. But now, no matter what it took, no matter how much effort she had to pour forth or what effect it had on her to find it, she *would* reach her magic again . . . she *would* bend it to her will . . . and she *would* repay all those who stood before her.

Renan began to read; Aurya recognized the words from the Thirteenth Scroll of Tambryn as surely as if she had penned them herself. She began to feel a little desperate, a little panicked as his voice continued, and she still found herself unable to call forth her powers. The magic was there—

she could feel it like a second heartbeat pounding within—but she could not find the way to reach it.

Renan grew silent . . . Selia came forward . . . voices were raised in surprise and objection . . . the Archbishop answered them . . .

Aurya ignored them all. There had to be a way . . . she poured her thoughts, her strength, her *will* farther and farther, deeper and deeper, blocking out everything else. No distractions, she told herself; there must be only herself and her magic . . . .

There . . . she touched it just as the sound of ringing crystal sang through the cathedral. As light exploded and filled the air, Aurya deepened and widened the new pathway to her powers. Finally, magic began to well up, growing stronger with each passing second. As the little procession of her enemies neared the top of the nave, she knew she was ready to strike.

She stood. Giraldus reached up and grabbed her arm; Aurya turned to look at him. Despite the anger on his face, he had made no move to join her—nor did he appear ready to take action. Aurya could not understand it. Why was he waiting?

She looked from Giraldus to Maelik and Rhys. They were still watching, obviously waiting for some signal or someplace in the ceremony they deemed more appropriate.

Appropriate be damned; she would wait no longer. The magic she had summoned was pulsing within her now, ready for release, almost as strong as her hatred. *Now* was the time to strike.

She started to step out, but Giraldus pulled on her arm, trying to hold her back. "Not yet," he whispered firmly. "Elon isn't—"

"Forget Elon," she whispered back, her voice even harder than his own. "Elon has *failed*."

"Failed? How do you know?"

"The cross the Archbishop is wearing," she answered with the last of her patience. "It's the *wrong one*."

Giraldus's surprise loosened his grip. She quickly pulled free and stepped into the aisle. There was nothing he could do, nothing he could say that would stop her. She would fight *him* if she must, but she would have her revenge.

"No," she shouted, putting all the force of her pent-up hatred into the word. It sliced through the cathedral like a sharpened blade. All eyes turned toward her, but she spared no thought for any of them. Her only thought, her only focus, was on the group clustered around Selia.

She heard the Archbishop call for guards, and she smiled at the foolishness. By the time they could push their way through the mass of people everywhere, she would be too strong for them to touch.

She began chanting as she walked forward. With each step, she could feel her power nearing the point of release. The feeling was sweet and heady, like sun-warmed wine pulsing through her veins.

Outside, the sun was nearing noon, and the rose window was ablaze with light, sending great shafts of color into the aisle before her. But she did not notice. Her only thought was of her enemies and of the revenge that she would now claim. She raised her finger and pointed at them, letting words and intent meet and meld in that simple gesture.

"Magic build and magic burn
Power stone as darkest night
Magic twist and magic churn
Give me what I claim by right . . ."

Each second that passed, each step she took, revenge continued to near. The power within felt like a living thing; it felt like a mighty serpent, coiling and at her command, preparing to strike.

"Power born of magic dark,
Power from beyond all time;
Ignite the fire, flame the spark
From depths of hate to my hands, climb. . . ."

Aurya saw that the group had gathered in front of Selia, as if to form a living shield. It made her want to laugh. *So futile,* she thought. *So foolish. You are nothing and I will destroy you. All of you.*

She raised both her hands, holding them out in front of her. Her whole body had begun to tingle. It came spreading up from her belly, from a place deep within that went far beyond a physical source of description; it was beyond the understanding of any who did not possess or who denied themselves the glory of *magic*.

Power ran down her arms, building into waves of fire that demanded release.

"Fire of darkness, Fire of death,
Fire born where hate resides,
Carried now on wings of breath
That none has power to turn aside. . . ."

The scene before her shifted as Selia's protectors tightened their shield in front of her. Behind them, the bishops of Aghamore were restlessly moving, torn between coming forward to aid their Primus and wanting to run away for their own safety.

Throughout the cathedral, the noise was building as people began to realize what was happening. Panic was beginning to find fertile ground, and its roots were spreading quickly.

As the voices grew around her, Aurya raised her own. She wanted her enemies to hear what was coming, and to know true fear.

"Fire of unending flame
Eat through flesh, consume the bone;
Sent to where my hatred aims:
With death enmesh, with pain enthrone.
Revenge is mine, I claim the life
Of she whose name is Wisdom's Font;
My hatred sharp as two-edged knife
Delivers now my deepest want."

Then, to her surprise, Renan stepped in front of the others. He lifted both his hands, palms flat outward as if to halt her progress. Then he began a counterspell:

"The time for hiding now is past,
Only Light salvation brings;
Light to hold thy Darkness fast;
Light that flies on faith's bright wings.
I summon Light and send it forth
Surround and bind thee, Darkness turn;
Consume the sender, not the aim:
Stop now they spell, or thou wilt burn."

Aurya's opened her eyes wide as Renan's counterspell began to reach her. *So, the little priest thinks he has enough power to stop me,* she thought. *Well, he shall soon learn otherwise.*

She raised her hands again, preparing to call up such dark power as Renan had never conceived. She was willing to give any amount of energy, of life force to achieve her ends. She would sacrifice her own life and that of her child in order to destroy those who had defeated and imprisoned her.

But before she could speak one final time, she heard someone yell, *"Now."* After a second of confusion, she recognized the voice of the accursed blind healer. Aurya's thoughts echoed the command. Her power welled. Despite

Renan's attempt to block it, it reached her fingertips and sparked like dark fire, flames filled with blackness.

At the same moment, the noon sun reached its zenith, and a brilliant shaft of sunlight shot toward the altar. As Aurya's power swirled, ready to shoot forth, she heard Renan's voice again.

> *"Light of day, by heaven sent;*
> *Light of hope, become our aid;*
> *Light as shield, no Dark can rent;*
> *Light now over all is laid.*
> *Light is gathered, Light sent forth;*
> *Light the power in which we stand;*
> *Light will prove Selia's worth;*
> *Light is the sword in righteous hand."*

With his words, the light from the window hit the diamond in the crook of the Archbishop's crozier, shot from there to the central diamond in the great chain of Office Eiddig wore. Again it refracted and shot a beam of light into the raised diamond of King Liam's crown, creating a mesh of Light that Aurya's magic could not penetrate.

She called up more power; felt it burning, searing through her mind. She sent it out just as, at Lysandra's shout, Selia raised the scepter. The beam of light shot from the crown into the scepter. The brilliant amethyst, now completed by the reunion of its Heart, absorbed the light, turned it, magnified it, and sent it straight toward Aurya.

The dark fire of her magic met it. For a single heartbeat the battle raged. Then, suddenly, Aurya felt a twisting, a churning deep within her body, as the child in her womb moved, responding to the wild magic coursing through Aurya's body. Again, she knew it was too soon. At five weeks of life, the baby should not be moving; her own body should barely know it was there.

Now the baby, caught in the forces battling for supremacy, struggled for its own existence. It twisted and drained Aurya's power to protect itself.

Aurya's magic began to recede. Fraction by fraction, second by second, the searing Light from the amethyst was coming closer. Aurya knew that in that Light was her death.

She was panting, sweating, as the battle continued. It had been only a few heartbeats, but it felt as if she had been fighting the Light for hours. Her strength was almost gone. She prepared herself for one final burst, ready to pour her last breath of life into her spell. She would die—but she would destroy her enemies with that death, and *that* was worth any sacrifice.

She spared Giraldus a single glance; his farewell. Then she closed her eyes and reached down . . . down . . .

"Aurya," Giraldus shouted at her. His voice was desperate, telling her that he had seen her intent in her eyes. She should not have looked at him, not have let him know. *I'm sorry, Giraldus,* she thought . . . .

Suddenly he was there, knocking her out of the way. The meeting of Light and magic exploded in a blinding eruption of power.

Aurya screamed as the power hit Giraldus. He stood for a moment, his whole body shaking violently . . . then he crumpled to the ground.

"Giraldus," Aurya screamed again, throwing herself on her knees at his side. Life was fading quickly. Aurya took his hand, hardly noticing anything, even Maelik kneeling beside her.

Giraldus looked at his sergeant, his friend. "Get her . . . away . . ." He forced the words out. "Keep . . . safe . . ."

"Aye, m'lord."

"Aurya." She bent close; his voice was barely audible. "Love . . . you . . ."

His breath came in one more ragged pant . . . then stopped. Aurya was struck cold. Giraldus could not be *dead*.

Throughout the cathedral, people were bewildered, stunned into silence as they tried to understand all that was happening. But it would not last for long. Maelik and Rhys began tugging on her, trying to hurry her away. When she did not move, Maelik scooped her up in his arms and began to run toward the door.

The still-stunned crowd opened before them, the fear of Aurya's magic giving them their slight—their only—chance of escape.

"Giraldus," Aurya said softly, still afraid to believe what bad just happened.

But then the reality crystallized. With it came the knowledge that she had to get away. Only then could she return and kill those who had just killed Giraldus. This time, however, it would not be with magic. This time she would plunge the knife into their hearts and watch their blood flow away.

"Put me down," she ordered Maelik, herself once more. "Rhys, run ahead and grab the horses. We're right behind you."

Rhys dashed off as Maelik put her down. Then, holding up her skirts for easy movement, Aurya ran by Maelik's side toward freedom.

Elon paced in the vestry beside the Lady Chapel, awaiting the summons that would call him to the glory he deserved. He had brought his most beautiful vestments of white, rose-marked brocade. The orphreys were made of hand-layered gold piping, couched with gold thread and bordered with tiny pearls. More pearls dotted the center of the roses woven into the nap of the fabric. Pearls and carnelians bordered the neck, around the bottom, and outlined the embroidered *Agnus Dei* that made the central design where the orphreys met.

The cope, stole, and maniple all matched the chasuble.

Elon had them specially made for this day, and they had never before been worn. He was also wearing a new purple cassock and cincture, with gold-couched piping and gold-covered buttons. The new alb and amice were made of purest linen and decorated with rows of delicate cutwork. These latter, like the brocade vestments, were only waiting for the Archbishop's word before Elon put them on for the first time, to go out to meet his destiny.

Elon heard the bell ring, calling the people of Ballinrigh to the cathedral. He was not quite certain what the Archbishop had planned or how long it would take, so to pass the time, he practiced the sermon he was certain he would be called upon to deliver.

Even so, the time dragged. Finally, he decided to crack the door just a bit and see for himself what was happening. From the door, he had an unobstructed view of the sanctuary steps and the quire. He stood for a few minutes, shocked into disbelief by what he was seeing. Then, finally, the reality of it sank in, and panic shot through his mind. His heart began to pound. His thoughts whirled as he closed the door quietly again and turned back into the room, trying to think of how to save himself.

Outside his door stood two guards, swords drawn and ready. There was no hope of escape that way. But they were not *watching* the door, only guarding it, and they had not seen it open. Their attention, like everyone else's, was fixed on the scene at the altar.

Elon's eyes swept through the room, trying to see something that might aid his escape. A moment later, a commotion started out in the church—a shout, voices being raised . . . *It's now or never,* he thought. But the room seemed devoid of anything to help him, anything to . . . then his eyes lit upon the tall cloak tree. It was made of oak, perhaps six feet tall, solid and strong, with a base of cast iron.

In the cathedral, the noise built. Elon had no idea how

long he would have before they came for him, but he guessed it would not be long. In one quick move, he picked up the cloak tree and, as the noise outside crescendoed, smashed the metal base into the window, turning the long wooden pole to clear away the broken shards.

The noise of it shocked him, made his already pounding heart race so that he could hardly think. He was used to mental action, to using his wits — and his voice — to get what he wanted, not to the noise and demands of acting as a soldier might.

But the moment was a desperate one. Elon looked at the gaping hole that had once been a thing of beauty, a delicate piece of art in glass, and it suddenly looked to him like the maw of some beast, ready to devour him.

He grabbed up the beautiful chasuble; it would do him no good now as a vestment. But it could serve him in another way. He wrapped his hand and arm well, and pushed the rest of the glass out of the frame. Then, using the room's one chair for a lift, he climbed up and out.

The drop was farther than Elon expected, and for a moment he lay on the ground stunned, unable to catch his breath. From within the cathedral, the noise built. There was a crash, a scream, voices raised in sudden confusion. The noise again shocked Elon into action. He forced himself to his feet, ignoring the pain that shot through his left ankle. He had to get away — back to his house, back to Ummera, then . . .

Then where? It was a question to which he had no answer. But later, on the road to Ummera he would have a day or two to think. Then he would decide. Surely, if he was quick enough now, he would have that much time before any danger caught up with him.

He took another step, and again pain shot up his leg. There was no way he could walk back to where his carriage was waiting, on the other side of the cathedral grounds.

The horses ridden by the Barons were tethered nearby. Hobbling as quickly as he could, he hurried toward them. He had nearly reached them when young Rhys came running, almost knocking Elon over.

"Your Grace," he said with a breathless surprise. "I . . . I must hurry—Lady Aurya be waiting."

"What has happened?"

Rhys shook his head. "There's too much . . . Lady Aurya must tell ye. But Baron Giraldus be dead, and we must get m'lady away. If'n yer with us, then hurry."

As he spoke, Rhys had grabbed the reins of the nearest horses. Elon did the same. Again ignoring the pain, he swung himself into the saddle and rode with Rhys toward the front of the cathedral. Aurya and Maelik were rushing toward them. One look at Aurya's face was all the confirmation Elon needed.

He thought of riding off on his own, abandoning Aurya and the others to whatever fate awaited them. But he was suddenly filled with the certainty that his future and hers were inexorably linked. So he waited, heart and head pounding off the seconds, while Maelik got a shocked Aurya into the saddle, then grabbed her reins and threw himself onto a horse of his own. He nodded to Elon.

The bishop led the way. At a gallop, they all rode—away from the cathedral, away from the known danger here. Together, they rode into the future and into the unknown but certain danger awaiting.

Chapter Thirty-six

Inside the cathedral, Lysandra's *Sight* followed them. The Archbishop ordered guards after Aurya, but Lysandra knew it was already too late. By the time they pushed themselves through the dazed crowds, Aurya and the others would be on their way.

It was the people now she was worried about—their welfare, and Selia's. It was important to complete the coronation. Once Selia was crowned, they could mount an organized search for the enemies of the kingdom—but they would do so with the people's support and confidence in their new Queen.

By then, of course, Aurya and the others would be gone from Aghamore; Lysandra knew it with the sudden certainty of prophecy. Whether or when they would return was unclear.

Lysandra also knew she needed to get somewhere alone. She needed to think about the events that had just taken place. Within them was the whisper of prophecy waiting to be heard. It was a gift so new, she was still uncertain how to use it; sometimes it overwhelmed her, and others, like now, it spoke in a whisper she had to struggle to hear.

Lysandra reminded herself that her *Sight* had once been as confusing. But time had taught her how to use her *Sight*—and she was certain that time would help her again.

At this moment, however, nothing mattered as much as

completing the coronation. Whether the kingdom knew it yet or not, Aghamore needed its new Queen.

Giraldus's body still lay in the long central aisle of the nave. At the continued sight of his lifeless body, the stunned inactivity of the crowd was beginning to wear off, and panic was starting to mount. Something had to be done and quickly, or all they were trying to do here would be lost. If Selia was not crowned, and with both the witness and support of her people, then Aurya would have won after all.

Lysandra stepped closer to Selia and gently put a hand on her shoulder. Then, letting the contact of her hand create a contact of their minds, she reached out to communicate with the speed of thought, undisturbed by the growing commotion.

You must act now, her mind said. *It is time to take control. You—not Renan or Eiddig or the Archbishop. The people need their sovereign to be strong if they are to give their trust and confidence—which you need. Show them that you are the Queen they need you to be.*

How? Selia's thoughts queried. *What should I do?*

Trust yourself, Selia, Lysandra told her. *You already know what must be done.*

With that, Lysandra withdrew both her hand and her thoughts. For weeks she and Renan had done all they could to help Selia become who she was meant to be. Now it was up to her. From here on, what she became rested in her own hands . . . and heart.

Selia stepped forward, past the group of protectors and friends who had encircled her. She touched each one of them gently as she passed: Talog, whose heart was both braver and more pure than she had ever known existed; Eiddig, in whom wisdom and faith sprang from the bottomless well that was his soul. As it blessed his own people, it also had blessed and taught Selia in wordless lessons she would always carry within her. And there was Renan, priest and friend, who moments ago had publicly revealed the secret he had protected for twenty years, not hesitating to use what he had once abandoned to serve his Queen, his friend, and his kingdom—even knowing the personal cost of the action.

Lysandra also felt Selia's thoughts brush with affection over her and the Archbishop. She was proud of the woman Selia was becoming and of the Queen she was now ready to be as she turned toward the crowd.

"People of Aghamore," she said in a loud voice. Her words, however, were swallowed up by the growing din. She tried again. "People of Aghamore," she shouted.

Lysandra used her *Sight* to watch the people. Toward the back, some were beginning to push their way to the doors, anxious to be free from the sense of danger they still felt. The Barons had drawn swords in their hands; thoughts of war and killing were pouring from them, thoughts that had, for a short time, been placated.

The bishops, too, had left their places in the quire. They were as confused as the people and were coming toward the Archbishop to demand answers.

All this, and more, had taken only a moment for Lysandra to see. Any more time and all would be lost.

Now, Selia, she thought. *Trust yourself and act. Now.*

She did not know if Selia actually heard her, but the younger woman took another step forward and raised her arms up over her head, hands reaching outward, fingers spread and pointing to every corner of the great room.

"STOP," Selia shouted. Her voice carried this time, reaching into every portion and corner toward which her fingers pointed. There was a new power in that voice, an authority and control Lysandra had not heard there before.

She smiled as it echoed through the great nave. The empty places of high, vaulted ceiling, corbelled arches, and spired bell tower, all amplified rather than swallowed the sound, sending it back over the people in a command they felt even more than heard.

It was a voice and a power Selia had never before displayed, and Lysandra could tell that it surprised her even more than the people. Yet, more than any crown or scepter, more than vows and blessings, rites and ceremonies, that voice had proclaimed Selia *Queen*.

Lysandra gave a deep sigh of relief. Her work here was over. She could go home.

Selia had to hide the surprise she felt at the command that came out in her voice. And she was surprised when the people obeyed. Everywhere they stopped their talking, their shoving and scrambling toward the doors. The Barons turned toward her; the bishops stopped in their tracks and waited.

The obedience was both gratifying and terrifying. It was all up to her now. Despite all that the others had done, no one could rule for her. No one could help her be Queen.

"Lord Iain"—she looked at the Baron, who put a hand to his heart and bobbed his head in the sign of obedience to his sovereign—"Baron Giraldus was of your House. I therefore ask you to take charge of his body. You may have it carried to the Lady Chapel and laid in state there. Despite his recent treachery, he was Head of the Third House and shall be given the respect that deserves."

Throughout the cathedral, the people were settling, responding to the decisive authority in Selia's voice and actions. She waited while Iain and his men gathered Giraldus's body and carried it from the nave. Once it was gone, the aura of Darkness went with it.

Selia turned to the bishops. "M'lord Bishops," she said, bowing slightly to acknowledge their standing authority as representatives of the Church, "you have held this kingdom together during this difficult time, and we all owe you our thanks. You teach us the ways of peace and obedience, and speak the voice of reason into moments of chaos.

"To you, I promise that you shall always have the ear of the Queen. This kingdom shall henceforth be known by its faith, and though the Crown shall govern in all things temporal, it—I—shall do so in obedience to God and His Church. But I can only do so, m'lord Bishops, by your grace. It is my hope that the Crown and the Church stand side by side, work hand in hand, so that the Darkness that so nearly destroyed this kingdom will never again gain foothold in this land."

Selia then turned to the Barons. "M'lord Barons," she said, giving them a little bow as well, "this kingdom owes you both its gratitude—and its very life. This is something that I shall not soon forget. I tell you all that I did not choose to stand in this place. I did not covet the crown or seek to be Queen. Rather, it chose me.

"Those who know me will tell you that I have come to this place reluctantly. But each one of you has heard the prophecies. Each one of you has held the scepter in his hand, and you know there was no trick to its opening. Just as the prophecy was given by God, His Hand opened the scepter and fulfilled the ancient words, thus demonstrating the Divine Will for the Crown. It is to that Will that I bow.

"Yet, my goal is not to gain power—but rather to serve. I seek to serve God and His Church, to serve all of you—and above all, to serve the people of this kingdom. This I cannot do without your help. I therefore ask of you, m'lord Barons, that just as you put aside your battles and fought together to repel the enemy of our land, will you now put aside whatever might separate us and support me, for the good of this kingdom? I stand here, m'lords, and my people, asking for your word."

At the back of the cathedral, a single voice rang out. "God bless ye, Queen Selia."

The cry was taken up, voices joining as the cry crescendoed ever louder. Then, like a reverse wave starting from the back, the people began dropping to one knee. The wave continued up to the Barons, and Selia held her breath. She knew she could not rule with their enmity. Then they, too, joined the people's affirmation, as they slowly dropped to their knees in sign of fealty. A moment later, in the quire, the bishops followed them.

Selia could hardly believe her eyes. A part of her had never truly believed this moment would arrive. She looked out, giving everyone one of her rare, sweet smiles. She turned to find her friends watching and smiling back at her. Finally, Selia turned to the Archbishop and was met with kind encouragement on his face. He gave her a little nod, wordlessly telling her that she had said and done the right thing.

"Well, Your Eminence," she said, "I believe there is a coronation to finish."

The Archbishop bowed to her. More than from anyone else, it was an odd sensation that the Archbishop, the Primus of the Church and once just a distant figure of reverence, should give her obeisance. To help ease the sense of oddity, Selia returned the bow.

The Archbishop stepped forward and held up his hand for quiet. Selia had no idea what was yet to come. She had read other coronation texts, and they had differed by the custom of the time and the desire of the King.

Would there be further questions or tests she must undergo, she wondered. Whatever it took to truly win the hearts of the people, she would do. They had given her one such show of support—now she would do whatever was necessary to let them know that she would keep her promise to serve them.

As Selia stood there beside the Archbishop, waiting for

the soft murmuring to silence, she steeled herself, ready for whatever should come.

"People of Aghamore," the Archbishop called out, "she who stands before you has fulfilled both the law of this land and the prophecies of this time. With these fulfillments, I say that it is right that she should be your Queen. By my authority as your Primus, I hereby set aside all questions save this, for this alone will decide your future. People of Aghamore— do you accept her?"

This was usually the final question, posed not to the would-be ruler, but to the people who would be ruled. It came just before the vows to serve the kingdom and the people, before the actual crowning took place. Having read all this, Selia now waited, hardly breathing, for what the people would say.

It began like a low roar, hundreds of voices mingling, building together into a single word. *"Yes,"* the voices cried, *"we will have her."*

The cry was caught up, carried forward and repeated as more and more voices joined in. Children, mothers, shopkeepers and tradesmen, guards, soldiers, Barons and bishops . . . soon every voice in the cathedral was shouting the same cry.

"Yes, we will have her. Long live Queen Selia . . ."

Selia felt unable to move, or to contain the joy that suddenly filled her. Tears sprang to her eyes and ran, unchecked, down her cheeks. She let them run—her personal baptism to her reign.

The Archbishop turned to her. "Are you ready, Your Majesty?" he said very softly.

Selia smiled at him. "Yes," she said, "finally, I'm truly ready."

The Archbishop gave her his hand and led her to the waiting throne. Then, after a silent moment in which he reassured

Selia with a proud, fatherly smile, he continued on with the final part of the Rite of Coronation.

The news went out with the speed of the Riders. It spread from person to person, town to town, until the entire kingdom was soon filled with celebration. Divisions and discords were forgotten as Aghamore rallied around the young Queen who had the support of everyone—Barons, bishops, *and* people.

Tales of the events, both at the coronation and in the days following, grew with the telling. Soon, Selia was more than the Queen to her people, she was a hero. She had destroyed the Darkness and vanquished the evil that threatened the kingdom. Even those who had never seen her were happy to vow their fealty and love.

The days following her coronation were busy ones for Selia. Her first act as Queen was to confirm and make permanent Iain's elevation to Baron of Kilgarriff. But that was not the only role she had for Iain's future. In recognition of the part he played in defeating the Corbenicans and protecting the kingdom, Selia created a new position. Lord Iain, Baron of Kilgarriff and new Head of the Third Ruling House of Aghamore, was named Commander of the Combined Armies.

Iain, unlike his cousin, had never craved power and was hesitant to accept this additional honor. But Selia was now his Queen, and though she could have commanded his compliance, she instead *asked* for his help. After all that had just happened, she said, the kingdom of Aghamore was like a newborn babe, and she would need much help in its protection while it grew strong again.

To such a plea, Iain could do no other than bow his acceptance. Selia felt better knowing that the armies of the kingdom were under the control of someone who thought of

Aghamore first and to whom personal gain was less important than personal honor.

Selia's next act was not nearly so pleasant, and she put it off until the next day so as not to distract from the joy and well-earned celebration that followed the coronation ceremony.

On the morning of the first true day of her reign, she sat for the first time on the throne in the audience chamber of the Palace, wearing the new crown that the Cryf had made and Eiddig had brought to her. Like King Liam's Crown, it was made from twisted ropes of gold and silver, though it was smaller and much more delicate. On the brow, instead of a diamond, was set a perfect amethyst. The stone was a deep and brilliant purple, an oval as long as Selia's thumb, and cut so that the many facets constantly caught the light when she moved her head. It drew all eyes to it, a shimmering reminder of the means by which she became Queen.

Selia still wore the Heart of the Scepter on the Cryf-made chain around her neck. Like the amethyst on her brow, it sparkled in the light of lamps and torches that shone in their many sconces on the pillars that ran in a long double line down the center of the room or poured in through the long leaded windows along both far walls.

To Selia, it was this necklace, more than the crown she wore, that was the symbol of her sovereignty. It was prophecy fulfilled, and Selia frequently touched it, as if to remind herself that it was all real.

The reality was a difficult one when Hueil of Rathreagh was brought forward, walking down the long aisle—the supplicant's walk—created by the room's double row of pillars. Selia had spent several hours thinking about Hueil and the problem he represented to the kingdom.

The charges were great, perhaps the worst that could be brought against an individual. Hueil had betrayed this kingdom; he had conspired with their enemies and brought an invasion force into these borders. All of this warranted Hueil's death. But he had also repented of his actions. Without his help, the Corbenicans might well have defeated the Armies of the Provinces.

Yet many had died because of Hueil, and there had to be some punishment and recompense for his actions. Selia knew it and, as he came forward with his head bowed and his shoulders slumped with the weight of his guilt and remorse, it was obvious that Hueil knew it, too.

Margharite stepped forward with him, although she refused to look his way. When Selia saw the pain on Hueil's face, she knew that his daughter's anger and rejection was hurting him more than anything she could do to him.

Still, she must punish him; justice demanded it.

"Hueil Ruairc, Head of the House of Cionaod, Ninth Ruling House of Aghamore, Baron of Rathreagh," she said formally, "stand forward and hear Our judgment."

Hueil took a shuffling step forward. Then, with a deep breath, he forced himself to straighten and meet his fate like the leader of men he had always been.

"By the law of this land," Selia continued, "your life is forfeit by reason of your treachery. Yet We do not forget that in the end you did repent of your treason and that it was your aid that turned the enemy from our shores. Neither do We forget that justice is best served when it is tempered with mercy, for that is the way of true wisdom. Therefore, your life We return to you.

"However, from this day forth, you are no longer Baron of Rathreagh. All wealth and honor, responsibility and title are hereby stripped from your keeping, never to be returned. You are, furthermore, banished from life within the Court of Rathreagh, that your words are not heard, nor your presence felt, nor your face seen by those to whom your former title and authority might cause misplaced obedience. You shall live the remainder of your life in quiet retirement. Be warned, should you ever again abuse the law or threaten the safety of this kingdom, We shall demand the life that We have this day spared."

Hueil bowed deeply and stepped back. He looked at his daughter, but she still would not meet his eyes. Selia sighed; she hoped that just as this kingdom was beginning to heal, this family would heal, too.

"Margharite Ruairc, daughter of Hueil, step forward," Selia said, "and kneel before Us."

Margharite looked surprised, shocked, but she obeyed. Little murmurs, that had begun with Hueil's appearance and grown quiet to hear his sentence, now took new life and ran through the room until Selia stood and with a stern expression, turned her gaze upon the onlookers in the room. Immediately, all grew silent.

"Let all now hear Our decree," Selia began again. "Margharite Ruairc, as your father did betray this kingdom, by your strength and bravery, you aided in its salvation. You proved yourself wise and intelligent, someone to whom the welfare of all the people, both of Rathreagh and of Aghamore, is of greater importance than personal safety. These are the qualities of a leader. Therefore, it is Our decision that from this day forward, *you* shall be the Head of the Ninth Ruling House. Just as this kingdom now has a Queen, the Province of Rathreagh shall now be governed by a Baroness."

A voice in the back of the room let out a sudden cheer. Selia, like many others, looked around to locate the sound. It came from Durkin, standing with the commoners in the far back. Selia smiled; it was a good omen, and she was suddenly sure that the people of the Province would generally feel the same way.

That done, Selia spent the rest of the day getting used to the business of the realm. Although she begged the patience of the court in finalizing the members of her Privy Council, she did officially ask the Archbishop to be her Chief Advisor . . . and she asked Renan to sit upon the Council.

Selia also asked Talog to remain and to represent the needs of the Cryf. Unlike Renan and the Archbishop, however, Talog declined. Both he and Eiddig were anxious to return to their people and their beloved Realm. Lysandra, too, declined Selia's offer of a place on the Council and a home in the Palace. Selia had not truly expected her to accept, but her heart still ached when she thought of how much she would miss this woman who was both mentor and friend.

It was Lysandra's gifts of prophecy and *Far-Seeing* that once again guided Selia's actions regarding Aurya and Elon. There was a part of Selia's heart that wanted revenge, that wanted to run Aurya and Elon to ground and exact the fullest punishment possible. But she knew she could not follow only her personal inclinations any longer. She was *Queen* Selia and must think with the kingdom's mind and heart.

There had been so much death already. The kingdom had suffered so much—not only in the recent battle but in the months leading up to it. Should she ask the armies to put off returning to their wives and families in order to chase after two traitors?

And the bigger question was Aurya's magic. Who, save the Cryf, would be safe from its threat? Selia knew she had to find that answer before she issued her orders to Baron Iain and the armies.

As she struggled with the question, trying to discern what her purported *Wisdom* directed, Lysandra and Cloud-Dancer sought her out. It was the morning after her coronation, before Selia went into the great Audience Chamber of the Palace. Lysandra came into the luxurious apartments that were now Selia's private domain, bringing the advice she most longed to hear.

Selia dismissed the servants that already seemed to be hovering everywhere. Then she and Lysandra sat together as they had so often before—and as Selia knew they would rarely be able to do in the future. It was a relief to be able to tell her concerns to this woman who had already taught her so much, given her so much . . . who was her *friend*. Even if Lysandra had no advice to give in return, her presence was a gift Selia cherished.

But she did have advice—or at least the information given by the prophecy she had felt in the cathedral.

"Aurya's future lies not in Aghamore," Lysandra told her, the look in her sightless eyes focused on something far away. "Though she will return in the end, the child she now carries will not be born within this realm."

"Aurya is pregnant?" Selia asked, incredulous. When Lysandra nodded, it firmed what Selia's heart had begun to whisper. Despite the mother's actions, the child was an innocent, and Selia would not claim an innocent life.

"And Elon?" she asked.

"His destiny, too, lies elsewhere. He will find that which he seeks, and it will bring him as much fulfillment as he will allow himself."

Selia nodded. It was settled then. She took the information with her when she went into the audience chamber and after dealing with the other duties of the day, she was ready to make her pronouncement.

The charges against Aurya and Elon were read out. She let the Archbishop speak first, and he declared them both anathema to the Church. The College of Bishops would meet the next day when excommunication would be pronounced, and they would begin the process of finding and consecrating a new Bishop-ordinary for the Province of Kilgarriff.

Once the Archbishop had concluded the Church's judgment, Selia took over. "Long into the night have We worried, knowing Our decision must be for the good of *all* Our people, which is always Our deepest concern and desire. Therefore, these are Our words and will:

"Aurya Treasigh and Elon Gallivin are hereby and forever banished from these shores and borders, and from all the Provinces of this kingdom. We have been told that their destinies lie elsewhere, and We release them to seek what awaits them. But should they ever return to Aghamore, it is here decreed that death awaits them. It matters not how many years pass or the reason for their return, to come again into Aghamore means their death. All within this kingdom are asked and ordered to remain watchful—for We will not be merciful a second time."

Once more, a general murmuring raced through the room—but it was Baron Iain who stepped forward. "Your Majesty," he began with a bow, "you have appointed me to head your army for the safety of this land. Forgive me if I speak out of turn, for you know you have my obedience in all things. But—I find myself compelled to ask, is not your mercy misguided here?"

Selia smiled at him. "M'lord Baron," she said, "you must always speak your mind to Us. For this, We rely on you. But put your concerns to rest. The word and gifts that have guided Us in this decision are without question. This kingdom has known too many rulers for whom mercy was but a word, too little remembered. As We begin Our rule, We would have mercy and the welfare of others be the ground upon which all else is built."

With a bow, Iain stepped back into his place among the crowd.

"Now," Selia said, "let those who have petitions come forward. It shall be Our intent each day to spend the hours between nine and noon listening to the needs of the people of this land. This is Our greatest duty, and be it known from this day forward, that all who desire it, no matter what their station, will be admitted here and We shall hear them."

This pronouncement made, Selia settled back into the merely relative comfort of the high-backed throne on which she sat and prepared herself to listen and try to help whomever chose to speak.

Chapter Thirty-seven

While Selia began her true work as Queen of Aghamore, Hueil returned to the chamber that had been his cell. He sat on the edge of the bed, staring dejectedly at the floor.

Selia's judgment had been more than fair, he knew—it had been merciful. Mercy was indeed the foundation of her reign. Hueil realized she would make a far better sovereign than he would have ever approached being.

Life away from his own court, from the Baron's Fortress—and the duties—that had been his home and his only occupation for all of his adult life . . . the prospect frightened him a little. What was he going to do with himself? Where would he live, what kind of future would he have?

But those questions were only a small part of his sorrow. The greater feeling came from the way Margharite had still refused to even look at him, let alone forgive him. Losing his status and power, his wealth, his authority were nothing compared to the loss of his daughter.

Into the silence and sadness came a soft knock on the door. "Come," Hueil called, expecting a servant with a meal or a messenger with further instructions from his new Queen.

Instead, the door opened and Margharite stood there. Hueil came immediately to his feet. He was overjoyed to see her, but he found himself suddenly nervous and unsure what to say.

He gave Margharite a small bow. "M'lady Baroness," he said.

"Hello, Father," she replied, ignoring the bow and stepping into the room. "I decided that Queen Selia was right—and like her, I do not wish to begin my new life on a foundation of enmity or anger."

"Margharite, I'm . . . I'm sorry. What I did, I thought was best—for you, for everyone."

"Oh, stop," Margharite said sharply. "Stop lying to yourself. The only one it was 'best' for was *you*—and that was all you thought about."

For an instant, Hueil felt as if she had slapped him. He stood there, stunned, staring at Margharite and saying nothing. She looked so much like her mother that it tore at his heart.

He could hear her mother in Margharite's voice, as well. She was the only one who could always talk sense to Hueil, even when anger or self-absorption made him unable to see past his own stubbornness.

Seeing her mother so plainly in Margharite did the same thing. "You're right," Hueil said slowly, hanging his head with the weight of his shame. "I wanted to be King. And yes, I went about it the wrong way. I made choices I should never have made—but I did think I'd make a good King, perhaps the best King from among the Barons. I did want the best for the kingdom."

"And the best thing for Aghamore was the Corbenicans?"

Again came the feeling of shame and sorrow. But Hueil straightened his shoulders and lifted his head. He would face her, and face the mistakes he had made, with dignity.

"No," he said. "I was wrong—wrong in that and in what

I tried to do to you. I'm sorry, Margharite. If I knew of a way to prove it, I would. Tell me what to do, and I'll do it. All I want is your forgiveness. I know now that nothing else matters—not title or wealth or power gained or lost. I accept the Queen's sentence as right, even merciful, and I shall abide by it. But please, tell me I have not lost you, too."

Hueil held out his arms and waited, praying with unspoken words that she would accept his contrition. It took Margharite several long seconds before she moved. He could see that she was considering whether, after all that had happened between them, she could trust him again. Like the Queen's words spoken such a short time ago, he knew that this, too, was right, and he continued to wait, letting Margharite take her time and make the decision of her heart.

Finally, slowly, she stepped into Hueil's arms and returned his embrace. Hueil felt the deepest wound to his heart heal as he held his daughter. He laid his cheek atop her head and sighed a breath of gratitude.

"Your mother would be so proud of you," he whispered as he softly stroked her hair, the way he used to when she was a child. "And so am I."

Lysandra stayed in Ballinrigh two more days, helping Selia settle into her new life. But as the days wore on, she began to feel an unrelenting restlessness that told her the time had come to go home.

Eiddig and Talog had left the night before, still preferring to travel when the sunlight would not hurt their eyes. But this time they traveled as honored ambassadors of their people and friends of the Queen, with the protection of an honor guard as escort.

Lysandra knew the good-byes would not be easy, but like all such things, it was better to face them now than later. So, with first light, while Renan was busy with the morning

Mass at his parish, she took Cloud-Dancer and went to the Palace.

She had no doubt of being seen and when she arrived, she was taken immediately to Selia's chambers, as per the Queen's now-standing orders. Selia was just starting her breakfast, enjoying the only private time she would have all day.

When Lysandra entered, she watched the young woman with her *Sight* and saw her expression quickly change from the joy of greeting to one of solemn understanding.

"You're leaving," Selia said. "How soon?"

"Today."

"But . . . but I still need you. I'm only getting started— I've still so much to learn, so much I don't understand."

Lysandra sat down beside Selia and took her hands— sitting, perhaps for the last time, as they had so often before. "Yes," she said, "there is still much for you to learn . . . and you *will* learn it. You don't need me anymore. There are others here who can guide you when you need it, far better suited to the present task than I. But above all, you must trust yourself. Remember that you *are* the Font of Wisdom, and that wisdom will always be with you."

"The Holy Words of the Cryf said that Wisdom and Prophecy would walk together. I thought—I hoped—that you would stay."

Lysandra heard the uncertain little girl in Selia's voice. But she knew that little girl would grow up, strong and whole; uncertainty was only passing and Wisdom awaited. Selia would soon be the shining light to her kingdom that she was destined to be.

Lysandra gave Selia a soft and somewhat maternal smile. "Prophecy comes when it is needed," she said, "but wisdom must always be present. And so it is with us. I shall always know when you have true need of me, and I shall come to you. Always. Wisdom and Prophecy *shall* walk together, Selia."

With the prophecy that was now part of her *Sight,* Lysandra looked ahead. She *saw* the woman Selia would become. Calm and serene, she would govern this land with the wisdom she was only beginning to realize. Under that influence and example, Aghamore would become a great and prosperous kingdom, far beyond their understanding now.

But that was not all Lysandra *saw.* The future for Selia held all that her past had denied her. She would have family, security, laughter, love . . . all these awaited in great measure. It filled Lysandra with more joy than if this had been her own future revealed.

Again Lysandra smiled. She had said all she needed to say, but this was the last time they would spend together for a while—how long, Lysandra did not know—so she would stay and talk about little things until Selia's own duties called her away. Then, while the Queen was too busy to notice, Lysandra would slip away.

There was one more stop she wanted to make before she and Cloud-Dancer returned to the guesthouse at Renan's parish to gather up her things. Then, she hoped by noon or shortly after, she would be on her way home.

The College of Bishops had once again convened, though its purpose was far different than its last meeting. This time, instead of a successor for the crown, it was one of their own they needed to replace—an ordeal that could be every bit as difficult.

Throughout the last few days, the other bishops, singly and in groups, had all come to the Archbishop's Residence, needing to talk to him about what had happened. He was their superior and, of obedience, they had supported him in the coronation of Selia. Now they wanted to know the full story of the Cryf, the prophecies that had been read, and all the other events that had led up to that moment.

Colm ApBeirne explained it time and again, patiently,

until each of the other bishops understood. Or, whatever they did not fully understand, they accepted through their trust of *him*. Now that Elon and his influence were gone, their trust in the Archbishop's decisions had returned, bringing again the harmony the spiritual shepherds of the kingdom were meant to have.

Today, as they sat in the large conference chamber, each of the bishops wanted to hear how the old man would direct them on the matter they must address. Colm ApBeirne felt a great lightening of the burden he had been carrying. He realized again that Elon's absence had taken the unexpressed, often unrecognized sense of friction that had been slowly tearing this body apart. The Archbishop shuddered to think what might have happened had Elon's true nature not been revealed in time.

But God had again protected His Church and they, as His representatives, would protect the souls of His people. That was their true purpose—not glory or recognition, not power or the elevation to rank. They must all remember that and be far more careful in their choice of Elon's successor.

The Archbishop had also planned to name his own successor after Selia was safely crowned. But Selia had been so earnest when she asked him to remain in office and help her while she learned to rule that he had agreed, putting aside his thoughts of quiet retirement once again in order to sit on her Council. His mind, however, had not completely dismissed the thought. Now, as he looked over his gathered brethren, he could not help but consider again which one would best serve the kingdom by wearing the triple-crowned mitre in his stead.

He struck his crozier three times upon the floor, calling their meeting to order. *"In Nomine Pater et Filii et Spiritus Sancti,"* he said, making the sign of the cross to bless their time together and the subject they would address. "We all know the reason we are gathered. Let us pray for guidance as we now consider who among the many is both ready and worthy of consecration, to become Bishop-ordinary of Kilgarriff—and may God protect us from repeating the mistake we made with Elon."

"Amen," came the many voices, both to his prayer—and especially to these last words.

Starting to his right, the Archbishop invited all to speak in turn and put forth any candidate they thought suitable. Everyone had names and reasons. It would take many days, he realized, to settle on the one person they could agree was the right one to heal the wounds left by Elon.

There came a discreet knock on the door. The Archbishop left the others talking and went to answer it himself, glad of the diversion—however temporary. Outside stood Brother Naal—and behind him were Lysandra and Cloud-Dancer. Colin had been expecting the visit. He dismissed the young monk. Then, pulling Lysandra's hand through his arm, he led her over to a small bench where they could sit together.

"So," he said before she spoke, "you are leaving and have come to say good-bye."

She did not ask him how he knew, but gave a soft smile. "My work here is done," she said, "and the thought of home grows stronger with every passing moment."

"For what you have done, daughter, this kingdom owes you a great debt. Won't you leave your solitary life and come live again among those who love and care about you? Both you and Cloud-Dancer would have a place of honor here in Ballinrigh."

Lysandra smiled but shook her head. "Surely you, of all people, understand the draw of the quiet life," she said softly. "I must return to where I belong, just as you must stay here. Selia needs your help and guidance now, not mine."

"Have you *seen* her future, daughter? Is there anything I must know?"

"I have seen some things, but not all. There are, I fear,

battles yet to be faced . . . yet in the end, all shall be well."
Lysandra gave him a warm and understanding smile. "Have
faith, Your Eminence, and all shall be well."

"Will I see you again? I am an old man, and the years
ahead grow short. But I should like to know I will see you—
and Cloud-Dancer—again."

Colm ApBeirne watched as Lysandra's expression
changed. It took on a look of distance, as if she were no
longer inside the body next to him, but somewhere far away.
Then, just as swiftly, her mind returned from wherever it had
just walked. She blinked—a strange thing for sightless eyes
to do. But her blindness had been replaced by prophetic
Sight, and she blinked as she returned to the here and now.

"Yes," she said slowly, "we shall meet again. I cannot *see*
the reason that brings me again to Ballinrigh, but I shall return."

"And for that, I shall rejoice. Then, daughter, take my
blessing with you as you go and my prayers each day until
we meet again."

As Lysandra bowed her head, the Archbishop raised his
hand to bless both Lysandra and her journey. But he could
not help but wonder what had been hidden from her? Despite
her assurance that all would eventually be well, the fact that
there was Darkness that even her prophecy could not penetrate, reawakened the knot of fear in his soul that he thought
had finally been laid to rest.

Renan was waiting for her when Lysandra returned, sitting in the rocking chair by the hearth of the guesthouse. At
his feet were three bundles. Lysandra, who had found that the
constant use of her *Sight* all morning had begun to tire her,
had begun using Cloud-Dancer's vision as they neared the
church, and so she could not *see* what was inside them.

When she entered the guesthouse, Renan smiled. It was an
odd smile, as if he knew something that she did not. The

smile broadened as she walked from the door into the main room. She was not quite sure what to say in response to it. She knew she could not leave without saying good-bye, yet she had dreaded this meeting most of all—and so she could not understand why he was smiling.

So far, Lysandra had been unable to think of the right words. How could she say good-bye knowing that half her heart would remain here, would always remain with Renan? Even the knowledge that she would someday return to Ballinrigh—and just as she would see the Archbishop again, she would also see Renan—even that was not enough to tell her how to say good-bye to this man she silently and so completely loved.

"Renan, I—" she began, but he held up a hand to stop her.

"Did you truly think I'd let you leave without me?" he asked. "Everything is packed—your clothes, mine, supplies for the journey. We can go whenever you're ready."

Lysandra felt dumbstruck. She did not know whether to laugh or cry. Instead she shook her head, not quite believing what he had said.

"How can you leave?" she asked. "There's so much for you to do now. Selia is relying on your help—and the people of your parish . . ."

"Selia knows, and she knows I'll be back. Don't worry, Lysandra. It's all arranged. Now, when do you want to leave? Now—or would you like to rest first?"

"Now," Lysandra said. "I want to go home, Renan."

"Then home we go," he said as he stood and hoisted two of the packs upon his back. Then he came over and helped her adjust her bundle so it was comfortable to carry. By the door rested her old walking stick. Renan retrieved it and handed it to her.

It felt right in Lysandra's hand, and she finally smiled. Soon, she would be out of the city; in a few days she would again be in her beloved forest . . . and she would be there with Renan.

It could not be forever, but Lysandra would accept whatever time they had as a gift and be grateful. Her heart was alive once again, and, because of that, she would never again live in darkness.

"Home," she said to Renan as she stepped toward the door he held open. "What a wonderful word."

Just then Cloud-Dancer threw back his head and howled, then he rose on his hind feet and lifted his paws, as he used to do when he was a pup, sharing his joy in the moment.

Lysandra laughed. "Yes," she said to him. "We're going home."

King Wirral of Corbenica stood on the heaving deck of his ship, staring back in the direction of Aghamore's shore. The winds that blew up the whitecaps on the waves and sent salt spray like tiny needles stinging his skin swallowed up the curses he was muttering. They stole the words from his lips and carried them away.

That was exactly what Wirral had intended. It was known that such a wind blew straight into the underworld, into the realm of the dark lord whose minions brought sorrow and Darkness into this world from the realm below. He wanted his curses to be heard—and carried out—by the dark lord.

But he would not rely only on the work of the nether realm. He had his own plan. No one betrayed him and did not pay the price; he would be revenged upon Hueil of Rathreagh.

And after that, he would march south, straight to Ballinrigh, and take by force the crown he had meant to have by marriage. He had been a fool to think there could ever be peace between Aghamore and Corbenica—except that which came after conquest. He had only brought a third of his fighting force this time, relying on Hueil's troops and his knowledge of the kingdom to supply the rest.

Next time it would be different. Next time he would bring every man who could carry a sword, an ax, a pike, or fight with his bare hands.

"I will be back," he suddenly shouted at the shore that had long since disappeared from sight. "When I return, the entire kingdom shall be my plunder, and all who oppose me shall die—beginning with Hueil of Rathreagh and not ending until your land is awash in blood. This I swear by mighty Doenaar, god of power, whose hand holds the sun in the sky. I swear by Krekin, the dark lord whose breath is death. I shall return and in their names bring vengeance upon you all."

Behind Wirral, his men began to shout, sending their war cries on the wind to join Wirral's curses as they were carried to the dark lord's realm, and let him know that the warriors of Corbenica joined their King in his promise of revenge.

Epilogue

Selia had sent a carriage after Renan and Lysandra. It caught up with them shortly after they had left by the Southgate, and although the driver had planned to take them all the way to Lysandra's cottage, Renan sent him back. Then he took the reins himself.

Riding back to the forest shortened the trip. It gave Renan a little more time to spend at the cottage before his duties demanded his return to Ballinrigh. Though they did not speak of it, they both knew that day was fast approaching.

Lysandra sat on the stone bench in her garden, listening to the sounds of the night. This time of year, when the nights were warm and the air clear, the forest was filled with a symphony of sounds, all of them welcome to her. After her weeks in the city, the sounds of birds and frogs, nocturnal creatures hunting or mating or foraging through the undergrowth that had grown high with the season, nighttime insects tapping against the windows of the cottage in an attempt to reach the lamps inside seemed music sweeter than all the angelic chorus.

She sat alone, drawn outside by a need to make peace with herself and the separation she knew tomorrow would bring. Tomorrow Renan would return to Ballinrigh, taking the larger part of her heart with him. Her only comfort was knowing that though they never spoke of it, Renan was leaving as much of his heart with her. What remained for both of them was her love of her life here and his of the people and the parish, the life that called him to return.

Lysandra had felt no need to use her *Sight* as she sat in the warm familiarity of her garden. The darkness held no fear; it was comforting and comfortable. Yet now, into the darkness, a light grew of its own accord. It was deep green, the color of growth and living things, the color of the forest and the plants around her. But it was lit from within, as if the sun from which all these things drew their life had come to rest within this brilliant color.

The living green became more and more intense and it called forth her *Sight* without her summoning it. What she *saw* shocked her into stillness and silence, too stunned to call for Renan or do anything but watch what was happening.

The brightness within the green grew until she knew it would have burned her physical eyes to look upon it. But with her *Sight,* she could see clearly. Deep within the heart of the living color, another form was growing. It started as a tiny speck, like something seen from far, far away. Then, quickly as a heartbeat, it sped forward until, suddenly, an old man stood before her. The brilliant green surrounded him, yet it was coming from him, too, as if he and it were inseparable.

He wore an old, much-mended monk's robe. His beard reached nearly to his waist and was as white as the hair that hung in thin wisps past his shoulders. Though his arms were empty this time, Lysandra recognized him from the visions she had *seen* so long ago, when his arms had been filled with the image of his scrolls. This time Lysandra knew him for who he was.

"Tambryn," she said aloud—and the vision smiled at her word. Do visions smile? She wondered briefly, and if he was not a vision, what was he?

I am the spirit of he who lived before, he spoke in her mind.

"Why are you here?" Lysandra asked him.

I am here to say you have done well with your first task.

"My first task? But Selia is safely on the throne, and all of the prophecies of your scroll have been fulfilled."

Again the vision smiled. *There are more,* he told her, *and Prophecy's Hand shall again be filled.*

With these words, he began to fade. "Wait," Lysandra called. "More what? More scrolls, more prophecies? Where? Wait—tell me what to do?"

But the vision of Tambryn was growing smaller almost as quickly as it had appeared. Then, softly, as if from a great distance, his last words reached her.

The heart will guide the Hand. Listen, and it will tell you all you need to know.

Then he was gone, and the garden was dark again. Renan came out of the cottage; Lysandra heard his footsteps and turned.

"What is it, Lysandra?" he said, hurrying toward her. "You look . . . strange. Did something out here frighten you?"

"I *saw* him, Renan. I *saw* Tambryn. He appeared and told me that 'there are more.' I think he meant that there are more scrolls hidden somewhere, waiting for me—for us—to find them."

"More scrolls?" he said eagerly. "Where—did he give you any hint, anything that might help us find them?"

Lysandra shook her head. "He said only to listen to my heart and it would guide my hand. I don't know what he meant or what he was trying to tell me."

Renan took her hands. "Come inside," he said, "out of the night air. Perhaps together we can find an answer."

Lysandra let herself be led inside. As the door closed behind her, leaving the darkness outside, neither of them saw the soft green light that suddenly erupted from beneath the little stone bench. It glowed for a few heartbeats of time, then faded again, once more leaving the garden in soft and silent darkness.

Far to the north, Aurya raised a weary head from off the pillow—and immediately regretted it. The movement made the small cabin in which she lay begin to spin, bringing another wave of bitter nausea. Her stomach began to heave, but having long since emptied all its contents, it could only bring up bile that burned the back of her throat.

Gently, with as little movement as possible, she laid her head back down. But the motion causing her nausea continued and would continue until they reached their destination. How many days that would take, she did not know . . . and at this moment, she was not certain she would survive the trip.

They had not gone to Ummera, as Elon intended when they escaped the cathedral. Thomas, his servant, had met them at the Westgate, riding one horse and leading another loaded with clothing, food, as much of Elon's secret library as he could quickly pack, money, and a few jewels. These latter had proved particularly useful.

Aurya knew it had been Elon's intention to send for Thomas as soon as they reached a town with a Rider outpost. With what she had learned of Thomas's budding prescience, she was only mildly surprised to see him. Elon was delighted. When they made camp that first night, he spoke to her, and to Thomas, about the possibility of still returning to Ummera so he could retrieve more of his secret library—the only thing he regretted losing. From there, he thought they might ride over the border into Salacar.

But Aurya had other plans. She had thought them out carefully, and she knew exactly where they must go and what they needed to do in order to ensure the revenge she was determined to have. Selia, Lysandra, Renan, the Cryf, the Archbishop—the entire kingdom would pay for Giraldus's death. As her child would live without a father, if her plan worked, then the people of Aghamore would learn what it meant to live without mercy or hope.

She could not accomplish her plan alone, or even with Elon's help. She needed someone with power, someone whose hatred for the people and the rulers of Aghamore equaled her own. There was only one person who fit those criteria, and it was to him they were now heading.

Wirral of Corbenica.

After what had happened during the battle, she was certain that he would be eager for revenge. If his hatred was not at the fever pitch she needed, she was also certain of her power to feed it, control it, turn it into a weapon to strike straight at the heart of her enemies.

But first, she had to endure this journey. With some of the jewels Elon carried, they had hired a ship and crew. Aurya had never traveled across the sea. The wind-stirred waves that buffeted the ship jarred it in ways that continued to twist Aurya's already emptied stomach. Only her determination for vengeance kept her from crawling into a corner, to welcome the death that must surely come; surely, no one could survive such agony.

She would survive it, she told herself, told the gods who seemed to laugh at her discomfort, told the universe so that it would know she would *not* be controlled. She would survive, and she would prevail.

"Do you hear me?" she said, though her voice cracked and her throat hurt from all the bile that had risen to burn it. "I *will* survive this, and I *will* return. When I do, it is death that will come with me, death that shall ride at *my* side—and death that shall set my son upon the throne. I swear now by Giraldus's lifeless body and by the life of his son, growing within me. All those who took Giraldus from me shall join him in death, and it matters not what it takes, whom I must use, or what I must do. While there is strength in my body, I shall not rest until death covers Aghamore, and the Nine Provinces are covered with the blood of my enemies."

Just then, another wave hit the ship, knocking it sideways. The sudden motion sent Aurya's stomach into another spasm, and another rush of bile rose and emptied itself into the bucket by her side. Weakness crashed in on her body, but her eyes burned with an unrelenting fervor that nothing could quench.

"I will return," she whispered, hanging on to the words like a mantra to get through the night. "I will return. . . ."

Appendices

Provinces and Houses:

Founded by King Liam Roetah I, the Kingdom of Aghamore, which means "The Great Field," is divided into The Nine Provinces. These Provinces were ruled by Liam's sons, now by their descendants, and the Houses each bear their founder's name.

Urlar is the central and capital Province; it was inherited by Liam II, who became High King upon his father's death. The Provinces are counted in this order:

Urlar, "the level place," First Province and House, House of Roetah;

Tievebrack, "the speckled hillside," Second Province and House, House of Gathelus

Kilgarriff, "the rough wood," Third Province and House, House of Lidahanes

Dromkeen, "the beautiful ridge," Fourth Province and House, House of Caethal

Camlough, "the crooked lake," Fifth Province and House, House of Nuinseann

Sylaun, "place of sallows," Sixth Province and House, House of Niamh

Farnagh, "place of alders," Seventh Province and House, House of Ragenald

Lininch, "the half island," Eighth Province and House, House of Baoghil

Rathreagh, "the gray fort," Ninth Province and House, House of Cionaod

Barons of Aghamore:

Urlar: Central and Capital Province, direct rule of the High King

Tievebrack: Baron Phelan Gradaigh, House of Gathelus

Kilgarriff: Baron Giraldus DeMarcoe, House of Lidahanes

Dromkeen: Baron Curran OhUigio, House of Caethal

Camlough: Baron Oran Keogh, House of Nuinseann

Sylaun: Baron Ardal Mulconry, House of Niamh

Farnagh: Baron Thady Cathain, House of Ragenald

Lininch: Baron Einar Maille, House of Baoghil

Rathreagh: Baron Hueil Ruairc, House of Cionaod

Bishops of Aghamore

Urlar: Archbishop Colm apBeirne

Tievebrack: Bishop Mago Reamonn

Kilgarriff: Bishop Elon Gallivin

Dromkeen: Bishop Awnan Baroid

Camlough: Bishop Dwyer Tuama

Sylaun: Bishop Gairiad apMadain

Farnagh: Bishop Tavic Laighin

Lininch: Bishop Sitric Annadh

Rathreagh: Bishop Bresal Ciardha

Pronunciation Guide to Cryf Words: The Cryf language is phonetic; if a letter is there, it is pronounced. The Cryf alphabet and sounds are as follows:

A, soft as in apple

B, as in boy

C, always hard, as in cat

Ch, breathy back of the throat sound as in Scottish *loch*

D, as in dog

Dd, soft 'th' as in bath

E, long "A" sound, as in able

F, "v" sound, as in very

Ff, "f" sound as in friend

G, hard, as in goat

H, as in heard

I, hard "e," as in east

L, as in long

Ll, breathy sound made by placing tongue behind front teeth and blowing air out the sides

M, as in man

N, as in nice

O, long as in open

P, as in peace

R, rolled

S, as in safe

T, as in toy

Th, long, as in bathe

U, soft "e", as in every

W, double "oo" sound, as in moon

Y, soft "i" sound, as in inch

Acknowledgments

As every writer will tell you, writing is lonely work. No one else can take the ideas in a writer's head and put them down on paper. It is also exhausting work, mentally and physically, and in order to accomplish it and do one's best work, a support network is essential.

Therefore, I wish to express my deepest gratitude to the following, without whom being a writer wold have remained an unnurtured dream and an unfulfilled longing.

To Jenn, my agent, who believes in me and all the things I want to write.

To Betsy, editor and friend, who is off to greener pastures, and to whom this book is dedicated.

To Jaime, equally patient, caring, and encouraging. I'm glad you're there to take over.

To Matt, who has helped me whenever I call. I think you're "Big Matt" only because of your big heart.

To Steve B., whose care and concern, whose encouragement and support, whose gentle friendship means more to me than I can say.

To Dolores, for all the rides, the phone calls, the understanding and encouragement, patience and help — without whom I don't think I could have made it through these last months.

To Donna, friend of my heart. Your spirit grows more beautiful with each passing year, and though time and distance separate, the love of true friends never fades.

To all my furry family: Grace, Bear, Itty-bit, Gabey-baby, Mama, Icon, Baby-face, Sweet-pea, Lady, Henry, Emily, Alfred, Anabelle, Fluff-butt, T.J., and Mickey. You fill my life with pets and purrs, with chased balls, grooming combs, and with boundless love.

And above all, and always, my dear husband Stephen. You are the light of my life, the joy and strength of my soul. Without you, nothing I do would get done, because without you, it would not have meaning. Thank you for the last twenty-two years—and here is to an eternity more.

REBECCA V. NEASON is the author of the bestselling STAR TREK: The Next Generation novel, *Guises of the Mind*, as well as two HIGHLANDER novels, *The Path* and *Shadow of Obsession*. Her most recent novel was *The Thirteenth Scroll*. She also has published numerous non-fiction articles which, along with her poetry, have been featured in regional, national and international publications. In 1988 she was awarded a Certificate of Recognition for Outstanding Literary Merit by the Pacific Northwest Writers Conference, and she is a graduate of the Clarion West Writers Workshop. A frequent speaker at science fiction conventions, Ms. Neason also lectures on pre-Christian through Medieval British History, Middle English, and the development of English as a written language.

Ms. Neason lives on ten wooded acres in rural Washington, sharing her home and her life with a husband and a large number of cats and dogs, all of whom are rescues—a cause to which Ms. Neason is extremely dedicated.

The Bitterbynde Books
By Cecilia Dart-Thornton

A young foundling—mute and scarred—struggles to unlock a lost and forgotten past. But unknown to the nameless one, somewhere a dark force is summoning the malignant hordes, determined to destroy the young mute's identity, history, and destiny. The world of the bitterbynde is a treasure trove of folklore—where goblins, peskies, knocks, and all the eldritch wights of the Unseelie haunt the land, and the stakes could not be higher . . . for in this foundling's fate lies the fate of the world . . .

ACCLAIM FOR THE SERIES

"Netted in golden prose. . . . Dart-Thornton's opener proves a sweet surprise." —WASHINGTON POST BOOK WORLD

"Not since Tolkien's *The Fellowship of the Rings* fell into my hands have I been so impressed by a beautifully spun fantasy." —ANDRE NORTON, AUTHOR OF BROTHER TO SHADOWS

"Generously conceived, gorgeously written. . . . might well go on to become—the potential is manifest—one of the great fantasies" —MAGAZINE OF FANTASY AND SCIENCE FICTION

BOOK I: THE ILL-MADE MUTE (0-446-61080-1)
NEW TO PAPERBACK

BOOK II: THE LADY OF THE SORROWS (0-446-52803-X)
AVAILABLE IN HARDCOVER

BOOK III: THE BATTLE OF EVERNIGHT (0-446-52807 2)
AVAILABLE IN HARDCOVER APRIL 2003

FROM WARNER ASPECT

1213

Masterful New Fantasy From
Diane Duane
Stealing the Elf-King's Roses

New York Times bestselling author Diane Duane now presents a startlingly original new adventure with a gripping mystery. Los Angeles prosecutor, sleuth, and forensic lanthanomancer Lee Enfield relies on her mystic Sight to gather the truth from suspects and crime scenes. But when she investigates the shooting death of an Alfen media exec, her powers, like those of her fayhound partner Gelert, uncover only deeper mysteries. Now, to determine the truth, Lee and Gelert must secretly infiltrate Alfheim, a universe forbidden to mortals—and crack the case before an inter-dimensional war destroys all creation . . .

"Duane is a craftsman, a player with words . . . She has moved, quite literally, into another dimension."
—New York Times

MORE ENCHANTING WORK FROM DIANE DUANE:

The Book of Night with Moon
(0-446-60-633-2)

To Visit the Queen
(0-466-60-855-6)

AVAILABLE AT BOOKSTORES EVERYWHERE FROM WARNER ASPECT

VISIT WARNER ASPECT ONLINE!

THE WARNER ASPECT HOMEPAGE
You'll find us at: www.twbookmark.com then by clicking on Science Fiction and Fantasy.

NEW AND UPCOMING TITLES
Each month we feature our new titles and reader favorites.

AUTHOR INFO
Author bios, bibliographies and links to personal websites.

CONTESTS AND OTHER FUN STUFF
Advance galley giveaways, autographed copies, and more.

THE ASPECT BUZZ
What's new, hot and upcoming from Warner Aspect: awards news, bestsellers, movie tie-in information . . .